Review

A shining light of a book, with bright writing, brilli'ant dialogue, compelling characterization and evocative description. It is what so much science fiction tries to be but fails. The plot is intricate and ambitious, but woven with such skill that it never even begins to unravel. Stefan Vučak wields words as effectively as the characters in the book wield their weapons, and that is with painstaking attention to detail and considerable suspense.

In the Shadow of Death is a fascinating read with a conclusion that justifies the journey. I don't need to tell you the ending because once you start reading you won't be able to stop until you discover it for yourself.

Midnight Scribe Reviews

I0592481

Books by Stefan Vučak

General Fiction:
Cry of Eagles
All the Evils
Towers of Darkness
Strike for Honor
Proportional Response
Legitimate Power
Autumn Leaves
All My Sunsets
F/X-26
28th Amendment
Night Sirens
Broken Rose

Shadow Gods Saga:
In the Shadow of Death
Against the Gods of Shadow
A Whisper from Shadow
Shadow Masters
Immortal in Shadow
With Shadow and Thunder
Through the Valley of Shadow
Guardians of Shadow

Science Fiction:
Fulfillment
Lifeliners

Non-Fiction:
Writing Tips for Authors

Contact at:
www.stefanvucak.com

IN THE SHADOW OF DEATH

By

Stefan Vučak

Stefan Vučak ©1997
ISBN-10: 0648473139
ISBN-13: 9780648473138

Dedication

To my father ... for he never gave up

Acknowledgments

Orion Nebula – Credit: NASA, NSSDC's Photo Gallery and C.R. O'Dell (Rice University).

Cover art by Laura Shinn.
http://laurashinn.yolasite.com

Map of the Serrll Combine

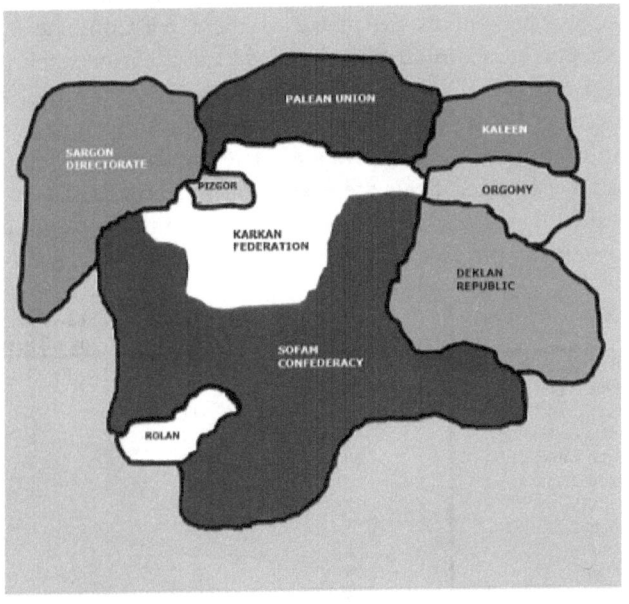

Composition of the Serrll Combine

The 238 star systems that make up the Serrll Combine is an association of six interstellar power blocks, split between two rival camps—the Servatory Party and the Revisionists. Each star system has a single representative in Captal's General Assembly from which members are elected to the ruling ten-seat Executive Council. Seats are based on a percentage of systems occupied by each power block in relation to the total number of systems in the Serrll Combine.

Name	No of Star Systems	Percentage of Total	Executive Council Seats
Sofam Confederacy	80	34	4
Deklan Republic	19	8	1
Palean Union	27	11	1
Karkan Federation	45	19	2
Sargon Directorate	30	13	1
Independents:		15	1
- Kaleen	8		
- Rolan	5		
- Orgomy	6		
- Pizgor	3		
- Other systems	15		
General Assembly	**238**	**100**	**10**
Outposts	44		
Protectorates	35		

Principal political blocks:

Revisionist Party:	Palean Union
	Deklan Republic
	Sofam Confederacy
Servatory Party:	Karkan Federation
	Sargon Directorate
	Nonaligned Independents

Composition of the Executive Council:

Security Council	Bureau of Colonial and Protectorate Affairs
	Bureau of Defense
	Bureau of Cultural Affairs
Administrative Council	Bureau of Administrative Affairs
	Bureau of Justice
Economics Council	Bureau of Economic Affairs
	Bureau of Technology and Development
Central Planning Council	Bureau of Central Planning and Development

Prologue

The little combie slued beneath her and corkscrewed into a savage right turn that pressed her into the padding of her seat. She grunted from the pressure of the restraining field and twisted her head to follow the orange beam as it flashed past. Her skin prickled and her hair tried to stand on end from the near-field effect of the beam.

Despite the loud thudding of her heart and the clamminess of her hands, she wasn't afraid anymore. Death would be a welcome release now. She had known a flash of real terror, gripping her chest in a vice of pain that made every breath a shuddering gasp. Earlier, with the incriminating intelligence safely recorded, she extracted herself from Kapel's executive offices as smoothly as she came in, as her training taught her. Waiting for the cable-tube to bring her up to the small landing ramp on the roof, she allowed herself a small smile of satisfaction. Garner's vaunted security turned out easier to penetrate than Kapel's lies. Or so she thought.

Running out of Kapel's offices, she scrambled into the combie and waited as the power plant spooled up. The combie gently lifted, then surged into the cold night sky. Raman's sprawl blazed with light beneath her. Above her, lines of traffic streamed in all directions. She activated the comms system and requested a voice-transmit-only link with Talia. Anonymity in her line of work was one of the minimal requirements. As she expected, the link came up quickly. The comms plate cleared and revealed Talia's quizzical small smile.

"Dama, I've got it all! I'm ready to transmit."

Talia frowned and her smile faded. Her oval yellow eyes clouded with a strange, almost mocking regret. "That will no

1

longer be necessary…Kadreen," she said softly.

A jolt of panic ran through Kadreen's body. She stared at Talia's image in confusion and felt the blood drain from her face. Cold dread froze her.

"How…how did you find out?" she managed to choke out.

Talia winced. "I'm sorry, my dear. I really am."

The plate turned dull gray, leaving Kadreen shaken. The whole exercise had been a plot to catch her!

To think it only happened an hour ago.

The night crisp, and the city lights behind her gave her scant comfort. Kadreen gave a rueful smile. The price she paid for playing the Family intrigues.

Another beam brushed past the combie and neatly sliced through the starboard impeller. The air suddenly smelled of ozone. Blue sparks arced at her from the curved console and the bubble frame, their touch sharp and burning. She yelped with pain and coughed from the acrid fumes filling the cabin. Some of the nav control pads flashed brown in warning of imminent failure. The power management system flickered between green and orange-white of total shutdown. The combie flipped over on its belly and nosed down.

Kadreen knew she had seconds at most. She glanced around, but could not see her pursuer. Fighting g-forces, she hurriedly punched in the transmission code, her breath a strangled hiss of frustration. The combie shuddered beneath her and began to tumble in its dive. The comms screen acknowledged her code and waited for the command to transmit. Grimly, she jabbed the commit pad.

She felt a silent explosion and the air around her flared with light. She didn't even have time to scream as the combie disintegrated around her. It all happened so slowly, like watching a scene in a Wall. Her last thoughts were about the message. Did it go through? For a split second, she had an image of her body torn apart.

In the Shadow of Death

Glowing wreckage fell silently on the dark countryside below.

Stefan Vučak

Chapter One

With absent dignity, Alasi twitched the crude garments around his stringy body and moved in for the kill.

Two suns peeked low over the stalls. Fat and orange, they leaked feeble warmth. Thin wisps of ragged cloud marred the intense blue of the sky. The wind sent dust and trash swirling among the vendor stands and pavilions, and made the awnings flap. Despite the keen morning chill, the soukh crowded and noisy, full of strolling, sometimes hurrying buyers and onlookers from nameless worlds, offered everything for a discerning buyer.

Smells of cooking from the food stalls were strong in the air. It made his stomach rumble. He ignored it. Somewhere in one of the rows of stands, a wail rose above the noise of bartering, yelling, and swearing. A thud nearby cut off hysterical laughter. Nobody paid any attention. Huddled in a corner of rough bricks, a bent figure gazed absently at nothing. Beside him, a chipped enameled bowl held a few coins and thin rods. Insects buzzed around his tattered and soiled garments. Alasi hardly noticed him. It was a common sight.

Leaning against a worn support beam, he studied the activity around the stand he chose to hit. Pavlir and his two boys had their hands full. They were busy serving odd fried tidbits to waiting customers, shouting and shoving each other for attention. One of the boys hurriedly scraped burnt bits off a large hotplate above the burner, then threw on fresh meats, vegetables, and slices of various breads. Aromatic steam gushed up and the plate hissed and crackled. Beside the stall, stacked tins, biscuit packs, and piles of dried fruit stood unattended.

Alasi allowed himself a grin. This one would prove to be

easy.

The noise of the soukh felt like a warm, familiar blanket. The only thing that could spoil his breakfast now was Pavlir's wife. Waiting for the right moment to strike, he watched her tending the credit register. Stern and formidable, she dispensed justice with a rough and heavy hand.

Like so many of the stray kids, Alasi ate at the soukh at the expense of unwary entrepreneurs. Not all traders could keep their eyes on both their goods and the crowd. Alasi remembered well the few who managed.

Despite the Proctor's laws, casual thieving was prevalent and impossible to curb. If caught, the priesthood guards exacted immediate punishment by whipping the luckless victim, to the gleeful hooting of onlookers.

He'd been lucky so far despite Maw's disapproval. "I run an honest farm, neh? We don't starve, and I won't have you hauling in useless trash, hear?"

"Yes, Maw," he would say, not hearing her.

He didn't spend all of his time prowling around with his gang. He had chores his Paw demanded be done. Herding a tractor around the farm was not his idea of honest labor. Besides, he did bring in useful plunder from his enterprises that were appreciated, albeit grudgingly.

A highborn Dama walked by. A hired attendant followed behind her, towing two squirming girls. One of the brats tugged at his hand and pointed at the stalls of steaming food. The lady turned and scolded her sharply. The girl pouted and kicked at a pile of stacked tins.

It was beautiful to watch.

The whole array came down in a rolling clatter, accompanied by a scream of indignation from the highborn lady. Surrounded by strewn merchandise the little girl burst into a howl. Pavlir's wife threw up her hands with a curse. The entire scene became an immediate attraction for the bystanders. While the attendant hurried to pick up the girl, Alasi bent down and helped himself to a few of the choicest packs.

"Gotcha!" A meaty hand grabbed his collar.

He aged ten years and almost dropped his plunder. Pavlir's wife shook him like a rag and swung her broad hand. He ducked and jerked free.

"Stop, you ruffian!" She hurled a piece of rock-hard bread after him.

Alasi laughed and sprinted into the crowd. He scrambled around the grinning onlookers and disappeared among the stands, followed by a lot of commotion and shouting behind him. He beamed hugely; it made him feel appreciated.

Maybe it would be a good idea if he avoided Pavlir's for a while.

A typical market day in the city of Raman, planet Elexi of the Four Suns.

Alasi opened a packet and dug out a biscuit. Munching, undecided, he rubbernecked through the soukh. Pockets bulging, he wandered past the slave section. It wasn't his favorite haunt and he didn't want to linger long. Too much chance of becoming one of the trade items.

The two suns had climbed higher and the wind had died down, but still crisp. The sky had developed a heavy gray haze. People muttered and shook their heads; another dust storm.

He didn't let it worry him. He checked his torn trouser leg and the grimy shirtsleeve. Maybe he should liberate something more appropriate. He needed to be careful not to overdo it, the mendicant business being touchy at best. Raising his status would cramp his style. Who would drop an odd coin or credit stick to someone dressed almost as well as the potential donor? It took craft to survive in the soukh and Alasi knew all the tricks.

Sticking to the broader avenues, he sauntered past the slave stands and the joyhouses. The owners who could afford it had gaudy holoviews of unholy pleasures waiting inside. Behind windows festooned with flickering lights, women, girls, and an odd boy, stood on display for the perceptive connoisseur.

Few of the slave pens had any shelter. The merchandise here all low rent, mature males suitable for heavy labor only. Most were illegals and aliens, with a few locals among them who had tasted her Benevolence's mercy. There was a lot of yelling and waving of arms as factors tried to encourage buyers to stop and examine. Alasi knew if a mark stopped, chances were he would walk away with a chattel he never really wanted.

Many beggars, pickpockets, and part-time muggers favored this popular tourist trap. Curiously, some of the offworlders felt flattered when ripped off buying a worthless trinket, something to talk about over a cocktail. The priesthood guards made sure such fleecing didn't get out of hand. Bad for business.

The stands changed as Alasi moved into the up-market area. Open platforms and simple corrals gave way to elaborate pavilions, viewing stands and observation lounges. The rarefied prices reflected the needs of the genteel clientele. Unobtrusive, hunched individuals slinked among the strolling citizenry, sweeping the paving clean.

A sale was in progress at Tarad's Circle. Alasi pulled up his hood and stopped to watch the Tridan factor at work. Tarad was all heavy bones and knobby muscle. A short, stocky runt, powerful around shoulders and legs; a good indicator of high gravity habits, if an unreliable one. He wore a long leather kilt, a narrow jeweled belt, and soft ship's boots. Despite the rawness in the air, his muscled upper body bare beneath a thin maroon cape. A jeweled armband adorned each thick wrist.

Alasi fingered the dull ceramic of the identification band around his wrist. Tarad had a large hairless head, a broad nose and small piercing eyes. His ears were vast black-veined flaps that sagged to his shoulders.

A burly keeper, hands crossed before his chest, glowered at the slaves. A vicious knobby whip hung at his belt. Standing in twos and threes, ignoring the waiting buyer in the paved lane, the slaves gossiped among themselves.

The Palean, dressed in the working grays of a master scout, gazed blankly at the stock arrayed on the viewing stand. Short and thin, he exuded an impalpable air of superiority. His hands twined in a characteristic gesture, the long fingers twitching. His delicate button nose glistened on a small triangular face. He had a pointed chin and enormous black eyes bulging beneath a high forehead. A thin mouth drooped at one corner.

Two rented attendants hovered behind the officer.

A muscled youth, dressed in a fine green tunic, stood aloof from other slaves on the stand. Tarad pointed at him and jerked his head. The boy was a bit slow and the keeper snarled.

"Bow, scum!"

Tarad flicked his bony wrist. The thin leather baton cracked against the youth's shoulder, staggering him. His eyes darted hate at the factor and he bowed slowly. The baton whistled again; another grunt. The muscles on his back twitched, but the youth remained bowed.

Tarad's mouth twisted into a scowl. "That'll teach you obedience, animal." He glared at the other slaves. "Anybody else, neh?"

He shoved the baton into his belt, fixed on an ingratiating smile and hunched in supplication. Clutching his cape, he turned to face the Palean.

"Your pardon, most excellent Tal."

His eyes skimmed over the officer's pressed uniform and the well-filled features with their certainty of fat Serrll credits. He ignored the hired help as beneath his attention.

To him the Paleans were nothing more than another form of scum, strutting around like they owned the universe. He regarded them as an arrogant, haughty people, but a pragmatist, he never allowed personal feelings to interfere with business. He would simply charge more. His hands fluttered in anticipation.

"The boy is one of the best I have and tractable with a bit of discipline. Tarad's Circle is reputed for the finest in living merchandise. If we don't have it, no one has it. That's my motto." Tarad cackled.

The Palean's enormous eyes roamed over the pitiful assembly of flesh. He shook his head in resignation. Not much of a choice, but this was the best of a bad pick. The other lots held only brutes, fit for heavy work and not much else. Certainly not fit to serve in his household. After all, as a senior Fleet officer on this station, he needed to maintain a certain standard.

"I can see how you administer your discipline, friend Tarad. No matter, he will do. I'll take him. And I'll take that one as well," he said and pointed a slender finger at a resigned specimen.

"A wise choice, gentle Tal." Tarad nodded eagerly, his ears flaring. "It's a pleasure to do business with a professional who knows his merchandise. Both are in top condition and only one owner. At least twenty years in each of them."

"If that turns out not to be the case, you can rely on me to be back," the Palean piped in a thin voice. His smile thin, without humor.

"Ah, the Excellency jests, neh?"

"Sure. Price?"

"This is your lucky day indeed, Tal. I've got a new consignment from Saiam, and you can understand I'm anxious to get rid of my current stock. Practically *giving* them away!" Tarad wrung his hands in despair.

"Do you hold any locals?"

Tarad looked around quickly, then shrugged apologetically.

"That's illegal, worthy Tal. Why, the Benevolent Proctor would have me strung up on the altar for even thinking of such a thing."

"Might not be such a bad idea, seeing the kind of starved trash you're trying to push on unwary customers."

"Don't tempt the fates, your Excellency. Her priests are everywhere and it's not wise to antagonize the powerful."

It was not always easy to do business on Elexi. The way to

stay off the sacrificial altar was to hand over the squeeze to the guards with a smile. Pay your altar dues to the priests and pray for forgiveness from her Benevolence. He had dealt with this in one form or another on many worlds. Elexi may be a hole, but one still needed to be careful.

The Palean dismissed Tarad's concerns with a twitch of his hand. His position as chief of staff to Prima Scout Cannan, the Four Suns Fleet commander, carried with it some privileges.

"I'm not interested in legality. What I *am* interested in is a female." It would make a welcome change to wake up, among other things, to a pretty face rather than the churlish expression from one of his servants.

"To brighten your dawns. I understand perfectly, eminent Tal," Tarad said with a knowing smile and drew closer to the Palean. "Just the other day, I got a perky little wench, part of my last Saiam consignment. She was the Praetor's fourth. You must know, worthy Tal, a Saiam courtesan is worth her weight in kerner stones." He grinned broadly, showing a row of uneven, blackened teeth. "Wait, I'll fetch her!"

The Palean scowled. "Hurry it up. I'm freezing out here!"

Tarad bobbed his head and disappeared through an ornately carved triangular doorway set into a stone wall behind the viewing platform. He'd spent a lot of his own money turning the pavilion into a major attraction, to the envy of some of the factors around him. He wasn't bothered overmuch by what they thought. He would happily carry any of them as part of his sales stock.

He appeared in the doorway, beamed and stepped aside. A tall girl stood beside him, almost a woman, and looked regally around her. Her sleeveless dress, sides cut to the hip, clung to her body, outlining a supple form. A simple strap crossed firm breasts. Her fine delicate features were expressionless beneath large green eyes. Copper hair fell in thick braids to her waist. The Palean hissed in appreciation and licked his lips.

Some of the males strolling down the line of pavilions

stopped and nodded in admiration. Most of the women hardly paid any attention. The highborn Damas had their chins in the air and daintily moved on.

The girl glanced at the Palean and raised her head in defiance. Wearing a smug grin, Tarad gestured with his arm and the girl walked with mincing steps to the front of the viewing stand. She stopped and turned her back. Tarad's features clouded and his baton rose. The Palean's long arm flashed out and clutched the factor's thick wrist. Tarad's head snapped around in surprise.

"Can't have the merchandise spoiled, can we?" the Palean said easily. He watched the play of emotions on Tarad's face with cold amusement, then released the hand.

"Heh? Certainly not, your worship. Certainly not." Tarad cackled and tapped the baton against his thigh in irritation.

"An exceptional item indeed." The Palean's eyes roamed greedily over the girl's figure.

Tarad nodded with satisfaction and jerked his head at the girl. She turned reluctantly.

"Now..." His hand moved sensuously along the girl's arm. "Look at that alabaster skin, the high features, and the vibrant shine of her hair. Believe me, Tal, she is no phony. Only the finest from Tarad's, neh?"

"How much?" the Palean demanded, suddenly feeling warm.

"Oh, very cheap, heroic Tal. I'm being most reasonable for one of our Fleet heroes. You understand, she's the best I've got. I can—"

"How much?"

"Couldn't go lower than six hundred," Tarad said, all cold business. The Palean chuckled.

"I appreciate your sense of humor, friend Tarad. Especially on a day like this."

"I'll take twelve hundred for all three. My last offer. I can't give them away."

"One thousand. Take it or leave it."

"Oh, yes, noble Tal! I'll take it. You're most generous." Tarad grinned and flashed a look at the keeper. "Guard her!" The keeper merely blinked.

Tarad jumped off the viewing stand and extended his hand.

The Palean rummaged in his pocket and brought out a handful of colored rectangular sticks. He counted out the money with maddening slowness while Tarad simpered with impatience. He would have preferred a credit transaction, but money was money. The officer placed the last finger-long stick into Tarad's hand and looked up.

"There, that should do it."

"Worthy Tal?" Tarad coughed self-consciously. "I think you're twenty short."

"What? You question me?"

The hard glare stopped Tarad's outburst. He swallowed and bowed quickly, ears drooping.

"Oh no, kind Tal. It's just…" The Palean scowled, towering over the little factor. Tarad cringed. "Must have been my mistake, Lord. I couldn't think—"

"Fool!" The Palean turned to the attendants waiting behind him. "Take them to the estate and see that they're taken care of. Especially her!"

"Tal," one of them murmured and bowed low.

With a last glare at Tarad, the Palean stalked into the crowd.

"May a thousand canal worms feed on his stinking carcass," Tarad grumbled after the retreating figure. Even for a lousy twenty credits, he felt sore at having a fast one pulled on him by one of the marks. He grunted in resignation and pocketed the proceeds.

He jerked his head at the keeper. The three slaves shuffled into Tarad's office. Working from hand to hand, he touched the identification band on each wrist with a small rod. Thin wafers slid out of the register console onto the dealing table. He motioned with a hooked finger at one of the attendants who hurriedly collected the wafers; copies of the sales contracts.

"Off, off!" He waved at them impatiently.

The slaves clambered off the display stand and gathered around the two attendants. After a whispered conference, they all disappeared into the crowd.

For Tarad, simply another sale. He swiveled on his toes and raised his baton.

"Here, here! Tarad's Circle, specialized dealer in slaves, houses of joy, and all the imaginable delights to suit everyone, rich or poor…" his voice lost itself in the clamor of the market.

Twirling his identification band around his wrist, Alasi watched the Palean officer vanish into the crowd and spat on the ground. Glaring hate beneath his tattered hood, he mumbled obscenities and bad wishes.

He twitched the thin garment around his shoulders and ambled through the mob. Undecided, he headed toward the outskirts of the city, toward the winding delta, the hilly grain fields and his home. He loved to drop in whenever he felt the city start to crowd him. Besides, he had to unload the pickings making a bulge in his spacious pockets. There was also a matter of some unfinished chores, and Paw wasn't likely to be amused by his lengthy absence, he thought gloomily.

Against the backdrop of Raman's towers, Alasi walked along the narrow meandering path that followed the riverbank. The wind had picked up, sighing through the tall grass. He stopped beneath the drooping branches of an old mud gum and looked back at the city.

Bush clicks chattered among gray branches of a nearby gum. In a flash of bright brown feathers, they swooped in a graceful curve toward the heaving grass. Alasi hummed some nameless tune he'd picked up at the soukh. His long hair whipped around his eyes. He ignored it.

A glint in the sky stopped his humming. Instinctively, he pressed himself against the gnarled bark of a mud gum. He watched as two personal combies, flat pebble-shapes, skimmed low over the fields, their dark blue inverted triangle emblems flashing. A Serrll Fleet patrol, lackeys to their Deklan masters. Alasi spat and wished pestilence on the scum. The combies vanished in low clouds, leaving him cold and alone with the setting suns.

Far to the north, a brown wall of dust drifted across a dark sky. The storm would blanket the city, grounding the communals and the little commuter sled-pads. The Deklans would curse the damned planet and its refrigerated climate, being colder than what they were used to at home. Alasi smiled happily.

He rounded a curve in the river, cut across a grass field and clambered up a steep hill. Breathing hard, he pushed through a thick clump of jeer brush and stopped beside an old rotten trunk. Tall paperbark gums bordered the narrow valley below. Nestled against the hillside stood a small, stone straw-roofed cottage. Gray smoke rose in a thin column out of a blackened chimney. Poultry fluttered around the yard, cackling in alarm. In the stalls, two cows stomped impatiently. On the yellow grass in front of the cottage rested the polished shape of a flat oval M-1 personal scout. Brandishing a phase rifle, a priesthood guard stood beside the extended landing ramp.

Alasi stared at the guard and his lip curled in distaste. To him the man was a pariah who had sold his soul to the Deklans in return for decent food and lodging. Alasi might foresee a remote possibility of being polite to a native Deklan, but there was a special kind of hate reserved for the slimy traitors of his own kind.

About to walk down, he saw his father stagger out of the cottage. A guard stood in the doorway laughing, his rifle held over his shoulder. Alasi stared, stunned by the scene. He felt the blood drain from his face and his mouth go dry. His mother ran out and flung herself at the guard. The goon backhanded her and she fell. His father rushed the guard and Alasi wanted to shout a warning. Standing beside the landing ramp of the M-

1, the other goon leveled his rifle and a thin beam of ruby light lanced out. Alasi's father fell in mid-stride.

"Paw!" Alasi yelped in helpless panic.

He knew what was going on. He had heard it described often. In the soukh the gangs would get together and talk. They'd talk of late-night calls where whole families vanished, never to be seen again. They dreamed about killing the Deklans, the slave traders and the corrupt city Proctors, sleek from their profiteering. It was only talk and they knew it, something to cheer them up. The priesthood guards kept things too tight to allow open dissent.

One of the guards motioned his mother toward the ship. The other tried to get his father to stand. Alasi's two sisters followed uncertainly. He gulped and clenched his fists. In a huddled procession, he watched his family being marched into captivity. He could not understand it. They held their farm out-right and didn't owe anybody anything. The farm wasn't much, but Maw managed to bring in valuable cash and his father worked hard.

The landing ramp withdrew into the craft. Its crimson nav shield pulsed and it climbed quickly into a dull sky.

Alasi watched for a long time the point into which the M-1 vanished. He felt strange, lightheaded, no feeling of disbelief, only a dull ache of loss. His family gone, it was likely he would never see them again. Deep down, he knew that. They could be anywhere, dragged off to some nameless labor camp, even Anulus. Life was bleak and unforgiving. If this was Serrll justice, he wanted no part of it.

Through gathering clouds the stars winked bright. Low on the eastern horizon a thick band of stars that was The Arch, stretched across the sky.

The wind felt frigid as it keened through the grass and the creaking branches of the gums. Alasi clutched the tattered garments around his body and gave a strangled sob. A heavy weight rolled over his heart and he whimpered at the pain. He hadn't cried in a long time, but hot tears of bitterness and rage slid down his cheeks now.

"Maw." He lay face down in the grass and sobbed.

* * *

"Second Scout Terrllss-rr, reporting as ordered, sir!"

He was screwed and knew it.

Not daring to move, he allowed his eyes to flicker over the silent figure sitting behind a gray-bordered, matte black desk. Prima Scout Anabb Karr was bulky and not very tall, but his presence dominated the office. His olive skin a wrinkled parchment on which the years etched deep lines, reflected a chiseled, narrow face stamped into a prominent scowl of disapproval. A ragged blue-veined burn from a phase rifle creased his left cheek. They said it tended to turn a mottled red when he got angry.

Terr figured he would probably have a chance find out.

The way he heard it, Anabb had made his reputation by being one crusty son of a bitch. Terr kind of hoped it was only a rumor.

Maybe he would find that out too.

Everything about Anabb looked ordinary, except for the eyes. Close-set ovals, they were brown pools smeared with flecks of amber. Hidden beneath ridges of narrow white eyebrows, they cut where they stared. If there was any sympathy in those eyes, Terr sure as hell couldn't see it. He disliked mixing it with high brass of any kind, and Anabb in particular. As COMDEKOPS, Commander Deklan Operations, Anabb was the most senior Serrll Scout Fleet officer in the Deklan Republic. Instead of occupying a cruiser-sized office on Deklan, he had chosen to plant himself on Talon, the Fleet's premier base and support facility in the sector, much to the annoyance of the base commander. No one liked having a flag officer breathing down one's neck, silently criticizing one's every move, but it appeared that Anabb was a rule unto himself and didn't particularly give a canal worm's butt about what others thought.

Standing stiffly at attention, Terr wondered which of his recent sins warranted this summons, and whether he would survive the encounter. Either way, it had to be serious.

Anabb looked up, pulled back his shoulders and gave Terr a slow, measured look.

"Sit down, Second Scout," he said in a cold, gravelly voice devoid of emotion, like stones being rolled in a barrel.

Terr winced. This was not good. As long as they didn't take *Ramora* from him.

"Thank you, sir." He picked one of the formchairs and made himself as comfortable as circumstances permitted. The thing squirmed as it molded itself around him.

Behind the wide expanse of Anabb's desk a window screen took up the whole wall. Tall slim towers of the Center reached toward low dark clouds. It only needed one bad thought and the rain would come down. Talon was a cold and miserable world even in summer, which this was not. Its only redeeming quality being its strategic location, sited almost on the Deklan/Karkan border. To Terr, the strategists on Captal didn't have comfort in mind when they picked the place, the planet only one of nine moons circling Cordia-Prime, a blue-green gas giant. Drawbacks or not, it made for lovely night skies.

On his left, a floor-to-ceiling full-dimensional Wall display station cycled through random color patterns. Uneven levels of transparent shelving crowded the opposite wall and held an assortment of campaign memorabilia; scalps more likely, he thought. He hoped his scalp wouldn't be joining the collection.

Anabb tapped a pad on the reactive surface of his desk. A plate lit up in the lower right corner. He studied the boy's record and only glanced at the display, then turned to scrutinize Terr sitting rigidly before him. The boy had firm, strong features, matured by the burden of command. The shock of brown-black hair needed some cutting, he mused wryly, telling him something of Terr's character. The face finely molded without appearing chiseled. A ragged scar above the left temple near the eyebrow added a touch of rakishness. With a hint of a chin cleft, his pink skin looked somewhat pale and drawn, as with all Kaplans. Cold gray eyes stared back at Anabb above an aquiline nose.

Handsome young rogue, he decided. With a pang of memory, he realized how much the boy looked like his father, an officer he was proud to have served with. What a loss. Not only a personal one, but for the Fleet as well. He cleared his throat, annoyed at allowing himself this lapse of sentimentality.

"I've been going over your record," he said heavily. "You're young to be commanding an M-3. Mmm, only twenty-eight. I'm glad to see it wasn't gained through your uncle's influence. Enllss-rr is a friend, but nepotism is a disease. You've been busy enough, I note. Two single ship actions against Palean smugglers, a survey flight beyond the Rolan group and a stint at the Serrll Moon Base, Sol. Mentioned in dispatches twice with decorations. You're independent and a low opinion you have of high command. Well, at your age that's not necessarily a bad thing. Provided you keep it in check. How do you like command?" he demanded suddenly.

"I prefer making the decisions that count, sir," Terr said cautiously, not sure where all this was leading to.

The mention of his uncle had thrown him. Enllss ran the Bureau of Cultural Affairs on Captal, Serrll's central intelligence organization and a very senior posting in the Security Council. They were family, but Terr hadn't seen any of his relatives for some time. The Fleet was a demanding mistress.

Impertinent young scamp, Anabb reflected, holding back a smile. He liked his officers to have spirit, and the boy certainly seemed to be full of it, but was that attitude hollow bravado or competence borne of hard experience? He needed to find out.

"So I've heard. You remind me of my own first command.

In the Shadow of Death

A converted M-2, it was. I learned a lot then, about men and ships; what makes them and what breaks them. A long time ago that, before your father died, but I suppose your family has already told you everything?"

"They've talked about it."

"You must have been just old enough to remember him. I was his commanding officer on an M-3, not all that different from yours. And like you, he had a low opinion of high command, but a good officer…and a friend."

Terr was a boy of six when he learned of his father's death, some sort of an undercover deal that went sour not very far from Talon when still a bare rock. His family never told him the details and he never found out. Even with his Fleet clearance, the information was classified. If he believed the rumor, his father's ship was sabotaged and he augured into Anar'on when the secondary drive plasma impellers failed. Terr's memory of his father was of laughter and games and glittering uniforms. Even now, he had trouble recalling his father's face.

"Your family, they're well?"

"It's been some time since I had an opportunity to visit Kaplan, or see them, sir, but they're all well, thank you."

"They forgiven you yet for joining the Fleet?"

"Resigned, if not forgiven," Terr said with a trace of bitterness and a rush of unpleasant memories. Parents cannot help managing their children's lives, he decided glumly.

Ever since his father's death, his mother tried to argue him out of his juvenile romance with the Fleet, as she called it. The House of Llss-rr was powerful, politicians and spacefarers all, and Kaplan needed her best at home. Although never voiced, he knew the underlying motive for her pressure. Instead of hunting for glory, he had a higher duty to continue the line. She never said it, but it was implied. The other thing, of course, his mother didn't want to lose him as well. The loss of his father had hit her hard. His stubbornness and refusal to bow to the family's wishes had been a source of ongoing acerbity ever since. In her eyes, he had no shadow. Despite the rejection, he reminded himself to call her sometime.

Then it hit him. The old fossil was setting him up, hoping to sidetrack him with sentimental family crap before jumping down his throat. Crafty old bastard.

"A different time it was," Anabb said moodily and nodded. "A better time, some would say, but enough reminiscing. Now, are you getting everything you need from Maintenance? I understand you're having problems with your phased array projector."

So that was it! Terr tried to keep his dismay from showing.

"A minor altercation—"

"A minor altercation?" Anabb exploded. "Is that what you call it? Let me list them for you. Haranguing Maintenance, you've been. Refusing compliance clearance. Insubordination. Conduct unbecoming. It goes on. The base commander bent my ear all morning. Is that what you call making decisions that count, boy?"

Terr admitted getting into a shouting match with a Maintenance first scout might not have been exactly politic, but the guy was a button-pushing asshole. Still, he never expected to be hauled before the Old Man himself about it. The base commander must really be pissed, but if he was going to have his butt raked, exemplary in its severity, as it seemed, it might as well be for the right reason.

"In my opinion, sir," he said forcefully, throwing caution out the lock, "Maintenance is more interested in paperwork and polishing the wheels of bureaucratic machinery than paying attention to my log reports. And they ignored two of them for my projector."

Anabb grunted. "I gather you don't approve of channels."

"Well, sir, you know what they say runs down channels," Terr said, his mouth doing his thinking.

Anabb bit his lip to stop himself from laughing. The boy had guts and confidence, something he wanted to confirm for

himself. Fitness reports didn't give the measure of a person behind them. Nevertheless, this was a matter of discipline. He
could not dismiss Terr's insubordination out of hand.

"I will not tolerate any impertinence from you, boy." His
eyebrows drew together into a thundercloud and he felt the
burn on his cheek begin to color. "You don't own that M-3,
and you certainly don't own this base. Yours isn't the only ship
Maintenance has to service. In case you weren't certain, bitching about your problems is not exactly a career-enhancing
move. An attitude adjustment would be more in order. You cut
across channels again and more than crap you'll find flowing
down. Am I getting through to you, Second Scout?"

Terr squirmed in his seat. Maybe making that crack about
channels hadn't been such a great idea. Rit!

"Copy that, sir!"

"I should kick your butt. On the other hand, Maintenance
exists to service my ships, and you cannot do your job unless
they do theirs." Anabb drummed his stubby fingers against the
desk. "All right, son. Out with it. What's your real gripe?"

The old father figure gambit now, is it? Confess all, fall at
his feet and plead for mercy? Since he'd already stepped in it,
he might as well go all the way. Well, *Ramora* had been good to
him while it lasted, Terr thought moodily.

"I know I shouldn't have blown my pad with Maintenance,
sir. But hell! They've been dragging their feet over my weapons
pod ever since I got here. I'm not about to lift off this
damned…I mean—"

"You meant damned rock, didn't you?" Anabb grated, but
his eyes twinkled.

"I meant Talon, sir," Terr said with a straight face.

"I know what you meant, boy. It's a damned rock, all right.
Go on."

"Well, sir, I'll not accept clearance until my projector is in
full operating mode. I would rather be ticked off for giving
Maintenance a hard time than have my weaponry fail in some

21

sticky situation."

Anabb sat back and gave the boy a long stare. He did not doubt that Terr was prepared to be grounded rather than knuckle under. It was not the first time he'd heard complaints about Maintenance, but thunderation! There were procedures.

"Tell you what. I'll see to it that the base commander tells Maintenance to read your logged incident reports. How about that?"

"That's just great, sir. He'll take it out on me in some other way and I'll never get *Ramora* off this rock."

"Don't worry about repercussions. You can leave those details to me, but you'll be counting rocks on Cantor if you're insubordinate again. I don't have patience for it. You read me, boy?"

"Aye, sir."

Anabb nodded, making up his mind.

"Very well. However, I didn't ask you here to chew over your problems with Maintenance. And I don't want to hear again that you've been bitching, whatever the reason. Now, I want to show you something."

He reached across the desk and tapped a panel on the inlaid console pad. The Wall cleared into a full-dimensional tactical grid of two binary systems, orbiting each other a scant tenth of a light-year apart.

"Recognize it?"

Terr should. It was part of his last patrol sector.

"It's the Four Suns. Kapel Pen is the current Prime Director and Controller of Elexi. It's one of four systems belonging to Deklan Republic's Third Prefecture, ruled by Anall-Marr," Terr told him crisply. He'd heard the Old Man expected his commanders to know their areas of patrol better than they knew their partners. More than one luckless officer had his head handed to him in a bucket because the unfortunate failed to do his homework.

"What else do you know about it?"

In the Shadow of Death

"Well, sir, Elexi is the major settled planet and contains the bulk of the Binary A system's population. The place is somewhat backward even by Deklan standards, and specializes mostly in agricultural export commodities. Raman is the capital city and houses the Four Suns' administrative center. Their culture is a matriarchy and, officially at least, is fully integrated into the Deklan Ecumenical Order. The religious dogma is enforced by priesthood guards who are accountable to the Controller and the city Proctors, not the Order, as is the norm in other systems of the Republic. That fact has been an ongoing source of irritation to the Ecumenical Synod on Deklan."

"That's all you got?" Anabb demanded as he tapped the table with stubby fingers.

"As you know, sir, what makes the Four Suns invaluable is Anulus, the fourth planet. It has the most extensive mining and refining operations of strategic metals and minerals in the whole Republic. Elexi provides some of the more sophisticated post-processing and acts as a marketing and distribution arm. It's a strategic and very lucrative economic asset for the Deklans. It also accounts for the Synod's veiled tolerance of the local administration's treatment of its priests. Two centuries ago, the Four Suns belonged to the Karkan Federation. At that time, of course, Anulus had nothing they wanted and they didn't mind giving it up. A fact they bitterly regret now. Binary B has four rocky planets, the third currently ecoformed, and three gas giants. Selius, the fourth planet, is practically a water world and supports the Fours Suns fishing industry."

"Not bad," Anabb said grudgingly. The boy had given a pretty good thumbnail sketch of the system. "You've been there, of course?"

"Twice."

"You'll find it handy," Anabb said and cleared his throat. Terr raised an eyebrow. "You must be aware that ever since the Deklans got hold of the Four Suns from the Karkan Federation, it's been an open wound for them, and lately, it has begun to fester. Elexi's ruling matriarchy has never acknowledged Deklan's dominion and sees them as a foreign occupation. If they had a choice, they would revert to the Karkans. Kapel Pen, the latest in her line, is particularly vocal in her opposition, to the extent of inciting other Deklan border systems to revolt. Without success, naturally. By all accounts, she hasn't given up her plan to see the Four Suns independent of Deklan rule.

"However, I wouldn't waste my sympathy on her. The matriarchy has kept the population in virtual serfdom despite the enormous wealth that Anulus brings in. Ordinarily, that would be an internal Deklan issue, but as you said, Anulus is a strategic asset and the Serrll government on Captal is wary of some of the things going on over there. What triggered Captal to act is that Elexi is engaged in slavery and the Bureau of Administrative Affairs has sent an Envoy to investigate."

"Under Ecumenical law, sir, slavery in the Deklan Republic is not illegal."

"Irrelevant." Anabb waved his hand in dismissal. "I'm not talking of expatriate or penal slaves. The problem, though, is that local Elexi citizens are being enslaved to meet the alleged labor needs of Anulus. That in itself is not our concern. Anulus has been a convenient penal colony for many Deklan systems. However, when supposedly free families are forcibly relocated, it smacks of corruption and possible sanction at official levels."

"Kapel Pen? Surely, sir, that's a local matter and should fall under Anall-Marr's jurisdiction. Or at most, handled by the Ecumenical Synod on Deklan."

"Ordinarily, that would be the case," Anabb agreed, pleased at Terr's perceptiveness. "Unfortunately for Elexi, the Deklans are more interested in maintaining output from Anulus than what happens to the local populace. They make a token protest and turn a blind eye."

"If I understand correctly, sir, Captal cannot act without a complaint from Anall-Marr or the Four Suns government. Why would Kapel Pen invite the Serrll government to rummage through her operation? Or did Anall-Marr make the complaint?"

Anabb gave Terr an appraising glance. "Some penetrating questions you ask, for a Second Scout, but not quite right. It wasn't Kapel, son, who made the complaint," he said with relish and grinned savagely, "but her own General Assembly rep, Relina Pen."

"Her own representative?"

"We need to shake loose some of that idealism. Don't think Relina was overcome with sudden remorse for the plight of her people. It means that someone on Captal brought pressure to bear on her."

"I don't get it, sir. Why has Captal developed a sudden rash about slavery in a backwater system like the Four Suns?"

"Ah, not so clever after all. You remember who owned the Four Suns?" Anabb tapped the inlaid console pad and turned to the Wall. The grid expanded to include the border between the Karkan Federation and the Deklan Republic. At a tangent, another line indicated the border with eight systems of the small independent nonaligned Kaleen group.

"Show the Four Suns," Anabb ordered the computer.

In the Wall, a bright blue dot began to flash near the Karkan border. "There you have it, the Four Suns. Caught between Deklan's economic expansion and the covert territorial ambitions of the Karkans."

Terr thought he understood it then. The Karkans wanted the Four Suns back, along with other border systems they were forced to give up in a political peace deal with the Deklans that had obviously not been to their liking. Gaining the Anulus mining concession was a major steppingstone in their campaign to regain control of the system. If they could not own the Four Suns politically, perhaps they sought to dominate it economically, but was the move entirely apolitical? Could the Karkan Federation be eyeing other border systems in some strategy to win them back? Destabilize the Deklan Republic and perhaps the Revisionist Party coalition itself? If successful, it could bring down the current Sofam-dominated government on Captal; something the Karkans have been working toward for centuries.

It probably wasn't that simple and he likely over-dramatized, but he was sure it covered most of the facts. Unless Anabb held something out on him, of course.

"Anulus is being mined by Kunoid Minerals, isn't it?"

"One of the most powerful mining conglomerates in the Karkan Federation," Anabb agreed.

"I think I see it, then. Should the Karkan Federation win full control of Anulus, Captal is worried they'll flood the Serrll Combine with cheap metals, destabilizing the entire market."

Anabb gave a sour chuckle. "Economic blackmail is what I'd call it. However, Anall-Marr is too careful to allow any such thing, even though he's cranking Anulus for all it's worth. At any rate, the political implications of a Karkan presence in Deklan space is not part of the Envoy's terms of reference, or yours, for that matter."

"Mine, sir?"

"That's right. We're handling the issue through other channels."

That meant the Bureau of Cultural Affairs, Serrll's intelligence arm. Terr would rather have fights with Maintenance any day. Obviously the Serrll government on Captal did not relish the idea of Karkans muscling in on their territory, whatever the pretext. Was the envoy really looking for incidents of slavery, or something deeper lurked behind his mission? A shadow fell across the window screen. Dark clouds had gathered and soft rain blurred the Center's skyline.

Somewhat appropriate, he felt.

"As of now, you're temporarily relieved of your command and attached to the Envoy as one of his two military aides for the duration of his mission on Elexi," Anabb said heavily.

"But, sir!" Terr protested in dismay. "I have *Ramora* undergoing critical repairs."

"Your executive officer will handle it." Anabb dismissed the matter with a wave of his hand.

"I am a Fleet line officer, sir. Not some creepy intelligence spook."

"I know what you are, Second Scout," Anabb said sharply. "The Bureau of Administrative Affairs has requested that the Envoy be supported by two military aides. You're one of them."

Rit!

"And my duties?"

"That's up to the Envoy. Distract Kapel's own intelligence machinery while the Envoy gets on with his slavery investigation."

"The only way I can distract Kapel's machinery, sir, is by finding something I'm not supposed to. You can use up a lot of officers that way."

"And I'm about to lose one right now if he isn't careful!" Anabb said with plenty of snap and leaned forward. The power burn on his cheek began to color again. "Now you listen to me. The government's motives are not your concern. The Envoy has a mission, and so have you. While you're a Fleet officer, and that might not be for much longer, given your impertinence, you carry out orders. Is that clear?"

"Perfectly, sir."

Anabb glared, then relented. "I know you feel uncomfortable and want to look after your ship. This may be outside your comfort zone, but it's an important assignment and a great opportunity for you to gain valuable experience. It's only a fifteen-day tour; plenty of time for you to get back and check up on *Ramora* and Maintenance. Besides, it'll take you out of the base commander's hair."

Terr didn't trust him. Anabb was smooth and glib like a Wall ad. Too many things can happen when you start digging into other people's business—unpleasant things. At least he knew the ropes with Maintenance. In contrast, Elexi represented a dark hole full of traps for an innocent like him.

"When do I start?"

"Have started already. An M-1 has been made available to you for the duration. I don't have to tell you not to bend it. Soft copy of your orders are in the ship's computer. Study them on your way to Elexi. And, Terr?"

"Sir?"

"Do your homework, son. This may be routine, but I don't want one of my officers getting caught by a low one because his head was stuck up his ass sightseeing. Stay focused."

"I'll take care of myself, sir," Terr said with more conviction than he felt.

"I can spare you, but I cannot spare the M-1," Anabb said gruffly.

For a minute there, Terr thought the heartless old bastard actually cared. He stalked out thinking evil black thoughts.

Chapter Two

Morning caught Alasi stretching stiff joints. He sat up and rubbed his eyes. Hugging his knees, he looked around the gloomy bedroom. The walls could do with a whitewash, he decided. A gauze curtain swayed against the wooden windowsill. The bedroom door open, showing a corridor that led to the kitchen. Against the wall stood a wardrobe cupboard, one door ajar. It did not quite fit. A chest of drawers stood beside it, one of them partly open. The double bunk next to him where his sisters slept was empty. Heavy exposed beams supported narrow ceiling boards.

He threw back the quilt and padded across the earth floor to the window.

The sky deep blue and clear, the two suns already up were bright orange bulges above the hill. A blanket of fine mist stretched low over the valley and hid the farm fields. He breathed deeply of the crisp air and listened to the background whisper of the river, the excited clatter of bush clicks, and the buzz of insects. Poultry cackled in the back yard and cows snorted in the corral. He would have to let them loose before he left.

Standing there, he hesitated, debating his next move. He could not stay at the farm. There was no telling when the goons might decide to come looking for him. Anyway, he would not find his family by brooding. How to go about looking for them wasn't exactly clear. The first thing to do, get in touch with the old gang. Together, they'd think of something. And there was always Tominoy the Wanderer. The old beggar always knew what to do, Alasi thought comfortably.

There wasn't much to pack. He changed his pants and put

on a fresh shirt. Gnawing a heel of dark bread, he went through the house and closed all the windows. With a last look at the kitchen, he latched the door shut behind him. This would be the first time he would leave the house without the usual clamor from the family. He felt lonely and the pain of loss weighed heavily on him.

Without looking back, he made his way across the valley and began the long trek toward the welcoming spires of Raman. Where else could he find a better refuge than in the masses of humanity that sprawled in the city? He had nothing anymore. Somewhere, someday, he would get even. Somber, with images of yesterday still crowding him, he walked through the dewy grass.

It was late in the morning when he arrived at his favorite haunt, the soukh. For the first time, he allowed himself to relax, safe here as though dead. Strolling along alleyways of merchandise, he kept an eye open for a likely breakfast and prowling priesthood guards who could spoil it.

He ambled past a stand of open trays and eyed a selection of cakes and bags of nuts. His stomach growled and he rubbed it absently. The local behind the bench flicked a cold eye at him. Reluctantly, he moved on.

All around him, people jostled and pushed their way between the stands. A buyer was haggling over a grain bag lying on heavy metal scales, waving his hands in agitation at the old farmer. Alasi knew the old guy. He held a spread not far from Maw's. Alasi and the gang often lifted items from the old man when no one looked. The farmer had a quick hand, but he could not watch everything. Besides, crowded now, Alasi hadn't hit the place for some time. He counted on that anonymity to pull a quick slide.

Blending with the crowd, he walked past the stand. He swept up several cakes when a gnarled hand clamped itself around his wrist. He dropped the cakes and stood there in shock. The old farmer leaned over him and glared.

In the Shadow of Death

"If you're not planin' to buy, boy, don't finger the merchandise, neh?"

"No, Tal! No indeed!"

"And I'm getting mighty tired of you and your gang messing with my stuff, hear? Next time, I won't be so understanding and it'll be the altar for you."

Alasi jerked, felt his hand free and took off. Laughter followed him as he ran.

After crossing several lanes of stalls, he slowed to a walk. It wouldn't do to advertise himself. He figured he would think better on an empty stomach anyway. The idea of being brought to the altar and caned unnerved him. He tried not to think what else could be waiting for him there. Still shaken, he followed the alleyways through the old city to the spaceport. With all the wild ideas in his mind, he might as well see which one of them he could afford to nourish. Lost in a daydream, he schemed of destruction and chaos he would bring on the Deklans and the acclaim his people would lavish on him. Only a dream, but it helped boost his somewhat cracked confidence. The Field opened out at the end of the alley.

Like most outposts of the Serrll Scout Fleet, the landing field in Raman a plain of stressed concrete fenced off by wire and a force field. This part of the city mostly deserted, old warehouses and crumbling terraces occupied by the seedier elements of the city. The priesthood guards did little to clean it up and it was a great place for gangs looking to bust something up. He and the boys had cruised around here plenty of times. Lots of fun to be had around the place.

He leaned against the wire barrier marking the first and last warning against the deadly orange shimmer of the force field. He watched and studied the sleek patrol M-3s, the small pleasure craft, ships landing and taking off. Service crews worked beneath some of the hulls, instrument pods hovering beside them. Sled-pads flitted between the terminal buildings and the craft.

Two huge M-4 cruisers, their triangle emblems glinting on their curved hulls, captured his total attention. They hovered above the apron, towering over everything. Imagine the hurrah if one of them met with an accident or something, neh?

"There he is!" The shout came from somewhere behind him. He didn't wait to find out whether it was him the voice referred to or not. He could do that later. Hanging around to satisfy his curiosity had landed him in trouble before. He raced down the nearest alley.

"Okay, kid. We gotcha. Come quietly before you're sorry."

Alasi glanced up. Two sled-pads, flat little platforms, were flying above him.

"Come and get me!" he yelled, searching the alley for doors into which he could disappear. Once in that dark maze, they would never catch him.

"Okay, kid. If that's the way you want it."

He heard a soft hum and a shaft of violet light stabbed at the wall beside him. The bricks blew out and masonry fell in front of him. Blocked, he headed back, only to meet one of the sled-pads coming down. Cornered, he backed against a brick wall. He would make them sorry if they touched him. One of the guards pointed a needler at him and grinned.

"No trouble, kid, or I'll have to get nasty. They didn't say in what condition I was to bring you."

"How'd you find me?"

The guard laughed. "Your band. It's not just a pretty bracelet."

Alasi looked at the dull sheen of the band around his wrist. A tracer! Some of the guys talked about the possibility, but no one really believed it, and it turned out to be true! No need for them to search the city. Let him come to them; guide them to him! He groaned and spat on the ground in disgust. Another betrayal. The wristband represented a symbol of freedom, not captivity!

"You come and get me, you traitorous sons of Deklan

whores!"

"Such language." The guard shook his head in disapproval and raised his needler. Ruby light lanced at him and Alasi staggered.

Through settling blackness, he heard harsh laughter.

* * *

This close to the system, the gravity waves were a complex swirl of orange and brown lines that twisted and roiled in a turbulent dance around two borderline G-type stars that made up one of the Four Suns binaries. Separated by a scant forty-eight light minutes, they would be ready to expand into red giants in about a billion years or so, merging into a single colossus that would swallow every planet in the system. Being so close to each other, their very proximity accelerating the aging of both.

A tenth of a light-year away orbited the second binary; a yellow-white star accompanied by its ravenous bluish dwarf. The accretion disk clearly seen as the dwarf stripped its hapless victim of surface material. A spectacular spiral of gauzy fluff that spun itself around the depleted star, a miniature galaxy of tortured plasma and light. When the dwarf decided it'd had enough, it would give a belch and life would end in the Four Suns.

Sprawled in the command couch, hands clasped behind his head, Terr sat in the darkness of the upper deck. Sullen and moody, he stared through the transparent navigation bubble that ran chest high around the deck at the creation process ahead of him. He'd been sullen and moody ever since he left Talon. A muted mosaic of colored contact pads from the sloping color-reactive control panels kept the shadows at bay. The main control plate before him a dark slab of gray.

"Approaching Elexi Surface Command and Control insertion point," the computer announced firmly. "Initial interrogative verified. All systems nominal for orbital approach. Preparing to egress transition mode."

If he strained, he imagined he could feel, rather than hear, the soft throb of the power plant a deck below, although only an illusion. One of the console pads blinked at him from time to time; otherwise silence reigned the ship. The two suns of Binary A slowly grew large in the nav bubble.

He could not see any of the planets, of course. They probably were not showing up as points of light anyway, even if he knew where to look. Elexi and its three rocky moons orbited the yellow suns. Two blue-green ringed gas giants maintained a cold vigil in the system's deeps.

Over the last four days, he'd gnawed over what little information Anabb had dolled out, taking the warning about being prepared literally. The way he saw it, Kapel Pen liked power and wanted to keep it. As Prime Director of two star systems, she had more than its measure. She hated the Deklans and spent a lot of her time stirring up other border systems in a joint demand for greater autonomy. In his view, that was unlikely to give her much change for her efforts. Anall-Marr would crush any move to destabilize the Deklan Republic or the coalition with the Sofam Confederacy. If Kapel wanted to expand her power base, how would siding with the Karkans accomplish that? What was in it for them? Just another mining concession, wasn't it?

Terr sighed and bit his lower lip. The whole thing could be a simple business deal and he was looking for motives that simply weren't there. She could be riding on the back of Deklan's agenda to expand its share of the strategic metals market, and Kunoid Minerals happened to be in the best position to help her out. Objectively, he could sympathize with Kapel's vociferous antithesis to Deklan rule. The Ecumenical Order had less than progressive ideas on what constituted individual enlightenment. He was not that naïve, though, to believe Kapel's struggle was anything but a personal exercise in Family power politics. And the wealth generated by Anulus gave her the economic and political levers with which to prosecute it.

What constituted the principal political driver for sending an envoy to the Four Suns? Captal's concern over slavery? Noble, but as he'd pointed out to Anabb, the issue really belonged in Anall-Marr's lap. Was Captal nervous that the Karkan Federation were peeking over the fence at Deklan's territory and wanted to know why? It couldn't be that they were miffed at missing out on the Anulus concession. After all, that was merely business and things don't always fall the way you want them to. Okay, if not business, it must be political. A simple binary problem.

Do your homework, Anabb had advised. Easier said than done. All right, he would pick at the basics. At the moment, the Revisionist Party called the tune on Captal, a coalition between the Sofam Confederacy and the Deklan Republic, with the Palean Union a nominal ally. The Servatory Party provided the opposition. Well, not exactly an opposition, as they shared power based on representation on the Executive Council. Shared or not, the Servatory Party, which really meant the Karkan Federation, wanted voting control of the Executive. The Sargon Directorate was more a partner of convenience than a true supporter. And that support might disappear if Sargon and the Paleans merged into a single block.

It all came down to an ongoing struggle for power between Sofam and the Karkans, the others being merely bit players. Important in the convoluted network of alliances and coalitions, but nonetheless, bit players. With the pieces spread before him, he still had far from what he could call a clear picture. One thing he did understand. Deklan had a good thing going with Anulus. The Karkans wanted it and Sofam maneuvered to stop them. He understood that part. What about Kapel Pen? Somehow, she was a pivot and a key to the whole mess, he could feel it, but how?

Caught in a web of frustration, Terr gave up. The corner

politics surrounding the ruling Pen Family was beyond unraveling. Way over his pay scale, he was happy to leave the muddle to the envoy.

He could not deny this represented a career-enhancing opportunity for him. But what *kind* of an opportunity? He wasn't happy about taking on new opportunities right now. Not these kind anyway. He was not happy about driving almost blind into an uncertain assignment either. And he certainly wasn't happy about leaving his ship.

Competent enough, but Terr couldn't help noting the dismay on his exec's face when told *Ramora* would be his for the duration. Face Maintenance alone? The exec almost wailed in anguish. Terr had sympathized. When asked whether his assignment was a punishment, Terr couldn't tell him. Perhaps, and Fleet command were good with gags like that.

All Terr knew, the exec was awfully young to be left all alone with his M-3. It was the first time since commissioning her that he wasn't with her, and it felt more than passing strange. It felt almost as though he would never see her again, which was ridiculous, of course.

Even the pleasure of driving *Pirana* only made him petulant. Ordinarily, the M-1's crisp responsiveness would have been a source of elation. Fast, maneuverable, the M-1 could outrun everything up to an M-4. Now, too full of uncertainty and doubt about the mission and the M-3 he left on Talon, he could not enjoy *Pirana* fully.

"State SC&C insertion time."

"SC&C insertion in eleven minutes. Landing configuration procedure nominal. Ship within acceptable flight parameters."

The nav bubble turned opaque and the tactical plot grid replaced the image within. Two ringed points of white stood between him and Elexi.

"Warning. K-band acquisition scans detected from two K/11 type picket M-3 sweepers," the computer said indifferently. "Navigation deflector and primary shield grid configuration only. Range, two point-two-five million talans. Closure rate is 25,280 talans per second. Effective firing solution in eighty-nine seconds."

Terr sat up and frowned. The scans themselves were not unusual. Pickets were bound to be prowling around the Four Suns. Nevertheless, his IFF should have satisfied any curious onlookers. So, why were these two so curious?

"Targets entering acquisition range."

"Mmm, damn peculiar," he muttered and scratched the scar above his left eyebrow. "Interrogate IFF of targets."

"Unable to comply. Targets have raised secondary shield grid and establishing weapons lock. Recommend full defensive posture."

Establishing weapons lock? Now, that *was* odd.

What in the pits were Fleet Scout units doing trying to interdict him? Surely those morons must see he was driving a Fleet vessel. Couldn't they? It wasn't as though he had stolen the M-1 or something. It had been done, but it wasn't worth the price.

He mulled over the obvious and didn't like it. If those jokers were not out joyriding, they must be under orders. Fleet units don't go wandering about without somebody knowing about it. Unless that somebody wanted to get him out of the way? He did not particularly care for the logical conclusion that line of reasoning led him to.

For a milk run, things seemed to have soured awfully quick. Soured or not, he could not allow those jokers punch him full of holes. And anyway, if he bolted, they'd only be waiting for him when he attempted another system insertion.

Should he outrun them, warn COMELOPS and wait to be escorted in with all the dignity of a cripple? Commander Elexi Operations was going to be something pissed if this turned out to be a false alarm—or a gag.

Gag or not, he had a ship to protect.

"Approved," he said at length.

For its size the Sofam-built M-3 medium interceptor had the speed of an M-4 cruiser, matching its mission profile as a general-purpose patrol craft. The M-3 had a particularly well-armored polymer construct hull. It mounted a single powerful Koyami 9A phased array projector housed in a dome slung beneath its belly. It could send 72 TeV in almost continuous traversing bursts of up to sixteen milliseconds at an effective range of 64,000 talans.

He should know, he commanded one just like it. Against them, *Pirana* had only speed in its favor. With only a defensive projector, he didn't even contemplate facing the M-3s in an exchange. He could think of more pleasant ways to commit suicide.

"Range to targets, 630,000 talans."

"Contact SC&C—"

"Unable to comply due to active jamming. Warning, targets are powering up in preparatory firing phase. Rate of closure increased by two hundred talans per second. L-band firing lock established." In the tactical plot, he could see the outer two shield rings around each M-3 brighten and begin to pulse.

Rit!

He told himself if he got out of this one in one piece, he would never again give a Maintenance joker a hard time; for a little while anyway.

They were not coming at him strictly line-ahead. The trailing M-3 slightly back and starboard of its leader provided an attack in depth. It gave Terr an opening to slip by the leading ship, albeit a slim one. The alternative was to drop his shields and hope it would be quick.

"On synchronization, initiate a maximum acceleration maneuver to port and below the leading target. When it commits to follow, keep it in line with the secondary target." A risky move, but if it came off, it should separate the trailing M-3 from its companion and inhibit its targeting solution for a vital few seconds. It would be enough. *Pirana's* superior speed should take him out of their range before they could regroup—he hoped.

"Acknowledged."

Before the M-3 could fire, it had to synchronize the pulse sequencer of the Koyami projector with those of the primary and secondary shield grid frequencies. That took several seconds. Once the shields stopped pulsing, the M-3 was ready to do business. The trick was for *Pirana* to maneuver when the M-3 started its firing sequence, thereby scrambling its solution.

Sometimes it worked.

A track of dull yellow ionization lanced out from the leading M-3 even as *Pirana* began to shift beneath him. The air around him suddenly smelled of ozone from the near-field effect. Small tongues of blue lightnings snapped and leaped from console to console. He yelped from the piercing pain as several little sparks stabbed at him from the armrest.

That one had been close.

The M-3 reacted quickly to *Pirana's* turn and followed, firing its projector in a traversing sweep. *Pirana* shuddered as the shields compensated from near misses, then staggered under a direct impact as the shields flared in a discharge of backsurges that arced against the hull, pitting and scarring the plating. The deck jolted beneath Terr. He grabbed the armrest as the internal gravitational field fluctuated. Some of the color-reactive panels pulsed a warning brown. The solid-light circuitry got a rattling, but at least nothing had failed yet.

"Power fluctuations detected in the aft secondary shield—compensating. SC&C insertion in four minutes," the computer said.

The trailing M-3 maneuvered away from his consort to clear its field of fire. Both warships fired in long continuous bursts. A ripple of yellow lines traversed along his track in a scissor pattern. Terr grimaced, expecting to be sliced up. The beams swept over *Pirana*, outlining the force lines of its flaring shields as it attempted to check its corkscrew tumble. The ship pitched as it struggled to regain attitude control, then everything became quiet.

In the tactical plot above him, the M-3s abruptly decelerated and dropped back, abandoning the chase, *Pirana* now beyond their effective range. If he'd been their commander, he would have prosecuted earlier, meeting him farther away from the Four Suns. This close to Elexi Surface Command and Control, and with a speed deficit, they had run out of time.

He wasn't about to question his luck. He let out a relieved sigh and slumped in the command couch. It squirmed as it molded itself around him.

"Damage control status," he rasped and ran a finger across his suddenly wet forehead.

"All systems within acceptable parameters. Autonomous diagnostics and repair routines initiated. Approaching SC&C insertion. Ready to transit."

"Very well. Drop normal."

"Transiting," the computer announced. The distortion field precursor changed polarity and began to collapse. Shields flaring, *Pirana* exited into normal space and fell below lightspeed.

"Send an advisory, Envoy personal with copy to Commander Deklan Operations and Commander Elexi Operations. Attach logs of the last fifteen minutes."

"Acknowledged. SC&C link enabled. Ready to copy."

"Approved."

The tactical plot in the nav bubble cleared and the stars wheeled as SC&C took command and swung *Pirana* into the Elexi approach pattern.

Fighting off reaction from the encounter, Terr clenched his fist and slammed it against the armrest. Someone would answer for this.

Elexi grew quickly, turning from a blue-green point to a thin crescent of swirling white, its shadow blotting out the stars;

a black hole that matched his thoughts. Its three moons were hard points of white. *Pirana* slowed perceptibly as Elexi filled the plot.

All around him shadows flickered from the status pads. Occasional murmuring of computer readiness reports broke the silence. He liked to come in with the navigational bubble transparent and the command deck darkened. At any other time, he would have enjoyed the sight of one of the Four Suns binaries breaking over the terminator, but not now. If he had any enthusiasm left for the mission, the gloss had definitely worn off.

He watched as SC&C brought the ship down. Raman was an untidy sprawl, nestled in a basin between two river deltas. A pall of brown smog hung over the city. He shook his head in resignation.

Pirana settled beside two M-4s blocking half the sky. In the repeater plate before him, he saw the M-1's landing skids deploy beneath him. The nav shield faded and the ship touched down with a slight bump. With the computer in housekeeping mode, he surveyed the expanse of the field and tried to suppress a grimace of distaste.

A grubby collection of maintenance hangars flanked the terminus building. A flat Palean tub hovered above the apron, tied to one of the landing rings by its access tube. The field obviously serviced both civilian and military traffic. Gaudy flags hung all around the terminus, fluttering halfheartedly on bright yellow masts. Terr doubted they were for his benefit.

A sprinkling of MPs hung around the buildings, playing with their rifles while looking around to shoot someone. He could see the city spires through the haze, its sky crowded with heavy cargo pads, public communals and an assortment of private combie bubbles.

The first thing he noticed when he stepped off the landing ramp was the depressing frostiness in the air. The hangar crews appeared indifferent to the cold, wandering about the cracked apron in short sleeves. He exhaled a thin cloud of white vapor and sealed his zip-jacket, deciding to dislike the place on principle. The other thing was the smell; sharp, raw and metallic.

He cleared his throat and suppressed an urge to sneeze, wondering if getting lung cancer was grounds for quitting the job. Nobody seemed to be paying any attention to him. Could he have landed at the wrong place? The way he felt right then, he would happily climb back into *Pirana* and take off. Counting rocks on Cantor, Serrll's premier penal planet, couldn't be any worse than this.

Across the Field, gliding low above the apron, an Armored Personnel Carrier came toward him at a fast clip. The APC braked hard and squatted down some four katalans in front of him. The almost black composite polymer armored hull fully opaque. A door hissed open and six dour-looking MPs with rifles slung at port arms, sprang out and stationed themselves around *Pirana*. As far as they were concerned, Terr didn't even exist.

An elderly Elexi Second Scout climbed out of the APC and glanced at the MPs. Satisfied, he walked toward Terr and smiled cheerfully.

"Second Scout Terrllss-rr? I am Halar, head of Field security. Welcome to our little corner of the Serrll Combine."

The Elexi native shorter than Terr by some three tetalans had a broad face, thin nose and button eyes. His skin dark brown with deep lines etched around the eyes and mouth. Terr wasn't fooled by Halar's casual facade.

"Thanks. For a while there, I didn't think anyone cared." Terr hooked a thumb over his shoulder at the MPs. "What's with them?"

Halar looked uncomfortable. "Your advisory caused quite a flap. You could hear Prima Scout Cannan bellowing all the way from the Center. Those two M-3s really jumped you, neh?"

"I wondered what I did to rate your personal attention, escort and all."

"You're catching us at a bad time. Security is pretty tight right now, what with the Prefect and your Envoy—"

"You mean Anall-Marr? I didn't know he was here."

"The correct honorific is 'Your Grace'," Halar said with a straight face.

"I'll keep that in mind," Terr said and nodded in the direction of the hangars. "What's with all the flags? A celebration or something?"

"Oh, that. One of Kapel Pen's little jokes. Whenever the Prefect blesses us with his beatific presence, she makes sure we're all suitably impressed. He hates it, of course. That's why she does it."

"No kidding?"

Halar's eyes kept sliding at *Pirana*. "Nice ship. Always wanted to drive one of those things, but don't worry. No one is going to steal it."

"I'm relieved to hear it," Terr said.

"I am to take you to the Dispatcher's office. Master Scout Ki-Tori, Cannan's chief of staff, is anxious to talk to you."

"I'll bet he is. Palean isn't he?"

Halar winced. "That makes him naturally mean, but he also works at it. If we weren't fellow officers, I'd tell you he's a stuffed end of a canal worm. Since I am, I can't tell you that. After you're finished with him, I'll haul you over to the Center where you can get squared away."

"The guy sounds like a challenge—"

"Copy that."

"Canal worm or not, you can take me straight to the Center right now," Terr said, making a decision. "If I'm seeing anyone, it will be the Envoy, not some local second-guesser."

Halar peered at him and rubbed his chin, obviously ill at ease. "I'm afraid, Tal Terr, I must insist."

"Am I under arrest or something?"

Halar chuckled. "That would solve only *one* of my problems."

"In that case, Mister, with all due respect to Master Scout Ki-Tori, I'll have to decline his invitation."

"Look, he only wants—"

"I know what he wants, and that's to ingratiate himself with me to get a handle on the Envoy. I'm not part of his TO and he has no authority to order me around."

"Unfortunately, Tal, I *am* part of his TO." Halar squared his shoulders and firmed his mouth. "Hath!"

A burly MP stepped out of the APC, strode up to Halar, slid his rifle down his side and snapped to. Terr looked up the two-katalan-high frame and met stony features.

"Escort this officer to the APC," Halar said, brooking no argument.

Rit!

* * *

Talia Pen lifted her head from the inlaid display panel in her desk and leaned back into the formchair. She rubbed her eyes, then absently swept a hand through her hair and allowed herself a small nod of satisfaction. The new plant, refining the halide metals from Anulus, finally online and in full production. Slightly behind schedule, but not unacceptably so. Some of the port facilities still needed work, but she was on top of it. More importantly, it did not prevent the freighters from loading and unloading.

At least it would get Kapel off her back. What was the rush about that plant anyway?

Looking around the plush expanse of her office, the trappings of power no longer seemed worth the price she had paid, but someone had to do it, neh? She was a Pen, and a Pen never complained. It wasn't as if she did not enjoy the power of her position, even though it left her little time to savor its privileges.

The comms alert beeped and she frowned in pique. She touched a pad on the sensitized surface of her desk and turned to the Wall.

"What is it? I said no interruptions." Her voice soft and modulated, betrayed none of her irritation.

"You wanted to call Tamara Lin, Dama," her personal assistant reminded her rather loudly.

Skies preserve me! She had completely forgotten about Tamara. Exasperated, she stamped her foot. The truth was, she had avoided making the call. Tamara could be so tiresome sometimes. Well, no use dragging her feet over it.

"Put her through now."

After a moment the random color patterns cleared and Tamara was there, smiling at some secret joke. An irritating, superior little smile that grated on Talia's nerves. Sometime back, Tamara had her hair coiffured in short waves of rich black. Clinging to her cheek the hair framed high cheekbones and rounded an otherwise long face. It looked good on her. She wore little makeup, a touch of frost and blush that set off wide, full lips. Her yellow eyes were alive, seeing everything, but no longer with innocence. Her nose thin and delicate, unlike the pinched beak Kapel wore, but still a distinctive Pen trademark. Talia remembered fondly the touting Kapel received from all of them because of that nose. She suspected Kapel was beyond caring now.

Then again, perhaps not. Talia's position demanded a certain isolation and loneliness. Power cannot be shared. At least she had the comfort of the other Proctors. What did Kapel do to vent her spleen when the problems crowded her, seemingly insurmountable? Kapel, though, would never consider consulting with her Proctors on a personal level. It just wasn't in her. Besides, her position did not allow fraternization.

Looking at her, Talia admitted Tamara was a strikingly handsome woman, a credit to the Pen line.

Tamara lounged back in the formchair and crossed her long legs in a feminine gesture.

"I see you managed to forget my call again, neh?" she said,

her voice rich and confident, faintly mocking. She grinned at her cousin's discomfort. Her teeth were perfectly shaped, even and white.

"Couldn't be helped, my dear," Talia said defensively. "Everyone's been after me this morning. It's not one of my best days."

"The new refining plant?"

"That and the Envoy—"

"And the Prefect, neh? I must say, that's quite a haul for one week. I've been warning you, dear cousin. You've allowed your bureaucratic machinery too much slack and it has landed you and Kapel in trouble."

Talia pouted. "You never did have a high opinion of my administration, or Kapel's, for that matter."

"Corruption is so unprofitable in the long run, dearie. I thought you and the rest of the Family would have learned such a simple lesson by now, but keep it up. It makes good copy for the *Morning Tribune* channels."

"Skies preserve me! As if I haven't had an earful already. You were never shy when it comes to pontificating on someone else's problems, were you, darling? Maybe that's what it takes to get a story, but not today. I'm not in the mood for one of your mealy-mouthed, patronizing, bleeding heart, simplistic sob lectures."

Tamara's eyes grew round. "My goodness, that was quite a mouthful. I am impressed."

Talia shook her head and sighed. "You wouldn't feel so superior if you had to sit behind my desk for a day. I haven't time to play, Tamara. What do you want?"

"I want an exclusive with the Envoy."

"An exclusive? The other channels will howl. Family influence and all that, neh?"

"That's what influence is for."

"Spoken like a true Pen," Talia said and laughed with delight. "Why worry about nepotism if it gets in the way of a story, right? Not so different from the rest of us after all, are we?"

Tamara raised a slender long-nailed finger in admonition.

"The difference between us is that I recognize the power of my name and use it responsibly."

Talia twitched an eyebrow in inquiry and Tamara had the grace to blush.

"Self-delusion is the first disease of a power megalomaniac," Talia told her with a smile. "We're all afflicted, my dear. You cannot help it. It runs in the family. Very well. I'll instruct my office to give the *Morning Tribune* exclusive access rights to the Envoy. You make your own arrangements with the other networks, but don't come to me crying if they want to scratch your eyes out. If that is all, much as I would love to chat, I have a city to run."

"Life of a Benevolent Proctor must be tiresome, neh?" Tamara said sweetly. "But that wasn't all. It's a small teensy thing, but maybe you could tell me why the Envoy is here. No one in Kapel's administration, or yours, will tell me. By the way, you wouldn't happen to know how his military aide came by his collection of lumps and bruises, would you?"

Talia grinned with evident enjoyment. "Tamara Lin, I'm surprised at you. Your own channel showed a four-minute clip about that aide last night. Didn't you bother watching it?"

"Come off it, dear cousin. That's your spin team talking. Don't try it on me."

"Try what? The truth is, I don't know. Have you asked Garner? He probably engineered the whole thing."

Tamara was silent for a moment, a slim finger stuck between her lips.

"And maybe you *don't* know. Never mind. Isn't Kapel overreaching herself? Interfering with a General Assembly Envoy could bring her some very unwelcome attention, you know."

"My dear Tamara. I imagine she already has more attention than she wants. Why do you think the Envoy is here?"

"As I was saying, why *is* he here?"

Talia smiled fondly at her cousin. Tamara was good, wasted at the *Morning Tribune*. If it were not for her opposition to Kapel, she could have had a very senior government position, even a Proctor. As it was, she seemed content slinging mud at the Family.

"I thought you knew," Talia said without any apparent guile. "He's investigating incidents of alleged slavery."

Tamara shook her head in disappointment. "Still playing the old games, neh? Slavery is not the issue and you know it. I think the Envoy is looking for something more and I aim to find out what it is."

Talia suspected she knew what the envoy looked for, but she couldn't very well say so. Not to Tamara anyway. *Especially* Tamara!

"When you do find out, let me know. It could be amusing."

Tamara uncrossed her legs and leaned forward. "You're keeping something from me, Talia. I can smell it."

"What you're smelling is the raw propaganda your channels are pumping out about my administration," Talia said primly. "Most of it untrue, I might add. Contrary to popular opinion, I run Raman well."

"Testy, aren't we?"

"If you're hunting for a lead, talk to Kapel."

"She wouldn't give me the time of day and you know it. If you won't tell me why he's here, at least tell me what he's like. You've met him, neh?"

"I've met him. He's from one of those awful rocky worlds in the Sargon Directorate. A ghastly place, I understand. He's short, scrawny, and looks like a boiled fowl, but don't let his bureaucratic nit-picking demeanor fool you. Rayon is sharp and knows Elexi and what makes us tick better than you do. He used to run the Strategic Branch—"

"Isn't that one of Commissioner Enllss-rr's branches?" Tamara interrupted.

"I think so. Why?"

In the Shadow of Death

"Simply curious. The Bureau of Cultural Affairs doesn't generally concern itself with backwater systems like the Fours Suns. Not unless something really nasty were going on. But you were saying?"

Talia had to agree, but wasn't about to say so. Not to Tamara. These were dangerous waters and she needed to steer Tamara away from the shoals.

"Well, Rayon is never likely to rise above branch director, but appears happy being a career ambassador."

"Seems somewhat of a personality, neh? But I never expected Captal to send us a dummy." Tamara gave a small smile and tilted her head. "By the way, my dear. Have you heard anything from Kadreen?"

"Kadreen? No, not lately," Talia said, hoping her emotions would not betray her now.

"Mmm. I received a message fragment from her the other night. Never mind, I'll get to the bottom of it. Thanks for the exclusive." Tamara nodded, waved and cut contact.

"You're welcome," Talia said softly to a blank Wall.

She frowned and chewed her lower lip. *Skies preserve me!* With everything going on lately, she didn't want Tamara getting inquisitive. Tamara's dogged persistence in pursuing a story was infamous. Better get this finished, dear Kapel, she prayed fervently, or we'll all end up counting rocks on Anulus.

What Kapel proposed held enormous potential for the Four Suns and their individual ambitions, but she didn't feel comfortable venturing into the uncharted and turbulent waters of Captal politics. Predators lay in wait there. Then again, life itself was a risk, she mused. Absently, she smoothed down her skirt, then tapped a private code into her desk pad and waited. The Wall cleared and Garner's heavy features stared back in surprise.

"Dama Talia, an unexpected pleasure." He tried a smile, but it never quite made it.

"Put me through, will you," Talia said impatiently. Stupid

male.

It took a minute for the Wall to clear. Ordinarily, getting hold of Kapel needed some arranging, which Talia understood. Neither of them exactly spent their time sitting on their hands, and right now, she suspected that Kapel had a lot to deal with.

When the Wall cleared, Kapel's smile was cool and reserved. Behind her, long gauze drapes stirred before an open window.

"My dear Talia," Kapel said briskly, a planetary executive doing one of the senior Family members a favor. "Wish I could say it's a pleasure, sister, but it would be a lie."

Chunky, but pleasantly so, her thick black hair wound in a curl above a finely sculptured brown face. It accentuated her long pale neck, adorned by a simple choker of small red kerner stones. Little yellow eyes regarded Talia above a thin beak nose. Her lips were wide and full, revealing even white teeth. She wore a daring cream business jacket, the sleeves running to just below the elbow, obviously enjoying the crisp morning air. A single yellow kerner stone clip held it together. It had no collar flaps, her knee-length skirt several shades darker. Simple elegance born of perfect design.

The jewel caused Talia's eyes to drift toward the shelves of mineral specimens and the brilliant fire stone on Kapel's desk. The thin fingers of translucent red and yellow gems looked like bristling spines of some petrified creature. She suppressed a frown of irritation. She had always wanted one of those things, but too proud to ask. Petty pride she knew, but that's how it was.

Kapel's desk was a single slab of polished, white-veined black marble. On one corner stood a carved globe of Elexi, made of some crystal, probably mined on Anulus. Shelves of mineral specimens took up most of one wall, reminding everyone of the source of her power. Looking at her, Talia came to the realization that Kapel had become arrogant and autocratic. She frowned, wondering why it had taken her this long to see it. Kapel needed reminding that she couldn't do it all alone, but Talia was honest enough to realize that same criticism could be applied to her.

"I could say this was a social call, Kapel, but it isn't. We need to talk."

"I dare say. Does it have to be now?"

Challenged, Talia would admit to nothing but scorn for her elder sibling, but deep down lay a layer of affection and grudging admiration for a professional and a worthy opponent. Kapel played rough, gave no quarter and expected none. That's how they all played the game, neh?

Especially now.

"If you're finding the life of Controller and Prime Director too demanding, darling," Talia purred sympathetically, "I would urge you to consider a long period of rest."

Kapel laughed. "Your concern is touching, my dear sister. It really is. And, of course, you would be happy to take over, neh?"

"If I had to. For the sake of the Family." Talia's smile predatory, enjoying the game they played.

"Keep that eagerness cool, my dear. If our plans work out, your turn will come soon enough."

Talia's gaze drifted back to the fire stone. Oh, *bother* with pride.

"That's a great specimen," she ventured uncertainly.

Kapel glanced at the desk. When she looked back, her eyes were sparkling, giving her a perfect opportunity to taunt Talia, make her squirm for the stone. She could sense Talia's anxiety and refrained. Begging came hard to all of them and she wouldn't achieve anything by humiliating her. They were not above scheming and clawing for power, ready to stab each other in the back politically, but when all was said and done, they were bound in blood.

"I will see that you get one, today."

Talia felt a surge of affection for her sister. "Thank you.

I always—"

"My pleasure. I would have sent you one already if I knew you wanted it. Now, about that weighty talk? I really am frightfully busy right now."

"Snappy this morning, aren't we."

Kapel grinned disarmingly, revealing a glimpse of real charm that few seldom saw.

"Forgive me. I'm about to have a session with Anall-Marr, our illustrious Prefect, and I'm not looking forward to it. That pervert always manages to annoy me unbearably, throwing veiled threats between aborted attempts at seduction. I cannot allow myself to forget that behind his cold Deklan façade lay seething emotions and the morals of an amoeba."

"What's his problem? The second mine, neh?"

"The man is infuriating! Here I am, breaking my neck getting that mine into full production—"

"While giving me a hard time over your cursed refining plant," Talia reminded her, looking petulant.

"—to cover his ever-increasing cut, and he's going to burn me for my trouble. Playing holier-than-thou high priest of the Path, while stabbing everyone in the back who gets in the way of his campaign to become Primate of the Ecumenical Synod. I tell you, dear sister, his sudden attack of righteous indignation has a hollow ring to it."

"That's nothing new. His concern is that Sofam will retaliate at our accelerated expansion into the strategic metals market."

"Rubbish!" Kapel shook a finger at her. "Don't get taken in by his propaganda, my dear. He cannot have it both ways. According to his policy, Anulus either expands production to finance Deklan's export drive to become a major metals player, or they cave in to Sofam and sell exclusively through their Paravan Trading Association's cartel, neh? But it's all a lie. Despite his brave words about promoting Deklan's trading independence, Anall-Marr is still toeing the Sofam line. The hypocrite talks about Anulus threatening the destabilization of the metals market, while demanding a bigger cut from the mining proceeds, which only extra production can get. I'll tell you what's being threatened, and it's certainly not the metals market. It's Sofam's dominance and profits, that's what."

"And his ambition to become Primate, should Sofam get seriously upset with Deklan, neh?" Talia said softly.

"You should listen to him. When I mentioned slavery, all he said, a stint in the mines would purify the souls of the sinners and make them fit to stand before the altar. I would like to put *him* on the altar! He disgusts me." She looked down and ran spread fingers from her chest down to her waist. "How do I look?"

"You look stunning, my dear, as always," Talia said irritably.

"It will do."

"Kapel, don't trivialize this. Metal markets aside, he's probably more worried about what the Envoy is doing here."

"He's simply worried about his cut, that's all."

"Perhaps, but they both smell trouble and some of the senior Family are getting anxious." This was a gross breach of custom, but skies above, she wanted answers.

"You never were one to waste much time on preliminaries and small talk, were you?" Kapel said bleakly. "Okay. Do *you* have a specific worry in mind, or were you only after a shoulder to cry on?"

Talia ignored the barb. "As a matter of fact, I do have a pet worry."

"Oh?"

"It's the Envoy's military aide. The one in the hospital, remember? You had Garner's goons rough him up, neh? Or was it one of your pet Scout Fleet thugs?"

Kapel bridled. "I did nothing of the sort! Before pointing a finger of feigned indignation at Garner, don't forget that a couple of nights ago, his goons saved all of us some serious embarrassment."

"Kadreen?"

"Did anyone else break into my offices lately? The trollop was one of our own and she betrayed us, or about to. Garner acted promptly and correctly to eliminate her. As for the Envoy's aide, why blame it immediately on me? Ki-Tori could have been acting independently, neh?"

"It's possible, I suppose," Talia conceded reluctantly.

"But, if I find out that Garner had something to do with putting that aide in the hospital—"

"He could have been interpreting your unvoiced intentions."

"If he was, he'll be doing his interpreting on Anulus. He's only a stupid male and wouldn't dare presume my wishes. I never touched that aide, and I know better than to interfere with the Envoy's people, no matter how much I loath the inconvenience."

"Inconvenience? Come, my dear. I'm sure if that aide was found with a terminal hangover in some dark alley, you wouldn't be mourning."

"Accidents happen, neh?" Kapel said sweetly.

"So long as you can maintain deniability, right? Don't tell me how the game is played, dearie. This is more than foolhardy; it's dangerous. The Envoy could unravel everything. Slavery is simply a convenient handle to get him here and we both know it. It was the excuse needed by the Bureau of Cultural Affairs on Captal for sending him here. Enllss-rr smells collusion between the Four Suns and the Karkan Federation, and the Envoy is here to get proof."

"There is a vast difference between suspecting something and being able to provide it, my dear," Kapel said, staring hard at her sister. "While we're talking about slavery, I would suggest that you take some steps, Talia, or I will. I told you before. You need to clamp down on some of the more zealous excesses of your subordinates. I'm serious."

"Heavens above! With the Envoy already here, it's a bit late for that now, neh?"

Kapel's cheeks colored with anger. "It's never too late! The Envoy will tire of his game and leave, and the Proctors will continue to profiteer behind my back. It's got to stop, I tell you."

Talia pursed her lips. She hated to admit it, but Kapel did have a point. Some of her own senior staffers could do with a lengthy vacation on Anulus.

"I'll take care of my administration, but the other Proctors are your problem, neh?"

"Indeed, but you've got me sidetracked. Forget the Envoy and Enllss-rr. They don't know anything, otherwise they would have acted already."

"How sure are you? Far too many people know of our plans as it is. Not all the Family are made of your stern stuff and one of them could talk. The Envoy's presence and your ill-advised interference with his operative, whether covert or not, will unnerve the Family and fuel further speculation."

"Let them speculate. Clatter of idle tongues, neh?"

"My goodness! When someone like Tamara starts clattering, I sit up and listen."

"That bitch? What does she know? I'll have her on the altar—"

"Calm down. She doesn't know anything, not yet anyway. Given enough time, though, she could put the pieces together. She is a Pen, never forget that, determined and stubborn like the rest of us. Her exposes have caused both of us pain in the past and we don't want her to start digging into our secrets." For a second, she thought of telling Kapel of Kadreen's message fragment, then decided not to. Kapel had bigger problems to deal with.

"Forget your nerves, I tell you," Kapel said. "The groundwork has been laid and all the wheels are in motion. Nothing can stop us now, not even the Envoy or Tamara's speculation.

All I need is ratification from the senior Family, a formality, neh? That shouldn't take too much longer, not if everyone stays calm and doesn't panic."

"There won't be any panic, provided the Envoy doesn't find something."

"He won't. By the time he chases down each lead, we will have made our announcement to the General Assembly. And that, my dear sister, will finish it."

"I hope so," Talia muttered. "I hope so."

Chapter Three

"Come in Second Scout, come in," the envoy said in perfect Pagish.

Terr suppressed a humorless smile. On his way to Elexi, he had taken the local language indoctrination under forced learning as an obvious prerequisite for the mission. Was the envoy testing him?

"I won't be a minute." The envoy gestured with his arm.

He sat behind a huge official-looking desk. The Wall beside him cycled through random color patterns, muddy and cold. On the other side of the office, a closed floor-to-ceiling window took up one whole wall. A real thing and not just a holoview screen. The office was big and opulent. More importantly, it was air-conditioned and warm. It was going to take Terr some time to get used to the local inclement elements. He didn't look forward to his stay.

"Thank you, Tal," he said formally in Pagish.

"Please, let's not stand on protocol," the envoy said, reverting to Serrll interlingua, and waved at one of the formchairs. "No protocol. I get too much of that around here now and it gets tiring. I'm buried in formality!"

While Terr made himself comfortable, the envoy continued to study his display plate, mumbling to himself. Rayon Tantour's large egg-shaped head hairless. He had slanting narrow dull brown eyes. He had no ears, only little black holes. The nose broad and flat above fat purple lips. They reminded Terr of Karkans with their green-scaled skin and fishy faces. Rayon's skin, though, was almost red. Nothing fishy about him, except...

Terr didn't relish the idea of working for an i-dotting bureaucratic stooge. The little language test did nothing to warm him over. He fought to keep his dislike from showing. He knew Rayon was in his second ten-year General Assembly term. A polished Captal official, he probably had a penchant for forms and procedures. To Terr, it only made things worse. Well, it was only for fifteen days.

Finished, Rayon leaned back into the formchair. His right hand fiddled with a record wafer. Reviewing the young man's personal file, he had noted Anabb Karr's comments with interest. Coming from the crusty old officer, hearty praise indeed. Terr's gray eyes showed nothing of the man behind them. Rayon guessed that he would find out quickly enough whether Anabb's recommendations were justified.

"I had the ambient temperature raised in here. Raised. Otherwise, I would have perished of exposure. Although Garner, that's Kapel's chief of staff, you know, finds it a bit overpowering. Yes. A bit overpowering."

"It's the first time I've been warm since I got here, sir," Terr said cautiously.

"And perhaps the last, I dare say. The last. You came from Talon, right?"

"Yes, sir. A short hop to Elexi. Just over four days."

"Dragged away from your command, I understand. An M-3 isn't it?"

"Currently undergoing maintenance."

"You must have done something right to have gotten such a command at your age. At least they haven't saddled me with a bureaucratic deadbeat," Rayon said easily and Terr stared. "No need to feel perplexed, young man. I can imagine what you must be thinking. From the security of an M-3, thrown into the uncertainty of diplomatic counterpointing with a Captal busybody." Rayon snapped the wafer against the desk and his eyes narrowed into slits. "I don't know the extent of your briefing from Prima Scout Anabb Karr—"

"I am aware of some of the…difficulties."

"Indeed? I'm gratified to hear it. Gratified. You seem to have come in for a share of those difficulties yourself already."

"I could have done without them. Is there any further information on those M-3s, sir?" Terr asked and crossed his legs.

"They seem to have vanished. An M-1 against two M-3s…Mmm. You were lucky to evade them."

"What about the logs, the SC&C trace…" Terr ran down when he saw Rayon's indulgent smile. "Of course. Logs can be altered."

"I'm afraid so. This is only the latest in a series of incidents plaguing my investigation, and one of my aides has wound up in a hospital through questionable circumstances. Questionable. That's why you're here as a temporary replacement. Despite *your* logs, Ki-Tori found your story hard to take. However, I find the incident extremely disturbing. Extremely. Whoever is behind it is running a frightful risk. Frightful."

"He reported to you?" Terr asked and leaned forward, his hackles rising from the memory of his recent interview with the prickly Palean.

"Hardly, but I'm not entirely without resources, young man. What he reported was his displeasure at your lack of co-operation."

"Lack of cooperation?" Terr snorted. "Dragged off the Field in what was for all practical purposes open arrest, did little for my cooperation. I also didn't care too much for the grilling he gave me, designed to get me to admit the whole thing was somehow my fault."

"Yes, an awkward piece of work. Awkward. He didn't take much of a shine to you, I'm afraid."

"I'll get over it." Terr shrugged and Rayon grinned.

"You will find the COMELOPS chief of staff a cunning and dangerous man, Terr. Dangerous. Remember, his position gives him powers far beyond those stated in the regulations; and Paleans never forgive. Never."

"The Chief of security—"

Rayon jerked his shoulders in dismissal. "The man was only doing his duty. No harm will come to him. Now, back to Anabb's briefing. As you may have gathered, the situation on Elexi has far-reaching implications. Far. It goes beyond any question of slavery or official corruption. The attempt to interdict your ship reinforces that and raises some disturbing questions in turn. However, those issues are not your concern, or mine, for that matter. Not directly anyway. No concern. Within the obvious limitations imposed on me by Kapel's administration, I'm here to investigate the complaint raised by the Four Suns General Assembly representative. Given all that, you're probably wondering what in tarnation is going on here, right?"

"The thought has crossed my mind, sir."

Rayon ignored the implied impertinence. "No doubt, no doubt. As Prima Scout Anabb Karr indicated to you, my real reason for being here is to find out the extent of Kapel's involvement with the Karkans. Slavery is a legitimate objective, provided I can tie Kapel with it. I have a staff of specialists who are conducting the actual investigation—on both fronts. You and my other aide are acting as a distraction."

"So I've been told. I must say, sir, that doesn't fill me with a whole lot of confidence."

"Let me put it this way, Terr. Unlike myself, you're a military man, used to clear orders and objectives. Clear. I, on the other hand, am used to the labyrinthine maneuverings of bureaucratic machinery. I harbor few illusions about the aims of this investigation. Few. My movements are totally chaperoned. Totally. It's unlikely I'll get to see or find anything I'm not supposed to. That will to a large extent apply to you as well.

"However, lacking specific intelligence training, you'll have a degree of freedom that might allow you to exploit any opportunity that may present itself. Any opportunity. You must use your judgment there."

"Surely, sir, Kapel's administration will be aware of all

this?"

"I expect so. Despite Elexi's provincial appearance, she is no amateur. Frankly, I doubt that you'll be in a position to find anything I can use. We may be able to prove administrative incompetence and a degree of pocket lining by elements of her bureaucracy and the Proctors, but to link that with Kapel in a charge of official corruption and slavery will not be easy. Not easy. Then there are the city Proctors to contend with; an entirely different dimension of politics. Rest assured, she'll use them to block all your investigative efforts. Assured. As far as her dealings with Kunoid and the Karkans are concerned, I hold even less hope. Less."

Terr's mind raced. According to Anabb, the envoy's terms of reference confined his activities to the issue of slavery. Obviously, Rayon thought otherwise. Did the envoy plan to dangle him as bait while Kapel and the Karkans took turns to nibble at him? What had he gotten himself into?

"Still, who knows?" Rayon went on. "I am a long student of history and a firm believer in the preposterous. A firm believer. Some of the most dramatic events in history have resulted from an improbable meeting of chance factors. Providence favors one who is willing to reach for luck."

"What exactly am I supposed to be looking for, sir?" Terr asked without enthusiasm.

"Confine yourself to the issue of slavery, nothing else. Nothing. How you go about it is up to you. Nevertheless, I can offer you a suggestion. Get into the city. Look around and get a feel for the local color, so to speak."

"You understand, sir, as your visible presence on Elexi, my neck will be out a talan."

"Kapel wouldn't dare interfere with a member of my staff!" Rayon snapped.

"The local Proctor or the priesthood guards may not be so careful. Meaning no disrespect, one of your aides isn't in the hospital having a rest."

Rayon's eyes twinkled. "Anabb did say you were sharp. I'm not being insensitive to your concern, young man. There's some risk involved, true. Nevertheless, the degree of media exposure that you will attract should provide some protection."

Terr was not exactly overcome by a warm fuzzy at that. In his view the media were notoriously good at explaining disasters, but not so hot at preventing them. He was sure his eulogy would be a literary masterpiece.

"I shall not interfere in your clandestine activities, Terr. Don't take it too seriously if you seem not to be getting anywhere. On the other hand, slavery is an ugly way to live. Ugly. Especially on Anulus. My opinion only, and not much good where the practice is an accepted one, as it is here." Rayon stood up, the interview over.

"I shall try and remember that, sir," Terr said, uncertain how to digest all this.

"Good. One more thing. One. Keep in mind that Elexi is subject to the laws of the Ecumenical Order. The priests administer the law here. Informers and spies are everywhere. Raman is a sprawling city with many dark alleys. Many. Be careful where you go, my boy."

Rayon appeared genuinely concerned and Terr realized he had misjudged the little bureaucrat. He may be a Captal busybody, in his element shuffling statistics and reports, but he seemed sincere.

"I'll make every effort to keep myself off the sacrificial altar, but you haven't given me much to go on with, sir," he said, still uncertain how to approach this assignment.

"Be thankful for that."

* * *

Small sounds filled the slave pen: guarded whispers, shreds of broken conversation spoken quickly, and the weary nodding of heads. A child suckled noisily at her mother's breast and whimpered. The mother stared at the far wall and rocked a child in her arms while humming a soft melody. Bare planks made the seats hard. A flickering light strip sent the shadows dancing. Someone shuffled about in search of a warm corner. Snarls of frustration followed the shape with a yelp when a reflex kick went home.

A new shipment came in yesterday and there wasn't enough room for everybody in the more comfortable observation lounge. Like himself, most of the slaves had the vacant look of resignation and quiet despair. Alasi leaned against the uncut stone of the wall and waited. In the days since his captivity, he learned to wait. He tugged at his finery—sales clothes given to him by Tarad. He was reluctant to squat in the dank straw lest he should soil them. He'd be beaten, then.

He glanced past the keeper near the doorway, taking in the hurried bustle of the soukh outside. He knew when a customer arrived. Tarad's voice would become a whine as he tried to induce a sale. Failure would bring angry scowls and the baton would lash some luckless victim. He winced at a painful memory and the welt on his side tingled.

There was a customer outside now, he could tell.

Tarad stomped into view and pointed. The keeper glanced sharply at Alasi and jerked his head.

"Move, you." The keeper reached in and yanked him out.

Alasi staggered, caught himself and slowly climbed up the scarred wooden steps to the viewing stand. Early afternoon and business was brisk, the crowd in no mood to haggle long. Invariably, some of the onlookers lingered. A hint of frost lay in the air. Under the pavilion lights, Alasi did not find it uncomfortable.

A highborn Dama, accompanied by a beribboned dandy, stopped and pointed a slender finger at him. She inclined her delicate head toward her consort, whispered then giggled behind a small hand. With a sideways glance, they moved on.

Alasi followed them with his eyes, thinking dark thoughts.

Let them laugh. He would show them one day. He'd show them all.

On the pavement below stood a young Scout officer. This one did not look like any dandy. Gray eyes stared back at him, remote and unforgiving. They were the kind of eyes that didn't miss much. Honest eyes, Alasi decided.

Tarad already well into his sales pitch.

"Rit!" Terr said and scratched the scar above his eyebrow. "He's too young. What the hell am I supposed to do with him? Change his diapers?" He shook his head with amusement and turned to walk away.

People pushed and jostled each other, hunting for bargains or just gawking. The constant background of shouting and inane chatter drove him to distraction. He hated crowds, wondering what he was doing bargaining with a slime like Tarad.

"Wait! Be reasonable, Excellency." Tarad's powerful hand reached for Alasi's shoulder. Terr could see the boy shrink back from the touch. "He's young, yes, but you can train him, neh? Think of all the innumerable little things that need doing in your ship."

"Worm crap," Terr said, trying to appear disinterested. Nevertheless, he was intrigued by the predatory technique of the factor. "I have a crew for that."

Tarad persisted. "They never give you that personal touch, noble Tal. I know."

"Like stealing from me?"

"Ah, I see the Excellency is jesting, no?"

"No. How come you hold locals in your stock? A bit unusual isn't it? It's supposed to be illegal too."

"Ah, a hurried deal, worthy Tal. I understand he was destined for one of the labor worlds. Maybe even Anulus." He leaned closer and grinned, showing a set of pitted dentures. "His captors figured on making a quick profit on the side and the boy is good stock. As for it being illegal, well, money smoothes many rough paths, heh heh. The Benevolent Proctor will not want from this sale, noble Tal."

"I am sure she won't." Terr glanced at two priesthood guards wandering about. They were obviously turning a blind eye, probably in on the cut as well. "How much did you have in mind for this wonder?"

"Three hundred," Tarad answered promptly. "Any lower and I'll have to give him away."

Terr turned and started walking.

"Tal!" Terr stopped and turned his head.

"Well?"

"Name your price, excellent Tal," Tarad said crestfallen, shoulders drooping. "I've got to get rid of him. I carry too much inventory already. I'd be better off letting him go. It's getting so an honest trader can't make a living anymore, neh?"

Terr really felt for the slaver. He studied the factor, then reluctantly walked back.

"Two fifty," he heard himself say.

"Done!" Tarad grinned and held out his hand.

The little bastard *was* a good salesman. Now that he had the boy, Terr still needed to figure out what he was going to do with him. He dug into his pockets and produced the money. Cash was a damned nuisance, but he didn't want to get himself entangled in the local electronic system, not for fifteen days.

Tarad sifted through the little rectangles, counting quickly. He looked up and motioned to the keeper.

"Okay, you." The keeper slapped his whip against his thigh.

Alasi looked at him with hate and shuffled toward the slaver.

"In there, boy." Tarad pointed at his office.

Alasi was ready. He kicked at the shins and his nails left brown furrows on the factor's hand. Tarad yelped and back-handed the boy across the mouth. Alasi staggered and tasted blood. It had been worth it. Rough hands reached for him. He jerked and twisted.

"Hold him, you fools!" Terr watched the boy slither beneath the keeper's outstretched hands.

Alasi jumped off the stand and ran, not even glancing back at the commotion and the screams of impotent rage that followed him. He laughed as he disappeared up the crowded lane, another figure among millions.

Terr stared into the crowd where the boy had vanished, and cursed. He lifted his head and his eyes locked on Tarad's slack face.

"If I don't get him back, unharmed, I will have you before the altar," he grated and the factor paled.

"But, heroic Tal!" Tarad looked nervous, his hands working in despair. "He could be anywhere!"

"Then find him! He still has his identification band. Trace him. When you do, have him brought to the Center—with the contract."

"Noble Tal, to whom do I—"

"Second Scout Terrllss-rr!" he snapped, furious with himself for getting talked into this mess.

* * *

Worrying a piece of liberated fruit, Alasi wandered in the general direction of the landing field. He needed a plan. His initial grandiose schemes had lost some of their luster while he'd been enjoying Tarad's hospitality. Instead of fire and destruction, he was prepared to settle for something more subtle, and he still had no idea how to find his family.

He dismissed the initial impulse to round up the gang. Time for that later. Besides, as a runaway slave, he would only get them into trouble. First, Tominoy the Wanderer! Tominoy would help. Tominoy would know what to do. And the band…He looked at his wrist and wrapped a hand around it as though that would stop its betraying transmission. He needed to get rid of it fast. The thought of being captured again made his skin crawl.

He made his way past the Field perimeter and headed for the ruins of the Old City.

A gust of wind flapped around his garments and sand stung his exposed legs. The sky dull brown and sullen red where the two binaries struggled to get through. The vendors grumbled and covered their wares with transparencies to keep out the sand. Stall awnings flapped and cracked. Disinterested customers, sightseers, pickpockets and mendicants vied for passing business. Dressed in his fine tunic, no one gave him a second glance.

Overhead, a combie skimmed beneath the clouds as it headed for the central spires of Raman. Alasi watched it disappear and spat on the lane.

People didn't hang around the Old City long. Alasi had often talked to Tominoy about that, but the ancient wouldn't say much. He would stare at nothing, lost among his memories while Alasi sat beside him studying the yellow, wrinkled face and the large rusted eyes with their vertical red slits. Whatever secrets the old man knew, he was not ready to tell them. Alasi was patient, and for some strange reason the old man had taken a liking to him. They would often talk about things and nothing in particular. Tominoy treated him as an equal, not a child, and Alasi appreciated that.

The old man lived in a small shack in a narrow alley among other small shacks. He sat cross-legged on one side of the doorway. Feeble street lighting fell around him, casting gray shadows. People walked by, occasionally dropping a coin into a shallow bowl. Tominoy never reacted. He sat there and stared at the street.

Alasi walked up to him and sat down. He wanted to tell Tominoy about his mother and the rest of his family. He wanted to tell him about Tarad and the young Scout officer and...

Somehow, it didn't matter. He felt that Tominoy knew and

understood. Alasi had known sorrow and pain, but sitting here now, waiting, he felt a measure of peace.

"You have suffered much, my son," the old man said after a time, his voice rumbling like the tremble of dying thunder.

Thoughts went through Alasi's mind that he didn't understand. He wanted to cry out in anguish and pain, but his tears were dry. He grimaced and tried to stop his shivering.

"Tell me what to do?" he asked in quiet desperation.

"Nothing."

"Nothing? But they's after me. I can't—"

"That will all pass," Tominoy interrupted gently. His eyes swept over Alasi's thin form. He reached out with a gnarled hand and wiped a streak of blood from the boy's cheek. "Tarad has a heavy hand doesn't he?"

"How—"

"Listen to me, my son. You are but a grain of sand flying in the wind. You have slipped through the net and the wind blows on. Do you understand?"

"No," Alasi said firmly and Tominoy sighed.

"Elexi is a large world, and Raman is not the only city. There are places where a free man can learn his worth. Go quickly now, my son. Spies are everywhere and people are not always to be trusted."

Alasi still didn't understand, but that would come later. It always did. One thing he agreed with, he had to get out of Raman.

"I need to see my home first."

"I would not advise it," Tominoy said. "It's one of the first places they will search."

"And my family?"

The old man was silent for a long time. Then, "They are beyond saving, my son," he whispered sadly. "It would take someone far more powerful than me to move the Proctor to act."

Alasi stared at him, not believing. "You won't help me,

then?"

Tominoy looked down, his face grave. "I don't have that kind of power, boy."

Alasi stood up and nodded. "No matter. I'll find them somehow."

"Wait, the band," Tominoy said and got stiffly to his feet. "In here."

Alasi followed him into the gloom of the room. The old man reached up to one of the shelves and produced a small rod, similar to the one Alasi had seen Tarad use. Tominoy took Alasi's wrist and touched the band. It glowed briefly, then faded to its previous dull sheen.

Alasi looked at Tominoy. "What'd you do?"

"I scrambled its identification code. I am not able to remove the band and you would be conspicuous without it. It will serve until you get away from here."

Alasi smiled. "Thanks."

Then that the priesthood guards came.

Alasi heard the soft whir of a landing sled-pad and paled. Tominoy glanced sharply at the doorway. He held out his hand and stared hard at the rod in his palm. The ceramic seemed to twist, glowed a dull yellow and turned black. He placed the charred rod on the bench behind him.

When he turned, two guards stood framed in the doorway.

* * *

Dusk settled slowly. Strands of mist began to gather among the lengthening shadows of Celean Park. The broad avenues were already bathed in light. The various administrative buildings of the General Assembly—columns of color-reactive ceramic, composite fiber and crystal—climbed into the early mist. Beyond the park, vanishing in the haze, lay the spires of Captal over which swarmed the stacked patterns of commercial and public traffic. A cluster of black towers stood outlined against the western sky.

The last rays of the sun waned and the internal lighting system compensated automatically. Enllss-rr canceled the response with a soft growl. The lights faded and shadows crept into the office. In the background, the Wall cycled through gyrating patterns of shadow to the accompaniment of unobtrusive music. This high up the Security Council tower was almost within reach of the lower traffic bands. Streaming lines of combies, private sled-pads and communals moved in radiating spokes toward outlying residential centers.

He leaned back in his formchair and took a sip of herbal tea. His eyes wandered along the colors of the sunset, then followed a line of traffic until it disappeared in the distance.

The comms alert beeped. He turned to the Wall and the office flared with light.

"Commissioner," the low tremulous contralto voice of his personal aide stirred distracting images in his mind. "Sill-Anais from the Diplomatic Branch is here to see you, sir."

"Very well. Show him in, will you?"

The large opaque panels slid away and Sill walked in. He wore his long white hair, streaked with twin bands of dark gray, in traditional Deklan fashion. Tall and wiry, thin white eyebrows outlined large, liquid wide-set green eyes that could cloud with anger, but were laughing now. His face, pinched and dry beneath an olive complexion, traced lines of age and responsibility. He carried himself with ease, assured of his power.

"Enllss." He bowed. Without ceremony, he sprawled his length into a formchair.

"Sill, you old sand slug! You still playing at catching moles?"

"Ach! Cleaning out all the ones you let in," Sill piped and slid a hand down the side of his head. "Apart from that, we're sweeping out the garbage your bureaucrats always leave behind after one of your schemes goes sour."

"By damn." Enllss grinned and poured them some tea. "I

wouldn't need to cook up schemes if your crowd did its job."

"The trouble with you, Enllss, is that you behave like you were still running my Branch. You are an important official now, not a lowly Branch director like me, to be bothered with trivia."

"Someone has to make sure that you do your job," Enllss said dryly and lifted his cup in a salute.

"Arrogant bastard." Sill picked up his cup and saucer, took a sip and winced. "Ghastly stuff." He always rubbished the tea and Enllss always served it. "I see that promotion hasn't made a dent in that infamous lack of tact. Enjoying your first term as Commissioner?"

"After a year the novelty has worn off," Enllss said easily, but he could not hide a tinge of pride in his voice. Only seven years into his first Assembly term, happily running the Diplomatic Branch, when they unexpectedly announced his promotion. A high compliment, as elevation to commissioner in a first term almost unheard of. "Your family, how are they?"

"Captal can be a dreary place and it's not home. Too clinical and impersonal. Ach! Necessary, I suppose, in a place that runs an empire."

"The Serrll Combine has never been an empire. The power blocks are all too independent for that."

"Mmm, perhaps, but the Sofam Confederacy has been its unofficial lord nevertheless."

"Let's say that we've been a stabilizing influence in our coalition with the Deklan Republic," Enllss said mildly and sipped his tea.

"Ach! Such modesty. But then, Sofam has always worn its power well. Like you, my friend. Ach!"

"It's like a cloak. Something I leave behind when I walk out the office."

"I think not. You know what I miss most of all? I miss my digits."

"Two boys, right?"

"Young men now, if you will pardon a father's pride. One is attending the Ecumenical Seminary and will shortly graduate as a priest of the Order. He's majoring in strategic studies and intends following in my footsteps into the Diplomatic Corps. The older one is serving with the Fleet. He is now a grade one Base Scout."

"You would have preferred both of them in the Order?"

"Ach! Times change, my sinful friend. The lure of far worlds is strong in our young, to the lament of the traditionalists."

"I haven't seen your partner in quite a while. You must bring her to my place sometime soon."

"She would like that, but you didn't call me here to discuss my family life."

"You're right, I didn't." Enllss placed his cup on the desk. "It's the Four Suns, and I'm worried. More so after going over Rayon's preliminary status—"

"By the way, sorry to interrupt, ach! I thought you would like to know that Anabb has assigned your nephew as one of Rayon's military aides."

"Terr? Do him good," Enllss said and shrugged.

"Command of an M-3 seems to have settled him down a little."

"You looked at his record? By damn. I don't mind admitting it to you. The boy reminds me too much of my own reckless and undisciplined youth."

"You? Reckless?" Sill piped mockingly.

"Better believe it. I had supreme confidence in myself and a sublime contempt for all authority. Why else would I have entered politics?"

"Arrogance," Sill said promptly and Enllss laughed. "I heard a rumor that you've been pushing Anabb to seek a nomination to the General Assembly, come the next general elections."

"It's no rumor," Enllss said. "Sofam can use him, and I

imagine after a lifetime in the Serrll Scout Fleet, playing Commander Deklan Operations has probably lost some of its gloss."

"I know how he feels."

"I can't say I blame him. He has an attitude, blunt to the point of insolence. It's probably just one of the reasons why he's warming a seat on Talon rather than commanding a battleship-sized office here in Captal, but don't get choked up with sympathy or anything. Anabb knows what he's doing."

"Like you. Power and responsibility has toughened you, my friend, but it has also made us old."

Enllss nodded and quietly sipped his tea. "I'll tell you something, Sill. Eight years ago, had I known the price I would have to pay, I might have thought twice about it. Then again, the load was lighter then…and I was younger then. But, enough of that. Talk to me about the Four Suns."

"Ach! After eight years, you're still to learn patience."

"I haven't time to be patient. Want any more tea?"

Sill shook his head and Enllss poured himself another cup. He took a sniff and nodded, apparently satisfied.

"Okay, what have you got?"

"Well, you've seen the reports. We can make out a fair case supporting the Four Suns Assembly rep's charges right now—"

"That's not good enough, Sill. Not nearly good enough. Rayon is not there to bury Kapel and you know it. I don't care about her or her miserable little world. I'm paying you to find out why she's coddling to the Karkans all of a sudden."

"Ach! Give me a break. They've only been on the case a few days."

"What are your vaunted experts doing? Taking up calligraphy?"

"No need to get nasty," Sill said.

Muscular and powerful, the bulge around Enllss' middle betrayed the effects of soft living. There was nothing soft about

Stefan Vučak

the square chin, determined and used to command. He had a habit of thrusting it out when emphasizing a point. Dark gray eyes that could turn opaque with anger, now looked at Sill with mirth. His hair almost pure white with a fleck of brown here and there that gave a lie to his age. The aquiline nose stood out sharply above a firm mouth.

Enllss shifted in his formchair and scratched his knee.

"Sill, we need to know what the Servatory Party, and by that, I mean the Karkans, are up to. There is more to this than Deklan's expansion into the strategic metals market."

"I know. That's why you pestered BueAdmin to send that runt Rayon to gnaw at it."

"What's the matter? The little guy still a burr in your pants?"

"There is something…unholy about him, that's all."

"Swallow that bias," Enllss admonished. "He's a very able ambassador. If anyone can sort out the mess on Elexi, he can. And I'm not talking about slavery, or Anall-Marr's political ambitions either."

"I understand your concern, my friend, but it doesn't seem warranted in this case."

"You think not? I'll tell you this much. If Anall is planning to destabilize the metals market, Sofam will crush him!" Enllss said and slapped the armrest. "He may be your friend, but I'll rip out his guts and hang them on one of his own altars."

"You can't accept it, can you, Enllss? For once, Kunoid Minerals has made a tactical coup without any suggestion of political influence."

"Apparent suggestion!"

"You're sore at us because Sofam and your precious Paravan Trading Association lost the Anulus minerals mining contract to the Karkans. Could the Commissioner be piqued perhaps, that Paravan got creamed by the opposition?" He had given his friend a hard time lately, not letting him forget the humiliation Sofam had received at Deklan's hands.

In the Shadow of Death

Enllss leaned forward and pointed a long finger at Sill.

"You couldn't be more wrong. Sure, I might be a little miffed, but I'm not sore at the Deklan Republic for what they've done. We might have done the same thing, had our roles been reversed. As for Paravan, that's business. What I cannot accept is Kunoid Minerals pouring megaserrlls into the Four Suns without some payoff in mind. They want something and I need you to find out what that is." He stood up, clasped his hands behind his back and paced around the office.

He had known Sill a long time and trusted his integrity. Nevertheless, he could not afford to forget that Sill was a high-ranking member of the Ecumenical Synod. As one of Deklan's representatives in the General Assembly, his job was to promote the Republic's interests, as Enllss promoted Sofam's.

He stopped and looked at Sill after a few seconds of silence.

"You know, I have always been fascinated by Deklan's peculiar approach to politics, colored as it is by the pervasive influence of your Ecumenical Order. That you managed to hold the Republic together and expand is not a testimony to your religious zeal or your professed devotion to the Path. Do you know what I think?"

"I am sure you'll tell me," Sill said, not certain what Enllss was getting at.

"I will. I think it's plain pragmatism over factional fanaticism. Above all else, you're realists. It's prudent to remember that your history is also a saga of blood and conquest. The robes of your priests are not red for nothing. You have always been a thorn in the side of the Serrll, sometimes pointing out things the Assembly and the Executive preferred not to think about."

"Like our business venture with the Karkans?" Sill could not resist that one. Enllss frowned.

"Perhaps, but I would start to worry if my Branch Director, swept up in a wave of patriotic fervor, suddenly lost his objectivity."

Sill slammed his cup and saucer on the desk. "You bastard.

Ach! What about *your* objectivity?"

They glared at each other. After a moment, Sill ran a hand through his hair. Did he react so strongly because the accusation rang true?

"Something for both of us to think about, isn't it?" Enllss said. "Will you listen to me for a second?"

"Of course—"

"Forget about Sofam and Deklan economic policy differences for the moment, will you? For centuries, we've had the Serrll Combine divided between two coalitions, the Revisionist Party and the Servatory Party. That means Sofam and the Karkans, if you discount the minor independent blocks. Between us, we've generally given fairly good government. As a rule, we don't interfere too much in the administration of individual systems."

"Well, now—"

"As a rule, I said. The Servatory Party has never abandoned its objective to hold the majority of seats in the Executive Council, thereby giving them control of the government. The fact that they hold far fewer systems than the Sofam Confederacy gives them a serious tactical problem. They can overcome that handicap in only two ways. The first is to form alliances with other power blocks. They succeeded with the Sargon Directorate. For all intents and purposes, they also control the nonaligned independents. That gives them only four out of the available ten seats, not nearly enough for them to wrest control. Who is left?"

Sill let out a long breath and picked up his cup. "Us and the Palean Union," he said. "But you control the Paleans. I mean, Sofam does."

"The Paleans are factional and their support is split with the Alikan Union Party," Enllss pointed out wearily. "And the AUP has been leaning steadily toward the Sargon camp. We hold their single vote now, but we cannot count on them forever, not if they succeed in their merger with Sargon."

Sill paused, his cup almost at his lips. "Are you saying the Servatory Party wants to dominate the Deklan Republic through the Kunoid operation?"

"It's possible."

"That's dangerous thinking, Enllss. We might have gone into a commercial venture with a Karkan conglomerate, but we never supported the Karkans politically, never. I cannot see us doing it now."

"But you don't make the decisions," Enllss told him bluntly. "Anulus spells power, a lot of power. Damaging in the wrong hands."

"You mean, when it's not in Sofam's hands."

"Let's not kid ourselves here, Sill. Your government made a deal with Kunoid simply to put the squeeze on us."

"You cannot leave it alone, can you?"

"Hear me out. The Executive Council told your Ecumenical Synod the optimum solution was to share Anulus with Sofam and the Karkans. The current situation is too unstable and can only lead to trouble. Don't forget that Deklan is more dependent on our support than we're on yours."

"Take it easy. Ach! I didn't mean it to sound like that."

"Sure you didn't. Just because I am Sofam's representative, that doesn't make me any less concerned for the welfare of the whole Serrll Combine. As commissioner, while I run the Bureau of Cultural Affairs, is my *only* concern."

Sill shifted in his seat and looked away. Enllss swore and reached across the space between them with an open hand.

"Forgive me. That was uncalled for, but this thing has me worried."

"Real bad, I can tell." Sill still did not like the insinuation that the current problem was all Deklan's fault. "You mentioned two ways."

Enllss sat down and took a sip of tea. "So I did. The second is territorial acquisition."

"Oh, come now! Ach! We're all guilty of that one. First, we

give a protectorate independence to quell their nationalistic fervor. When they get tired of their nonaligned status, we swallow them. Where does Kunoid's operation fit into that scenario?"

"The Karkans might be getting ready to do some swallowing of their own."

"Are you trying to tell me the Karkan Federation wants to invade Anall-Marr's prefecture because Kunoid Minerals happens to be involved? Come on! Any way you look at it, that's a fantastic conclusion based on a grand leap of imagination. Ach!"

"That might be," Enllss admitted. "I want you to do something for me. Shift your focus to Kapel Pen and the other three Controllers in Anall's prefecture."

"Care to tell me why?"

"Axiom, Sill. Politics is the art of plotting. Diplomacy is the art of counter-plotting. I have a hunch, or a leap of imagination, as you call it. I need to know what Kapel and the Karkans are plotting. Something is going on and it spells trouble. I can feel it."

"Ach! That's paranoia talking, you old fool."

"See to it, Sill."

Chapter Four

Across the circular interior of the shopping plaza, the native tailing Terr leaned against the second floor gallery railing and looked directly at him. A rusty trench coat belted tight around the middle hid a tall gaunt form. The dark eyes were expressionless, something to see with. A thin mouth beneath a spare nose an empty gash worn on a long bony face.

Transparent cable-tubes packed with shoppers glided up and down the interior walls. Beneath them the plaza floor was a cauldron of hurrying, strolling citizenry. A distraught mother burdened with colored packages and bags, dragged children in her wake. No one seemed to mind the impersonal pushing and jostling that went on, but this was a common market and the more refined of the Raman's female citizenry spurned the place. In the center of the floor the tinkle of falling water from a multicolored fountain lost in background noise. Terr found the bright display lights, the booming speakers and the clamor of countless voices a shield. Ordinarily, he would shun such places. The press of humanity was not a blanket he wore lightly.

With a last glance at his shadow, Terr walked to the nearest tube. The guy supporting the railing didn't move. He was still there when the tube whispered down to the ground floor.

Terr expected to be under surveillance, but this was altogether different and open. The two items keeping him company during the evening looked mean and didn't bother hiding it. They were not subtle about it and made sure he knew it.

Outside, he pulled his liner closer about him and blew white breath into his hands. The feeling of being watched was a tingle at the back of his neck. If those two wanted something, he would make it easy for them. He cast a searching look

79

around the crowded sidewalk. His two pals were nowhere to be seen.

The so-called tradecraft he'd been trying to employ was not as easy to do as the thrillers made it out. He smiled wryly and walked down the mall, his footfalls loud. Above him, glidewalks and tubeways spanned the buildings. Public communals stood parked in hovering clusters along the mall. Bored drivers waited for customers.

Terr pushed through the crow and made his way behind the plaza where he left his combie. A dark figure leaning casually against the building straightened as Terr approached. When Terr was about to walk past him, the figure turned and pushed a hard elbow against his side. Terr saw a glimpse of a rusty trench coat as the figure disappeared in the crowd.

Okay, so they wanted to play. He liked a brisk game as much as the next guy. He absently massaged his side.

The parking lot behind the plaza well lit. Enough people were coming and going so that he didn't feel lonely. Hovering rows of stacked combies and sled-pads packed the open quadrangle. A shopper punched in his code at one of the open control booths and turned to watch the parking system extract his combie out of the stack and bring it down. Public communals cruised around like scavengers waiting for prey. At various levels cargo liners hovered around the plaza's landing ramps.

He needed to find out what the goons following him were really after, but he wanted to do it without attracting attention. He took a shortcut through a darkened alley between two buildings. A tall figure stepped out of the shadows ahead of him, the trench coat clearly outlined against the glare of the parking lot. Padded footfalls sounded loud behind him, then stopped.

Terr glanced over his shoulder at the silent figure standing several paces behind him, then stepped sidewise until the alley wall was against his back. The two figures stood there and waited for him to get comfortable. On cue, they both pulled short saps out of their coats and walked deliberately toward him. He guessed that chatting wasn't high on their skill list.

They closed in without stopping, figuring to smother him from both sides. It was a dirty way to fight and very effective. When they got to within two katalans from him, Terr crouched, skipped toward the nearest one, and lashed out with a straight leg.

Instead of countering, the figure stopped and leaned back—only to receive a boot in the face as Terr kicked up with his other leg. Terr felt the satisfying jar of breaking bone and the figure bounced hard against the opposite wall. He didn't wait to see the body slide down, but swiveled as the other thug swung down his sap.

Pain exploded against his head and left shoulder. The thug continued the swing in a vicious flat circle, aiming for Terr's right side—the kidneys. In reflex, Terr crossed his hands and blocked, only to receive a boot high on the chest that sent him sprawling along the alley.

Rit!

His shoulder burned with fire, but he didn't think it was broken. Wheezing, he coughed to get his breathing working again, but he didn't have time to pick himself up. The thug jumped toward him and lashed out with his foot. Terr swung out his left forearm and partially smothered the kick. Needles of pain exploded in his side and he grunted, rolled with the blow and lashed out with his left leg in a sweep.

The thug's legs slid away beneath him and he crashed down heavily. Terr continued his roll until he was on his back. He raised his right leg and brought the heel down hard against the thug's chest. There was a rush of expelled air and a deep grunt as the thug tried to double up. Terr got to his knees and brought a smashing elbow against the thug's head. The body twitched and slumped back.

Kneeling, he placed both hands against the cold paving. Deep coughs racked his body. Next time he felt like sightseeing, he would resist the urge. He looked around, but the alley was empty. The whole attack couldn't have taken fifteen seconds, but it felt longer than a minute. Massaging his left shoulder and side, he looked down at the two sprawled bodies.

His search revealed nothing, except for the ship's boots they both wore. He wore a pair just like them.

He let out a loud sigh and leaned against the wall. If shopping was going to be this exciting, he would be staying indoors from now on. He plunged his hand into his pocket and pulled out a little pebble communicator. Time for the envoy to do some work for a change.

* * *

Brooding, Terr stared through the closed window at the jumbled profusion of towers that surrounded the Center. In the distance a brown blanket of pollution hung above the city. Morning found him bruised and sore, wallowing in self-pity. He allowed himself a few moments to savor the feeling.

He reminded himself to ask Rayon for the incident report on the aide still in the hospital. If the attack last night meant to discourage him, he was discouraged. Who wanted to send him that kind of a message? And those ship's boots…

Could Ki-Tori be pissed enough at him to remind him who was the big kid on the block? Possible, but Terr considered it unlikely. Why would Cannan's chief of staff bother himself with a lowly second scout? It seemed more to do with the envoy's side of the business than a matter of personal revenge. He wondered if there was an open season on military aides these days.

The entry monitor tinkled sharply and he scowled.

Frustrated, he turned to the Wall. Two priesthood guards waited outside brandishing drawn needlers. Between them stood his little runaway slave.

Terr was appalled by the boy's appearance. The garment he wore dirty and torn, he had bruises on face and arms. Terr could see ribs outlined on the boy's thin body. Standing there, recaptured, not knowing his fate, he looked sullen and defiant. Terr shook his head.

Even now, he couldn't really explain why he allowed himself to be suckered into buying the boy. Against regulations and…he cursed for being a sentimental fool. He wanted to convince himself the boy would have been an ideal means of plugging himself into the local color. Undistorted by official propaganda, it would have given him a handle on what everyone claimed to be an impossible job. It would…

Rit!

The bottom line, he knew something of the quality of human suffering. He had seen it on too many worlds. He suspected this to be a futile gesture, though. Still, the boy had touched some part of him that meant he couldn't simply walk away. The squalor of the soukh and the open misery of some of its inhabitants came as a rude shock to him. He wasn't used to seeing life in such raw detail. Anabb told him this would be a valuable experience, although he figured Anabb hadn't been thinking about the soukh when he said it. Futile gesture or not, he was committed.

"Open," he said gruffly and the door slid into the wall. The guards glanced curiously around the luxurious apartment, then stood to.

"Second Scout Terrllss-rr?" one of them asked diffidently and Terr nodded.

"Tal, we have delivered your slave as ordered, with the contract. If you wish to press charges against Tarad's Circle, you have two days within which to do so."

"I shall keep it in mind," Terr said and took the proffered wafer.

The guard lifted his needler in a salute, then both marched down the corridor.

Holding the wafer, Terr placed the other hand on his hip and looked closely at his new property. The boy had his fists clenched and returned Terr's gaze with defiance.

"You want to come in or were you planning to make a break for it?" Terr asked pleasantly.

Alasi took a quick glance down the corridor and weighed his chances. How far could he expect to get before the goons caught up with him again, and then more beatings? Right now, he had a brand new opportunity and there were always angles he could play. With a cautious glance at the alien standing before him, he stepped in. The door hissed shut behind him. His eyes darted around the room, round with wonder. He never imagined himself in such opulence. When he looked at his new master, wary and alert, he had his guard back in place.

"What's your name, boy?" Terr asked.

The boy hesitated, petulant. "Alasi…master."

"I'm Terr, and you don't have to call me master."

Alasi smirked. If the guy thought to soften him up with phony sympathy, he wouldn't get much change for his trouble. Sooner or later, his master would make a mistake and that would be it.

Terr looked down at the boy, painfully aware of Alasi's resentment.

"Before we go any further, I want to get one thing straight. Whatever hard knocks you might have had, I'm not your enemy. I may even be able to help."

Alasi snorted with contempt. "Help? I've seen the sort of help your kind hands out."

"All right then, a straight proposition. A deal."

"Like the one that got my parents taken away, neh? You can shove your deals. And if you think that you can keep me here…"

Terr's hand came up and Alasi flinched. Terr appeared not to notice as he touched his scar.

"I don't know anything about your parents, but before you spit in my eye, I want you to hear me out."

Alasi stood there, unsure of himself. He'd been prepared

for hunger and beatings, but not this. To be hanging around a pad like this the alien had to be rich and powerful. A deal? The alien was asking for the moons.

"Why'd you want to do all this anyway? What do I matter to the Serrll?"

Not sure how to answer, Terr tapped the wafer against the side of his leg.

"Let's say I want to see a little justice done," he said, and Alasi's smile was grim.

"Tarad gave me a taste of justice in the pens."

"The deal, kid. Interested?"

Alasi wasn't about to fall at Terr's feet in gratitude. Still, this could have possibilities. It couldn't hurt to talk.

"What kinda deal?" he asked cautiously. Terr relaxed a bit.

"Information. No strings attached. You tell me things and you get your freedom."

Alasi chuckled. "I'd been free before. That didn't help me any."

"Yeah, I know. But you can't have it both ways. You either trust me or you can turn around and go," Terr said and pointed at the door. "There will be no one to stop you. And I won't set the guards after you, but once you're out there, you'll have to take your chances. Before you make up your mind, think about this. By helping me, you could prevent some other family from being taken away. I cannot promise I can get yours back, but if you want to tell me what happened to them, I'll see what I can do."

Alasi lifted his head and glared. "Why should I trust you? On Elexi, we don't believe'n much. Not the way things is run. One thing we did believe in. If you have your wristband, you're free, neh?" he hissed and shook the banded wrist at Terr. "That turned out to be just another lie."

"I haven't told you any lies, Alasi."

"Hah! You haven't told me anything."

Terr felt a wave of helplessness. How could he hope to

break through a lifetime of hatred and suspicion? Better to forget the whole thing.

"You can still use that door, boy," he said wearily.

"With a scrambled wristband, how far do you think I'd get? And besides, who are you to change the world?" Alasi glanced at the insignia on Terr's chest and sneered. "Even a Second Scout needs help, neh?"

"Something like that."

"Find my family," Alasi demanded firmly, not wanting to believe, but hoping anyway. Tominoy did say it would take someone powerful, and this Scout officer may be his ticket.

"And our deal?"

Alasi felt tugged in conflicting directions. He couldn't afford to trust, not now. He'd been through too much. What the alien offered was impossible, a fool's dream. Yet, what choice did he have? *Maw!* Suddenly, the fight went out of him and he stood there, eyes pleading.

"Find my family," he whispered and his shoulders sagged.

Terr silently cursed the fates that have reduced the boy to this.

"I'll do my best," he said and cleared his throat.

* * *

Terr nibbled at his food. Alasi worked at his plate with undisguised gusto. It must have been a while since the boy had a decent meal, and certainly not one like this. All the time Alasi shoveled it away, his eyes were darting around the room, figuring the situation. In the uncertain world he lived, it was a case of taking advantage of every opportunity as it presented itself.

Alasi wore a simple coverall that Terr had the Wall dispenser run out. He squirmed and fidgeted, unaccustomed to wearing such garments. They were warmer and better than the tunic Terr threw away, but he longed for his tattered soukh outfit. He hated feeling conspicuous.

In the Shadow of Death

When they got to the teeth-picking stage, Terr leaned back in the formchair and folded his hands across his chest. The boy had relaxed somewhat after the meal, his eyes no longer wild, looking for hidden traps, but still wary. He also looked better after Terr had treated his cuts and bruises.

"Tell me, Alasi. Are there many other slavers in Raman besides Tarad?"

"You've seen them at the soukh. They're all over the place and not only in Raman. Most of them are under the protection of the local city Proctor."

"Protection?"

"Sure. The factor pays a contribution, a cut of his take, neh? For altar sacrifice, you know."

"Mmm." Obviously, Alasi had seen more than one operator in action in his time. "Do most of them trade in local slaves?"

"Depends. It's not done much, though. Mostly, they just snatch you. The guards, I mean. A farmer can't pay his way and the landowner will sell him off. Family, the lot. He can get himself into trouble with taxes. There is always some new tax or other. Lots of ways you can cross the priests. Before you know it, they come some night and you're gone."

"Don't the people complain?"

"You don't know much about the local setup, do you?" Alasi looked knowingly at the alien and Terr suppressed a smile. "And anyway, who'd they complain to? If you talk to the priests, all they want is an altar sacrifice for the privilege of bending your ears with a sermon. They do nothing to fill your stomach. Besides, no one believes that Path nonsense anyway. We got our own gods and they'll be around long after the Deklans disappear."

"I gather their presence isn't appreciated much," Terr said and Alasi grimaced.

"There's talk at the soukh. About getting rid of them, I mean. They've held the Four Suns a long time, but it's only talk.

Can't see them leaving 'cause we don't like 'em, neh?"

"Alasi? Why do you think they took your family?" Terr asked gently and the boy sagged, despair all over his face.

"Don't know," he said miserably. "We was poor, but we had land and Maw managed the farm all right. Maybe they took them to Anulus. Some of the guys at the soukh are saying that this year, lots of families have disappeared. These days, if you cross the priests, they send you to Anulus, like as not. So I've heard, but we haven't done nothing."

Terr frowned. Without realizing it, Alasi had told him a great deal. If all Captal wanted was evidence of local slavery and official corruption, they need not have bothered sending an envoy. Kapel Pen must surely know that. On the other hand, she might not necessarily know what all her Proctors were doing.

He didn't believe it.

"Have you seen any Karkans hanging around Raman?" he asked on impulse.

The envoy had hinted he shouldn't get mixed up in that side of the investigation, but Terr couldn't see how the two could be separated.

"Lots. You see them crawling around the place. I've seen their ships at the Field. It's like the old days."

"The old days?"

"Don't you know? Elexi was part of the old Karkan empire long time back. So my old man said."

Yeah, two centuries ago, Terr mused.

"Come," he said suddenly and stood up. "We have work to do."

Alasi got out of his chair with some reluctance. "Your will, master," he said and hung his head.

"The name is Terr, remember? Didn't we make a deal?"

"Yeah, but—"

"No buts. Let's find out what happened to your family," Terr said and the boy's eyes lit up.

In the Shadow of Death

* * *

Tall, lumpy trees lined the boulevard on both sides. They exuded a sharp citrus smell Terr was not sure he liked. Behind manicured lawns sprawled the polymer-glass and color-reactive facades of the administration buildings.

Despite the sharp breeze the avenue was crowded. Boxed vendor stands stood clustered in ragged lines, peddling foods and trinkets. All too often, huddled beneath a tree, holding a chipped bowl, a disheveled figure would stare vacantly as they passed.

Terr dropped some coins into one of the bowls. Alasi tugged at his arm and shook his head.

"I wouldn't waste my sympathy on them, master; I mean, Terr. They're pros on a cut with the goons. Strictly for tourists."

"Like me, you mean," Terr said and cocked an eyebrow.

Alasi gave a disarming grin and shrugged. "I've worked the game myself. Without a license, of course," he said with disdain and Terr laughed.

He could have taken a combie he had at his disposal, but he preferred to get a personal feel for the local culture by walking. Alasi's casual comments explained far more than any officially sanitized tour.

The building he wanted loomed beyond the trees. Even from here, he had to look up to see its twin points reaching into a cloudy sky.

"Is that where we're going?" Alasi wanted to know and Terr nodded.

"Social Administration and Records. If anyone can tell us what happened to your parents, they should be the ones to do it."

Alasi didn't look happy. "Don't like the idea of messin' with no officials."

Terr patted Alasi's shoulder. "Relax. They'll be anxious to cooperate. Take my word for it."

They climbed a set of wide steps crowded with people. Translucent panels slid away as they approached. They found themselves in a large hall lined with inquiry counters besieged by long queues. Women clutched infants on hip, gesturing heatedly with a neighbor in the line. Small children ran shrieking, chasing each other through the hall. The place noisy, and the smell of unwashed humanity hung heavy in the air.

Terr hated the sight of packed bodies and their cloying intimacy. Maybe that's why he preferred the sterile microcosm world of a starship. He picked a line and waited stoically. He received a few curious glances, but was largely ignored. Alasi fidgeted beside him. It took a while to move up the queue.

"Yes? What is it?" a harried official demanded from behind the counter when their turn came. He didn't bother taking his eyes off the computer display plate.

"I want to register a manumission," Terr said and Alasi gaped.

"Contract," the official condescended to look at Terr. Small fingers tapped the counter.

Terr laid down the thin wafer. The official scowled at it before passing it against a sensitized plate. His scowl deepened as he stared at the screen.

"This is some kind of joke, neh? I don't have a sales registration for this transaction. Where *was* the sale?"

"Tarad's Circle."

"Tarad…Tarad…" He searched the plate and his eyes lit up. "Ah, I have it. Wait…something is wrong here. There is no notation against this subject."

"What does that mean?" Terr said.

"The contract is illegal…Tal. That's what it means. Here, let me have your wristband, boy." Alasi glanced at Terr who nodded.

The official touched the band with a small rod and stared at the plate. "This band has been scrambled!" He looked scandalized. "I cannot issue you a manumission on an illegal contract and a band that's been tampered with. This is highly irregular."

"I don't know anything about this tampering," Terr said, getting a bit tired at the clerk's attitude. "Check his permanent records and let's see what they say about his status."

The clerk glared at Terr before issuing instructions to the computer. He shook his head and looked up. "This is highly irregular. They show him to be a free citizen."

"If his records show him to be a free citizen, what's the problem, then?"

"The problem, Tal, is his wristband, neh?"

"He is a free citizen, you said so yourself. I want his band to reflect that," Terr said and added a touch of frost to his voice. The official was shocked.

"I cannot just alter his band! What about your contract?"

"I don't give a damn what you do with it. Cancel it!"

"I'll need to look into this more closely. Come back tomorrow and I'll see what I can do, neh?"

"I want this cleared up, now!"

"My man, others are waiting behind you. I cannot spare the time to look at your problem now."

"Then maybe your supervisor can. Get her."

"Now, see here. I have done—"

"I know what you've done. You've been a procrastinating officious pipsqueak!" Terr bellowed. The onlookers cheered, glad to see one of the powerful put in his place. "Either you get her now or I take this up with the Proctor's office."

"Now just a—"

"And why do you want to go to the Proctor's office?" a pleasant soprano voice inquired behind Terr. A sudden hush fell over the crowd.

He turned and saw a pert young woman. She had deep midnight eyes in which flecks of yellow sparkled. Her hair black and long, she looked at Terr with frank engagement.

The official jumped to his feet. "Dama, this—"

She waved him back and glanced at Alasi. "Come with me," she said to Terr, then turned and walked quickly toward a row of offices lining one of the walls of the hall. The crowd parted respectfully before her.

In her office, they made themselves comfortable. She placed the tips of her fingers together and leaned back in her seat.

"Now tell me, Tal. Why do you want to go to the Proctor's office? Surely not to report that fool's lack of courtesy, neh?"

Terr held up the wafer. "I have a sales contract for this boy. When I wanted to register his manumission, his permanent records showed him to be a free citizen. I simply wanted the matter cleared up."

"Mmm. Things are seldom that simple." She held out her hand for the wafer. After studying the computer plate, her eyes flickered at Alasi.

"We get such cases from time to time, Tal Terr; the contract has your name," she said and her eyes widened. "Now I know who you are! The media has been full of the Envoy and his mission. You don't waste much time, neh?"

"You were saying something about the contract?" Terr prompted and she gave him a thin smile.

"Yes, well, some landowners or unscrupulous traders pick up children wandering the soukhs and sell them. This is what apparently happened to your slave. Of course, you will be fully compensated."

"I don't want to be compensated. I want to find out how he came to be handed over to a factor like Tarad when he's supposedly a free citizen."

"Rest assured, Tal Terr. Tarad's Circle will be prosecuted. We don't tolerate slavery of local citizens."

"Not officially."

"I beg your pardon?"

"Never mind. I also want to know why his whole family

was taken away and where they are now."

"Family? I don't understand."

"I was there," Alasi said, clearly agitated. "I watched from a hill above our farm when the goons took 'em!"

She bit her lip and tapped the desk with the wafer. "Just a moment." She leaned back and whispered instructions to the computer. After a moment, she looked up, clearly puzzled.

"His family is still registered as free citizens, having a small freehold on the outskirts of Raman. They have no outstanding claims against them by the Proctor to justify confiscation or slavery."

"An overzealous exercise of authority, perhaps?" Terr suggested and watched her squirm.

"It would seem so, Tal."

Terr stood up, his eyes boring into hers. "I want you to correct the information in his identification band, Dama. Now. Then I want you to find his family."

"Tal Terr—"

"Now," he said evenly. She glared, weighing up the implications, then made her decision.

"Your wrist." She snapped her fingers and Alasi extended his hand.

"His band has been tampered with." She looked up from the plate. "That's a punishable offense."

"I wouldn't worry too much about it. Not in this case."

She studied Terr for a second, then issued instructions to the computer and touched the band again. It glowed briefly.

Terr held out his hand. "The contract."

She glanced at the wafer and hesitated. "It's invalid, of no use to you—"

"Of no use to you either. I shall find some use for it, or the Envoy will."

She didn't want to give it to him, but smart enough to realize the trouble it could cause her. In the end, she shrugged and slid the wafer toward him. After all, it was not her problem.

"Thank you, Dama. I want a status report on his family this evening. You know where to reach me," Terr said and left her glaring after him.

Outside, Alasi fiddled with his band. A huge smile shone on his face. "I'm really free?"

"That's right."

"I'm free!" Alasi shouted and began prancing. Then he stopped and his smile faded. "Don't get me wrong, Terr. I got nothing against you and you helped me like you said you would. I know we made a deal, but I got plans. Watch out for tourist traps, neh?" he said and, with another shout, ran down the steps.

"Wait!"

It was no use. Standing at the edge of the steps, Terr looked down at the sea of anonymous faces. The boy was gone, swallowed by the throng.

Rit!

* * *

Hidden in the crowd, Alasi followed Terr at a discrete distance. In his old rags, he would have been invisible, just another beggar. His new clothes had already drawn more than one curious stare and he could see the questions in some of the faces. Where did he steal them? He didn't let it worry him. First thing he would do is get rid of them and find something more appropriate.

Leaning against one of the stalls, he looked at his hand and rubbed the dull band around his wrist. He still couldn't believe he was free. Could it be a trick? He dismissed that out of hand. The whole setup was too elaborate.

He smiled coldly as he watched Terr walk down the boulevard. The alien appeared uncomfortable surrounded by people and customs he didn't know. It was gratifying to see one of the high and mighty reduced to confusion.

In the Shadow of Death

Still, he conceded that Terr had done as he promised. This offworlder was different. He didn't behave with the haughty disdain for the locals that marked the Deklans. So what? They were all the same, neh? Scum!

He bit his lip and ambled with the crowd, keeping the alien in sight. One thing he couldn't understand. Why would Terr bother with a nobody like him? Now free, he could round up the old gang and…

Do what? No amount of talk would bring his parents back, he realized bitterly. And talk is all he could do. The unpalatable truth? He had no influence and didn't know anyone who could do anything for him. Tominoy? He meant well, but the old Wanderer was only a helpless cripple. Could Terr really deliver? Could Alasi trust him?

* * *

Walking down the boulevard, Terr felt disappointed and a little betrayed, but he could not blame the boy for running, not really. In his place, he guessed he would have done the same thing. It was unfair to think Alasi would care for his problems, or owed him any loyalty.

At least he had learned something of the local setup from the experience.

He stopped at one of the food vendor stands and picked up two sweet pastry rolls. He took a bite and chewed. The thing spicy and tangy, and gods alone knew what was in it. He hoped he wouldn't find out the hard way. He looked around the stalls at the hurrying figures and the nameless faces. Where were they all going? Surrounded, he felt lost and out of his element. Right now, he would gladly swap this to be back in his *Ramora*.

Alasi appeared from behind one of the stalls and walked up. He eyed the pastry and licked his lips.

"I could use one of those," he said reluctantly and Terr handed it over without a word.

They munched in silence. Thin sunshine broke through heavy cloud and the wind seemed to die down. It was almost pleasant.

Terr picked one of the trees lining the boulevard and relaxed beneath its canopy. Alasi wiped his fingers against a trouser leg and Terr smiled. Squatting down, Alasi ran his hand through the pale yellow grass.

"Before you say anythin', I couldn't leave you stumblin' around all by yourself. The cudfish cruising around here would chew up a tourist like you in no time."

"I appreciate that," Terr said and sucked at a piece of pastry stuck between his teeth.

"I just wanted you to understand."

"Right."

"How come you bossed that Dama back there? You don't do that kinda thing around here."

Terr leaned back against the warm bark of the trunk. "Let's say I got some pull."

"Looks like it. I haven't seen one of them squirm like that for quite a piece. Who's this Envoy she talked about anyway?"

How much to tell the boy? How much would he understand?

"Let me put it this way. The Envoy has been sent from Captal to investigate the reasons behind local slavery and put a stop to it."

"Serrll justice." Alasi frowned and spat on the grass. "I had a taste of it and don't like it much."

"Don't confuse Elexi law with that of the Serrll Combine. He's here trying to help."

"Like you, neh? But that's gonna be tough. The Proctors got things pretty much sewn up around here. Nothin' much happens that they don't know about."

"Maybe not."

"You one of this Envoy's guys, neh?"

"And I still need you, Alasi."

In the Shadow of Death

"Figures."

"Tell me. Why did you come back?"

"Told you." Alasi kicked at the grass. "You wouldn't last a day out here all by yourself."

Terr grinned and patted the boy's shoulder. "I'm glad to have you with me. Now, if I wanted to find out how things are run around here, who would you suggest we talk to?"

Alasi's eyes instantly became alive. "Tominoy!" Then his shoulders sagged. "He might not be home. When the goons collected me, they also took him."

"Let's find out."

* * *

High fog streamed around them, hiding the ruins of the Old City. A collection of collapsed towers, faded brick and stone and rubble-cluttered streets—a home for those who had none. It served as shelter from the law or somewhere to lie down and die.

The sprawl of the soukh lay on their starboard side, a confusion of stalls, pavilions and alleyways—teeming with humanity from the Serrll worlds. They could see the crowds between the drifting streamers of fog. Directly ahead lay the expanse of the main Field, mostly empty. A few ore freighters clustered near the terminus, tied to the landing rings by access tubes.

The combie turned and the port side sagged. Alasi clutched the edge of his seat and gave Terr a worried glance.

"You sure you know how to drive this thing?"

Terr smiled. "Trust me."

The combie settled with a sigh in the middle of a narrow alleyway, drawing few glances. In this place it did not pay to be noticed. The curious melted into the shadows. Terr could sense eyes following his every move. Raw sewage flowed along an open ditch beside the street. Cracked, sagging fences filled the gaps between small houses. Somewhere a gate creaked.

The plant spooled down and Terr opened the bubble. Alasi pointed at a lonely figure, head bowed, sitting in front of a streaked red brick wall. Thin sunshine broke through the fog and the shadows fled.

"That's him," Alasi said eagerly. "I wasn't sure he'd be here."

The Wanderer was thin and gaunt, his yellow skin drawn tight over the bony ridges of his long face. The wide mouth with its drawn lips pulled into a tight line. A sprinkling of rusty white hair covered his head, falling straight across bent shoulders. He wore a plain brown robe that hung on him like a sack. Unaccountably, Terr hesitated, sensing coiled power in the frail frame.

Hovering a few tetalans above the dried mud alley, the combie shifted beneath them as Terr stepped out. Alasi jumped and ran toward the bent figure.

"Tominoy!" He knelt down and hugged the old man's knees. After a while, he looked at Terr and motioned with his hand.

Terr walked over and stopped before the Wanderer. Alasi tugged at his leg and patted the ground beside him. Reluctantly, Terr squatted down in the dust.

"What—" Terr began, but Alasi cut him off.

"Wait," he said and flashed him a smile.

Terr wasn't going anywhere and he realized that he was tired. Not tired physically, but drained emotionally. The suns were warm on his back and he took in the sounds around him. He could hear the shuffling of feet along the alley, an occasional shout and the scampering of children. Much of the mortar that held the brick wall before him cracked and worn, leaving gaping black lines. He felt dreamy and relaxed. Time whispered by.

After a while the Wanderer stirred. His orange eyes with their vertical red slits, were bright and searching. Terr could not look away.

"So, you're the one who rescued my misguided young

friend," he said in a heavy voice that made Terr think of deep wooded hills, of rumbling thunder and stormy skies.

Near him, he felt the old man's calm and a measure of peace. Like everyone else, he had heard the stories about the Wanderer Discipline that supposedly gave the natives of Anar'on strange powers. It was only talk, but those eyes…

"I couldn't walk away," he said after a pause and the Wanderer nodded in understanding.

"Tominoy." Alasi pulled at the old man's leg. "I saw them drag you off. How'd you get away?"

The Wanderer smiled, revealing even brown teeth. His face a crossed trail of clefts and valleys. "I told them nothing. When they grew tired of their questions, they let me go. They must have been watching me to come so quickly."

"More likely followed the boy's wristband tracer," Terr said.

Alasi looked stunned, then reached for the old man's hand. "They didn't hurt you, neh?"

Tominoy inclined his head. "Pain has been my companion for many years, my son. It is almost a friend, but tell me of this one."

"He bought me from Tarad. I'm free now and he's going to get my family back."

"I said I would try," Terr amended hastily.

Alasi beamed at him. "I know you can do it."

"Come inside where we can talk," Tominoy said and his joints creaked when he stood up.

Terr dusted himself off and followed the tall, thin figure into the gloom of the doorway to a small room. Tominoy had to stoop to move around. An open sooty fireplace occupied one of the corners. Jars and tin containers lay in neat lines on shelves that lined a side wall. Blackened pots and pans of various sizes hung above the fireplace. A wooden bunk with a straw-filled mattress lay beneath the shelves. The open doorway provided the only light. The shack may have been modest, but they seemed to satisfy the Wanderer.

The old man pulled some cracked wooden chairs around a small table and extended his hand in invitation.

"My humble lodgings are yours." He folded his veined hands over the gaping boards of the table and looked down at Terr. "How can I help you, Tal?"

"Must we stand on formality?" Terr asked and Tominoy nodded once. "My young friend here trusts you," Terr said, inclining his head at Alasi. "I'm prepared to listen to what you have to say."

"But not necessarily believe. That is wise and I am not offended. Here, unwary words can lead one to the sacrificial altar. Even an Envoy's aide."

Terr wanted to ask him how he knew, but it didn't seem important. "If you know who I am, then you know why I'm here."

"I sense anger in you, my son. Uncertainty and a searching for fulfillment."

Terr stared.

The old man had touched something he thought hidden. He turned his head and looked through the open doorway. The street sounds seemed muffled and far away. How could he tell this alien of the emptiness in his soul that he yearned to fill, but he did not know with what. How could he tell him of a longing to stand on far lands beneath strange skies, of a need to master himself, his ambitions and drives?

"It will come with the waiting," Terr said finally.

When their eyes met, there compassion lay in Tominoy's. "Tell me, my son. Why *are* you here?"

The question demanded more than falling back on orders. Injustice is only a violation of custom. To judge implied a position of moral superiority, and there were so many moral norms in the Serrll. Terr gave a brief chuckle.

"I have already answered that question, old man."

Tominoy's eyes widened and he gave a rueful smile. "Yes.

So you did. Likewise, I have answered yours."

It was Terr's turn to smile. The old man was wily and Terr would hate to debate morality with him, uncertain as he was of his.

"If I knew anything of consequence, Kapel Pen might not hesitate to move against me, but I don't. And my position does carry with it the authority of the General Assembly."

"Captal is many light-years away and the alleys of Raman are dark and sinister, my son. Even a starship commander such as yourself, out of his element, may be vulnerable before a naked blade."

"Yeah, someone reminded me of that the other night."

Alasi looked at Terr, his eyes round. "You command a starship?"

"Hush, boy," Tominoy admonished. "Terr, you don't understand the absolute power wielded by the ruling Family matriarchy. If that were not enough, the cursed Ecumenical priests have spies everywhere. Kapel is a ruthless administrator and cares little for the plight of the populace. The Proctors are no better. It has always been like this on Elexi. What is slavery to her as long as those activities don't interfere with her objectives. Before you ask me what they are, I don't know. Whatever you're trying to find, you'll not do it from without. It must be done from within."

"You mean someone in her administration?"

Tominoy shook his head. "No. All her senior staff are females in her Family line and personally loyal to her, openly at least. What I mean is, to run a planet, even an insignificant one like Elexi, takes a large bureaucracy. The passion of all bureaucracies everywhere is their love of order, forms and records. If a ship leaves this planet the fact is recorded in many places: manifest, crew, flight plan, and clearances. All of these leave a trail."

He reached out with a long arm and placed his hand on Terr's shoulder. "But you're not here to establish proof of local slavery, are you?" Tominoy rumbled.

"What makes you say that?"

The old man looked weary. "Slavery is common on many worlds of the Serrll. As for the Deklan Republic, the Ecumenical Order finds no inconsistency with this practice and the tenets of the Path. The Deklans are pragmatists and rule by persuasion rather than domination. For that matter, so does the government on Captal. Even that is more a council of consensus than a ruling body." Tominoy folded gnarled hands over each other.

"You must have realized by now, my son, that Captal could have resolved Kapel's administrative excesses through the official Ecumenical Synod machinery. Sending an Envoy was a superfluous gesture. Therefore, it's obvious that he must be serving another purpose."

Terr stared hard at the old man. Who or what was he really? Tominoy obviously had a grasp of Serrll politics and an understanding of Elexi's power structure far beyond that of a simple mendicant.

"You will have to pardon my saying this, but there is an inconsistency about you as well. A Wanderer, far from his native world, begging in the slums of Raman? You're obviously not a beggar."

"Let me say I am also searching for fulfillment."

Terr smiled indulgently. It didn't take much effort to figure out why Anar'on would be keeping an eye on the Deklans. The watched doing the watching, perhaps?

"As you say. And I'm only a lowly Second Scout, old man. I have no desire to get caught up in the wheels of Captal's or Kapel Pen's political machinery. Whether I'm wasting my time or providing a diversion in some grand scheme, I intend to follow my orders."

Irony tinged Tominoy's smile. "I am sure Alasi appreciates that."

"You spoke of getting at Kapel from within. How?"

Tominoy pondered that one for a while. "There is one social organ which Kapel has not managed to silence completely."

"The media!" Terr said.

"Indeed. Of course, the media is tightly controlled and heavily censored. That doesn't mean it's not active and a source of irritation to Kapel. She has the power to silence it if she wanted to, but it has its value as another intelligence medium. Even with absolute power, her bureaucracy doesn't always tell her everything she wants or needs to know. The media sometimes fills in the missing pieces. I can give you a name of a well known, or notorious if you prefer, investigative journalist. Ask her your questions."

"Why should she help me? After all, she is a female and would be enjoying the privileges of her position."

"My son, rivalry in a matriarchy is as intense as in any other political system. Anulus is filled with females who failed to appreciate that fact."

"Take care that you don't join them, old man."

Chapter Five

The *Morning Tribune* was a gray, drab six-story structure on the edge of the central business district. Like other buildings on the block, it had seen better times. Despite its rundown seedy appearance, there was something solid and reassuring about the grimy facade streaked with bird dung and pollution stains. Around this area, like in most of Raman, life held little glamor.

Behind the metallic darkness, the glare of streetlights hid the stars, but two of the three moons glowed yellow low over the city. Even some of the more modern structures clad in reactive panels shone with mute enthusiasm.

The combie settled on a small parking lot beside the building without attracting attention. Combies and sled-pads cruised above them, soundless teardrops of pearly light. A public communal hovering near the entrance, its bubble and doors open, disgorged what Terr presumed was a news team.

Alasi stood patiently while Terr locked the combie. The breeze plucked at Terr's jump jacket. He pulled it around him and caught Alasi grinning.

"I'm cold," he grumbled and Alasi nodded.

"I can tell."

"Your sympathy is appreciated. Come on. Let's get on with it."

It wasn't much warmer inside. For a media center, the lobby was almost empty. A relief depicting Raman's skyline covered one wall. The other wall showed four full-dimensional news channel clips. Terr stepped to the help desk and asked the computer where he could find Tamara Lin. A melodious female voice asked him to identify himself, then told him that Editor Lin had been paged.

In the Shadow of Death

It didn't take long.

The cable-tube doors slid away and revealed a tall, slim woman. She wore her hair coiled above her head, accentuating high cheekbones and searching yellow eyes. Her figure pleasantly filled the knee-length gray skirt and dark sweater. Terr was struck by her elegant poise that only comes from total self-confidence.

Before she stepped out, her eyes flicked over him and noted every detail, her face expressionless.

"Tal Terrllss-rr, the Envoy's military aide himself," she said thoughtfully in a pleasant voice. "Not much military action in my line of work, Second Scout."

"Is it me or do you hate all Scout officers?" Terr demanded peevishly.

A smile lifted some of the heaviness off her face. She stepped out of the cable-tube and the door hissed shut behind her.

"And why would an Envoy's aide want to see me?"

"I'm not sure I do," Terr said and she raised an eyebrow. "But Tominoy said you might be able to help."

He saw her eyes cloud. It was impossible to tell what went on behind them. They were the kind of eyes that had seen and lived everything. Old eyes, like Tominoy's. She bit her lip.

"In here." She jerked her head and strode toward one of the side doors.

"Alasi, hang around while I have a chat with the charming lady."

"But—"

"This shouldn't take long," Terr said and hurried after the retreating figure.

The door opened into a small room. Several formchairs lay arranged around a low stone table. Large holoviews from past news scoops cluttered the walls. The floor was of some soft brown cork and his shoes made no sound as he stepped to one of the formchairs.

Tamara sat on the edge of her chair and hugged her knees. "You said something about Tominoy?"

"I'm surprised that you came down so promptly," he countered.

Lights danced in her eyes. "I was curious to see a real Envoy's aide. I have never been close to one before."

"And…"

She took her time calibrating him. "I don't know. We'll see, neh? Now, about Tominoy?"

"You know what I'm doing on Elexi, don't you?"

"From Kapel's point of view, nothing good," she said and chuckled. Terr grinned.

"Tominoy told me you're an expose editor with your own Wall segment on one of the *Morning Tribune* channels. He also told me you would be able to answer some of my questions."

Her laugh was rich and even. Terr decided she would be fun to be with in a different setting.

"He did, did he? The old fossil could have done that himself," she said. Unconsciously, she pushed the sleeves of her sweater up to her elbows.

"I don't understand."

"Of course, you don't. And I suppose you didn't know that he's here mousing around on behalf of Anar'on and the independents, neh?"

"On behalf of the Kaleen group, yes," Terr said cautiously, feeling his way. "I suspected that. But the independent systems in general?"

"It's the same thing." She waved a delicate wrist. "He doesn't want to antagonize Kapel by being too open about it. She barely tolerates his presence as it is. He hasn't exactly done anything illegal, so she can't just throw him to the priests. One day, though, she'll get tired of him and old Tominoy will end up as altar bait."

Terr took his time studying the woman, not at all what he expected. Being a female, her directness and a certain aloofness was understandable. Then it hit him. She behaved like any other male executive would in her position. In a female-dominated society, her bearing probably came automatically. It wouldn't do to underestimate her.

"Look at it from his point of view," Terr said. "The Deklan Republic has had its eye on the Kaleen systems for some time. After the first Deklan takeover attempt failed, the Kaleen group is understandably wary."

"Then Tominoy should be spending his time on Deklan, not this backwater world," she pointed out reasonably.

"Depends on how you measure these things."

Tamara sniffed. "Look, Tal Envoy's aide. You're getting into things way over your head. Seeing Tominoy was a mistake, but not too much of a mistake. You're simply ignorant, neh? Then you went and spoiled it all by coming here and compromising me. That's all right too. I've been a thorn in Kapel's administration for years and everybody knows it. By seeing me, you're likely to find out things best left uncovered. The priesthood guards take a dim view of people turning over old garbage. If you persist, you could find yourself on an altar slab feeling somewhat different."

"I should imagine," he said pensively.

They both laughed. It made her much more attractive, and he became very conscious of her presence. He allowed himself a moment of pleasant distraction.

"Tell me, if I'm not being impertinent, how does a nice woman like you get to be so hard and cynical?"

Her shrug a pleasant movement of shoulders. She shifted in the formchair and folded her arms in her lap.

"By seeing life in the raw, that's how. For most people on Elexi, it's not a pretty sight. Some years back when I was naive and green—like you—I had dreams of becoming the local General Assembly rep. Kapel wasn't in power then. She was Proctor of Raman, but even then, she had her eyes on greater things. She also wanted to be a rep and we campaigned against each other. We both lost in that round."

"So you became an expose writer?"

She grinned. "It was easy, with no shortage of material." She paused, momentarily flustered. "I don't know why I'm telling you all this anyway."

"You have never been close to a real Envoy's aide, remember?" he reminded her and she chuckled. "I noted a certain icy breeze when you first saw me. Do you hate all Scout officers or is it seasonal?"

"The ones crawling around Elexi, at any rate," she said primly.

"Any particular reason?"

She touched her lips with a slender finger. "Yes, there is a reason, if you must know, and I can tell you. As far as I know, you haven't been contaminated. Fleet command on Elexi is corrupt, some of the senior officers at any rate. Don't look so shocked. You think the Proctors and their priesthood guards alone can keep the population in check?" Terr stared at her and she gave him a pitying smile. "You don't believe me, neh? Never mind. I didn't expect a still-moist idealist like you to know what's going on."

Her features firmed and the facade was back in place, but he had seen something of what lay beneath.

Corruption in Fleet command? That was a bit hard to take. Still, what she said could be true. All Kapel had to do was buy off the first two levels of the command structure, three or four officers at most—like Ki-Tori? How much would it cost to have your own tame master scout? Tame enough to send a couple of M-3s after him?

Rit!

He was getting as paranoid as Tamara.

"Tell me something. At the landing field, I saw flags. Even in the city, you can see one or two fluttering about."

"Hah! One of Kapel's private little jokes," she said. "She hates the Deklans, which is no surprise. We all do, neh? She does it to annoy Anall-Marr. A subtle campaign of passive sub-version has been running for years to undermine Deklan's presence." She pulled at one of her sleeves and he nodded thoughtfully.

"Interesting. Then again, could it be public conditioning perhaps?"

She looked at him with a trace respect. "A novel interpretation. My goodness! Behind that military facade the Envoy's aide has some smarts. However, I wouldn't give that idea too much attention." She unfolded her hands, wanting to cut this short. "Now, what can I do that a squad of Envoy's specialists cannot? I gather your personal efforts have not been altogether successful, neh?"

"I prefer to call it an exercise in character building," he said dryly and she smiled. "I want to find out if Kapel Pen or her administration is involved in local slavery. And I want to know why Kunoid Minerals and the Karkans are getting so chummy with the Four Suns."

"Is that all? Darling, you *are* naive. First of all, everybody knows that city Proctors all over Elexi have their snouts in the public trough, with the priest hierarchy on the cut, of course."

"That doesn't necessarily implicate Kapel's administration," Terr protested.

"You've been reading too much political theory. Reality is altogether less pleasant. Most of the Proctors and senior administrators are women from her Family line. The General Assembly rep is her own sister. And who do you think is the Proctor of Raman?"

"Another sister?"

"Talia Pen. That shakes up you theory a bit, neh? As you may have figured, Kapel and Talia have been trying to gouge each other's eyes out for years. Both are power mad. It runs in the Family, of course. Kapel herself is a greedy bitch," Tamara said bitterly. "Bleeding the populace while sitting on top of a planet of riches. She's like that. Even if they wanted to, they cannot break from the Family mold. The Pen line has ruled Elexi for over two hundred years. Continue the Family line, that's all that matters to them."

"Can't they see that their own excesses will end up hurting them?" Terr ventured.

"Who would replace them?" she retorted. "The Pen line may be torn by factions and divided loyalties, all clawing for personal power, but when threatened, they close ranks."

"What about the Prefecture? Anall-Marr is supposed to control the excesses of the planetary Controllers under him."

"He would if he weren't in on it himself."

"I find that hard to believe."

His preconceived notions of political oversight were taking a heavy beating. He was not sure that he wanted to know this side of Elexi politics, anyway. Sometimes it was better to remain ignorant. He certainly didn't want to annoy any master scout, on the take or not. That kind of exposure wasn't good for a promising career. As for the city Proctors, well, rit! Was *everybody* corrupt?

"The wheels are starting to turn, neh?" Tamara looked at him indulgently. "Have you any idea of the gross annual income from Anulus? Especially now that Kunoid has brought its second mine online? I'll tell you. It's enough to abolish all the misery you see on the streets and make everyone rich."

"Like one or two Fleet officers?"

"You will have to make up your own mind about that, Tal Terr. I'm not talking just about money. I'm talking about economic and political power."

"And how long has Anulus been mined?"

Her small nose crinkled. "I don't know exactly. On and off, several centuries, I'd guess. Those metals were not always strategic. Why do you ask?"

"Just a thought. If the place is so valuable, why did the Karkan Federation release the Four Suns to the Deklans anyway? I take it the Karkans would give a lot to have Anulus and the

Four Suns back in their hands."

"You're not kidding, but there isn't much chance of that happening. Besides, two centuries ago, Anulus didn't have anything that anyone wanted. Karkan is regretting their decision now."

"Nevertheless, Kapel Pen seems determined to hand it to them."

Tamara shook hear head. "Giving Kunoid the right to mine the place is not the same as giving the Karkans political control. And the Deklans will never give up the Four Suns. Why should they?"

"For a supposedly backward planet, you seem to be well informed."

Tamara bridled. "You forget yourself, Second Scout. Just because most of us run around in rags doesn't mean we're ignorant."

Terr winced. "I apologize, Dama. I did not mean it the way it sounded. Now, about my questions?"

"You don't care much for my sympathies, neh?"

"I didn't—"

"Never mind, Envoy's aide. You have me intrigued despite my better judgment. Your first problem shouldn't be too difficult. It will take some digging into computer records, but it can be done. Mining on Anulus is dangerous and there is always demand for labor. It's the second one that's hairy, being political, and you know it."

"I need evidence," Terr said. "Proof that she is directly involved in slavery."

"Not so fast. I may be able to get you evidence, but not necessarily proof."

"I'll settle for that. How do you propose to tackle the second question?"

"Let me gnaw on it for a while, neh?"

"It could have been an objective decision. Giving Kunoid the contract, I mean."

"For a supposedly naive Envoy's aide, you ask the most unusual questions."

"Yeah. So I've been told."

She laughed. "I don't doubt it. Could it be one of the reasons why you're here?"

Terr smiled in admiration. She was sharp. "I've been wondering about that."

"Your problem is certainly worth looking into and it would make a great story, neh?"

"Do you suppose Kapel still harbors ambition to sit in the General Assembly?" he asked suddenly.

"Mmm. Now that is an interesting question. She could be, but she wields a lot of power now, more than any General Assembly rep. It would take a lot to make her give that up. Quite a lot."

* * *

The gloom outside highlighted the few lonely pedestrians hurrying beside the glidewalks—dark shadows among silent buildings. The wind swirled rubbish around the parking lot. Terr rubbed his hands and tightened his jump jacket. Day weather was bad enough, but this was torture.

Alasi breathed deeply and grinned wickedly. "Crisp night," he said, enjoying Terr's discomfort.

Terr swung his hand and Alasi ducked, chuckling. "Let's get out of here, you scamp."

"Did you get the stuff you wanted?"

"I don't know. Some of it. Don't worry. You're not out of a job yet."

Terr turned toward the parking lot when a big beefy bruiser in a dark outfit stepped out of the shadows. He wore mufti, but the casual way he sauntered identified him as one of the priest-hood heavies. An ordinary citizen carried himself low, trying to be inconspicuous. This guy was pug-ugly, mean and spoiling for action. Terr heard a scraping sound and he turned slowly. The guy standing there could have been the pug-ugly's twin. He held a worn rifle casually by his side, looking for an excuse to use it.

Alasi pressed himself against Terr's side. Pug-ugly walked up to them and smirked.

"It's not safe wandering around in the dark. Lots of nasty people looking for trouble out here."

"That so?" Terr said.

Pug-ugly's eyes glittered. "You wouldn't happen to be one of those nasty people, would you?"

"Simply minding my own business."

"That's nice, but I gotta make sure, neh? How about showing me some ID, huh? Your wristband."

"Would this do?" Terr dug into his jump jacket and produced his Diplomatic Branch tag. Pug-ugly barely glanced at it.

"Second Scout Terrllss-rr? Aren't you—"

"That's right, I am. You boys lost or something?"

Pug-ugly chuckled. "Hear that, buddy? A good one, neh?"

"Yeah. Real good, Skin," the other grunted behind Terr.

"Okay, funny man," Skin said. "We're gonna take a little ride uptown."

"I can get there without an escort, boys," Terr said easily, keeping still.

It was clear that Skin had known who Terr was without the ID tag. He was only demonstrating his control. Was this a pinch or a one-way sightseeing trip? With Alasi at his side, Terr's options were limited.

"I wasn't asking, pal. Let's go." Skin jerked his head.

"You maybe got a warrant or something?" Terr prompted and Skin smiled nastily.

"Listen to the man, will you? A warrant, he says." He pulled away his jacket revealing an ugly snub-nosed needler. "This is my warrant. Want me to show it to you, maybe? Now, get moving."

They walked through the parking lot. Around the corner of the building, Skin had an armored combie waiting. He opened the back door while his partner pointed with the rifle. Terr got the hint and climbed in. Alasi jumped in after him. The door slammed shut with a certain finality.

The inside smelled of sweat, fear, and dirty socks. The bubble opaque, they only had the green safety strip around its edge for light. With a surge of power the combie lifted. Alasi pulled at Terr's sleeve.

"I don't like this. Where are they takin' us?"

"Some guards precinct, I'd imagine," Terr said with more reassurance than he felt. "And I don't like it either. Try not to worry."

"I always worry when the goons is after me," Alasi said with grim resolve. Terr had to agree with him there.

Wherever they were going, it didn't take long, even if it felt like it. The combie slowed and sagged beneath them. It was not a comfortable landing. They braked hard and Alasi muttered something pithy about heartless Elexi goons. Terr grinned.

Skin opened the door and Terr squinted. The landing ramp glared under harsh lighting, designed no doubt, to disorient an already terrified prisoner. It wasn't a bad ploy. He could not see anyone else around.

The city lights lay sprawled all around them. This high up the wind gusted and swirled. The goons waited impatiently for their guests to climb out before hustling them into a small foyer. Heavy transparent doors barred the entrance to the empty offices beyond. Slim passed his wristband against an ID plate and the cable-tube doors opened.

They filed in and dropped down in silence.

When the door opened, Skin motioned Terr out. Their footsteps were hollow echoes in the long narrow corridor that seemed to have an endless number of doors. The walls were drab gray. A black strip ran chest high along both sides. The ceiling glowed dull white. Muffled voices sounded somewhere and a door banged. Terr had a feeling like he was inside a cellar. Some way down the corridor, Skin stopped and jerked open a plain white door.

"Inside," he said, looking hard at Terr.

Terr glanced at Skin's partner fingering the rifle and slowly walked into the room. It was painted the same cheerful gray as the corridor. In the center stood a small table surrounded by several metal chairs. The room probably had thick walls too, to keep in the noise, he suspected. He'd seen its kind before. He could not see any obvious signs of surveillance monitors, but he felt certain the room was wired. It had to be.

Terr crossed his hands before his chest. "Nice place you've got here, Skin. Are we expecting company?"

"I'll ask the questions. Sit down."

"Not until—"

"If you don't sit down, *Tal*, I'm not gonna be polite anymore," Skin said softly, eyes malevolent.

Tempted to show the goon what being polite meant, Terr decided against it. He pulled one of the chairs toward him. It scraped loudly on the concrete floor. Skin parked himself on the edge of the table and glanced at Alasi, who quickly sat beside Terr. The other goon smirked at them, eyes alert.

"Okay, Tal Terr," Skin said almost pleasantly. "Envoy's aide. I just want to be sociable and ask you some questions."

"All right. Go ahead then and ask."

"Now you're being smart. What were you doing in the *Morning Tribune* building? With Tamara Lin, neh?"

"What makes you think I was there?"

"Huh?" Skin glanced at his partner. "We've got ourselves a wiseguy. Look, Second Scout, you've been seen in the company of a known subversive."

"Then why don't you arrest her?" Terr snapped.

"I asked what you were doing there."

"Oh, discussing your delightful climate."

"Last chance."

"Screw you."

Skin was on his feet in an instant and backhanded Terr on the mouth.

"That's for being cute," he said and massaged his knuckles.

Working his tongue inside his cheek, Terr tasted blood. He wiped his mouth on the back of his hand. His ears buzzed. Skin had a heavy hand.

"Let's try that again. What were you doing—"

Without any windup, Terr lashed out with his foot and got Skin between the legs in his multiplication machinery. Skin went white, made small mewling sounds and clutched his balls. He folded like a soggy Serrll fiver and slid to the floor. His partner spread his legs and swung the rifle down, but Terr was already moving.

"Hold it right there!" the guard bellowed.

The phase rifle is an ungainly weapon for close-in work and the guard wasted a precious second training it.

The orange beam swept above Terr's head. He chopped down on the goon's kneecap with his boot. There was a crunch of splintering bone and the goon screamed like a child. He sagged against the wall and cradled his knee. Terr relieved him of his rifle and stepped out of reach.

The whole fight couldn't have taken four seconds. Alasi gaped at Terr, his mouth wide in surprise. Skin still clutched himself and Terr left him there to enjoy it.

"Come on, Alasi. Let's get out of here. I'm sure these two won't mind us leaving."

"Wow! You'll hafta teach me to do that. Might come in handy prowling the soukhs," Alasi said in open admiration.

"Forget it, you little hoodlum."

The door opened then.

An armed squad waited outside. Holding his hands loosely before him, the officer stood framed in the doorway and scanned the room. The guy looked like some high ranker judging by the ribbons and little colored pins on his chest. Terr had him covered with the rifle, but the officer ignored him. He strode in, glanced at the two men on the floor and shook his head in disgust. He straightened then, his mouth set in a grimace.

"You'll not be needing that," he said to Terr and glanced pointedly at the rifle. Terr thought about it, then carefully set the weapon down against the wall. The officer relaxed a little.

"Tal Terr. Please accept my profound apologies. These two…scum!" he grated and swept a hand at the two bodies, "exceeded their authority."

Terr didn't know who the guy was. Frankly, he didn't care for any more of their hospitality. That two thugs could bring in a prisoner without due process and without anybody else being around smelled too much like a setup. He only wanted to get the hell out of there before they thought up some other cute funny.

"Are you going to resume where they left off?"

The officer had the grace to wince. "You're free to go, Tal," he said rigidly, gave a small bow and stepped aside.

"Don't bother with an escort. One of them might stumble and hurt himself."

"I assure you, Tal—"

"I imagine you'll have some explaining to do tomorrow. The Envoy would love to hear it. I would also appreciate it if someone could bring my combie back to the Center." Terr brushed past him and walked out. The guards outside reluctantly made way for him. Eyeing them nervously, Alasi stayed close to Terr.

The echoes of their footsteps were loud as they walked down the corridor. Terr felt an itch along his back all the way to the cable-tube.

* * *

"That's all I know, sir," Terr said. "After the stunt in the

117

plaza, this one may have been clumsy, but equally as effective."

Rayon nodded and a deep frown creased his face. He shifted in his seat.

"Garner was profuse with his apologies. Profuse."

"I'll bet he was," Terr said sarcastically.

"Understandable that you should be annoyed. Understandable. Garner promised to have the matter thoroughly investigated."

"They will deny everything!"

"No doubt. From what you told me, the two incidents don't appear to be connected. Then again, it could be a clever piece of misdirection." Rayon sat back and sucked on a tooth. "In your short stay here, you managed to attract more than the usual amount of attention, young man. Much more."

"Just getting the local color, sir, as you suggested."

"Hah! Are you sure you're all right?"

"Nothing broken, sir. But I think I'll avoid the *Morning Tribune* building for a while," Terr said and Rayon grunted.

"This is not the end of it. I'll not stand for any intimidation from Garner or anyone else. My first aide hurt and now you. If Kapel thinks that she can harangue my people with impunity, I'll have to start getting nasty myself. We'll talk about it later." He reached across the table and picked up two record wafers. "I was going over your status reports. Frankly, my boy, you have done more than I expected. A whole lot more, but what in perdition makes you think Kapel is involved with the Karkans, despite the fact I told you to leave that matter alone? Yes, alone."

Terr did not flinch at the criticism. He took a few moments to put the events of last night behind him and sort out his ideas.

"Well, sir, I have no evidence, only a gut feeling."

"A gut feeling, eh?" Rayon's long fingers tapped against the table and Terr realized how foolish the whole thing must seem to Rayon.

"I realize that—"

In the Shadow of Death

"Please." Rayon raised a hand. "I was considering the ramifications of the idea. Considering, not criticizing. One of my other, ah, operatives has made a similar observation. A low probability event he called it in their particular obfuscating, bureaucratic parlance. Why can't these undercover types speak in plain language? Plain," he demanded petulantly. "Never mind. As for your gut feeling, even if there was something to it, why do you consider it relevant?"

"I don't have a hypothesis, sir. I can only tell you how I see the possibilities. First of all, I suspect that Anulus is being used as a focal point between the Prefect and the Karkans in some power struggle. Maybe two different power struggles, I don't know," he said, aware how thin the explanation sounded.

"It's interesting to note, though, with the coming Ecumenical Synod elections, Anall-Marr is one of the principal candidates for Primate. Such campaigns cost a lot of money and that money has to come from somewhere. Anulus perhaps? It could be an innocent coincidence. What is not a coincidence is that Deklan is using Anulus as a bargaining chip with Sofam to gain a foothold in the strategic metals market. I gather Deklan has little love for the Paravan Trading Association. As for the Karkans, Anulus has given them a foothold into the Revisionist's sphere of influence. It *could* be an innocent commercial venture and everyone is chasing shadows. Whatever the real situation might be, the Diplomatic Branch was sufficiently concerned to add its own specialists to your investigation."

Rayon looked faintly amused and Terr suspected he was being humored.

"Go on. This is all very interesting. Very."

Damn the bureaucrat, Terr thought.

"Frankly, I don't believe Sofam is all that worried about the metals market. Logically, neither are you, but you already told me that." He paused then took the plunge. "I submit that through its control of Anulus, the Karkan Federation intends to expand its influence into the Four Suns."

"Well! Are you suggesting political dominance?"

"That's exactly what I'm suggesting, sir."

Rayon stared thoughtfully at Terr, his fingers tapping against the table.

"Mmm. The borders between the Deklans and the Karkans, you know, have been stable for two centuries. Two centuries. The Deklans have no reason to contemplate giving up the Four Suns to the Karkans, or any of their other systems, for that matter. Why should they? You're not suggesting some kind of military operation?"

"Of course not."

"What then? A revolt?"

Terr didn't say anything. Rayon hissed impatiently.

"You're serious, aren't you?"

"Have you noticed the flags around the city and the Field? It's a gesture of defiance. I suggest that Kapel Pen is conditioning the populace to an increased level of antipathy against the Deklans. You would only do that if you wanted to secure support for a major decision, like an insurrection."

"All this based on a few fluttering flags? Really, my boy. A grand leap of imagination, wouldn't you say? Grand. Tamara Lin has obviously made an impression on you."

"She did, sir. Quite a woman. She told me a lot of interesting things."

Rayon's eyes sparkled as he looked fondly at the boy. "I am sure she did, but she may not have told you that she is also Kapel's first cousin," he said and Terr gaped, chagrined that he'd missed the obvious.

Rit!

"No, she left that out."

"To hold such a position, she had to be connected," Rayon said gently.

"I should have seen it. She spoke too glibly of the administration's failings, and Kapel's."

"Not all traps are obvious, Terr."

"Related or not, that doesn't necessarily invalidate her arguments, or my conclusions," Terr plowed on stubbornly and Rayon laughed.

"You're dogged, I'll give you that. It's an incredible idea, if somewhat farfetched. Incredible. However, I cannot ignore what you told me. I cannot. The possibility and the consequence of you being correct are far too serious. Far too serious, but a rebellion?" He shook his head.

"Did you know, sir, that Kapel Pen once tried for the General Assembly?"

"Why, yes. It's in the records."

"From what you told me of her, she doesn't strike me as a type of person to give up or be sidetracked by a setback."

"She does seem to be a pretty determined individual. What are you getting at?"

"People will do a lot for power."

"Indeed." Rayon chuckled knowingly. "But if you're suggesting that Kapel has struck some sort of a bargain with the Karkans to help her drive out the Deklans, you don't appreciate the power of the political process. Even Kapel has to observe due form."

"As a military officer, I am trained in strategy and tactics. Those principles apply equally well to non-military situations."

Rayon nodded tolerantly. "I am sure they do, but you shouldn't be surprised when I tell you that political reality seldom lends itself to classical tactics. Seldom."

"I have one other thing, sir. I hate the very idea, but it's possible that elements of the Fleet command are supporting Kapel's slavery activities."

Rayon's grin faded. "Yes, I know. And I appreciate you telling me this, however hard it must be for you. Appreciate. It's being looked into," he said and there was a twinkle of amusement in his eyes. "Between getting harassed, you managed to get yourself a slave."

"Not exactly a slave, sir."

"Of course, I understand. This family you speak of. I gather you want me to pursue the office of Social Administration and Records until they're found. Is that it?"

"A word from you would do far more than any posturing on my part."

"Mmm. Highly unorthodox. I don't need to tell you that getting personally involved could jeopardize your objectivity."

"I realize that, sir. However, Alasi has provided me with a picture of Raman life which I could not possibly have obtained in any other way." Terr could not help smiling. "He also provides direct evidence supporting slavery claims made by the Elexi Assembly rep. Although not against Kapel."

Rayon grinned. "A novel interpretation I must say. Novel. For that matter, his family is an even better source of evidence, if we can get them back. You did well to save the contract. Very well."

He laid the wafers on the table and turned serious. "You obviously have a talent for getting yourself into trouble and your movements have attracted too much attention for my liking. Too much. It doesn't matter who was responsible, or why. If Garner or someone in the Fleet is behind it, it's unlikely that we'll find out. At least not in the time left to me here. So far, you've been lucky. The next attempt may involve something more permanent."

Terr shrugged. "What I don't understand is why it's being done?"

"Yes, an interesting scenario. It *could* be a case of pure intimidation, since they cannot get at me. I have requested permission to go to Anulus and see something of the mining operations for myself. The request is a formality, of course. I have full authority to go wherever I please. Full authority, but it's better to observe the conventions."

"And you want me to go along, is that it?"

"That's it," Rayon said firmly. "If the family of this young friend of yours, Alasi, happens to be there, so much the better.

At any rate, Anulus may provide both of us with additional information to support your, ah, gut feeling. You have given me much to think about. Much."

Chapter Six

"Fool!" Kapel glared at Garner who stood rigidly before her desk. "The Envoy doesn't need my permission to go anywhere. Why did you think I would try and stop him?"

Dealing with his temperamental charge, Garner had learned to be phlegmatic. When she decided to become difficult, like now, he wore her down through sheer perseverance, or got out of her damned way. He also knew when to stand there and take it while she raged at him, venting her spleen. He didn't take it personally.

"Dama, if he goes to Anulus, he will find all the evidence he needs to support the charges made by our General Assembly rep, neh?"

"He's got that already." Kapel's beaked nose flared with annoyance. "Besides, I *want* those charges supported."

He stood there, his mouth working. "But…but the repercussions!"

She patted her skirt and smiled at him. "What repercussions, you silly man? The Envoy returns to Captal and makes his report, taking his meddlers with him. The General Assembly passes a censure motion against me for lax administration and Anall-Marr gets a rap over the knuckles for his complicity. Not a bad outcome, neh? I wonder what that will do to his nomination as Primate? Nothing good, I hope. And the pervert sought to remove me."

A gust of wind shook the window panels smearing them with rain. Heavy clouds obscured the Center. The lights from the buildings were blurred and washed out. Sleet pinged against the panels. There wasn't much traffic in the air.

In the Shadow of Death

Kapel leaned back behind her desk with evident satisfaction and beamed at Garner, almost laughing out loud at his comical expression of grave concern.

"It's perfect, darling, don't you see? With the Envoy gone, old Enllss will find himself with a lot of questions and no answers."

Garner did not share her disdain for Captal's political machinery, but his job required him to tell Kapel things she didn't necessarily always want to hear. That, of course, carried with it its own element of risk.

"Dama, the Bureau of Cultural Affairs never gives up. And neither does Commissioner Enllss-rr. If he even suspects—"

"I told you before, it's mere speculation, and he cannot act on speculation. Everything is falling into place, I tell you," she said and rubbed her hands with pleasure. "When we're finished, it will set an example for other border systems to follow. We'll be rid of the Deklans once and for all, them and their cursed Path. What's more, the resulting factional recriminations will see Anall-Marr swept into oblivion. He'll be finished!"

A most satisfactory outcome, she thought. She allowed her eyes to stray to the delicate crystal arms of the fire stone. Poor Talia. She could have had the thing long ago. She only needed to ask. Pride, that's what kept all of them apart, but that was the way of things.

Garner allowed a small silence to build between them, his way of showing disapproval.

"Unless the Envoy manages to undo everything," he said at length.

"There is nothing he *can* do," she said impatiently, tired of his defeatism. "The preparations are almost complete and there is nothing to link me with the Karkans, neh? You worry too much."

"I worry because I care, Dama."

Her eyes softened. "I know you do, silly man."

"There is always Kunoid Minerals."

"Forget them. That's purely a commercial venture, haven't you heard? By poking his nose into our business, Enllss is simply proving to everybody that Sofam are sore losers."

"If I may be so bold, Dama, there is still the question of the senior Family ratifying your proposal."

"A formality, even if it is dragging on. Call them and give them a prod. Now, about that new military aide, what's his name?"

"I still say we should not dismiss the Envoy too quickly."

"The name, Garner."

He sighed in resignation. Maybe he could pick this up later.

"Second Scout Terrlss-rr. A Fleet line officer with no intelligence training that I can find. Shadowing agents have seen him with that Wanderer—"

"Tominoy?"

"That's him."

"I think it may be about time we sent that particular Wanderer to the altar," she said frostily and tapped her teeth with a finger. "His beggar's facade is wearing pretty thin and I'm getting tired of Anar'on's spying. What else?"

"Terr was seen entering the *Morning Tribune* building."

"Tamara? I should send *her* to Anulus!"

"Ah, that would not be desirable, Dama. Not while the Envoy is here, at any rate. You cannot afford to have open brawling in the Family, neh? Not now."

"I suppose you're right."

It galled her to have Tamara hold up her administration to ridicule. Something appropriate would need to be done about her once the Family ratified the decision.

A peal of thunder shook the windows.

"After all, she is your first cousin, neh?" Garner pointed out.

"Cousin? My sister in cabal, more likely. Waiting for her chance to sink her claws into me like the rest of them, but not yet, dear one. I wonder if Talia had something to do with this latest attack of nerves among the Family? It has her stamp. Was there any connection between Tamara and Kadreen?"

"None that I could find, Dama."

"Mmm. That doesn't mean none exists. Keep an eye on her and this officer. Find out if she suspects anything. If she attempts to communicate with him…"

Garner understood the look in her eyes.

"Dama, I know what you're thinking," he stammered in sudden alarm. "Getting rid of her wouldn't be very wise, no matter what she may suspect." With the whole Serrll Combine focused on them, he was horrified at the possible consequences.

"Who said anything about getting rid of her?" Kapel said sweetly. "At most, Tamara may be able to provide this Scout with additional proof of administrative corruption. On the other hand, should she stumble onto something that could conceivably threaten our plans, you know what to do." Her eyes suddenly blazed.

"I don't like this, Dama. It could spell trouble." Brawling within the Family made him uncomfortable. Casualties usually wound up with more physically oriented careers—in mining. He was too old for that kind of crap.

"You don't have to like it. Just do it."

Garner allowed himself a small shrug. "I shall increase our surveillance coverage."

Kapel nodded and arched the tips of her fingers over her lap.

"A report came across my desk this morning, Garner. Something to do with this Scout Terr. Care to tell me about it?"

Garner squirmed. He had hoped to avoid this. After a blistering session with the envoy, he did not look forward to another dressing down from her.

"Well, Dama, the priesthood guards hauled him in for questioning and bungled the job. It seems that he disabled both of them, even though unarmed."

"Those inept dolts! I told you to keep an eye on him, neh? Nothing else!"

"The officer responsible has been disciplined." Garner had him assigned to a tour on Selius, his career ruined.

Kapel glared at him. "You told me it was a routine operation. You told me that nothing could go wrong, neh?"

"Dama, it *was* routine."

"Silence!" She sat up, her posture suddenly menacing. "If you have any more schemes like that, in future keep them to yourself. Do I make myself clear?"

"Perfectly."

"I'm glad we understand each other. After having put one Envoy's aide in a hospital, one more blunder like the one last night and we'll all end up on Anulus. Now, what about the rest of the Envoy's agents?"

"We've got one of them compromised, but we cannot—"

"Never mind. Let them have their moment of glory."

Garner did not look convinced. Those people were professionals and it would be a mistake to underestimate them. But who was he to keep digging up a dead subject?

"What do you propose to do with Relina, Dama?"

"My General Assembly rep sister? I want her recalled, stripped of everything."

"Ah, I don't think that's possible."

"She carries out policy, she doesn't make it!" Kapel raged, her voice shrill. "Sister or not, I don't give a sniff what pressure Enllss or anyone else may have brought to bear on her. She is supposed to be my voice. Nothing else!" she snarled and Garner squirmed.

"Dama, Relina's term cannot be rescinded. She will have to serve out the remainder of her two years."

Kapel pinned him with her eyes. "No excuses, Garner. I want her off Captal, you hear me? I want her here where she can explain to me, if she can, by what authority she saw fit to make that statement to the Bureau of Administrative Affairs."

"I will issue the recall immediately."

"You do that."

"It...it might be several days before she can comply."

"As long as she stands before me. Anything else?"

"Ah, a small matter, Dama," he said, suddenly very nervous. "Insignificant in itself, but it has the potential, remote as it is, to escalate into a symbolic representation of the Envoy's whole mission."

"What are you babbling about?"

"Ah, it seems that Terr, the Envoy's aide, has purchased a boy at the soukh—"

"So?"

"Well...I..."

"Make it march."

"It appears, Dama, that someone has ordered his whole family to be deported to Anulus. The boy was caught later and sold to a local slaver—"

"And?"

"A supervisor from Social Administration and Records filed a report on the matter after Terr went there to record the boy's manumission..."

Kapel looked at him in disgust. "Don't tell me. They were free citizens, neh?"

He wrung his hands. "I'm afraid so."

"Of all the...And I suppose the Envoy has asked you to look into it, neh?"

He nodded and felt a trickle of sweat run down his back.

"Then find them! How many times did I tell you to clamp down on the Proctors? Now this. Call Anulus and have them ready when the Envoy gets there."

"But, Dama..." Garner bit his lip, really afraid now.

"What's the matter with you? It's only one..." The awful implication sank in and color drained from her face. She looked at him with death in her eyes.

"No!" She jumped out of the formchair and slapped both

palms against the desk. "If that family is there without a veneer of legality, hasn't it occurred to your simple brain that he'll ask how many *others* might be in the same predicament? It has, hasn't it? I can see it in your stupid face. When he finds out, he'll demand their release, and I won't have any choice but to comply, neh? Tell me." She walked around her desk and stood nose-to-nose with him. "How many people are we talking about?"

He gulped and pulled back. "Quite a few, I'm afraid, Dama," he whispered.

"Quite a few," she repeated and sneered. She pressed her fists against her temples to stop herself from screaming. She clasped her hands, trembling to control her urge to lash at him. After a few deep breaths, she felt herself regaining composure.

"What can we do about it?" she demanded softly.

He hated this part. If there was only a way to spare her…

"Ah, it's not something we can cover up or deny," he muttered lamely.

"No, I suppose not. This has gone far enough. There must be an official or two in Talia's administration who is anxious for a change of scenery. I want your proposal for appropriate measures against all the Proctors on my desk, today. Now, get out. Get out!"

Garner fled, his knees weak with relief.

* * *

Thick mist raced low over the apron. A rolling rumble shook the ground. Slanting walls of rain came in cold, sullen sheets. The rain softened and blurred where it touched. The air became white and outlines melted.

The Field, suffused by the pearly glow of polyarcs mounted on the corners of the deserted terminus. Even the civilian liners tied to the landing rings were mere smears in the rain haze.

A sharp gust tilted the sled-pad and slued it around before

it righted itself. The howl of the wind momentarily died to a hiss. Protected from the wind's fury by the sinister shape of a towering M-4, *Pirana* was a nucleus of darkness in its shadow. The other M-4 bearing the envoy had already left for Anulus.

Terr glanced at Alasi sitting beside him. The boy's face glowed with rapt attention, his eyes never moving from the approaching M-1. Back at the Center when Terr told him they were going to Anulus, Alasi just stood there in enthralled wonder.

"In a real starship, neh?"

"Not a large one. It's only a scout."

"A starship," Alasi repeated dreamily. "Wow! Wait till the gang hears this one."

Terr did not share his kind of enthusiasm, glad to be leaving, even if only for a few days. The sled-pad glided beneath *Pirana's* curved belly and settled gently beside the extended landing ramp. The repeller field dropped and the wind swirled around them. Sharp pricks of icy rain hit Terr's face. Shivering, he hurried up the ramp and pressed his palm against the glowing access plate. The hatch stirred above his fingers, then slid away, spilling a shaft of warm light.

"In you go." Terr jerked a thumb over his shoulder. Alasi broke into a broad smile, jumped off the sled-pad and ran up the ramp.

The wind cut through Terr's light zip-jacket. He hurried down the ramp muttering curses. He leaned across the sled-pad's console, touched the flickering recall strip and stepped back. The sled-pad rose a few tetalans, turned and disappeared into the gloom.

Alasi waited for him on the lower level, looking keenly at the glowing cable-tube that ran to the command deck.

"Come on," Terr said and stepped into the tube.

The navigation bubble ran chest high around the deck. It cleared as the tube brought them up. Alasi gaped in awe at the sloping control panels molded into the curve of the hull.

"Status?" Terr inquired.

"Nominal," the computer said.

Alasi nodded in appreciation.

"Secure for lift," Terr ordered. "Clear with SC&C for immediate departure and file a flight plan for Anulus."

"Landing ramp retracted and all exterior connections secured." Terr felt a slight pressure surge when the hatch closed. "Nav deflector grid activated. SC&C has cleared for lift. System check complete. Lift sequence enabled."

Inactive panels began to glow soft amber and yellow, a mosaic of colored contact pads. Alasi almost pranced with excitement as each new panel activated. When the projected flight plan appeared in bright lines on the curve of the nav bubble above them, he clapped his hands with glee. The main control plate before them glowed into life. A repeater plate flickered in front of Alasi.

Terr sprawled into the command couch and pointed at the spare beside him. Alasi lowered himself and wriggled in the clinging seat.

"Ready?" Terr asked and Alasi nodded. "Good. One other thing." He inclined his head at the consoles around them. "Don't touch anything. All right? Not even for fun."

Alasi shrugged, his eyes mischievous. "Sure, got it."

Terr didn't trust the little imp, but decided not to worry about it. Only a short hop and the boy wasn't going to be out of his sight. The computer would refuse the boy's commands anyway. He quickly scanned the status boards.

"Proceed with lift."

"Lift sequence active. Confirm."

"Continue."

The landing skids retracted and the M-1 hovered. *Pirana* lifted without any sensation. When they broke through the cloud cover, brilliant sunshine flooded the deck through the transparent nav bubble. They were suspended above an endless sea of rolling white cloud. Then the sky faded, turned purple and the nav bubble became full of stars.

Terr tilted the ship. Alasi grabbed the sides of the couch and gave a little yelp. An instinctive reaction, as there was no shift in the internal gravity field. Elexi stood suspended beside them, blue-green and smeared with thick bands of white. He stared at his world etched against the backdrop of The Arch.

"I never thought it would look like this," he said soberly.

"Not a bad view, is it?"

"How long does it take to get to Anulus?" Alasi asked as he stared at the receding world.

"Oh, about four hours."

"Four hours?"

Terr laughed. "It *is* a starship, remember?"

"Sure, but four hours?" Then his face clouded and he became serious. "Terr? I'm really gonna see my family, neh?"

Terr could only guess at the boy's feelings. Alasi's last few days must have been bewildering. Captured, sold, bought again, then daring to hope. He probably still could not believe it was really happening.

"Alasi," Terr said gently, "the Envoy himself will be there when you meet them."

"I guess there is Serrll justice after all," Alasi said brokenly and his eyes filled. "I don't know how..." he began, struggling to keep his emotions under control. Then he jumped out of the couch and flung himself at Terr.

"It's all right," Terr said softly and patted the boy's shoulder, feeling a lump grow in his throat. "It's all over now."

* * *

Even from orbit, Anulus looked grubby and used. A small world with a thin atmosphere, broad equatorial deserts and tiny icecaps. It had several lake systems, but no seas. Smears of green smudged the temperate latitudes, but still cold and forbidding. It might be a mineral treasure, but Terr could understand why the place had never been settled; probably too many heavy metal pollutants in the biosphere.

They came down at the main administration complex field; a collection of low buildings, dreary rows of accommodation housing, lighted processing complexes and towering vent stacks belching steam and chemical smoke. A thick brown haze hung over everything and extended to the horizon. Long lines of colored tailings and mounds of preprocessed minerals surrounded the complexes. They stretched as far as Terr could see. Clustered around the complexes lay bulky freighters from all parts of the Serrll. Conveyor belts laden with ores moved endlessly into cavernous holds. Quite an operation.

Despite himself, he was impressed.

The envoy's M-4 already down and tied to the terminus landing ring. At the edge of the field stood a cluster of M-3s and a couple of M-1s, all shepherded by an M-4. Clearly, Kapel took no chances with her reluctant labor force, and had no intention allowing anything to happen to her valuable installations.

SC&C brought *Pirana* down beside the M-4. The access tube was already sliding out from the terminus to meet them. There came a thump when it connected. Terr glanced at Alasi and twitched an eyebrow.

"Ready?"

Alasi nodded eagerly and scrambled out of the couch. They rode the cable-tube to the lower deck. The curve of the corridor took them to the main hatch. Terr palmed a glowing yellow panel on the frame and the hatch slid up, revealing the bright interior of the access tube. Alasi sniffed, screwed up his face and snorted.

"Gah! The air stinks like a garbage dump."

Terr wouldn't have used that exact expression, but it accurately described the heavy chemical odor.

"You'll get used to it," he said uncertainly and crinkled his nose.

A third scout, dressed in rumpled working grays, met them at the tube's end. He snapped to and waited while Terr looked him over. A Karkan, somewhat taller than Terr. Beneath a thin ridge of dark green scales, cold fishy eyes stared at nothing. Terr's frown deepened. The Karkan had a wide flattened head on a slender neck. His pale green head covered with broad scales that glistened, changing color when he turned. Terr imagined he could smell the dank stink of the swamp about him.

"Well?" he demanded.

"I am to take you to the administrator, sir," the third scout hissed as his tongue flicked in a blur.

"The administrator?"

"Yes, sir. The Envoy is waiting for you there."

"Let's get on with it, then." Terr hoped there weren't any more like him hanging around, although he wasn't surprised to see Karkans on Anulus.

The terminus complex stark and utilitarian. An unusual number of MPs sprinkled around the various entrances, their rifles held by their sides, appeared out of place. Well, the place *was* a penal planet. Nevertheless, all that hardware made Terr uneasy.

After going up two levels and down some corridors the youngster stopped before a door guarded by another MP.

"With your permission, I will resume my duties now, sir," the Karkan said briefly, turned and walked off.

The Elexi MP stood at attention as his eyes slid over Alasi. When Terr approached the door, it split down the middle. The sides slid into the walls and revealed a large room. Before an entire transparent wall, the whole landing field stretched on the other side. On Terr's left a Wall that showed a pattern of traffic, which presumably covered the installation. The hard, polished gray floor echoed his footsteps.

He looked down at Alasi. The boy stood there and stared at the group before them. The woman could not have been very old, but life in the fields and the stress of captivity had aged her. The man beside her thin and wiry, his black hair peppered white, he carried himself with dignity. Two little girls tugged at his hands, then broke away and ran toward Alasi.

"Alasi! Alasi!" They swarmed over him, and the woman smiled indulgently.

"Brats." Alasi quickly hugged the girls, then hurried to stand before his parents. "Maw," he whispered in a choking voice. The woman nodded and reached for him.

"My boy," she sobbed and they embraced. "My boy. Oh, it's good to see you well, neh?" The little girls stared, somber, eyes round.

His father clasped him by his shoulders. "Son," he said, man to man, his voice trembling with emotion.

Terr felt all puffed up with virtue. This one small thing made it all worth it, even if nothing else was achieved out of this sordid exercise. He glanced at the envoy. Rayon's eyes were fixed on the scene before him. Terr nodded and walked toward him. Rayon clasped his hands behind his back.

"We watched your ship come down."

"Is anything wrong, sir?"

"Later."

Alasi turned, smiled and motioned for Terr to come over.

"Maw, I want you to meet Terr," he announced proudly.

The woman's appraisal frank and penetrating. "So, you're the one who delivered us from this horror, neh? I don't know how to thank you, Tal."

"You can be proud of your boy, Dama," Terr said and bowed formally. She gasped and her eyes filled.

"Nobody…has ever called me that." She dabbed at her eyes. "My family is in your debt, young master," she whispered and her hand touched Terr's chest.

"How have they been treating you?"

Her eyes clouded, her mouth firm. "We were given quarters. It's somewhere in this complex, I don't know where. Since my man didn't know nothin' but farming, they had us out in the open working the slag tailings." Her eyes filled with desperation. "There are so many others."

"Others? I don't—"

"Terr?" Rayon jerked his head at the door and walked out.

"You have nothing to worry about now," Terr told her comfortably. "Everything will be all right. I'll see you all later." He ruffled Alasi's hair and followed the envoy.

Outside, Rayon paced up and down. When Terr emerged, Rayon stopped, turned and pointed a finger at the MP.

"You. End of the corridor."

The MP brought his rifle to port arms, stood to and marched away briskly, his footsteps loud on the hard floor.

Rayon gave a low growl and clenched his fists.

"You know what those people told me? There are hundreds more like them all over Anulus. Hundreds. I should have realized it back on Elexi. Can you imagine those families toiling in this purgatory? Toiling! The thought makes my blood boil and I'm really looking forward to hearing Kapel's explanation. Really."

He turned abruptly and began pacing again. Obvious in hindsight, but Terr didn't tell him that he should have seen it as well. Rayon suddenly stopped and prodded Terr in the chest.

"And that simpering stooge—"

"Sir?"

"The administrator of this miserable rock. Some distant Pen relative. A political appointee, no doubt. A payoff from Kapel for past favors, I should imagine. Favors. She had the effrontery to suggest that most of the families here were actually volunteers. Can you believe such nonsense?" He shook his head and snorted in disgust.

Terr felt flattered that the envoy should see fit to unburden himself to him. He was a lowly second scout with no political pull. Well, not quite true. His uncle was a commissioner, but no one could accuse Enllss of nepotism, certain Rayon knew all that. The truth was, he came to have quite a lot of respect for the little man. The envoy was nobody's fool.

Did that mean his investigative efforts were not entirely off the mark? He liked to think so. More likely, Rayon was acting on information supplied to him by his own specialists. Then again, had Terr been fooling around among the fleshpots of Raman, he wouldn't be here now.

Either way, it gratified him to share confidences with one of Captal's shakers and movers. Rayon probably had no one else to talk to anyway. His specialists? Stuffed dummies probably.

"Quite an operation they have here, don't you think?" Rayon said, amused.

"And not the only one either," Terr said. "From orbit, I saw evidence of vast open cuts all over the place. That kind of work could use up a lot of people."

"Officially listed sites show twenty-five installations of various sizes. But—"

"There could be others not so official," Terr finished for him. "Away from prying eyes and visiting dignitaries."

"Exactly. I've got to know if Kapel has a mine or two tucked away somewhere off the main track. It wouldn't be hard to do with an underground installation either. It wouldn't. As a routine matter, I had the official list compared against the one I got from the administrator. The two matched and I expected nothing else. Nothing. It would have been amateurish in the extreme if they didn't. Kapel may be a lot of things, but she is no amateur. No amateur."

"Even if we find something, sir, what would it prove?"

Rayon shrugged. "Probably nothing. Then again, a lot. But I like to indulge in an occasional gut feeling of my own. Consider. If an unofficial mine happened to exist somewhere, it could only be set up with Kapel's approval. Kunoid doesn't operate independently here. Doesn't. It would lend some credibility to your preposterous notion that Kapel has an ulterior agenda in her dealings with the Karkans. Yes?

"I want you to do a few survey circuits around Anulus. A few circuits. Who knows? My belief in the preposterous might just bear fruit." He rubbed his hands with satisfaction. "Even if we don't find anything, Kapel cannot possibly plead plausible denial for holding all these families here."

"What do you intend doing, sir? It will take some time to identify the people. Not all of them are from Elexi. It could be enough time for records to be altered or lost."

"I am not without resources, my young friend. Nevertheless, you make a valid point. Valid. I shall need to make use of my M-4's communications center. That boy's family and others will be quartered in my ship as my guests for the duration of our stay. When we get back to Elexi, I intend to see to it that all of them get proper restitution. Proper. Heads will roll over this.

"By the way. We have an official reception tonight, courtesy of the administrator. Nineteen hundred local time, if I have the military jargon correct."

"Quite correct, sir," Terr said and smiled. "I'll be back in plenty of time."

"Good. Alasi and his family were invited. Profuse apologies and all that, I suppose."

"I hope they appreciate the gesture, sir," Terr said waspishly and Rayon grinned.

"You will have to learn to be more diplomatic about displaying your feelings, my boy. Much more. Now, let's get back in there and help your young friend celebrate."

* * *

Leaning back in the command couch, Terr studied the overlay window image superimposed over the background of the nav plot. Blue points of officially listed mines burned on the surface view of Anulus. Bands of color showed veins of alkali metals and halogens. Mined from huge expanses of halide salt flats, they were vital in the manufacture of artificial alloys and machine ceramics used for just about everything.

Given the extensive geological survey of the planet, surprised to see how few mining operations were actually in place. That was until he scanned some of the individual sites. Most of the complexes were underground. The surface installations were primarily final processing and shipping terminals. The warren of layered tunnels in some of the installations could hide a city.

Most of the mining complexes were in a ragged belt running through the western part of the northern hemisphere. The nearest mine far to the east some four thousand talans away. A perfect place to have something going where someone would prefer for it to remain hidden.

He didn't intend to poke around and make a nuisance of himself. People who wander around generally fall into things, not all of them pleasant. All he needed were a few sub-orbital circuits around the planet to locate any strange energy sources, above or below ground. Provided, of course, they were there to be found.

He asked SC&C for an unspecified flight plan and got the ship ready for lift. Responding to computer prompts, he scanned the panels around him: plot, environmentals, internal gravity, power core, comms; all the things meant to keep him alive and get him to where he wanted to go.

Suddenly, the computer announced it received coded transmission from Tamara Lin. The Anulus Admin message system was holding it. Did he wish to scan it?

Getting ready for lift, he decided to save it. Opening it would require an uplink, but then again, Tamara would not have gone to the trouble of sending him a message if she did not consider it important.

"Upload and hold. Proceed with lift sequence."

He could always look at it later.

In the Shadow of Death

Pirana shifted beneath him, lifted and the landing ring dropped away. The terminus a pattern of lights that faded as the ship climbed. From ninety-four thousand katalans up, still within the effective atmosphere envelope, the curve of Anulus etched sharp against a purple sky. Following the west-to-east rotation, he steadied and programmed the sub-orbital sweeps. Two hours would be more than enough time to finish up and get ready for the official breast-beating ceremonies that evening. He had a strong streak of official cynicism the passage of time had only reinforced.

This high up, he couldn't see a thing. The world below all shades of white, green, and brown. The computer-managed TLM scan, telemetry, faithfully recorded for later analysis.

Letting his thoughts wander, he watched the pulsing dot of his ship move against the ground nav plot. *Pirana* was a very nice ship to fly, responsive and agile enough for an interceptor. If he wasn't careful, the feeling could grow on him. After all, he only had the thing on loan and he might as well enjoy it.

He made one circuit of the northwestern hemisphere when they jumped him.

And he was just thinking about people who wander.

When the computer announced a K-band scan lock, his eyebrows twitched. Nothing unusual about that, but somewhat unexpected nevertheless. His SC&C flight plan should have identified him to any picket ships.

He glanced at the nav plot where his IFF pulsed a steady blue. He sat up and switched to tactical. Two M-3s, one slightly below, the other up on his four o'clock, were pacing him. K-band interrogative scans swept across *Pirana*.

"Comms," he ordered.

"Comms link established," the computer said. "Channel open."

"Very well. Visual."

A small full-dimensional window opened in the nav plate. A Karkan first scout walked into view. Terr stared at the image for a few seconds before the alien opened his mouth, revealing a row of small sharp teeth.

"General prisoner LK-26995/211. You're ordered to assume neutral status and prepare for boarding," the Karkan hissed, his tongue a blur.

Terr stared at him. Was that a sample of Karkan humor? Then again, perhaps not.

"First Scout. You have my IFF and must know—"

"Not receiving your comms. Assume neutral status immediately or you'll be interdicted. Comply!"

That sounded pretty definite. Terr canceled the comms pickup interface in case the Karkan listened in.

"Verify comms link," he demanded.

"Comms link active, channel open. Negative on fault diagnostics. Confirm target ship receiving comms."

Rit!

What the hell were they up to, then? He glanced at the tactical plot and frowned. The two rings of the primary and secondary shield grids were visible around the M-3s. Clearly, the Karkan was not here to chat.

"Status of targets?"

"Targets have positive K-band acquisition lock and are powering up to preliminary firing phase. Recommend bringing up defensive shield grids."

"Negative. Send a status burst to SC&C and stand by for full evasive," he said and activated the interface link. "First Scout, I'm on an official mission for the General Assembly—"

"Warning, leading ship in preparatory firing phase. L-band firing lock established. Primary and secondary shield grids raised. Ship on primary alert status. Link with SC&C now under active jamming. Shield grid raised."

The comms link window in the nav plate cut off. A dull track of yellow scintillation lanced from the leading M-3.

"Evasive!"

Pirana staggered and slued beneath him, shields flaring. The

142

restraining field was a second late in activating. He was flung from the couch and the deck got in the way. He landed hard on his left shoulder with a soundless explosion of light and pain. The same shoulder that had already been given a workout by the goons in the alley. Small blue sparks arced at him from the deck. He blinked back tears of agony, heaved himself up and looked at the navigation bubble. The M-3s were still pacing him.

That shot meant to disable him. In open space, it might very well have done just that, but all energy weapons lose some effectiveness in an atmosphere envelope. Reduced effectiveness or not, *Pirana* could not sustain many more such hits. Watching the plot, he wondered whether those were the same jokers who jumped him earlier. He did not relish the idea of another encounter, and he suspected they'd be wary of any cute maneuvers. Explanation for this absurd attack would have to wait until later, if there was a later.

Pirana shifted orientation and streaked across the face of Anulus, the computer obeying Terr's last command. Two beams of yellow death stabbed after him, close enough to collapse the secondary shield grid. The ship trembled and skidded beneath him. The near-field effect made his hair stand on end. Some of the color-reactive control panels pulsed a warning brown. One panel changed to glowing green and began to arc as it fused in blue discharge. In seconds the ship punched through the atmosphere, momentarily throwing off the M-3s.

"Stand by to transit, maximum acceleration." Massaging his shoulder, he climbed into the command couch.

"Unable to comply. Within the gravitational boundary envelope of Anulus, cannot bring up the distortion field precursor. Transition possible in eighteen seconds."

Rit!

He might not last eighteen seconds. "Status of targets?"

"Both M-3s still within the atmosphere envelope. Breakout in three seconds. Stand by to transit on present course. Confirm transition."

"Approved!"

Terr cleared the nav bubble into transparent mode. Space seemed to rush at him and some of the stars ahead turned shades of blue. What had been blackness before was now filled with faint patterns of dark orange, red and brown lines; gravity waves that had become visible. Still within the Four Suns system, the density of waves was relatively high.

If this was a horrible case of mistaken identity and they were indeed after an escaped criminal, the M-3s would break off and alert COMELOPS on Elexi. On the other hand, if he was the intended target, they would follow.

Why were they attacking him? Did his sensors pick up something someone wanted kept hidden? Whatever the reason, he doubted they would give him a chance to find out, and he didn't have time to worry about it now.

Some of the control panels still pulsed brown, warning of partial failure or severe damage to that subsystem. One of the panels was the comms board.

"Damage control status."

"Overload on port primary shield grid regulator—compensated. Failure of the general communications module. Short range ship-to-ship facility available only. Repair not possible with components on board. Predict complete failure of the primary reactor containment field in twenty-eight point-four hours under current flight parameters. Recommend sub-light speed only and immediate reduction in power setting."

He smiled grimly. Reduce power? It was the only thing keeping him alive! Then again, if the M-3s didn't get him, *Pirana* was likely to fuse into slag around him, and Anabb had asked him not to bend it.

"Warning, target M-3s have successfully transited and are maintaining full boost. Have identified K-band interrogative scans. Negative on weapons lock."

Well, that was definite enough. It seemed like he was the

intended target after all.

"Tactical," he demanded, studying his unwelcome predicament.

Elexi far on his starboard beam, with Anulus directly behind him, the M-3s had positioned themselves to cut off any possibility of him reaching Elexi. That wasn't good. With system damage, he did not feel like finessing them by engaging in fancy maneuvers. If these jokers were the same M-3s who jumped him earlier, they would have learned from their previous mistake and he would be pushing his luck beyond the credible. A straight attempt to outrun them, then?

He projected his current flight plan. The nearest accessible world that held Fleet units was Anar'on in the Kaleen group of systems. One small detail made him uncomfortable about that destination. Flight time to Anar'on was twenty-nine hours at full boost. Scowling at the plot, he didn't fancy his chances, not with a bum containment field. Would the reactor last the distance?

He could try for Talon; it had been his first choice. But he would need to get past the M-3s first. The other small detail wrong with the plan, his containment field would give up a quarter of the way there.

"Transmit on Fleet emergency—"

"Unable to comply. DES module not operational."

Rit!

He had forgotten about the damned comms. He couldn't even cry for help. Should he dump the emergency beacon? The trailing M-3s would probably cream it before it let out a beep, even if it could get through their jamming. What if it did manage to put out a signal? Without a declared emergency and an unspecified flight plan, SC&C wouldn't even raise an eyebrow. By the time the mess was sorted out, he would be dead.

Terr stared at the tactical plot and pursed his lips. Well, after meeting Tominoy, he always wanted to know more about the Wanderers. It looked like he was going to get his wish.

Chapter Seven

Rayon paced around the administrator's office like someone caged, shaken by the sudden turn of events and angry with himself for being so careless. The incident with Terr two nights ago should have warned him. *Stupid!* The plain fact, he was not used to violence. It was so *dated.* Normal Captal intrigues were verbal battles where a deadly thrust delivered through blackmail or a simple vote on the floor got results.

Dated or not, violence seemed to be very much alive here, and effective.

He was also angry with the Anulus administrator. She had been polite without helping, sticking to the letter of the law, obviously protecting Kapel and wasn't about to commit a transgression that could jeopardize her own position. He could understand that. Still, with or without her cooperation, he was going to get to the bottom of this.

What he could not figure out was why? The boy didn't know anything. He didn't have *time* to find out anything. Or did he? Rayon no longer believed that this was an indirect attack against him. Maybe the whole thing was a legitimate mistake after all. Possible, but not very likely. His belief in the preposterous did not stretch that far.

Those cursed M-3s!

What really galled him was the blatant way in which someone did it. Such arrogant confidence displayed a total disregard for his authority and presence. A distracting inconvenience, that's all he was.

So, a General Assembly envoy an inconvenience, was he? He would show her inconvenience.

The administrator sat uncomfortably behind her desk.

In the Shadow of Death

Outside, darkness had settled like a heavy blanket. They could hear the thin whistle of the wind even through the insulation of the windows. Beyond the confines of the Field, low clouds glowed dull yellow and brown reflecting the light from the processing complexes.

She might have made a bad mistake here. Getting involved in Family politics was always a chancy proposition. Listening to Garner may have been an even bigger one. She should have had the order confirmed by Kapel. *Heavens above!* She was already thinking in terms of a cover-up, recriminations and reprisals. If there was an ensuing fallout, relying on Garner's orders was not likely to protect her. She did not relish the idea of carrying the blame should this incident turn out to be a screwup, a distinct possibility now.

Still, it was unlikely the envoy, despite his pacing and fulminating would get much change for his efforts.

Abruptly, he stopped pacing, stomped to her desk and glared at her.

"I cannot believe what you're telling me, Dama. Cannot. One of your prisoners manages to commandeer an M-1 on the other side of your miserable world and takes off. The mine superintendent of…"

"Complex Fourteen," she said and her cheeks burned at such impertinence.

"Complex Fourteen," he repeated like it was something dirty. "He sends out two M-3s in pursuit. Two. Why didn't he send guard interceptors? Why? And who authorized him to use military vessels?"

"As for your first question, Tal, we have nothing on the ground that can match an M-1 in speed—"

"Hah! An M-3 cannot match it either!"

"Secondly," she said, ignoring him, "the mine superintendent has the authority—"

"Has the authority? From whom?"

"From me, Tal Envoy."

"You, Dama?"

She arched her head and glared at him defiantly. "As the effective head of this planet's administration, I have a mandate to call upon any resources at my disposal in support of civil authority. That includes units of the Serrll Scout Fleet, as you no doubt know."

Rayon growled with impotent frustration. As much as he disliked the fact, she was technically correct.

"You cannot simply let them loose. There is due process to be followed. Due process!"

"There wasn't *time* for due process, neh?"

"All right. So you had the authority. Why is it then that SC&C can only identify the M-1 belonging to Second Scout Terrllss-rr? There is no sign of the supposedly stolen ship or the pursuing M-3s. No sign. We'll go into the matter of how a military vessel could have been thus appropriated later, if it has been appropriated. Right now, I want you to contact those M-3s and order them recalled. Immediately!"

The administrator may have been a political stooge, but also very capable. Kapel Pen brooked no incompetence, especially on Anulus. This was serious trouble, but her responsibility was clear. Annoyed at being thus harangued, she stood up and jutted out her chin.

"Tal Envoy, you may carry a lot of weight on Captal, but you have no authority here. I have been ordered to cooperate—"

"Then cooperate!"

"—with your inquiries, and I have done so. I shall not stand for any interference in my administration from you or anyone else. The superintendent of Complex Fourteen is handling the matter. Until I receive his report, I suggest that you regard your aide as overdue, neh?"

"Overdue?" Rayon dropped all pretense at diplomacy. "Dama—"

"Enough of this!" she snapped and made a chopping motion with her hand. "You don't have any facts, Tal Envoy, to accuse me or anyone else of anything. I suggest we wait for the superintendent's report before you contemplate taking any hasty action."

"If you're after facts, Dama, why are we unable to contact *Pirana*?"

"There could be any number of reasons for that, Tal, all legitimate," she said primly. "Hardly sufficient reason to warrant drastic action such as you propose."

Rayon held himself in check with an effort. Chagrined, he realized she was right. Without additional facts regarding Terr's status or why the M-3s may be in pursuit, it was premature to begin throwing accusations. Suspicions were not enough, no matter how plausible, but by the time additional facts emerged, Terr could be dead! Rayon feared for his young aide. This was not the time to be sitting on one's hands following protocols.

"You want facts, Dama? Very well, let's get some facts," he said and pointed at the Wall. "I want a channel to my ship."

She hesitated, but could not very well refuse. She tapped the combination on the sensitized surface of her desk and the image in the Wall cleared. The duty officer on the M-4's command deck stiffened to attention.

"Mr. Envoy. Is there anything I can do for you, sir?"

"I want an immediate link to COMDEKOPS, personal for Prima Scout Anabb Karr. Personal." Rayon nodded with satisfaction at the administrator. She seemed to shrink as her bluster melted away.

"Sir, it's early morning Talon time—"

"Son? Did I ask you for a time check?"

The young officer blanched and colored. "No, sir."

"Then make the connection."

Rayon clasped his hands behind his back and turned to the administrator.

"Your actions under law may be technically correct, but

149

you underestimated my authority, Dama. I want your logs, all of them: comms, SC&C, ship-to-ship, everything. I want to cover the last four hours. Four."

The Wall cleared and Anabb's scowling face swam into view. He had obviously been asleep and didn't appreciate the interruption. His brown eyes flickered at the administrator before sweeping back to glare at the envoy.

"I wondered who had the pull to get me out of bed," he grumbled peevishly. "Rayon, I hope you appreciate the time here."

"Sorry about that," Rayon said, deriving sardonic pleasure from Anabb's discomfort. "This is important. I want you to issue a frag order to two M-3s currently en route to Anar'on in pursuit of an M-1. They are to break off contact and return to Elexi. It is imperative that they comply. Imperative! If they refuse, I want them interdicted.

"I also want you to stand down all Scout Fleet units in the Four Suns. No flights unless cleared through COMDEKOPS. No flights. And I want an M-6 here soonest to enforce that order."

Anabb's face grew longer and longer as he listened to Rayon's demands.

"Thunderation! What's going on there? You haven't started a war or something, have you?"

"I'll fill you in later. Briefly, one of my aides is missing and I am gravely concerned for his safety. Gravely."

"And who is the unfortunate to warrant all this fuss?" Anabb demanded, his sleep ruined.

"Second Scout Terrllss-rr."

"Terr? What's he gone and done now?"

"That's what I need to find out, Anabb."

"You don't need an M-6 for that."

"It's not for Terr. I want to relieve your Fleet commander on Elexi, Prima Scout Cannan."

In the Shadow of Death

* * *

Anar'on hung there, washed in hues of red, brown and long patterns of yellow from the deep desert.

Fractal tendrils reached in jagged fingers from the southern polar cap to vanish in faded muddy patches of green and flashes of azure from the small shallow seas. Scattered cloud moved slowly north in semi-spirals, spreading and fading long before reaching the rusty yellows of the equatorial deserts. A long stretch of open water glittered purple-blue that reached down from the northern ice fields, waning into washed greens of giant coastal flats.

Terr sat in the darkened command deck with only the console lights and the small ship noises for company. He watched the desert world grow before him. Just looking at the bleak landscapes made him thirsty. Like everyone else, he'd heard stories about the Wanderers, their strange powers and what they did to nosy strangers. He hoped they were only stories, tourist propaganda. Stories or not, he had nowhere else to go.

Around him, some of the color-reactive control consoles had already failed. Too many of them had showed a steady brown pulse for most of the flight. The primary engineering panel now glowed orange-white, indicating imminent power failure. *Pirana* refused to die, but the ship had little left to give. The way he'd been pushing it, he was surprised it held together this long. Sofam Industries builds them well, he decided.

The tactical grid, traced in blue lines on the navigational bubble dome above him, showed the two M-3s closing. That had been inevitable once he started to slow for orbital insertion. The information mockingly repeated on the main plate before him.

After twenty-nine hours of pursuit, Anulus was but a distant memory. During the long tense hours, he'd had a lot of time to think about things, perhaps too much time. And he was tired. The long flight had drained him, and the rage and indignation of betrayal by his own service had faded into a dull throb of unfairness. Unless he managed to avoid the M-3s, *Pirana* would be destroyed. He only hoped his death would count for something, but the M-3s would have to catch him first.

Had he already accepted defeat? That attitude would guarantee he'd be defeated. He set his jaw in defiance. Mud crawling worm slime! Not dead yet, and until it did claim him, there were always alternatives.

"Have you tried SC&C again?" he asked the computer, knowing the answer already.

"Affirmative. Status of communications system unchanged. Unable to establish comms link with Anar'on SC&C due to sustained damage."

He should have ejected the emergency beacon pod while still over Anulus. If nothing else, it would have attracted the attention of Surface Command and Control. Damn it, he was a fighter jock, not some merchant weenie who cries for help when things got a bit sticky. He was supposed to *handle* sticky situations.

He exhaled in simmering frustration, realizing that he had allowed the situation to carry him along instead of thinking about his mission. The pursuing M-3s clearly meant to finish what they had started the first time. He doubted that fancy maneuvers on his part would do him any good this time, even if he had a healthy ship. An escaped prisoner indeed. Tamara was going to be disappointed in him, falling for such a beginner's trick.

After endlessly picking over every word, he had committed her message to memory. Any way he cared to look at it, Fleet command on Elexi appeared hip-deep in slave running, and his vinegar-faced Palean friend seemed to be behind it. Was Ki-Tori acting on his own, or was he only the point man for Prima Scout Cannan? Even as chief of staff, Ki-Tori would find it hard to disguise Fleet unit movements around the Four Suns as innocent exercises. Sooner or later the web of procedures would have caught up with him, unless Cannan provided him with the necessary veneer of legitimacy.

So what? They were just skimming the haul, greasing the bureaucratic machinery of the city Proctors. Compensation for being stuck in the ass end of nowhere. Right? Unpalatable as it might be, Terr was forced to accept that the Fleet arm on Elexi itself was not above corruption. The thought galled him. It ran contrary to everything he believed the Fleet should be. Tamara had been right again. He *was* naïve and innocent.

Okay, so the Serrll Combine was a rotten place and some of its unsavory citizens would be better off counting rocks on Cantor, or digging them up on Anulus. Captal knew about slavery on Elexi and Anabb as much as admitted it. Rayon hadn't been sent to the Four Suns to stamp out slavery or clean up obvious excesses of corruption. That was merely a diversion, he knew that much. In his quest to tie Kapel in with the Karkans, would Rayon be prepared to turn a blind eye to Fleet profiteering? He did not want to believe it. Rayon seemed a straight shooter. Captal was playing power politics and Elexi merely a pawn, as was he.

Rit!

Politics or not, he still wasn't about to lie down and allow himself to be smeared.

His fingers drummed against the armrest while he fought against mounting exasperation. He reviewed Tamara's message again. It still said the same thing. Okay, let's sum it all up. Kapel Pen had engineered the first overture to Kunoid Minerals for the right to mine Anulus, not the government on Deklan. Normally, as a Revisionist coalition partner, Deklan would have been wary of any entanglements with a Karkan conglomerate. Anulus meant power, a lot of power, political as well as economic. Deklan wanted to show they could handle the deal on their own. Sofam's scramble for a cut of the pie only served to prove the point. Still, that was only interstellar commerce at work, wasn't it? Just business.

Terr reminded himself that Kapel was ambitious. Her career exemplified a ruthless climb to power over crushed opponents who were rash enough to stand in her way. And she didn't try very hard to keep her antipathy toward the Deklan Republic a state secret. Given all that, it was natural she would approach the Karkans to develop Anulus.

The Four Suns also used to be Karkan territory, he reminded himself. Karkan territory…

He thought he had it then, but it looked as though he wasn't going to get the chance to tell anybody. Could Tamara be right, and Kapel sought more from the Karkans than merely economic cooperation? People would do a lot for power, he remembered saying to Rayon.

"Emergency beacon primed?" he asked softly as he studied the tactical plot.

"Standby mode only."

"Warm it up. I want you to change its message text."

"State new message. Warning, trailing M-3s will have L-band weapons lock acquisition in three point-two minutes."

"Message follows," Terr said.

It took just over a minute. When he finished, he got the computer to repeat it. He changed some of the words, then leaned back into the couch. Maybe he would get a chance to atone for his mistake above Anulus after all—if Rayon got the message. He checked the tactical display plate. The M-3s were getting awfully close.

"Still no sign of Fleet support units?"

Where the hell were those Anar'on pickets? One ship was supposed to be in orbit all the time. He'd been counting on that picket to ward off the M-3s. Having an afternoon nap no doubt, he thought savagely.

"Negative. No activity within detection range. Warning, advise immediate reduction in power setting. Primary containment field will fail in three-point—"

154

"Life support to minimal," he cut in. "Divert all power to the stern shield grid."

The brown glow of the environmental panel flickered to pale green in overload. He scanned the weapons board and shut it off. Against an M-3, his small single-phased array projector would be a drain of vitally needed power.

"Initiate landing sequence—"

"Warning, leading target's shield grid are pulsing in preparatory firing phase. L-band lock established."

In lines of yellow ionization a pattern of fire from the leading M-3 rippled along *Pirana's* port quarter. The stern nav grid flared in orange discharge and spectacular backsurges. He smelled ozone in the air and squinted against the glare as the M-1 staggered beneath him. The bubble above him flickered, lost its transparency, then cleared. He put up his hand to cover his eyes as the engineering panel sputtered. It arced in coiling lines of blue before fading to pulsing white of total failure.

"Condition critical! Primary drive reactor containment field has failed. Initiating escape sequence. You have thirty-one seconds to purge and counting. Thirty—"

"Eject emergency beacon!"

The secondary lighting system cut in and the deck lit up in amber gloom.

Pirana staggered again and the deck heaved. He grabbed for the armrest, missed and crashed against the console bank with his already injured left shoulder. Blue sparks crawled over the deck, stabbing him with little pinpricks of fire. This wasn't fair. He massaged the tender spot and uttered a few pithy words. Most of the panels were in overload brown, failed white or already inactive. One more pattern and the ship would be nothing more than a cloud of iron filings.

"Emergency beacon destroyed," the computer went on remorselessly. "You have twenty-two seconds—"

The patterned computer display suddenly turned dark gray. Smoke drifted in from the cable-tube shaft and quickly filled the command deck. Between being roasted inside or roasted by the M-3s outside, there didn't seem to be much of a choice. Coughing, he staggered across the deck and leaned against the emergency hatch. He jammed his palm at the winking yellow pad. The hatch snicked up into the bulkhead. He ran toward the survival blister, its hatch already open.

He dived in, checked the displays and jabbed the pulsing yellow purge pad. It stopped pulsing and the hatch clanged shut behind him. He barely had enough time to lay back into the couch when the blister surged along the ejection tube and cleared the tumbling shape of the M-1.

Yellow lines streaked past him, bracketing *Pirana*. Under concentrated fire the shields failed in a corona of blue discharges. Mottled lines of orange and red spread over the unprotected hull. Plating turned white and melted, then exploded out as jets of atmosphere vented from the rents. Debris tore away and spun lazily into space. A burst at the drive spaces and the ship broke up. He turned away and shut his eyes. The glare from the exploding primary drive reactor left afterimages, then the shockwave hit. Control panels flashed brown and green, fusing and arcing as the blister tumbled. Anar'on whirled above him, filling the display plate. The blister shuddered and began to whine as it bit through the upper atmosphere.

The artificial gravity surged. The near-field effect squeezed him into the couch and the blister skidded violently to port. The M-3's beam must have just missed, but it had saturated his feeble nav grid. The air smelled of ozone and blue sparks arced across the front panel and his hands. He grimaced at their sharp bite and his hair stood on end. The whine turned into a high-pitched screech that made him wince. He prodded at the almost useless maneuvering controls. The tumbling seemed to check, but Anar'on still whirled above him. If the shield collapsed now, he would never know it.

Another beam ripped past him and the restraining field gripped him hard. Glancing at the nav screen, the M-3s didn't look like they were following him. Were they waiting to see if he burned up, or was Anar'on SC&C finally getting its act together?

The way the blister shuddered, it looked like the M-3s may have managed to do their job after all. He tried to right the jawing ship, but it refused to turn over. The shuddering increased as the blister ripped through layers of upper turbulence. Hand poised above the console, he watched the amber sky fill the display plate. After a while, he let his hand sag. He was in terminal descent.

The surface reached up for him.

He felt his stomach clamp and ripples of fear danced inside. What would it feel like to die? It looked like he wouldn't even have enough time to worry about it. His father was somewhere down there. They would be together now. The blister shook badly from the buffeting as the surface lost its fuzziness and distinct features clarified into sharp reality. Desert lay everywhere he could see, stretches of never-ending yellow and orange sands, rolling dunes, and a mountain range. He seemed to be heading straight for it.

Jagged red cliffs rose up and he tensed, waiting for them to tear through the soft hull. The rocks looked awfully close as they flashed beneath him, opening into salt flats and more dunes. The blister tipped side on and sagged down as the sands rushed by him. The restraining field gripped him hard as the blister plowed into a dune. A curtain of sand rose up on either side of it and cascaded down in its wake. With a lurch that snapped his head around, the blister bounced once and slammed down hard.

* * *

He lived in a brief moment of silence where the images of the crash still echoed in his mind. Hard against the bulkhead, the deck sloped steeply beneath him. The interior of the survival blister not quite dark. Blinking amber and green the control panels cast dark shadows.

He felt something ooze down his cheek. When he wiped at it, the hand came away covered with blood. He gingerly probed the lump on the side of his head and winced. His left shoulder throbbed. Weary, he groaned and sagged against the bulkhead. He was alive, but this was too much. Nothing was worth this kind of treatment.

Then he noticed how hot it was inside.

Beside him, the power plant inspection plate smoldered and started to glow blue. He could feel the heat building up from the deck. There was no mistaking the crackle of the arcing power coil below the plates. He sat up in alarm. When the containment cell failed, the blister would brew up and turn into a pile of scrap metal. He didn't want to be around when that happened.

He looked about, searching frantically for the emergency hatch release. Acrid smoke curled up in lazy fingers from the inspection plate, forcing a spasm of coughing from him.

Where the hell was the damn release?

His eyes wandered to the deck beneath him and he uttered an obscenity. With the blister on its side, he was sitting across the hatch and its emergency release. He shifted, spread his palm across the pulsing bright yellow pad and pressed. The pad stopped pulsing and the hatch stood outlined in white. He moved to one side, propped himself against the canted console and pressed the pad again.

The explosive bolts detonated with sharp cracks. The blister lurched beneath him, throwing him against the bulkhead as the hatch went flying. A shaft of searing light lanced through the opening, followed by a cloud of sand and a wave of dry heat. Coughing, eyes streaming, he groped toward the open hatchway.

In the Shadow of Death

He saw the metallic sheen of an amber sky and the emptiness of rolling dunes stretching in waves of yellows and reds into a shimmering blue-gray heat haze. Nothing stirred on the vast barren sands.

The cell's inspection plate blew and he was engulfed in smoke and flame. With a yell, he threw himself out and rolled. Spluttering gritty sand and vile curses, he cast a quick glance around. The smoking blister lay in a shallow valley between two dunes some fifteen katalans high. Thick gray smoke billowed from the blown hatchway. He scrambled through the burning sand and pushed himself over the lip of the dune. A cascade of sand hissed after him.

The blister cooked off then and the shockwave rippled through him. Debris was hurled high and he watched with apprehension as it rained around him. He covered his head with his hands and winced at the hot sand. Something heavy landed beside him with a thud and a spray of sand. Then the deadly rain stopped.

Ears ringing from the explosion, he turned on his back and felt his body sag in utter weariness. He yelped and sat up in a hurry as the heat seared through his zip-jacket, the sand was that hot.

Rit!

His whole body began to tremble. Reaction was setting in from accumulated stress of being shot at and bounced around. The crash had sent him into shock and he hugged himself, waiting for the cold spasms to pass. He realized that death hadn't missed him by much.

His hand shook as he wiped sweat off his brow. It came away smeared with blood and the back of his head throbbed. He breathed deeply of the strangely scented air, thick with the smell of burnt rock and sand. Above him oily black smoke writhed upward in silent agony. The sands whispered and he thought he could sense the dunes move. In the silence, he heard a faint crackle of fire from remains of the burning blister.

He could feel the heat of the sun on his naked skin, palpable and almost soothing. The air hot, but not unbearably so, and dry. Very dry. There wasn't a trace of humidity. He looked up and stared for a while at the strange amber sky, willing himself to relax. Eventually the spasms stopped and he let out a loud exhale.

With the sand shifting beneath him, he crawled to the lip of the dune and peered over the edge. The valley between the two dunes littered with smoldering hull plates, panels and torn control boards. The blister was a jagged, twisted shell from which the blackened skeletal frames stood like stripped ribs. Small flames licked at the remains.

His eyes scanned the strewn wreckage. Beginning to get anxious, he spotted the emergency hatch. Slipping and sliding, ignoring the hot sand, he crawled down the dune and knelt beside the hatch. He took a minute to blow at the singed palms of his hands. Squinting at the sun, he rolled his tongue around his mouth. This heat was going to take some getting used to. The sooner he found or build some sort of shelter, the better— before he ended up crisped like his blister.

On the hatch a small panel above the supply pack glowed orange. He pressed his palm against it. The hatch seamed along its middle and the halves slid into the frame. There wasn't much there: a thermal blanket, rations, a jump jacket…and water. The container pitifully small. In this heat it was not going to last him long.

He took off his zip-jacket and shirt. The dry heat immediately sucked moisture from his skin. He savored a moment of pleasure as his body greedily drank in the warmth. An ugly puffed bruise ran down along his left forearm. The shirtsleeve scorched, and so was the shirt's back. His left shoulder was swollen and already colored.

It simply wasn't his day.

Picking through the supplies, he found the medical kit. The spray soothed and took away some of the sting. He sprayed his palms and rubbed his back as far as he could reach. He flinched as pain lanced through his left shoulder. He could not tell how badly he was burnt. And anyway, there wasn't anything else he could do for it. He closed his eyes and directed the cooling spray at his head, hoping it would close the scalp wound.

He slipped on the light zip-jacket, wrapped the shirt around his head and felt immediately better.

Looking around, he stared at the flowing sands of his domain. In a blur of shimmering heat the dunes merged into an amber horizon. A sea of frozen waves, the sides a pattern of wind-swept ribs and piled-up drifts. The sand crystals sparkled and caught the sun as he turned. Some of the dunes were covered with tough-looking grass. Their broad white edges were turned toward the sun, presumably to conserve moisture. Spare thorny brush poked timidly through the grass. Nothing moved. The silence had a density about it, a quality he could almost feel.

Standing there, he was struck by the haunting beauty of the empty landscape of red, orange and yellow sands. Once, long ago, as a child on Kaplan, his grandfather had taken him to the world's single ocean. The memory vivid in his mind: of booming surf, the foaming, hissing white water, the iodine smell of the beach, and the blue-green of the sea that merged with the deepness of the sky. Later, on the water with waves bubbling and frothing against the boat's hull, he stood alone on the deck, surrounded by the ocean. He felt very humbled and a little afraid then. It wasn't water surrounding him now, but an endless sea of sand. Nevertheless, he felt that same sense of awe, and a measure of inner peace.

It may hold a certain fascination, but the desert was also dangerous and deadly for the unprepared.

His eyes followed the gouged furrow made by the survival blister. Barely visible, a line of shimmering red cliffs lined the horizon. Twenty, thirty talans away, perhaps? Without reference points it was difficult to judge distances. The eye simply skidded helplessly over the dancing, twisting waves of air.

Somewhere in the depths of those cliffs could be water. From orbit, it didn't look like it rained in the deep desert. He doubted his chances of finding standing water at all. The heat would have sucked any moisture dry within hours. Still, some of the sheltered gorges may hold open pools. It wasn't uncommon for groundwater to well up…Sure. And his crash was just an unfortunate accident too, he figured.

At any rate, he had no other choice but to make for the hills.

To wait for rescue that may never come meant certain death. Maybe SC&C had picked up the emergency transponder when the survival blister purged and tracked him down, if they had time before the blister brewed up. Then again, SC&C *could* have picked up the millisecond message burst before the M-3s destroyed the ejected beacon. Rayon would know what to do.

His training said to wait in the area of a crash. His instincts screamed at him to get away. If SC&C had picked him up, so could the M-3s. Would they follow him down to make sure the job was finished? In the end, the desert made the decision for him. Without special equipment, it would be madness to cross this desert in the heat of the day. Okay, if he was going to hang around, he needed to build some cover.

He looked about for large hull panels. Hands on hips, he glanced up to check which way the sun went. A searing ball high in the northern sky, the shadows fell to his right. That meant he was somewhere in the southern hemisphere, then.

It was hot work hauling the plates, but after twenty minutes, it was done. Propped against the side of the dune the clumsy collection of panels and struts wasn't much, but it would keep out the worst of the sun. Right now it beat the luxurious rooms at Raman Center all hollow. With a piece of plating, he scooped out the sand from the enclosure. With the floor more or less level, he spread the thermal blanket over it.

After carrying in his survival supplies, he took two mouthfuls of water and sprawled on the blanket. He groaned with contentment, vaguely hoping that this was as hot as it got around here, but he had shade and it made him feel better. He turned on his side, away from the burnt shoulder to reduce the irritation.

A shaft of light leaked down through a crack between the panels. His eyes drifted to the lighted circle beside him. After a while, he closed his eyes and listened to the whisper of the sands.

* * *

Kapel Pen unleashed her full fury against Garner.

He stood in the middle of her office while she raged. Hands waving, she brought her face close to his and screamed.

"An M-6 is going to be hovering over my head in a day and you tell me to relax? Production on Anulus is at a standstill and Anall-Marr has gone orbital! The whole cursed Ecumenical Synod is in a flap. And it's all your fault, you stupid man. You couldn't have caused more trouble if you were a paid subversive! Are you?"

She was livid and Garner tried to endure her lashing stoically as he waited for the storm to break. Maybe he had exceeded his authority just a little bit, neh? Still, it was unfair to blame it all on him. No one could have predicted that a simple operation could have gone so drastically wrong.

Anyway, the knocks came with the territory. He'd had these sessions before and survived. This time, though, her fury had a different quality and he wilted under the onslaught.

When the histrionics finished, she planted her fists on her hips and kept throwing stabbing glares at him. Gradually, she calmed down, but it felt more like being in the eye of a hurricane.

"There is a full COMDEKOPS team crawling all over Anulus, and I'm a virtual prisoner in my own Center! I only hope the fishy-eyed slime at Complex Fourteen rots for all eternity in mud," she hissed, stomping around the office. "Did they at least finish it?" she demanded over her shoulder.

"We don't have positive confirmation, Dama," Garner answered carefully. Kapel snorted in disgust. "The M-1 was destroyed, but the pursuing M-3s saw a survival blister crash in the deep desert. They had to break off after being challenged by Anar'on's SC&C."

"After all that, you bungled it, neh?"

"The probability of survival is negligible."

She pointed a slim finger at him. "But it's there, isn't it?"

"I'm afraid so."

"Then remove it!"

The implication of what she was asking slowly surfaced and Garner squirmed.

"But, Dama—"

"You started it, now finish it! Even if you have to scour the whole planet for him."

"Interfering in Anar'on's space—"

"Get it through your head, Garner. If there is even the remotest chance of that officer being alive, he must be prevented from talking. Ever. Even you can grasp a simple idea like that, neh?"

"I will see to it," Garner said confidently. "We know where he crashed. We'll be waiting."

"Good. What about our cover on Anulus?"

"I ordered the administrator to crash an M-1—"

"With a body, I hope?" she interjected sarcastically.

He winced and nodded. "There will not be any SC&C trace. The ship flew low. The superintendent of Complex Fourteen can claim a regrettable case of mistaken identity and there is no evidence to prove otherwise. The Envoy won't find anything."

"Provided Terrllss-rr doesn't come back to haunt us," Kapel finished for him, looking disgusted. "What about the logs in the M-3s? They have to corroborate our story or the whole thing collapses, taking us down with it."

"Ah, that might be somewhat more complicated to arrange."

She raised both her arms. "I don't want to hear it! Just fix it. I still cannot believe you did this. Male and stupid, that's what you are, Garner. Your first bungled attempt to scare off this Second Scout should have been a warning, neh? You chose not to heed it, or my warning, and it's landed you in trouble. When you start something, finish it!"

"Dama—"

"Silence! I told you to watch Tamara, not that Scout officer!" she raged, her small fists clenched.

"Ah, if I hadn't ordered the intercept, your plans may have been compromised, neh? After landing on Anulus, Terr would have received Tamara's message and—"

"And what?" Kapel walked to her desk and tapped the sensitized surface. In the Wall, text appeared against a pale blue background. "Tamara's intercepted message, neh? All it says, she has evidence linking me with the Karkans. Speculation, nothing else."

"Terr would have passed the information and his suspicions directly to the Envoy," Garner said lamely.

"What suspicions? There is nothing *there*, you idiot! To someone who doesn't have the necessary background knowledge, it's just innuendo. You overestimated the significance of Tamara's message and overreacted in your response. Instead of discussing it with me, you brought the whole weight of the Serrll Scout Fleet on my head! Not only that, you compounded your first error by going after Tamara. And you bungled that as well, neh? Who told you to touch her?"

"Dama, if you recall—"

Her small fists pounded the desk. "How could you have been so dense? You were to silence her only if she *knew* something!"

"But, Dama, if Tamara and Terr are permitted to exchange their—"

"That's why that Scout must die, you fool! Not Tamara! Instead of solving my problems, you've added to them. Your actions have brought all the Family factions against me just when I desperately need their support. You managed to undo in three moves what all my dear relatives have failed in years of trying, and that's to bring me to the brink of ruin. I should have you burned where you stand. Oh!" Her eyes tore him apart as she shook with fury.

Garner smoldered with humiliation as he realized his mistake, one that could prove politically fatal to Kapel. Devoted to her, he endured her outbursts because she needed someone to rage at; and he needed her companionship, no matter how one-sided. But to knowingly hurt her?

He bowed deeply. "Dama, I should have consulted you," he murmured humbly. "I was in error and I'm prepared to accept the consequences of your wrath."

Kapel glowered at him, torn with indecision. She wanted to hurt him as he had hurt her. Although he did what he thought was in her best interest, it was small consolation. Who could have counted on events turning out as they did? She should have given him more explicit instructions. Her mistake was in relying on him to act as she would have acted. He was only a stupid male after all.

"We shall all have to accept the consequences, Garner," she said gruffly. "Much as I would love to send you to the altar, I can't spare you."

Garner did not know what to say. He mistrusted emotion of any sort. They merely got in the way. Now, he was as close to experiencing love as he ever hoped to. After what he had done, she managed to rise above her desire to lash out and actually forgive him.

"I am your humble servant, Dama," he whispered and bowed again. She looked at him fondly.

In the Shadow of Death

"You're a fool." They were both fools, she decided. "I want you to deliver my personal apology to Tamara—"

"But, Dama—"

"Silence! I want the driver of that communal delivered to the priests. And I want Tamara to know it."

"The altar?" Garner looked at her in dismay. "But…he's one of my best Fleet operatives."

"Do you want to take his place?" He dropped his eyes and she nodded knowingly. "I didn't think so. Although misguided, you failed to kill her and I don't tolerate mistakes. At the first opportunity, I also want that Karkan piece of swamp mud off Anulus. Kunoid can scream if they want to."

"The mine superintendent? I wouldn't advise it, Dama," he said, slipping naturally into his role. "He was only following the administrator's orders."

"Your orders, you mean. It's a sign of my displeasure. She should have queried your order. Executive decisions come only from *me*, neh?"

"I take note of your displeasure, Dama."

"I know you do, Garner."

* * *

Troubled, Enllss leaned back in his formchair and sipped tea. Troubled not only by what occurred on Anulus, but also about Terr. The House of Llss-rr had lost many of its sons to ventures of dubious value. His own brother, Terr's father, had met his end on Anar'on during a murky undercover operation for the Fleet. Now, Terr himself missing, also on Anar'on. Were the fates playing with the House of Llss-rr?

When the comms alert beeped, he reached across the desk and tapped a rectangle on the sensitized surface. The random tumbling of soothing patterns in the Wall dissolved. Sill's face dark with anger, eyes unnaturally bright.

"Been expecting your call," Enllss said. "What's ruined *your* day?"

"Ach! It's the Four Suns fiasco, of course," Sill piped and waved his right hand in agitation.

"Tell me about it."

"I just finished talking to Anabb on Talon. He has relieved the Elexi Fleet commander on the spot. There are bodies everywhere. One of them is Master Scout Ki-Tori, Cannan's chief of staff. There will be plenty of courts-martial to follow, I should imagine. Anabb wasn't exactly in a forgiving mood."

"He's a born hatchet man," Enllss said comfortably, "and is probably loving every minute of it."

"I wouldn't count on it, Enllss. We're talking serious dereliction of duty here. It doesn't make Anabb look good."

"Not his fault."

"Maybe not, but as COMDEKOPS, he has to carry the can with CAPFLTCOM." Referring to Captal Fleet Command.

"That's his problem. Just give me the short version, Sill."

"Ach! He has the whole Fleet inventory in the Four Suns grounded pending an investigation into the Elexi command and control structure. My people went over some of the logs taken by Anulus SC&C. So far, we found nothing that cannot be explained."

"What about those two M-3s? They were ordered to break off pursuit."

"That's the curious part," Sill admitted. "Their logs don't show them receiving any comms from COMELOPS or *Pirana*."

"Eh? Preposterous!"

"That may be. They followed the M-1 all the way to Anar'on where they had an exchange. *Pirana* was destroyed. There are some irregularities, but Anar'on SC&C confirms the action."

"What about comms from Anulus? Didn't those bovine poltroons try to authenticate *Pirana* with Anulus SC&C? What about that?"

Sill shrugged. "Apparently, when challenged, *Pirana* simply took off."

Enllss growled and bared his teeth. "Are you telling me we don't have any comms logs from *Pirana* or the M-3s?"

"That's about the size of it."

Enllss growled in frustration. "That sucks and you know it. It's too convenient. Even I know you cannot go wandering about the Serrll without SC&C control. They must have had *some* comms."

"We'll keep checking, Enllss, but it seems that someone went to a lot of trouble to see to it that Terr never touched dirt again."

Enllss felt a pang of loss, but he refused to dwell on it. "You're sure it was *Pirana*?"

"I'm afraid so," Sill said, aware of his friend's pain, but helpless to do anything to help him. "Anar'on SC&C received a two-part burst from his emergency beacon before it too was destroyed. When SC&C saw the Diplomatic Branch prefix codes, they forwarded the message to Rayon."

"What did the message say?"

"Ach! He didn't get around to telling me. Right now, all the evidence points to a regrettable case of mistaken identity. The real prisoner crashed his M-1 soon after taking off. Hugging the terrain, SC&C never picked him up."

"Some bloody mistake. Why wouldn't Terr communicate? It doesn't make sense, Sill."

"Damaged comms?"

"It's possible. Keep at it. Have those M-3 commanders properly debriefed. And I want the M-3s stripped down to their seams. I want to know why they failed to pick up their orders. If they had a comms fault, their diagnostics computer should have been screaming in alarm."

"Anabb is already on it."

"One M-3 with faulty comms I can swallow, but two of them? That's pushing your luck beyond the credulous. It's a setup and we both know it. What else you got?"

"More than we bargained for, but not necessarily what we wanted. Ach! It pains me to say it, but I must admit Rayon has proven to be very competent. The Bureau of Administrative Affairs will need to send a team out there to sort it all out."

"The bottom line, Sill."

"Patience, I'm getting to it," Sill rasped and ran a hand through his hair. "If anyone else was involved except Kunoid Minerals, I would say forget the whole thing. Kapel Pen has been severely embarrassed and no doubt heads will roll. She has a lot to answer for. On the surface at least, there is no case for impeachment. However, Rayon has reported some disturbing findings that were corroborated by my team. One of those findings came from Terr. It could establish a possible link with the Karkans and his subsequent misadventure."

"And what finding is that?"

"Before I forget, your hunch about Kapel was right. She was the one who initiated the negotiations with Kunoid. Anall-Marr got in only when the deal required his ratification and he saw a profit in it for himself."

"I told you." Enllss nodded with satisfaction. "And?"

"She once ran for the General Assembly."

"Is that so?"

"That's where Terr's observation comes in. He suggested to Rayon that Kapel might still be cultivating that ambition."

"It's possible," Enllss mused. "I cannot see her being satisfied with a mere General Assembly seat, though. Not after ruling a whole system. This is all very interesting, but it doesn't give me that link between her and the Karkans."

"Ach! Without Terr, we're still stuck."

"Kapel Pen in Captal, eh?" Enllss said and pulled at his chin. It made him forget, at least for a while, Terr's loss.

* * *

In the Shadow of Death

Terr sat up suddenly, still seeing the hurtling survival blister around him, seeing Anar'on whirl above him and the fire of the M-3s. The sensation so powerful, he had to struggle consciously before that reality melted away, leaving him shaken.

A pearly, diffuse light enveloped the darkness. Black shadows lay heavy among the pale silver outlines of the dunes. He crawled out of his makeshift shelter, stood up and stretched his arms with a satisfied grunt. His left shoulder stiff and still sore, he spent a minute massaging it. He breathed deeply of the crisp, heavily scented air and looked up. The canopy of stars that was The Arch reached unbroken all the way to the horizon, cold and brilliant. The sheer density and profusion of stars was overwhelming. They seemed to almost press down. A meteor tore a silent orange streak across a quarter of the sky. A half moon stood high in the west and glared bright. Low on the horizon its smaller companion glowed buttery yellow.

At any other time, he would have enjoyed that sky and those moons. There was something protective about the night and the silence of the desert. Under other circumstances, he could easily learn to love this land. The stars stared indifferently at him, bringing him back to harsh reality.

After spraying his burns again and swallowing two pills against infection, he made a production of gathering his survival supplies. He stared at the bulky jump jacket and decided it would come in handy when the night turned really cold. It didn't weigh that much anyway. Using his shirt, he tied the booty into a loose bundle. Taking a bearing from the furrow the blister made in the dunes, he searched the sky and picked two marker stars as near south as he could make. Even if he was out a bit, during the day there wasn't much chance of him missing the formidable line of escarpment cliffs.

He heaved the bundle over his right shoulder, glanced around the camp one last time and headed into the night.

There was only the sound of his ragged breathing and the whisper of shifting sands beneath his feet to break the silence of the desert. The moons were now high above his left shoulder, glaring milky white. Occasionally, he would pause and stare at the dunes. The mineral crystals along their sides sparkled like fields of frozen snow. He could easily imagine himself walking through a cool snowfield. Then he would move and the magic would fade.

Not that there was much magic in dragging himself through the shifting sands.

At first, he found the going stimulating. He played pretend mind games, imagining himself an explorer, a Wanderer. He tried whistling, but scrambling through soft sand or up a steep dune face broke his rhythm. He settled on talking to himself. The thing he didn't talk about was his predicament. Bad enough having to live through it without dissecting every step he made. As the night wore on, even talking felt too much like work.

After what seemed an eternity of dunes, he clambered up a broken slope. Small stones rattled behind him. He reached the top and stood on a rocky plateau. He took several deep breaths, bent over and started coughing, the air rasping raw in his throat. The way he felt, he didn't have to worry about running out of water, he would have a coronary long before morning.

He straightened and took his time studying the ground. Stony flats stretched far into the desert, broken by patches of pea-gravel and shallow dunes. He squatted down, pulled off his boots and poured out the sand. He wriggled his toes, luxuriating at the freedom. Reluctantly, he reached for the water container. The thing was heavy, but he decided grimly it would get lighter all too quickly. He bit on the spigot and felt better after a couple of cool mouthfuls.

Standing up was a reluctant process of groaning and moaning. Unaccustomed to such abuse, he realized if he didn't keep moving, his legs would stiffen and seize up. He needed to keep walking while he still felt strong. He tried not to think about his aching body, burning shoulder, or about tomorrow when the water would start to give out. Checking his marker stars, he headed into the darkness.

* * *

Above the sands, the purple sky gave way to a smear of deep red. In the predawn chill, the stars merely blinked, aloof and indifferent. Even with his jump jacket on, he found it bitterly cold. His breath a white fog before him. He blew on his fingers, then vigorously rubbed his hands, longing for some of the day's heat.

Feeling more than a little abused, he stood there, too weary to admire the breaking dawn. Somewhere back in the eternity of night, he had lost that spring in his step, his walk reduced to a determined weary slog. He ached all over. His legs were numb and his arms were tender from the chafing of the awkward pack. He was worried about the burning sensation in his left shoulder and hoped the burns were not getting infected.

Clambering up and down those damned dunes, that's what did it. If the government was looking for a penal colony, this desert was better than Cantor.

Maybe it was just as well he headed out when he did. He certainly would not have been able to cope with those dunes now. Slowly, the desert lit up. All around him the ground was either all soft sand or rocky flats, covered in places with grass and small prickly brush. On his right, not one hundred and fifty katalans away, perhaps two hundred paces, stretched a flat plain of hard mineral salts, smooth as a glidewalk.

He stared at it for a while without blinking. He didn't even have the strength to laugh. Gods knew how long he must have been paralleling it, killing himself over broken ground and shifting sand. He cursed weakly and sagged down to his knees, utterly spent. This was cruel.

Ahead of him, dividing the sky, stood the black ramparts of the escarpment, its top tinged with pearly light. They looked close, but he wasn't kidding himself. Maybe by tomorrow

173

morning, he would reach the foothills. Shafts of yellow light lanced out over the cliffs like a gauzy fan.

He hoped to find water somewhere in those gorges or this was going to be a hell of an effort just to pick a rocky grave. He knew he should keep going until it became too hot to walk, but he couldn't do it. He only wanted to curl up and sleep. His mouth tasted like the inside of his boot and his throat tender.

Rit!

It was getting light rapidly. He looked around for a handy gully to crawl into. Groaning, feeling sorry for himself, he staggered to his feet. Pain prodded and stabbed from protesting muscles. Thinking dark and evil thoughts, he began shuffling toward a ridge on his left.

The sun became a thin wedge of gold that peered over the horizon. The shadows abruptly fled, and where the light touched, it burned. From dark gray the rock and sand suddenly filled with color. In an instant, it turned into another world. The magic of the night faded into memory, replaced by another kind of magic. He paused to look at the new landscape.

This early the air had a dreamy soft quality to it. In the deeper valleys still in shadow, strands of mist hung like a protective blanket. Where did water come from to form a mist? It came to him a transitory thought, not really important. Nothing stirred and the silence was total. Eerie and serene at the same time. In this place where the world held its breath, he felt a strange protective peace. Then again, it could be the peace before a somewhat unpleasant death. With a nod, he reluctantly turned to the task at hand.

The grass was tall, wide and spiky and seemed to move around him. He stood at the lip of a narrow ravine winds have carved out beneath a wall of dark brown rock. The ravine ran roughly north-to-south. What he searched for was an overhang or a hollow. He wanted a place that would give him shelter all day long. Peering down, there didn't seem to be any easy way down. On his right was a small drift of sand. When he walked to it and looked down, it went all the way to the bottom. The place dark, full of shadow.

He slid down the slope in a cascade of loose sand. Spluttering, he brushed his hair and patted himself down, then examined his kingdom. It wasn't much, but it was his. A few paces from him in the rock wall where he came down, a jumble of smooth slabs covered what looked like a deeper fissure. He walked to it, supported himself against an overhang with an outstretched hand and looked under it. The cave shallow, filled with drift sand and it offered cover. Not much, but it would keep out the sun. It would do.

After scooping out the cold sand, he picked some dry grass and laid it on the cave floor. He covered the grass with his thermal blanket, sat back and admired his handiwork. It made a tolerable bed. The way he felt, it could have been a piece of rock for all he cared. He lay down trying it on for size, grunted with pleasure and smiled. He considered this little achievement a major life's accomplishment. Wriggling around a bit, he let his head sink back. The grass rustled beneath him, its oily smell strange, but not unpleasant. His legs throbbed and his shoulder painful. He thought about having something to eat, then things became fuzzy. Wearing a wistful grin, he drifted away among images of red desert sands beneath an amber sky.

* * *

He woke with a start. For a second, he stared vacantly at nothing. The air oppressively hot, his hair was slick with oil and sweat. Stiff and sore, he propped himself up on an elbow and wiped his face. His mouth tasted vile and he probably looked it. While he slept, he must have pulled off his jump jacket, for it lay beneath him in a crumpled bundle.

Fumbling with the water container, he brought the spigot to his mouth. Biting on it, he took one long swallow. When he finished, he shook the container and frowned. It was less than half full. He licked his lips and shrugged philosophically.

Outside, the opposite wall of the ravine glared and shimmered with reflected heat. Nothing stirred and he wasn't sure whether there were any predatory animals about. His knowledge of Anar'on sketchy at best, he didn't remember reading about any prowling or crawling things. He recalled a passage about rock rays, but the details eluded him.

Muscles protesting, he crouched and shuffled out. The heat burned his skin and dried the sweat. He stood there and allowed the heat to soak into him. He stretched his arms upward and grunted. Joints creaked and popped and he grimaced. His left shoulder very sore and was going to be a problem. After a few deep breaths, he looked along the gully floor. The place was littered with strewn boulders and jumbled rocks. The wall of the ridge towered above him.

The air full of strange smells: baked rock, sand and grass and others he couldn't identify. Then there was the silence. It lay thick and heavy over everything like a blanket, and the shadows crowded around him. Shielding his eyes from the reflected glare, he looked up. The soft amber sky free of cloud. He suspected it might have been quite a while since this place saw rain, if ever.

Back in his upholstered cave, he stripped off his trousers and immediately felt better. Down to his undershorts, squatting on the thermal blanket, he rummaged through his pack of supplies. Picking over the plunder, he stared skeptically at a small packet of concentrate. According to one of the labels, the pack guaranteed to be full of nutrition and vitamins, sufficient for one day. Sealed, it yielded to his touch. He decided to give it a go over some of the drier and bulkier items. This one held some liquid and he was mindful of his dwindling water supply. Food would never be a problem anyway. He would run out of water long before he ran out of rations.

He placed the packet beside him and took out the medical

kit. His throat raw from dehydration, he worried about infection. He swallowed a pill and hoped it would be enough. Next, he took out the burn spray and wetted his palms. Reaching back over his left shoulder, he sighed with contentment at the cooling touch. When he prodded the cut on his head, he felt dry scab. At least that was healing.

Lying on his back, knees drawn up, one hand behind his head, he sucked at the goo in the pack. It wasn't really bad, but he wouldn't want to live on it.

Apart from some aches and pains, scrapes, burns and broken blisters, he didn't feel too bad. He knew that by tomorrow morning, it was going to be a different story. Once he ran out of water, he wouldn't last long. He didn't underestimate the seriousness of his predicament, but lying there, reduced to basics, he had no fear. There was something elemental about his impersonal struggle with the desert. It stripped away the veneer of artificiality and reduced life to a simple question of survival. Issues a day ago that seemed critical were now something almost inconsequential. His perspective had broadened and shrunk at the same time.

He hadn't felt such a keen thrill in a challenge for a long time. This one, though, he mused, was likely to kill him. It was not simply the bite of danger that drew him. Only a fool walks openly into the jaws of death. No, it was the prospect of a personal and direct struggle against an unremitting environment. Here, the desert ruled and he either adapted or died. Unfortunately, he wasn't going to last long enough to adapt.

Even if he somehow managed to live through this, what then? Return to the comfortable shield of his uniform? Charge about in his *Ramora*, pretending he was righting the wrongs the races of the Serrll inflicted on each other? Remain content to act as a small piece in a complicated game played by faceless bureaucrats on Captal? He didn't know the answer to that one, but Alasi was free and with his family again. Whatever happened, he had the satisfaction of knowing that at least one life he had touched had benefited from it. Maybe death wasn't such a high price to pay for that.

He tried to sleep. The afternoon wore on in snatches of semi-wakefulness. When he moved, the dry rasping of grass under the blanket would jolt him awake. The more he tried to ignore it, the harder he listened for the faintest sound. It made the day about a hundred years long.

As the shadows thickened, he was tempted more than once to set out to relieve his fidgeting. He wanted to be moving, to be doing something. He may have been thinking about it, but he had enough sense to restrain himself. Still too hot out there to be wandering about. Even if the sun didn't fry him, he would be losing precious bodily moisture from sheer exertion. He was drying out as it is. Restless, he picked out another ration pack and forced himself to eat. He did not feel hungry, but it took energy to walk. He could not afford to drink even if his body craved water. This experience at least gave him a new insight into the luxury of unlimited water.

Chapter Eight

Through the night as he walked, Terr talked to himself to shorten the burden of time. He held elaborate debates with imaginary adversaries, and some not so imaginary. He decided the envoy meant well, but the whole thing was screwed even before it started.

When Rayon finishes his investigations, what then? After a brief flurry of excitement, Elexi would quietly sink back into anonymity and things would revert to their old ways. It was so pointless. Captal, he realized, didn't give a damn about Elexi or slavery. The Four Suns was a small arena in an endless struggle between the Servatory Party and the Revisionists. Then again, wasn't everything?

Absorbed in his thoughts, it took him a while to realize that a light breeze had sprung up. It drove fine sand across the salt flats, forming waving, twisting lines. He licked his lips and swallowed. His throat painfully raw and he was running a degree of temperature. So much for modern medicine. Clearly, the local bugs had found him acceptable. After centuries of interspecies contact, he could expect the environment would be filled with an assortment of microbial cultures, something for everyone. More likely, the extreme dryness of the air allowed his personal fauna to flourish.

Somewhere during the night, he decided he wouldn't make it. He guessed he must have known it all along. It wasn't fatalism, and it didn't mean he was giving up. The desert would have to fight him, and maybe he'd get lucky. He was simply facing up to a harsh reality. Gazing up at the sweep of stars, he figured the naked face of death wasn't so grim after all.

In the silence, he had the thin keening of the wind and the

soft crunching of mineral salts beneath his feet for company.

He kept walking.

It was still dark when he saw the loom of black cliffs against the backdrop of stars. The salt flats gradually gave way to stretches of packed sand and smooth rock, and he knew he was getting close. He didn't know why, but that line of cliffs, forbidding and remote, sent his emotions churning. He picked up his steps.

Morning was long gone by the time he reached the foothills. The cliffs were high and he had to look up to see their jagged faces. The bare walls of the escarpment lay unbroken before him. Nothing grew here, not even the tough grass of the desert. Muscles twitching from fatigue, he desperately wanted to lie down and sleep.

Thirst had been his companion for most of the night. He needed to make the precious little water he had left last, although he wasn't exactly sure why. Standing before the cliff wall, he looked left, then right. Wearily, he turned right for the hell of it and followed the unbroken line of rock. He needed to cover as much ground as he could before the heat of the day forced him to take shelter, already uncomfortably warm. If he didn't find water today, he knew it wasn't likely he would see another dawn. The thought of finding water kept him going. There wasn't much else to live for and he felt too cranky to roll over and simply die.

The sun had not reached the top of the escarpment when he saw a break in the line of red stone. The gorge wide enough for an M-4 to go through without scraping the sides. Huge drifts of brown sand were piled up almost to the rim of the break, something like sixty or seventy katalans high. It would make for a tough climb and he didn't look forward to it, but this side of the wall had nothing. The shadows had fled and the air had lost its crispness, becoming thick and heavy. He looked past the gorge at the unbroken line of cliffs and groaned. He couldn't walk any farther.

In the Shadow of Death

His legs buckled beneath him and he sagged down to his knees. He moaned and stretched out on his back to stare at the soft amber of the sky. There was no wind to disturb his thoughts. It felt good to take the weight off his legs. His shoulder throbbed, but the pain now almost a comforting companion. He ignored it.

He didn't know how long he lay there. When he opened his eyes, it was painfully bright. He cursed himself for falling asleep, but realized he'd needed the enforced rest. Slowly, he unwound the shirt off his head. Picking over his collection of supplies, he stuffed some concentrates into his pockets. Maybe he shouldn't have dragged all that stuff with him. There was no way he could eat it all before the end came. Still, it seemed like a good idea at the time.

With his thermal blanket around him like a cape, he headed for the break.

High now, the sun beat down without pity. Climbing the drift guarding the gorge, he gritted his teeth and cursed softly. Anger gave him strength and he needed every bit of it. The soft sand shifted beneath him and he slipped more than once to slide down the steep face.

Wheezing, his face pressed against the hot sand, ignoring the burning, he figured that living wasn't worth this kind of effort. Ridiculous and no one was around to appreciate his struggle. There would be no medals. If there wasn't even a medal in it, what was the point? Chuckling, spitting sand, he pulled himself up.

When he reached the crest, the smooth cliff walls fell away on either side of him. Before him, orange and yellow sands stretched into endless distance, merging with a brown sky. Hot and dry, a faint breeze stirred the air around him, giving him an illusion of coolness. Dejected, he squatted down and stared into the open empty vastness. Nothing out there but an endless sea of more sand and more heat. Who would want live out here anyway? There wasn't even a Wanderer around. Probably holed up in some nice air-conditioned cave, no doubt. Smart…

Panting, racked by small coughs, he licked his cracked lips and examined the cliffs on either side of the break. On his left, they seemed to form into more gorges and wadis. On his right the rocks were smooth and unbroken.

There was no question of looking for water now. He must get out of the sun or the problem of water would become academic. He would start in the afternoon when the sun fell below the line of the escarpment and there was shade. He nodded, liking the idea. After a weary sigh, he started shuffling and sliding down the drift.

Little more than a crack in the cliff, it was dark and just wide enough to crawl into. The stone cool and he spent a minute leaning against it. Behind him the drift towered up, furrowed and creased where he stumbled and rolled down its face. Groggily, he threw down the thermal blanket and sprawled across it.

* * *

He stirred uneasily and coughed. A spasm of shivering ran through his body. He opened his eyes to darkness. For long seconds, he stared stupidly at nothing. Then he cursed and sagged weakly against the blanket. It was already night. He had overslept, or been unconscious more likely.

Absently, he rubbed the grit out of his eyes. Still in a daze, he groped for his jump jacket and dragged it on, comforted by its warmth. He knelt, clasped his hands in his lap and glowered at the water container. What the hell! He was tired of lugging the bloody thing around anymore. He picked it up and shook it. There didn't seem to be much in it.

He clamped his mouth on the spigot and sucked. The water was still cold and he almost choked gulping it down past a raw throat. There were probably four good mouthfuls in it. A wave of dizziness swept over him and he held his head between his hands. His forehead burned and he shivered and clutched his knees, waiting for the spasms to pass. He thought of eating, but couldn't bring himself to it. That was bad. He guessed there was worse to come. He should take some medicine, but it seemed too much effort. With a moan, he sank down and curled his legs up against his belly.

Just a little longer, he thought, and then he'd get moving. The muscles in his legs jumped with tension. He turned over to relieve them. His legs still felt like chopped blocks of wood. Instead of putting himself through this torture, he should have stayed with the burnt remnants of his blister. If the M-3s came, at least it would have been quick. Sleep came as a welcome distraction.

When he opened his eyes the sand seemed to whisper and shift beneath him. He was stiff and cold and his throat burned. That degree of temperature was now a fever. Mumbling obscenities, he crawled to the lip of the fissure. Judging by the shadows, it was late in the morning and high time for him to do some paid work. The dry wash into which he had wandered was narrow and the red cliffs rose smoothly toward a honey sky. Still cool, the sun would not come here until early afternoon. Staring at the cliffs, he tried to remember what he had to do. Ah, water…

Mechanically, he wrapped a strip of shirt around his head and loosely draped the blanket over his shoulders. His footsteps echoed faintly on the hard-packed floor of the gorge. He couldn't feel his legs anymore, they ended somewhere below his knees. His arms were stone. That was okay; it helped with the walking.

He must have fallen several times. He would find himself breathing heavily, coughing, his face in the sand. He ran his tongue across swollen, broken lips. His mouth was dry and had a bitter taste. He lay there panting, wondering what he was supposed to do. He giggled weakly, then laughed. The cliffs threw back his laughter. He was supposed to keep walking, that was it.

Patches of grass lay in some of the crannies, taller than the stuff in the open desert. Then he saw the tree, a weird looking thing with a smooth ringed trunk. It had broad drooping leaves suspended from gnarled spines that bristled with thorns. The stuff dark green, tough and leathery. A sharp odor permeated from it, faintly sweet and redolent. He figured that kind of plant needed lots of water. That didn't necessarily mean open water. Water! *That's* what he was looking for!

He crawled toward it on all fours. He leaned against the trunk and decided to rest for a while. Its leaves hung over him in mute sympathy, like a blessing. After a time, he closed his eyes and slowly toppled over. It seemed too much effort to move and the sweet smell of the tree was everywhere.

He didn't know how long he lay there, but it must have been a while. The cliffs seemed to melt around him as they shifted, crowding him. He thought he could hear the bubble of running water somewhere. The sun was high overhead and he could feel its heavy heat on his skin. Then a cold spasm shook him and he clutched the thermal blanket to him, shivering. He knew he must keep moving, but the reason eluded him.

When he heard the footfalls and the soft shifting of sand, he squinted at the shadows. They finally fell across him and he turned up his head. The tall silent shapes were black outlines framed against the red cliffs. The shapes seemed to move in slow motion. One of the figures reached up and pulled back his brown hood.

All he could see were two enormous orange eyes filled with fire. He knew who they were; the fabled Anar'on desert no-mads, the Wanderers. He saw in their hands lightning and death. One of them knelt beside him and reached for him, his eyes burning. Terr drew back and gave a strangled scream of terror.

* * *

"The bitch tried to kill me!" Tamara snarled in cold fury.

Talia squirmed, not enjoying this at all, but sure her face betrayed no emotion, a minimum requirement in her position. She had expected the call and was surprised it took Tamara this long. What was Kapel thinking of anyway? Didn't the woman realize this could ruin everything?

Enraged, Tamara pressed her lips into a thin line. She looked the picture of indignation.

"You look lovely, my dear," Talia said charmingly. "Anger sets off the color of your cheeks."

"Don't evade the issue!"

"My dear, Kapel may be a lot of things—"

"And she's done most of them, neh?"

Talia smiled thinly. "Well, I won't argue with you there, but to suggest—"

"I'm not suggesting anything. If that communal driver hadn't been so anxious to save his own hide, I would be a news item on my channel."

"How do you know it wasn't a real accident? How do you know anything? Communals have been known to crash, neh?"

"You can save it for someone who doesn't know her as well as I do, dearie. That goon was one of her Fleet scum, too professional to be anything else. Why are you protecting her?"

Talia bit her lip. "Even if you're right, it doesn't necessarily mean Kapel is involved. It could be Garner acting on his own."

"You don't believe that any more than I do. I can spot a security blanket as well as you, and I've had one draped over me ever since that Envoy's aide paid me a call. This is Kapel's handiwork, all right, whether she sanctioned it or not. You know that Garner doesn't dare breathe without Kapel's permission."

Talia realized then why Kapel tolerated Garner. She needed him to voice her concerns and have someone to rage at. A woman assistant would never do. She would be connected to the Family and would no doubt try to play the Family game.

Garner was only a male after all, and hardly counted. It was an interesting insight.

"She apologized, or Garner did it for her," Talia pointed out. Tamara's laugh was less than humorous.

"My dear, if I were dead, she would be gloating, not apologizing. I want the senior Family to look into this. This time, Kapel has gone too far. If we allow her to get away with this, no one will be safe and you know it. Anyone who stands in her way will get a visit some night from one of Garner's goons and they're gone, just like she got rid of that Envoy's aide. She is dangerous, I tell you. And if you don't do something about it, I'll have it on tonight's clip. Everything!"

Talia sat up in alarm. Whatever Tamara knew or suspected, she could not be allowed to leak it, not now. The situation was delicate enough without panicking the senior Family. Some of them were already wondering whether they were making the right choice supporting Kapel. If their plans failed, Kapel herself may or may not fall, but it would certainly upset Talia's ambition to become Controller of Elexi and Prime Director of the Four Suns. With Kapel in Captal, coddling to the Karkans, Talia's ascension would be automatic.

Could it have been Garner acting on his own? It was possible, but unlikely. Still not outside the realm of plausibility. It would explain the apology.

Curses on Kapel and her high-handedness.

Then again, if she could engineer Kapel's downfall, the wayward elements of the Family may be suitably grateful, neh? All they faced now was an altogether perilous course of action with little profit and considerable risk. Talia dismissed the thought. Any serious repercussions would more than likely see all of them swept into political oblivion, or worse. She could all too clearly see herself in one of Anulus' holes. The contemplation made her flesh creep.

Why couldn't Kapel be happy with simply running the Four Suns? Wasn't that enough? What did she know of Captal and the naked cut and thrust of Serrll politics? Talia guessed that Kapel was only testing the limits none of them had dared contemplate before. No one could accuse Kapel of being timid, but Talia had allowed herself to be swept up in Kapel's grand vision, forgetting the more immediate problems facing her at home. Perhaps not too late to remedy things.

"That wouldn't be very smart, my dear," Talia said softly, the threat clear in her voice. "And you don't have anything worth saying. Innuendo, mere speculation."

Tamara stared through the Wall and grinned.

"Did I touch a raw nerve? That stern facade of yours is starting to show a few cracks, neh? Perhaps all I have is speculation like you said. Then again, perhaps not. Some time back, I received a message fragment from Kadreen, remember? It made for very interesting speculation. The next day, I learned that her combie had crashed, what was left of it. They never found her body. It could have been a coincidence, but I don't believe it. What did she find that demanded her death? I kept asking myself another question. What could *I* possibly know to make Kapel want to kill me? And I keep coming back to the same answer. You want me to go on?"

Talia sat tense in her formchair, wishing she could reach through the Wall and wipe the smirk off Tamara's face. Nevertheless, she had to admire her persistence, a true Pen.

"Listen to me—"

Tamara chuckled with unfeigned delight. "You should see yourself squirm, Talia. You would think that the Four Suns was at stake..." She paused and her eyes went round. "That's it, isn't it? You're planning to cede the Four Suns, aren't you? Gods above! And I was a fool not to see it. Are the senior Family supporting her?" When Talia said nothing, Tamara shook her head in disgust.

"How stupid of me. *You* must be in on it, have been from the beginning, neh? And to think I came to you for support. Do you also want me killed, cousin?"

"Stop talking nonsense," Talia snapped. "No one wants you killed. Not even Kapel, despite what you may think. We don't do business that way."

"In that case, I could be closer to the truth than I know."

"Closer to a place on an altar slab than you know," Talia retorted angrily.

Tamara chuckled. "What a plot. All this maneuvering right under Anall-Marr's nose. Poor fool. The last thing you would want to see happen is for him to hear about it. All that anti-Deklan propaganda, subversive campaigns, accelerated mining on Anulus. It all makes sense now. And that Envoy's aide Terr, he saw it. He saw it all."

"A lovely theory, my dear," Talia murmured, regaining her composure. "But you've been looking at too many of your channel's thrillers."

"Don't patronize me, Talia. This is big. It could blow the whole Deklan Republic wide open, destabilize the border systems—"

"As if you cared, neh?"

"I do care, and so should you. I also care about myself. You either cut me in on a slice of the cake or you better tell Kapel to finish what she started with that combie."

Talia stared at her, then laughed with genuine admiration. "The Pen self-interest rules after all. All along, I thought you were on some high moral campaign for the people."

"You admit it, then?"

Talia shrugged helplessly. "It would be pointless to deny it, neh?"

"What about Kapel? What does she get out of this?"

"A commissioner's post in the General Assembly on Captal," Talia said and Tamara arched an eyebrow.

"Commissioner? My goodness! You can't be serious. That would be a blatant flouting of the conventions. It is impossible to make senior post in the first term, and I cannot see Kapel waiting two more years until the next elections."

"She made a by-election deal with the Karkans. They will keep their end of the bargain."

"But commissioner?"

"Enllss-rr made it in his first term."

"So he did. And you succeed as Prime Director, neh? I wonder whether that will mean as much under Karkan rule. What of the Four Suns, dear cousin? Do we exchange one set of overlords for another? Kapel gets what she wants, but what does the Family get out of this arrangement? What do the border systems get out of it?"

Lately, Talia had been thinking very hard about that.

* * *

It was the awful flags that really got under Anall-Marr's skin.

Hung around the terminus building they fluttered gaily in the stiff breeze. The two escorting Armored Personnel Carriers, APCs, lifted quickly off the apron. Looking down, he grimaced at the gaudy display. He had spoken to Kapel about it already. She simply shrugged, relishing his annoyance. She was following protocol, showing respect, she said.

More like throwing down a challenge, he raged.

The combie and the escorts headed for the Center. For once the Raman skyline clear, washed by wind and recent rains. Feeble sunshine struggled through the cloud, painting the city below a muddy yellow. Their flight corridor swept of normal traffic, heavy lines of commercial traffic still wound all around them.

Instead of putting up with her insolence, he should have had the bitch rayed. What had him bristling was the final humiliation of having to obtain clearance from the picket M-6 before being allowed to land. He never heard the like! To be treated like some minor functionary in his own prefecture…it was infuriating.

Even he could not believe Kapel would be so naive or arrogant to interfere with a member of a general envoy's mission. Bad enough to have one of his systems investigated, he could ride out the ensuing personal embarrassment. The confusion among his supporters on Deklan was harder to face. What was especially galling were the mealy-mouthed predators who sought his demise. They positively glowed with glee at this unexpected propaganda windfall, brother priests of the Path. Sinners and heretics, all of them!

He knew what they were saying, even if they didn't dare say it to his face. If he was not capable of managing the Four Suns, how was he going to cope with the Deklan Republic if he were allowed to become Primate?

Blasphemous scum. Ach!

Even his contingency plan for taking over the administration of the Four Suns had somehow been leaked and the Synod was in a flap. It was one of those routine things prepared by his bureaucracy, never intended to be taken seriously, until now.

As Prefect, he had the authority to have the plan implemented. There was no question of its legality, but taking over any of the prickly local administrations carried with it considerable political risk, especially with the Four Suns. The Synod became paranoid whenever Anulus came up in a discussion. He knew other Deklan systems practicing questionable policies would bitterly resist any such interference, justifiably fearing intrusion into their own administrations. He also knew that many Karkan border systems held the Path in open ridicule. An intolerable situation. Discipline must be restored for the salvation of the sinful, he thought grimly.

The road of righteousness was a path strewn with thorns, he reflected stoically. And thorns were not the only things that lay strewn along his path. That was but a test of character and resolve. The skeletons of many crushed careers and lives lay beneath his feet. The price others paid for his ambition. It was not ambition for his personal glory, he told himself. People needed guidance to reach the Path, and his leadership would give them that. The Synod had turned weak, seeking the pleasures of flesh. Time for Deklan to return to its true calling and adherence to fundamental tenets. A calling he heard very loud and relished the prospect of following.

They came down on the landing ramp of the executive complex. Two rows of MPs in working grays stood to as he climbed out. He exchanged polite greetings with Garner as they rode up in silence.

With severe dignity, Garner ushered him into Kapel's office, exacerbating Anall's irritation at seeing a competent male subservient to a mere female.

Kapel stood demurely beside an open window, her hair shimmering against the city backdrop. She wore a long gown, dark brown with discrete red stripes that showed her figure to best advantage when she turned to face him. A choker of kerner stones adorned her throat with yellow fire that matched her eyes. The sleeves of her gown were broad and their backs hung to her knees. She wore it just to annoy him, he knew. His eyes stumbled on the low cleavage of her gown.

Seeing her standing there, soft and elusive, he felt a stirring of desire. Again, he experienced a confusion of emotions in her presence. It made his skin crawl to look at her, displaying herself so shamelessly. It was also her power and self-confidence—a very destructive combination in a female—that drew him and clouded his judgment. He was caught by the sheen of her hair, the creamy lines of her…He pulled himself up and cursed silently. She was a temptress of wickedness! It grated on him to look at her, hands folded, showing not a trace of respect his due. It was infuriating.

He knew he should rise above the weakness of the body, but he wished the cursed window were closed.

"Your Grace," she murmured and her voice tingled down his spine.

Forgetting control and the calm of the Path, he passed a

hand through his hair.

"Dama," he grated, moved to her desk and sat down in her chair. She raised an eyebrow, but said nothing.

"It is always a pleasure to welcome the Prefect," she purred maliciously. "But I had anticipated this visit."

"Ach! I dare say you have."

He had an image of her on the sacrificial altar, screaming for his forgiveness while the priests worked on her. The thought helped to steady him. After all, she was only a female. He stretched his long legs and leaned back into the formchair.

"Let's dispense with the pleasantries, Kapel. This time it's serious and I aim to have your explanation."

"Explanation? About what, your Grace?"

How self-important he looks, she thought contemptuously. And he sought to rule the Republic. He was tall, corpulent and sleek. Sleek with the fat stripped off Anulus and the other Deklan border worlds, she reminded herself. Something not to be forgotten. His hair completely white, streaked with the twin bands of dark gray of a mature Deklan male. Beneath thin white eyebrows, his long dour face framed large liquid-green eyes.

She knew why he was here, of course. He wanted to remove her from power. Recent developments now gave him a perfect excuse to do it, but procedure demanded a protracted course of action that required time. Time Anall didn't have. She would announce the secession long before he made the first official steps.

Nevertheless, none of this would be necessary if it were not for Garner's bungling interference. Stupid man.

"I shall not delve too deeply into your antics with the Envoy," Anall said coldly. "I dare say you have enough problems with Captal as it is. My concerns are more immediate. You allowed Kunoid to bring two mines on stream this year against my express instructions. Now I learn that you authorized development of a *third* mine, and that it will be ready to come on stream within the year."

Clever, she admitted grudgingly. He was going to hang his whole campaign against her based on that spurious mine.

"Your office has been receiving my reports, Your Grace," she said and flashed him a smile. "I have done nothing to be reproached for."

"Ach! Bureaucratic doubletalk."

"Doubletalk or not, darling, plans for that mine were under negotiation for over nine months. Five months ago, you gave Kunoid your personal approval to begin implementing the necessary infrastructure, neh? Why are you bringing this against me now?" She looked hurt, pretending wounded innocence.

"Ach! That was for the second mine, not the third one!"

"Now, wait a—"

"I expect my Controllers to use their initiative. The last time I was here, I told you to cut back production from the second mine. I expected you to take the next logical step. I'm not in the habit of having the Synod on my back asking awkward questions."

A flush tinged her cheeks. "If you wanted development of that third mine stopped, Your Grace, you should have said so, neh? I'm not a mind reader," Kapel retorted primly.

"Ach! And I'm not going to argue this with you, Dama," he said comfortably. "You're to freeze all work on the third mine immediately. You take any liberties over this and I'll have that M-6 up there reduce your Center to rubble, and anyone else who dares to interfere."

Her smile was anything but amused. "Really? You're prepared to throw me away just to retain your nomination, neh? It's not that simple and you know it. Closing an operation that size is not like shutting off a Wall. There are long-term commitments and contracts to consider, and penalties for breaking them. I have to look at asset disposal, equipment, and freighter charters. Technical staff and the general workforce to be considered, not to mention our obligations to Kunoid."

"Ah, I'm glad you brought that up, my dear. We certainly

cannot forget our Kunoid friends. Ach! Especially when they are indirectly responsible for interfering with the Envoy's mission."

"A regrettable case of mistaken identity, Your Grace," Kapel pointed out evenly.

Damn the envoy and his aide. And damn Garner.

"Indeed, Dama. You don't know how regrettable that is. Remember what you told me the last time we spoke? The Envoy will find nothing, you said. You would see to it personally, or words to that effect."

Kapel pursed her lips and fumed.

"Despite your assurances, the Envoy *has* found something, hasn't he? Ach! Quite a lot, as a matter of fact. Wouldn't you say? A fourth mine in the northern hemisphere!" he thundered and crashed his fist against the desk. He had the bitch now.

Kapel winced, composing her thoughts. Evidently, Anall had gotten hold of Second Scout Terr's TLM and was using it to maximum effect. Whichever way she cared to look at it, this was an unwelcome development. Not exactly a disaster, but it also wouldn't make life any easier for her.

"Nothing to say?" Anall asked maliciously. "Well, I have. Skimming profits off the mining accounts—"

"You cannot make that stick without implicating yourself!" Kapel snapped.

"Any monies my office happened to receive were treated as altar donations, Dama," Anall said and smiled nastily. "All perfectly legal. Not so legal is your violation of Deklan Synod directives. My directives! I've got a whole load of charges here. Open contempt by the general populace for the way of the Path, corruption of your Proctors, illegal slavery of local citizens. It's a grand haul.

"Now, I accept that you might not have been personally involved. Nevertheless, such open disregard of your own laws suggests a degree of incompetence on your part. It's clear to me that you're not fit to hold the office of Controller and continue to discharge the duties and responsibilities that go with it."

She looked at him sitting there all puffed up with self-importance and broke into helpless laughter. Color drained from his face and his eyes glittered with fury. Clutching her stomach, she groped for one of the formchairs and slumped into its embrace. After a moment, she dabbed at her eyes.

"You should listen to yourself, Anall. You're such a pompous bag, darling. What's more, it is you who isn't fit to be Primate of the Synod. And you won't be."

Anall stood up unable to believe her insolence.

"Ach! In all my years of political life, no one has dared display such open contempt for the office of the Prefect. No one! Do you think this is a titular appointment? How dare you speak to me in such tones? I represent the authority of the Ecumenical Synod—"

"You represent nothing, darling," Kapel said archly. "Or at best something that no longer has any relevance. I told you before, neh? I rule here. If you try to move against me, I will rally the sympathy of the border systems. No matter how I may be implicated, you don't dare risk making your allegations public. Not now. Not when you're so close to securing your own nomination."

Fuming, he accepted the unpalatable truth of her words. He wanted to crush her, but not at the cost of his career. And he was so close! Patience was a guiding light of the Path and he had learned how to be patient. He tightened his lips, wanting to wipe Kapel's insolent smirk off her face and the way she was taunting him with her body. It was beneath him, he knew, yet the prospect of ruining her gave him a sinfully pleasant glow of anticipation. Mouthing the second litany of subservience to the Path, he prayed for forgiveness and enlightenment.

"The Four Suns has always been a thorn in my side—"

"Well, it won't be for much longer!" she snapped and cursed for allowing herself to be goaded. Fortunately, Anall-Marr seemed to ignore her rash remark.

"As you said, I cannot risk a controversy, Dama. Not now, but you misjudged me. Appeasement serves to weaken an opponent until he is forced to concede the struggle. That has never been my policy. Facing Sofam or anyone else.

"I haven't the time or desire to indulge in a protracted process of formally relieving you of your office. From now on, all policy decisions regarding Anulus will be handled by my office. You'll have *advisors* to help you manage the Four Suns. After all," he piped and smiled with grim satisfaction, "the Envoy will probably recommend that very thing. And we don't want to antagonize the Bureau of Administrative Affairs, do we, *darling*? Ach! Anulus is a vital Deklan resource, too great a responsibility to be shouldered by any one person. Don't you agree?"

She admitted it was a clever maneuver. It stopped short of an all-out brawl that would have erupted at any attempt to remove her. He had also sidestepped the prickly possibility of open protest from the other systems. She was under no illusion as to his motive. When he secured his position as Primate, she expected him to move against her. By then, it would be too late.

"If one of your flunkies tries to interfere with my administration, I'll have him on the altar... Your Grace," she hissed, maintaining a fiction of outraged indignation.

"That would be an act of rebellion, Kapel. The Synod would not take kindly to that."

"I'll take this to the Bureau of Justice on Captal!"

"Ach! You do what you want," he said with contempt, gratified to see her on the defensive for a change.

* * *

Afternoon shadows stretched black across the dunes. The children, clad in long brown surtaf robes, chattered and laughed while they drove the lumbering oark toward the corrals for the night. Snuffling, their long tails swishing, the oark sought to impale their tormentors with their short corkscrewed single horns. Poultry cackled in alarm, scampering between the soft pads of the oark's feet.

Along the desert, clumps of tarad grass lined the slopes of the dunes. They stirred in the light breeze, their white undersides flashing. Tall peelath clustered around a stone well and clearing, creating an island of shadows in a sea of sand. The air cool beneath their majestic wide branches. Women worked around an open trough, washing, talking and arguing. Toddlers sat in small groups and played their pebble games. Youngsters ran among the peelath, shrieking in their chase.

Other women were preparing the communal meal, to be eaten when the sun touched the horizon. Everyone in the village would be there, sharing in the telling of the day's activities, resting from the day's labors. It was also a bonding with other villages should a visitor arrive. Later perhaps, there would be dancing.

Young unpaired maidens collected in separate groups. Heads bowed, they giggled among themselves as they chatted. Their earthy humor directed at the young men working around the corrals. The girls wore plain surtafs with loose sleeves rolled above their elbows. A thin red band of cloth wound around the forehead kept their long hair in check and proclaimed their unpaired status.

Every now and then one of them would look up from her pile of dry peelath cones and wipe her brow. Getting the seeds out of the tough cones was hard work. There was a regular sound of thumping of stones used to soften the outer casing. Once broken they would pry out the round black seeds and spread them on rough cloth to dry in the shade.

The girls enjoyed their work. It gave them a chance to chew on the raw delicacy.

Nestling in a shallow valley the round straw-covered mud huts of the village lay scattered among the tall peelath. Gray smoke rose from some of the huts and filled the air with a sharp smell of boiling herb tea. A small group of elders sat before the communal hut, discussing the serious business of the village. The youths walked quietly near them, showing respect, leaving the Rahtir to their deliberations.

Generally, the women could not walk before the communal hut unless summoned. They had their own gathering place. The elders sipped their fermented juice and talked. Not a very large village, some 120 odd souls. Even this group had complex social problems to resolve, issues to discuss, family disputes to settle, barter to arrange and joinings to be made. Everyone treated these issues as a grave responsibility.

Sidhara sat alone on the dune's crest, his thoughts lost among the rolling sands. Tarad grass snuggled against the steep dune sides, their tall stems turned away from the sun. A deep breathless silence held time in check. Cape stirring behind him, he subconsciously noted the background sounds of the village, ready to become alert should something unusual disturb him. He liked this time of day. The harsh colors softened and the waning heat pleasantly melted into his body without burning. The first touch of an evening breeze renewed and reconnected him with the Saffal. The colors became richer, deeper, and the desert itself assumed a solidity altogether different from the bright harshness of raw sunlight.

His face a mass of deeply wrinkled lines worked on by time. The years may have laid their heavy hands on his shoulders, but the sparkle in his eyes still bright. The eyes, with their vertical slits, used to be orange and the slits red. Now they were faded, like the rest of his body. A thin membrane protected the eyes against fine abrasive sand. They were up now while he gazed absently at the stillness of the desert. His once ocher hair now brown and streaked with gray. It spilled around his shoulders in thick braids. He wore a plain surtaf robe with a brown hood. A sign of humility and an acceptance of his failings.

Sidhara was old, and some claimed not without wisdom. The young showed him respect, as was his due. Sometimes, he would debate manifold questions and decide troublesome issues with the other Rahtir. The way of the Discipline made for few arguments and the rulings of the village elders were absolute.

Staring vacantly into the dark amber of the sky, he recalled the days of his first trial before the gods that lived in the escarpment of Athal Than. A youth could not be considered complete, or able to call himself a Saddish-aa Wanderer, without facing the trial. The trial was a culmination of years of intensive training, and a test of faith and mortality, as well as a transition into somber manhood. It also gave him a voice in the Rahtir council.

Sidhara had endured the judgment of the gods, forever changed by the experience. Afterward, strong with power from the god of Death, he had proudly worn a yellow hood. Years later came the second trial where his soul hung in mortal danger. His youth was wild and he had misused his power. It was a time of harsh inner appraisal, but the gods forgave him his transgressions. Surviving the trial, humbled, he wore a red hood then. In the years that followed, others saw him as a sober man of maturity and dignity.

The gods called him late in life to walk in their shadow for the third and final time. By then, he had outgrown the rashness of his youth, abandoning the hollow victories of dominance over other men. The trial was but a confirmation, another step into the mysteries of the Discipline. He wore a purple hood then, a figure of reverence and respect. After ten years, he discarded the outward trappings of his power for a plain brown hood and the cycle was complete. The irony and the meaning of that cycle was not lost on him. No matter what his power, from the Saffal he had sprung and into its sands he would return, for only the gods were forever.

Now, women brought their newborn to him and men listened attentively when he spoke. He spent his days in contemplation trying to understand the terrible relationship the gods had with the people of the Saffal—and the power of Death that lay in their hands. For it was a terrible power indeed, one that could crush worlds if unleashed. One did not toy with such matters.

This day did not rest easily on his shoulders. He sensed the shifting of ponderous forces and knew that events were drawing to a cusp. He'd had the dream again last night when the gods spoke to him. He saw an alien, cloaked in the shadow of the god of Death, suspended in space, arms upraised, two stars adorning his feet. Before him, a painted world hung against the tapestry of night, and there was lightning in his eyes. He leveled his arms and the lightning went forth and lashed at the world. Sidhara heard the cry of billions and the alien laughed, his laughter shaking the heavens. When the world exploded around him, there was only the sound of thunder.

The alien alone, suspended in night with two stars at his feet.

Sarumajan, the destroyer of worlds, the thought came unbidden.

Sidhara had wakened badly disturbed. Destiny was being shaped and he seemed to be in the middle of it. He did not feel comfortable with the idea that his decision could set fates into motion. His relationship with the god of Death was a complex one. The god had given him power and he had grown comfortable wearing its mantle. What disturbed him was having to be part of something he didn't really understand. The dream told him the gods thought him worthy of shaping time. It was a dubious honor.

"Tah, the gods will tell," he rumbled heavily and made his way slowly to the village below.

Someone shouted and he turned to see children running toward robed figures emerging from among the dunes. One of the tall youths carried a slumped body in his powerful arms. Sidhara paused and brushed sand off his surtaf. He watched the four youths make their way toward the village well. One of the youths wore a yellow hood, showing that he had undergone the first of his three trials.

Children crowded around them, chirping excitedly about the alien the youth carried. Everyone fell into subdued silence as Sidhara appeared and they made way for him. He nodded and they laid the body down. A disorderly chatter rose through the gathered crowd. The women whispered urgently among themselves and pointed at the still form. The alien's face and hands were badly sunburned and his gray uniform bore scorch marks. The alien moaned and moved, twisting in silent pain.

Sidhara stared at the prone figure and felt a shock of recognition. It was the alien in his dream!

Energy emanated from the body as though the god of Death held his hand over it. He found that disturbing. Not being of the people, of the Saddish-aa, how could that be possible? The alien bore the working grays of a Serrll Scout Fleet officer and Sidhara wondered how he came to be in the deep of the Saffal. This was very strange.

One of the older women quickly knelt beside the body and started probing along his arms, torso, and legs.

"Some cuts and burns, but nothing broken," she said, her voice deep and urgent. She looked briefly at Sidhara. "He has lost a lot of water and we may be too late."

"Master." The young Wanderer pulled back his yellow hood, stepped up to Sidhara and placed his right hand over his eyes in respect. "We found him near the Katai Than Pass. He was near death. He could have been searching for water. We were crossing the pass when we saw his tracks. We trailed him into the Taalika gorge."

"I know the place," Sidhara said, his voice rumbling deep within his chest.

"No water there, of course," the youth said. "Not this time of year. By the looks of him, he must have wandered around for days."

"Will he live?" Sidhara forced himself to ask. The old

woman shrugged and he nodded knowingly. The alien would live, he was certain of it.

"He is delirious with fever and has suffered much. Tah, the gods will tell," she said simply.

"That streak of fire we saw in the sky two days ago, master. It could have been a survival blister," the youth ventured.

Sidhara brooded, contemplating the torment etched deep in the alien's face. This wounded being was a far cry from the image in his dream, an alien suspended in space with two stars at his feet, a lord of Death. In the end, the decision was a simple one and the future yet to be written. Right now the injured alien needed help.

"Perhaps. Care for him," Sidhara ordered and the women gathered around the prone figure.

* * *

Dhar tilted the combie and looked down. The barrier of steep dunes fell away and gave way to gently rolling slopes. Thin patches of brown tarad grass grew in the lee of the dunes, rippling and swaying in the breeze. Clumps of peelath clung stubbornly to the sides of a shallow gorge. Their broad flat branches hung heavy and limp in the afternoon heat. The peelath grew more thickly as the gorge opened, its sides falling away into a shallow valley. The rounded mud huts of the village lay amongst the shadows of tall peelath. His feelings were complex as the valley drew near.

He circled the village once and the memories came rushing back. On his way from Kanarath, he told himself he wouldn't get carried away with emotion that this was just like any other visit, but it didn't work. The memories were warm, of laughter and play and discovery, memories of a happy childhood. He missed that life and that time. A carefree time without duty or responsibility. They were only memories and he was a different man now.

In the Shadow of Death

Coming in for a landing, the young boys gathered excitedly around the hovering teardrop of his combie. He waved at them and shut down the plant. He paused and looked about, drinking in the familiar images of his youth. It was all there as he remembered it. Despite his resolve, he was uncertain of the emotions threatening to overwhelm him.

It had been too long.

He opened the bubble and climbed out, the heat washing palpably over him. He breathed deeply of the intimate smells, of burnt rock and sand, the tang of tarad grass and the oily fragrance of peelath leaves. As the desert talked to him, it felt good to have the scented wind run through the tumbling hair around his shoulders. Nothing had changed and he belonged again.

They crowded around him chanting. "Dharaklin! Nightwings! Nightwings!" A large group followed him down into the village clearing. Some of the younger men clustered near him in greeting. He recognized several faces. Touched by their open welcome, he laughed and his cares dropped away. The boys surrounding him followed his laughter.

Briefly, he allowed himself to forget the demands of the Fleet. He had waited long for this period of leave and he wanted to abandon himself in the simple life of his yesterdays. Tomorrow did not exist. There was only the now.

In the clearing, the youths and the unpaired girls made way for him, touching him as he went. They were proud that one of theirs rode the fires between the stars. An old woman stood holding dried brush gathered in the desert. He stopped before her and touched his forehead to hers.

"Mother, your son has returned."

There was a murmuring of approval around them. She looked at him, her face dry and wrinkled, and smiled broadly.

"There shall be dancing tonight, Nightwings," she said gruffly and he hugged her.

"And my father?" he asked and pulled back.

"Away with a scouting party. Looking for new winter pastures." She patted his arm. "Worry not, he will know."

"Why—"

"Have you forgotten our ways already?" she chided him, amused. "We will be moving to the low grounds soon, but you better go and pay your respects to the Rahtir."

"Later, then," he said comfortably.

He was glad to see his mother again and well, but saddened that his father was not here. He last saw his father through the eyes of a youth, eager from his venture into the unknown of the Fleet Academy on Captal. He was a fresh graduate then. Now grown, he needed sober man talk. He was not concerned. There would be time for talk and renewing later.

The children followed him as he walked toward the men's communal hut. He stopped before the elders, covered his eyes with his right hand in respect and knelt.

Sidhara nodded solemnly, but his eyes were alive with pleasure. He reached with a gnarled hand and touched Dhar's head.

"Nightwings, your shadow is a light among us, my son. You have our blessing."

"Master, I fear the light has faded, for I was not a dutiful son of the Discipline."

"Time will heal all," the old man said kindly.

Dhar stood up and beamed with pleasure. He was home.

"Sit with us and let the desert sing to you," his venerated teacher offered and Dhar felt a surge of pride at this honor. This was not done to honor his father, but himself. One of the Rahtir proffered him a stool and he sat down among them.

"Go!" An elder waved his hand at the youngsters crowding before them. His growl kindly and they laughed and skipped away.

A maiden walked up to them carrying a gourd of fermented peelath berry juice. She poured for him and smiled shyly. She wore a red band around her forehead.

"Tabe," Dhar mumbled his thanks and she lowered her head, hiding a smile.

He drank the cool tart juice and exchanged pleasantries with the elders. The branches of the peelath rustled and swayed above them. In the distance the dunes took on the shadows of evening, standing dark and sharp against the gathering night.

"We shall have a feast," Sidhara decided and turned to one of the youths near them. "Make it so."

"A feast!" the youth cried, hurrying away. Others took up the cry. "A feast!"

After a time, Sidhara looked searchingly at Dhar. "Has the Fleet been a kind mistress to you, my son?"

Dhar considered the question. "It has been a challenge, master."

Sidhara smiled and nodded knowingly. "Your spirit has prospered."

"Not without some cost, master," Dhar said gravely, remembering the trials life in the Fleet had imposed on him.

"As it should be," Sidhara said simply. "You come to us in a time of need. For another of you is among us."

"A Fleet officer?" Dhar stared at his old teacher in amazement.

"An offworlder, found at Katai Than," one of the other Rahtir said heavily. "The gods have touched him and his soul wanders the sands of the Saffal," he added with mild regret and others murmured assent.

"He could be the officer who has the whole COMDEKOPS in a flap looking for him. Master, I need to see him," Dhar asked diffidently, unaccountably disturbed. "If he's here, I must report him to Fleet command in Kanarath immediately."

"That will not be possible, my son," Sidhara said gently, but his resolve was firm.

"But—"

205

Stefan Vučak

"As long as he is with us the gods will decide his fate," Sidhara said with finality that brooked no dissent. "Now, tell me of yourself."

Dhar could not argue. What strange fate had brought the two of them together?

The wind stirred the dust about his feet and poultry cackled contentedly, searching for grass seeds between the huts. There was a buzz of insects in the air and life was clean and simple again. He looked about him. The elders still sat before the communal hut like they used to when he was a child. The women went about their chores. Everything was as it had been, but he felt some quality missing. Dismayed, he realized why he could not recapture the innocence of those times and the purity of his youth. His experiences in the Fleet had contaminated him.

"Nothing has changed, but I cannot grasp the days of my yesterdays. I have tasted the fruit of far worlds and my eyes have seen beyond the desert of the Saffal."

Sidhara nodded at the wisdom of the words. "The dunes change, yet remain the same. The shapes may change, but the sand is always there," he said gently. "We also change with the desert. Do not force your feelings. It will come of its own accord."

Dhar nodded. "Your words are true, but I see the life of our fathers being crowded by demands of the offworlders."

"In the cities, perhaps. Out here in the Saffal, the sands still rule."

"I needed to replenish myself, master. The Fleet is a demanding mistress and the temptations many."

The old man's eyes understood and he placed a gnarled, veined hand on Dhar's thigh.

"I feel your confusion, my son. Your life may be fulfilling, but this land will always be a part of you. The desert makes no pretenses and you need to find yourself again among its sands. Do not search. You need merely to reach for it."

Dhar lowered his head, his thoughts in turmoil. He was

happy to be back with his family and his spirit soared among the shadows of the dunes. He was also troubled. He was trying to recapture an impossible past in a still unclear future. The conflict of his heritage, the need to keep his power hidden, weighed heavily on him.

"It is difficult not to interfere, master," he said, revealing his true fear. "I hold Death in my hand, yet I feel helpless."

Sidhara nodded. "That is the beginning of wisdom. The use of power requires checks and balances and a measure of restraint. Remember the lesson of the pond. A stone cast into the water creates ripples whose effects are unknown and may be unintended. A momentary gratification of pride and ego that you may feel when unleashing the hand of Death for a perceived injustice, may be far more damaging than the good you sought to achieve."

"I have not revealed my power," Dhar said. "Even when using it would have prevented suffering."

"Only the gods know all effects," one of the Rahtir said heavily, and the others nodded. "That is why they don't interfere with their creations. Likewise, only you can judge when the power within you must be revealed and the consequences to you and those around you when you do use it."

Dhar turned to Sidhara. "Master, tell me about this officer. Permit me to see him."

The old Wanderer's shoulders slumped. "I see that you are troubled about this offworlder. Come, then."

He rose and took Dhar to a nearby hut. They walked in and the shadows lifted. Lamps filled with oark oil burned, suspended from overhead beams, and cast thick yellow light. The hut smelled of smoke, cooking, and the sweat of living. Sidhara swept back a curtain of oark hair and stepped into a small room. An old woman inside nodded to him and made way for them. Dhar looked down at a body lying on a mat of peelath leaves, sunburned and naked beneath a rough blanket. A tingling shock made him stop and stare.

Fear and terror lay in those oval gray eyes. There was also a throb of power like the touch of Death itself. Bewildered, Dhar looked at Sidhara.

"Master—"

The old man nodded. "I know, my son. I feel it also."

Confused, Dhar looked at the alien. His pale skin dry and cracked, drawn tight over strong features. He whimpered and tossed his head at the torment within him. Dhar stepped to the mat and the woman moved aside. A hushed silence filled the room. After a momentary hesitation, he reached out and grasped the alien's hand.

"Do not fear, my brother," he said softly and stared down at the tortured face, wishing his strength to flow from his hand. "Rest, I am with you," he heard himself say in a deep voice.

The alien returned his grip with surprising strength, but the eyes were elsewhere, lost in some private nightmare.

"Nightwings," Sidhara called behind him and Dhar reluctantly turned away. "I sense in you an affinity with this alien. Why is that, my son?"

Dhar stood there confused, torn by conflicting emotions. "I don't know, master," he said and looked back at the tormented body. "I…I felt compelled to reach out—"

"Just so," Sidhara rumbled.

"Master, what will happen to him?"

"He will heal in time."

"That isn't what I asked."

"I know," Sidhara said and walked away, leaving Dhar wondering after the hooded figure. He took another look at the tortured face and followed. The experience had left him deeply disturbed.

* * *

Beneath the blaze of stars, the fires rose high that night. They sent glowing embers shooting among the branches of the peelath to dance against Rima's glow, the moon yet to climb fully into the sky. Everyone in the village sat around the big fire. The sounds of talk and laughter mixed easily with those of children at play. Sharp shadows flickered among their open faces. It was a happy time and the night full of laughter and light voices.

The Rahtir sat farther back from the fire in a place reserved for them. They talked quietly, watching, nodding approvingly from time to time. The old women sat on the other side, opposite the elders. The young paid them equal respect.

Above the licking flames a young calf turned on a spit. Small boys crowded around the roasting meat and plucked at an opportune piece of loose skin. They scampered away when the older men scolded them, laughing gaily. From time to time one of the youths would pour berry juice over the meat and the aroma would drift appetizingly in the breeze. The unpaired girls moved cheerfully among the men, filling cups from gourds hanging on their shoulders. Other girls clustered in small groups, talking of girl things, laughing, some of them looking pointedly at the youths. It was an innocent, distracting pastime.

The evening meal had been light in anticipation of a feast. What had not been eaten was saved for tomorrow. In the village, they wasted nothing. Having a feast was a rare event; young calves being valuable trade goods, and fuel for the fire hard to come by. But life needed gaiety from time to time or it was reduced to mere existence. The Rahtir were wise in the way of the Saddish-aa.

Wearing a surtaf with a yellow hood pushed back, Dhar sat at an honored place with the Rahtir, silent and thoughtful. He watched the children run heedlessly among those sitting. Sometimes tripping on an outstretched leg, they would sprawl into the dust and he would smile.

He allowed himself to be immersed in the sights and sounds around him, letting his spirit merge with his people again. He accepted that he could not recapture the images and emotions of his past. There was a barrier and a quality of experience that separated him from these people, which he could not cross. He considered himself sophisticated.

Even now, his mind was on his duties and responsibilities as a Fleet officer. Yet he was also one of the people of the Saffal. As the surge of inner rebellion of his youth receded, he came to treasure that feeling of belonging. Right now the Fleet was far away and his past called strongly to him. Relaxing, he abandoned himself to his feelings. Here was a moment of rare peace and happiness and he did not want to lose it. Wasn't that why he had returned?

The youths brought with them small drums, flutes, and leetas. They settled themselves near the fire and got ready. The drums beat in a slow rhythm and the flutes tugged at the air to the haunting strands of the leetas. Men slowly tapped the ground in time with the melody. Occasionally a faster tempo and a beat of drums would bring with it shouts of approval and a furious round of tapping. The sands echoed the sounds of the drums and the stamping of feet.

A hush fell as the boom of drums faded and the leetas led into a new, slow melody. Then the drums began to beat again, unhurried and deliberate, harmonizing with the leetas. Several of the unpaired girls suddenly jumped to their feet and began to dance before the fire. The flickering light of the flames revealed their laughing faces and outlined the slim forms beneath the robes. Their feet moved from side to side and their bodies swayed sinuously. Arms held high, they weaved slow patterns in the air. They stomped their feet and dust shrouded their legs. The drums quickened their rhythm.

After a time, one of the girls drew away and slowly moved toward the youths sitting around the fire. Others shouted with glee when she stopped, tapping the ground before the chosen youth. With pushing and good-natured suggestions from those around him, he stood up and raised his arms. Weaving a similar pattern, he shuffled his feet in time with the girl's.

In the Shadow of Death

They weaved about each other, oblivious to the urgings around them. Their eyes held each other, burning with a secret desire. Gradually the tempo of their movements increased to the urgency of the flutes and the drums. The dance ended with a final stomping of feet and the boom of drums. Chests heaving they stared at each other and the watchers shouted approval.

Sidhara gestured at Dhar. "They danced well, don't you think?"

Dhar had watched the pair, his thoughts lost somewhere in memory.

"Yes, it's been a long time since I saw it last."

Sidhara looked at him, wearing a faint smile of amusement.

After a while the girls resumed their solitary dance. The drums were silent while the flutes and the leetas whispered their magic. One of the girls broke away then and the drums started again. Dhar watched her body move in slow weaving patterns.

It was the girl who brought him the berry juice earlier.

In dismay, he realized she was making her way toward him. The men around him roared in approval. He cast a panicked look at Sidhara, but the old man only nodded indulgently. The girl stopped before him and tapped the ground. Her eyes blazed and she looked at him with consuming intensity.

"Dharaklin!" they chanted. "Dharaklin!"

It was custom and he had no choice. They broke into another wave of roaring when he reluctantly stood up.

Her close presence was overpowering and her eyes burned into his. A ripple of heat flashed through his body and his feet began to move through the old, almost forgotten steps. He was disturbed and excited by the intensity of his feelings. The music loud in his ears, he fell under its spell.

The young men around them urged him on, shouting, but he did not hear them. There was only the girl and the fire of her eyes. He moved with her, his arms high, swinging through the slow movements. Their bodies twined and touched, her skin velvety and cool when their arms met and her scent clean and

211

enticing. The tapping of their feet were the echoes of his yesterdays.

His movements became more intense. There was nothing
else in his world but the girl, the dance and the flames around
him. They seemed to roar to him, or was that shouting? He felt
a release, a oneness with the all and an urge to cry out at the
force of his emotions. Then he did cry out and the hand of
Death was on him.

Blue lightnings crackled between his hands and a rumble
of thunder echoed among the dunes. The girl laughed with secret excitement and her eyes blazed. The men stood up and
chanted his warrior name.

"Nightwings! Nightwings!"

A sheet of blue light flashed from his arms and the shadows
jumped.

When the dance stopped, he stared into the girl's eyes and
felt her hot breath.

"Tabe," he whispered huskily. Breathing heavily, she
looked boldly at him.

He slept that night in her hut.

* * *

Dhar spent his days with the young men of the village. He
mended the corrals, gathered fallen peelath logs from deep
gorges, hauling them in on the backs of lumbering oark. With
other youths, he searched for new pasture grounds for use
when they returned from the low country in the spring. He
found the simple physical work stimulating and satisfying and
his spirit was renewed. In the evening, beside the crackle of the
fire and the scent of burning peelath, he would talk of the Serrll
with those who sat with him. He would talk of the Fleet and
the ships that moved between the stars. Boys would crowd
around him to listen in rapt attention as he described the awe-
some power of an M-4 firing its twin projectors.

In the Shadow of Death

Sometimes an elder would ask a question and Dhar would pause. Others would wait in silence while he deliberated. The questions were often complex, involving interstellar commerce, the origins of the rivalry that existed between the Revisionists and the Servatory Party. They would ask about Captal, the fabled world where the Serrll government held court in the city of the same name. Often, he struggled to come up with a ready answer, but he had seen several worlds and remembered something of what he saw. They listened to his words and paid him homage for his wisdom, which embarrassed him.

He talked with his father and began to comprehend some things better. His father had always been stern and aloof, and to Dhar unreasonable. Now his father gave of himself and there was approval in his voice. Dhar appreciated that acceptance, needing it more than he realized. He had known rejection and the pain that followed it. Grown up and able to see other points of view, his father's words now washed away the childhood disappointments and he felt that each at last understood something of the other's life.

In the slow pace of the village, he found fulfillment. He also found a measure of contentment and peace. Dawn often met him in the open desert, waiting for the stars to fade. Through meditation, he renewed his bond with the god of Death. When the villages heard a rumble of dying thunder and a flicker of light against the dunes, they would nod solemnly in understanding. Resolved once again in the ways of the Discipline, following the words of the *Saftara*, Dhar considered himself fortunate. Yet the alien presence in one of the huts continued to trouble him. He was also troubled that his master did nothing to ease the torment of a wounded spirit, alien though it might be. It was almost cruel, although he did not dare to express it like that. He only knew that he should do something to ease the creature's suffering.

As the days passed, Dhar's resolve grew. In the end, he confronted Sidhara. His master listened attentively, nodding from time to time. When he finished, Sidhara's orange eyes were on him.

"To enter his mind would mean exposing yourself to his subconscious self where he has now fled. It is a grave risk, Nightwings, my son. He may overcome you and both of you will be lost. You must remember one other thing. If you are successful, he will forever be a part of you as you will be a part of him. He is not a Saddish-aa and you may be setting a cascade of events into motion that later may cause an intolerable conflict within him, as his personality and memories might do to you. Are you prepared to take on that responsibility and its consequences?"

"I am compelled to do it, master," Dhar said with more resolve than he felt. "I don't know why, but we cannot leave him like that."

The old man nodded in understanding. "Your feelings do you justice and the knowledge and insight into offworlder thinking that you will gain will be valuable," he said and raised his hand when he saw Dhar's alarm. "Alien he may be, my son, but the help you so unselfishly give is not diminished if I choose to see the broader benefits this may provide all Wanderers in our cause for independence. The Deklans would take our worlds, were it not for the constraint imposed on them by the Sofam Confederacy. But we cannot rely on their continued goodwill. Anar'on and the worlds of the Kaleen group must be free to shape their own destiny. We may live simple lives, far from the cities, but that does not make us ignorant. We follow closely domestic and Serrll politics."

Dhar did not doubt it. He had seen the Wall station in the communal hut of the elders.

"I accept the wisdom of your words, master, but I am disturbed that all our acts seem to be measured in political coin," Dhar said, greatly daring.

Sidhara merely smiled, revealing worn brown teeth. "It is good that you question, and so your spirit grows," he said and pointed. "The branch from the peelath provides us with many things and sustains us in the desert. It also has thorns to protect itself from the unwary. Thus we too must protect ourselves from the thorns of the Serrll Combine and take of it that which will sustain us."

"Right now, master, I care little for the Serrll or the Unified Independent Front's cause. I only know that I cannot leave a fellow officer in endless torment."

"I know," Sidhara said, resigned to the fates. The dream strong in his mind and the gods would not be denied. "Very well, you have my permission. Do not fear, my spirit shall be with you and guide you."

And there came a day when Dhar crossed the barrier of minds separating him from the alien. A furtive breeze tugged at his cape and surtaf. The whispering of sand lost itself among the shifting dunes and hot air burned beneath an amber sky. Peelath leaves hung limp in weary acceptance. The pecking poultry and the contented grunts from dozing oark broke the drowsy silence.

Only the children moved about the village, restless and ever ready to play. In the heat of the day everyone rested in what shade they could find. If anyone worked, they did it in the cool gloom of the huts. The hut where the alien lay seemed to swim in the heat and Dhar fancied the gods were waiting. Yet he hesitated. He had seen a joining done before and knew the forms dictated by the *Saftara*, but this was the first time that he contemplated such an act alone. As a youth, he flirted with a friend, as boys would, an innocent game that meant nothing. When he was older the Rahtir allowed him to witness a joining with another, but for the solemnity of the ritual, the experience meant little to him.

Taking a deep breath, he went inside.

For a time, he watched the tortured lines on the drawn face. Gray eyes stared inward at some private hell. He hesitated when those eyes suddenly turned and sought him out, but there was no light of intelligence in them. When he reached with his hand the alien moaned and returned his grip with a strength born of desperation.

They were alone, for this was not for women or children. He knelt beside the bed and closed his eyes, the words of the *Saftara* burning bright. Still clasping the alien's hand, he allowed his mind to probe delicately along the barrier that stood between them. He felt power pulsing in that mind unlike anything from another Wanderer. Surface impressions of confusion, fear and terror coiled about each other like twisting lightnings.

He probed the barrier with delicate touches, recalling Sidhara's words of warning. He hesitated, realizing that he feared personal oblivion. Done hastily, he could end up trapped, consumed by the torment of the alien's mind. For a moment, he was tempted to withdraw. He felt Sidhara's reassuring presence and took a deep breath.

The searching grip of the other's hand decided him.

He moved gently along the surface of the alien mind. When he found a fissure, he paused, then thrust firmly, allowing the barrier that lay between them to topple away. There was a resistance, a tearing, and he almost pulled back. With a cry of pain, he felt himself swept along the whirlwind of shadows into the other mind.

Once past the barrier, he found it easy. His fear of insanity and endless torture, of losing himself, held him back. It was an interesting insight. He needed to be careful here, lest he added his nightmares to the alien's horrors. The other mind lay open to him now and he took of it and they merged.

His name was Terrllss-rr of the House Llss-rr and in joining, he became Dhar's brother. In him, Dhar saw a reflection of a searching, wandering spirit, free and without purpose. There was ambition and a power lust, unchanneled and undisciplined. Yet beneath the turmoil of loose morals and blurred loyalties lay a capacity for compassion, love and a need for fulfillment not so different from his own.

In the Shadow of Death

Images of another world, Elexi, crowded his senses. There was also a boy, a beggar, who seemed to hold a special significance. Immersed in the images, it all became clear to Dhar. The alien was indeed the officer everyone searched for. What he saw were only surface images and emotions, turbulent and heaving like a stormy sea, a dark barrier that kept the inner horrors from breaking out. And it was those horrors he had to confront if he were to free Terr. Yet those horrors could also consume him. Gathering his resolve, he sank deeper into the murky depths of Terr's subconscious and he knew everything and understood everything.

Another world waited there, Kaplan, Terr's home. It all came tumbling out and he struggled to keep the flood in check. It was impossible. Once the process began, the merging seemed to take on a purpose of its own and he found himself swept into a whirlpool of memories from which he was helpless to escape. Only when he plunged into sudden darkness did he experience real fear.

It was not fear of the desert. Terr seemed to have a strange fascination and a love for the Saffal. It was the elemental struggle for life that threatened to overwhelm them both. There was a memory where Terr looked at a robed figure with red eyes and blue lightnings playing between his hands. Surrounded by the horrors of Terr's mind, Dhar found a spark of light that flickered uncertainly in the darkness. In his trek for survival, Terr's spirit had been overwhelmed by the harsh demands of the Saffal. There was something else, as if Death's shadow lurked within. Dhar thought that impossible. Terr was an offworlder. He touched the light with his being and the shadows parted while the two lights merged into one.

He felt Terr's struggles subside and the terrors retreat. They were one and Dhar bathed in the glow of pure energies as their personalities integrated. It was an intoxicating feeling, being himself and being Terr at the same time. After a timeless moment, he withdrew and pondered at the heritage they both now

217

shared.

Finally over, Dhar sat beside his newfound brother. He saw himself reflected in Terr's eyes. There was peace at last in their depths and something else. Horrified, he stared at the shadow of the god of Death. How was that possible? The alien had not undertaken the trial, yet he could not deny the power pulsating from Terr. Sidhara had warned him, but he had not understood, or chose not to understand. Done, he would indeed have to live with the consequence of his action. But could Terr? In his desire to help another, has he unleashed a different nightmare?

He sat there a long time holding the alien's hand. When Terr finally slept the nightmares did not return.

Before leaving, Dhar looked down at the sleeping form.

"My brother, what have I done to you?"

Chapter Nine

Terr blinked and it was morning. Dawn had not yet broken and the room still gloomy and thick in shadow. Looking around, he found himself in a small bedchamber of a mud hut. Suspended from sooty rafters a lamp flickered weakly. In the gloom, he saw two other beds beside him. Both were empty.

Bachelor quarters, the thought came to him unbidden. He didn't know what he was doing there. Mildly puzzled, he pondered the thought. In the end, he gave up. It wasn't important. Nothing had any importance. He threw back the thick oark-hair blanket, stood up and breathed deeply of the chill air. Far from making him shiver, he enjoyed its keen bite. A plain brown surtaf hung on a hook beside his bed. Absently, he pulled on the coarse robe and tied the sash about his waist. Crouching, he stepped out of the room into the living chamber. The fire in the hearth nothing but cold cinders. Cooking utensils hung from blackened rafters. Clean dishes were stacked on a low bench. Hardly noticing them, he walked down a narrow corridor. The small door made of dark peelath wood creaked as he pushed it open. Outside, the air crisp and smelled of smoke, dry tarad grass and the musky scent of oark. He could hear them snorting in the corrals.

Shadowy figures moved between the black outlines of the huts. Somewhere behind him, an infant whimpered dejectedly. After fumbling for them, he put on his sandals, open and comfortable. A red streak tinged the eastern horizon. He hesitated, then walked uncertainly across the open space toward a rise that cradled the valley where the dunes began. Peelath clustered around the well, pillars of black shadow against the backdrop of night. Short tarad grass grew in clumps on the sheltered dune

219

slopes. The air held its breath and the branches above him were still.

He stood on the dune's crest and watchedthe stars fade and the sky turn pink. He recognized the pattern of stars that was Amulran the Damned and the Stalker, waiting to loose the arrow of doom at his enemy. He didn't know where the memory came from. It didn't matter. He was content just to look at the stars. After a while, he sat down and absently played with strands of tarad grass while the eastern horizon turned pale red. When the sun did come, it was bright yellow and cut across the horizon, and the soft shadows fled around him. It climbed quickly into an amber sky. He could feel the heat on his face, but it wasn't uncomfortable. The reds and yellows of the desert took on an intensity and clarity of full color pleasing to look at.

As he sat there, images and half memories flashed through his mind. He saw strange faces and stranger skies. He saw towering red cliffs and he was there with thunder and lightning pouring forth from his hands. He saw a face of a boy and felt he should know him, but the knowledge eluded him. There was also thirst and fire and a need to escape. He thrust the memories back.

Looking out at the endless sands, he felt a deep bond with the desert and a sense of belonging. He felt comforted, sheltered as he stared at the desert and he allowed it to fill him. He gave of himself freely and opened himself to the impressions that flooded him. Time held no urgency and he had nowhere to go. There was only the breeze and the sky and the cradle of the dunes. The sands whispered to him and he listened to their song. There was a stirring of unease deep down where it was dark, which made him frown, but for the moment, he was content.

Later, when he walked down, the youths of the village looked at him strangely and left him alone. The Rahtir kept to themselves near a large hut and ignored him. They did not permit him to enter there. Some of the children were minding poultry and shaggy oark that browsed on the grassy dune slopes. When they saw him, they ran and pranced around him, shouting, pointing, jeering at him. They threw small stones at him and ran screaming with glee until one of the men scolded them. He didn't know why the children did that. The men left him alone.

For long periods, he would sit in the shade of a mud hut and stare vacantly at the flowing dunes, pondering the whisper of the sands. The oark stomped and snorted in the corrals and he would listen to the women talking, preparing meals and doing women things. The buzz of insects a comforting, drowsy melody. He stared at the swaying tarad grass and watched the majestic branches of the peelath. When they gave him food, he would eat mechanically and the days changed to nights.

All this time, he kept seeing visions of strange shapes that seemed to move between the stars. He saw slim, shining structures piercing the sky, crowded streets, people wearing exotic clothing, and things he didn't understand. He remembered a fire and the heat of the desert and images of alien hooded figures that hovered over him. There were moments when he struggled to climb up from the black, dusty corners where his mind hid—the basement corridors of insanity, terror and living death. He visited them all.

He would wake at night screaming as the lightnings tore at his body, only to find he was dreaming. Wet, shaking, he would whimper, curled into the comforting warmth of the rough oark blanket. The two youths sleeping beside him would look at him and shake their heads. He feared to sleep, because that was when the images came to haunt him. When he did sleep, his spirit was lost in visions he didn't understand. Then the dunes would come and the sands would talk to him and he would be at peace, if for a moment.

On some days they allowed him to mind the oark. Always at dawn or late in the afternoon. He would walk the ponderous animals into the desert in search of grass. He liked that, for he would be alone with the sands. The shaggy beasts never wandered far from him, grunting with contentment as they sought the moist olive shoots. Some of the bulls would butt their heads in play. The single twisted horns made hollow echoes when they struck. Calves would nuzzle him where he sat, breathing noisily, and would snort when he slapped them away.

Finished, the oark would get restless and start making their way back to the village. He followed in their tracks. His thoughts drifted with the sands and he would have a waking dream. With a little prodding the oark shuffled into the corrals and he would drop a long peelath trunk across the gate. The flimsy structure could never withstand a determined prod from one of the bulls, but they seemed satisfied.

As the sun dropped toward the horizon, the youths assembled the long tables and the women brought out dishes and other things. Sometimes, he helped with the heavy cauldrons or dug out succulent meats and vegetables cooked under the hot sand, wrapped in peelath leaves. They gave him food and he would eat in silence.

On other days, he would go out with the children. Carrying large peelath-woven baskets on their backs, they searched the old grazing areas and collect dried dung. The dung, he came to learn, had many uses. Sometimes the women used it to fuel the fires. They soaked the brittle pads and mixed them with sand to spread over the small gardens. Or they used them in a mixture of grass and mud to patch up cracked walls of the huts.

The children still teased him, but with less passion. This was work. Even though he didn't know it, his efforts were respected.

The youths showed him how to care for the corrals and muck out the enclosures. The oark were placid animals, content to chew on their cud, their tails swishing to drive off insects. Sometimes the women permitted him to milk the cows. The first time he tried it, his effort was rewarded by a thin trickle of thick yellow milk and earthy laughter from the women.

In the Shadow of Death

He learned how to pleat short strands of tarad grass into long sections. The men used them to repair the straw roofs of the mud huts. They showed him what needed to be done and when. Wordlessly, he would do it.

From time to time a young man in a plain surtaf, wearing a yellow hood, would come to him and talk in various tongues. Terr listened, struggling to comprehend, but the words meant nothing. There was a teasing of understanding, but it eluded him. He wanted to reach out, his eyes begging for acceptance, but he didn't know how. In the end, he could not say anything and only stared at the youth. After a while the young man would shake his head sadly and walk away.

Terr couldn't talk.

Then again, he had no need of words, for the dunes spoke in their own way. Drawn by their whispers, he walked among the moving sands and listened as they sang to him. It filled something within him that thirsted for more than simply food. He couldn't tell why he was compelled to wander the dunes. Perhaps their emptiness helped to keep the lurking shadows of his nightmares at bay.

Whenever he had an urge to set out into the desert, one of the unpaired maidens would always be there with a small gourd of water for him and a few rough cakes of peelath nuts mixed with vegetables. He accepted the food in silence, not wondering how she knew. A particular place not far from the village became his own.

Sand crunched and whispered as he walked silently in sandaled feet. The drifts grew smaller and gradually gave way to rocky flats that echoed his footsteps. Two needles of red rock guarded a low mesa that hid a steep canyon. Clumps of tarad grass grew among the more sheltered boulders.

A solitary peelath guarded the entrance. It opened before him suddenly, dark and full of shadow. Tall strands of tarad grass covered the steep slopes of the gorge, waiting for a breath of wind to get them whispering. Short peelath clustered along the sandy floor, their branches limp and lifeless. Sand drifts piled against boulders sent thin trickles into the gloom below. They hardly made a whisper.

Sometimes while he waited for morning in his private retreat, he would sit against the trunk of a peelath or the smooth side of a boulder. He liked to wait there for the first rays of the sun to light the gorge entrance. Dark shadows reared and fled as dawn touched them. Warmed by the sun, he sat there, his eyes unfocused, lost among the shadows of his mind. It was long into the afternoon before he stirred and headed back toward the village.

After one sleepless night, he woke to the thin keening of the wind and the hiss of drifting sands. He dragged on his brown surtaf and went outside. Lightning and thunder tore the clouded sky and the air became charged with tension. The women were hurrying to collect washing from the lines and the men were tying the oark in the corrals.

Alone on a dune, cape flying behind him, an old man stood gazing out across the desert. Terr knew him only as one of the Rahtir, venerable but aloof. He watched the lone figure for a long time, summoning his courage. Haltingly, not sure what he was doing, he approached the figure, his emotions churning inside him. The old man looked down at him dispassionately as he plodded up the face of the dune.

Lightning crashed from the sky.

Terr stopped a few paces before the old Wanderer. The wind swirled the sand around his feet. Gazing up at the lined face and the burning eyes, he seemed to remember such eyes in another place and another time. Standing before the Wanderer, he struggled to make a sound. In helpless anguish, he clenched his fists, moaned and sank to his knees. There was pain and a tearing that seemed to rip something deep within him. Head bowed, he reached for the old man's robes and managed a cry torn from his soul.

"Tahalik aka," he sobbed in agonized relief, able at last to utter the words, and lifted his head. Blinking back the sting in his eyes, he stared at the old man in a silent plea. "Help me," he mumbled in another language, and there was a stirring of memory. He saw a figure in strange gray clothes outlined against a shape he thought familiar, but the image eluded him.

Sidhara was undecided as he studied the alien creature. He had waited for this moment ever since the alien first appeared in his dream. Still he hesitated, uncertain what his action could unleash. The silent pain and the torment of hidden terrors lurking in the alien's eyes finally decided him, and a sense of obligation. He had taken the alien under his wing and he could not abandon him now. He could have stopped Nightwings, but he did not. Hidden deep within the alien's eyes, he saw something else, the shadow of Death. It was as he had feared.

Tah, the gods will tell, he reflected and reached out with his hand.

Terr felt the touch on his head and flinched. Power raced through him like something alive and he shuddered. There was a stirring within him, something more than a mere memory.

"Rise, foolish creature," Sidhara rumbled in a timeless voice that sent a shiver down Terr's spine. It was the language of the villagers and he understood the words.

His eyes never leaving the old man, he got to his feet. The Wanderer's expression softened.

"What do you want of me?" the old man asked, his voice filled with compassion and sadness.

Terr wanted to still the rage of images crowding his days and tortured his nights. He wanted peace and a release from the terrors that pursued him. He wanted to know who he was.

"Make it stop…the images, they never leave me," he moaned, relieved that he could say the words. "Why do they haunt me?" He felt his vision blur and hot tears burned his eyes.

Sidhara shook his head and turned to gaze at the desert. Perhaps it would have been kinder to have left the creature to the Saffal. Still doubting the wisdom of his actions, he nodded and sat down. He motioned with his hand. Terr wiped his face and sat before him. Loose sand swept around them, but neither noticed.

"You are torn between two worlds and two memories, foolish creature," Sidhara said gravely. "The Saffal has claimed you and you must find your way back. I will help you find your way and your destiny, but the price you must pay could be terrible."

Terr didn't understand the meaning of the words, but the powerful presence of the old man and his soothing words gave him comfort and his fears faded. Something shifted deep within him and his mind whirled with untold questions.

"I sense the uncertainty in you, and the force of Death," Sidhara said quietly and turned to face the open sands. "No matter. Just watch." Together they sat on the crest of the dune, letting the wind and the desert fill them.

Thus began Terr's first lesson.

* * *

The children no longer mocked Terr or laughed at him. The young unpaired girls gave him respect he found unsettling. Almost daily, in the morning or afternoon, Sidhara would take him into the desert where they could talk.

At first, it was about survival. Sidhara showed him how to drill a hole beneath the base of a peelath branch. He would then insert into the hole a small tube with a bulb at its end. After a time, he removed the stalk and bade Terr drink. The liquid bitter to the taste, but cool and refreshing. Sidhara sealed the puncture with a patch of grass gum so the tree wouldn't bleed.

Then there were the shoots of young grasses hidden in the center of dry clumps. Before dawn when the bush spread its leaves to catch the last moisture of the night, the shoots could be taken to draw water and a measure of sustenance. Not all plants were edible. Painful lingering death would be the price of a mistake.

Some roots yielded soft pulp that did not hold much water, but were nourishing. Terr learned their signs and the places where they grew, sometimes having to dig deep into the sand to find them. Not many things in the desert gave their moisture willingly. He came to read the sands and the shifting dunes, where to walk and what places to avoid, where there was water and how to find it. He had a lot to learn about life in the Saffal, but in some strange way, he already knew these things.

The old Wanderer was patient and Terr expanded under his tutelage. The desert was harsh, Sidhara reminded him often. It was a cruel master exacting unremitting respect. It knew no mercy, but it could also be a friend to those who knew its ways. Some parts of the desert even the Wanderers avoided, or crossed quickly.

Mostly, Sidhara would talk of life, of other villages and the wanderings of the people of the Saffal. Some of what Terr heard seemed hauntingly familiar.

The sun dipped low in one evening sky. They sat facing it, the dunes behind them were deep in shadow…and they talked.

"Master," Terr asked diffidently, still marveling that he could talk. "There is something I don't understand. Your teachings about the Saffal. Why is it that I seem to know all these things? The words are there in me and I feel that I have lived through this before. Yet it's all hazy and disjointed."

In the distance a line of brown-red cliffs rose above the sand, swimming in the heat. Terr recognized them as the Katai Than range. He felt a strange dread of that place, a place where the youths found him, so Sidhara said. What he was doing there, the old Wanderer declined to say.

"In a way, you have lived through this before, foolish creature," Sidhara murmured after a time, noting Terr's discomfort. "When you were brought out of the desert to the village, it was one of our own, Nightwings, a star wanderer such as yourself, who gave you those memories."

Terr had an image of a young Wanderer dressed in a plain surtaf wearing a yellow hood, hovering over him. And what was a star wanderer?

"Why did he do that, master?"

"To free your mind of the terrors from which you had fled."

Terr squirmed as the buried memories threatened to surface. Sidhara nodded solemnly.

"You wandered in the Saffal for two days. Your mind and body were not prepared for what you went through and your spirit fled. At great risk to himself, Nightwings allowed his spirit to merge with yours. It was the only way to make you want to live. The process left part of himself with you and took part of you with him. His knowledge is now entrusted in you and brothers forever you shall be. It is his experiences and knowledge that you now feel."

Terr's skin crawled as he listened to the old man's words, not really understanding. Some terrible force stirred within him then. When it happened, Sidhara looked at him strangely.

"If that knowledge is with me—"

"Like your memories, foolish creature, it is still buried. What you are experiencing are merely fragmentary flashes from your past life."

Terr showed him his arm, the skin tanned, but still not the deep leathery yellow of everyone else.

"I know that I'm not of the Saddish-aa. Who am I, then?"

Sidhara's eyes were troubled, but he did not look away. "Someone without a memory, without a past," he said and Terr gaped at him.

"You said I am a star wanderer."

"You came to us from another world. Do not be troubled, my son. Our blood has mingled and this will always be your land. Have you not a brother?"

"These teachings, master." With his eyes, Terr traced the ancient lines on the old man's face. "What are they?"

In the Shadow of Death

"It is the way of the Discipline," Sidhara said and his voice was the voice of the desert. "They are the words of the *Saftara*. You have their measure."

"From Nightwings—"

"His common name is Dharaklin. When your spirit has been freed, you may then call him Nightwings."

"Dharaklin...he sought me in my mind?"

"Just so. In you the words of the *Saftara* lay dormant and must be wakened if you are to remember."

"Wakened? How?"

"Out in the desert there are places where the gods gather. Places of power. These places usually take the form of an escarpment."

"Like Katai Than?"

"Just so. Such places affect the mind, enhancing some functions, erasing memories and curing illnesses. The forces there can also kill the unprepared. The randomness of the effects can be controlled to a certain extent by someone who has been trained to discipline his emotions, desires, hates, and jealousies." Sidhara paused, his mind far away, reflecting on the training of his own youth. "Thoughts must be turned outward, embracing the all, not centered on self. The way of the Discipline enables us to survive in the desert. Through its teachings, you learn how to control the body and recognize those things that sustain life. The process also reveals about self. Entering the escarpment, you must be prepared to face transformation of your very being...and also total obliteration."

"You mean death?" Terr said.

Among the shadows, he heard the soft stomping of oark and the laughter of scampering children.

"Death would be a release," Sidhara said heavily. "The fate of those who fail is much more terrible. Don't mistake the Discipline for a religion, foolish creature. There, worship is offered to an abstraction in the absence of reality. A living god only requires reverence and due respect. The Discipline is a bridge between the Saddish-aa and the gods. It is also a way of existing and thinking in an environment some would call forbidding. Death is part of living and can sometimes be a transition to another level of being. Unprepared, those who enter one of these places always die. For those who return, most possess the power of Death in their hands. When willed, their touch can kill, even at a distance. No one who has sought the power ever received it. That is not the way of the Discipline. The trial with a god is a test of self over the power of chaos." Sidhara sighed and plucked at his robe. "Only men can be shaped thus, foolish creature. And not every man. It is death for a woman to venture into such a place."

"Why is that, master?" Terr ventured, struggling to comprehend the flood of meanings the old man's words implied.

Sidhara remained silent for a long time. The western sky painted his face with wane light. When he spoke, his words were muted rumbles.

"In the end, all life belongs to Death and they war constantly for ascendancy. And a woman is the embodiment of all life."

Terr wasn't sure he understood.

"Master, why are you telling me these things?" he asked, afraid he already knew the answer. The old man grunted.

"As you suspect, you must face such a trial. You will have no peace until you do. Nightwings has left part of his union with the god in you and you must complete the joining. To find yourself and recapture your past, you will have to confront one of the gods and be prepared to face his judgment. I sense the latent power in you and I know you're disturbed by it. It is a call, a pull if you will, from the god who has chosen you. You will have no rest and no peace until you answer it."

"You mean I must test myself at Katai Than?" Terr murmured, his fear barely suppressed.

"No, that is a different trial altogether, merely a test of my humble training in the ways of the desert. For you, there is another place. To answer the call, you must confront your inner self at Athal Than, the Keep of Death. The place where the gods reside."

"But I'm not prepared," Terr protested. "I know nothing of the Discipline."

"Your brother knows and his spirit is with you," Sidhara said firmly. "You have everything you need."

Forces seemed to shift within Terr and Sidhara nodded.

"You can feel it even now, I sense it in you. Until you free yourself from the shadows of your mind, nothing more can I teach you."

Looking into the old man's eyes, Terr understood what he was being told. If he didn't survive the experience, further effort in his instruction would be a waste of time. It was perhaps a bleak conclusion, but the Saffal allowed little room for sentiment.

* * *

A blue-gray haze obscured the horizon, softening the harsh afternoon colors of the desert. Hot and still the air had a heaviness that made any exertion an uncomfortable necessity. Still, there was movement. The women were stirring, checking on the cooking of the evening meal being baked beneath the hot sands. Children were driving in the lumbering oark, occasionally prodding the reluctant shaggy beasts with long sticks. The poultry cackled contentedly, pecking absently around the bases of the peelath.

Terr slung his riding pack on a corral fence post and leaned against the railing, watching a young calf's determined effort to suckle his mother. With a grunt and a lazy backward glance at her impatient offspring, she at last deigned to stand still. The calf's head disappeared beneath her long coat to the sound of contented slurping.

Sand crunched behind him in shifting footfalls.

"For a while we feared she might reject the calf," a deep, resonant voice said beside him. Terr turned and looked curiously at the young Wanderer.

The youth wore a plain brown surtaf, the yellow hood pulled back. His reddish hair framed a long, narrow face before it spilled across the shoulders. He was thin and wiry like all the desert nomads. The yellowish skin drawn tight over the bony ridges of his face. The orange eyes with their vertical red slits were bright and searching.

Terr felt a stirring of memory, like he should know this man, then it passed.

"Yesterday, I watched as you brushed the calf, then her, then the calf again…"

"The mother would not touch the calf—"

"Because it smelled wrong?" Terr said.

"It was her first and sometimes touching is difficult."

Terr glanced at the suckling calf. "It appears to have worked, but I don't understand why."

"Touch is a powerful need in all living things and is often overlooked, even by us," the youth said seriously.

"You are Dharaklin," Terr said, uncertain how to go on. "My master told me what you did. I should feel something…"

"Don't be troubled. It will come with the waiting."

"Sidhara said that we are one, that we're brothers. Tell me who I am," Terr whispered, fighting to keep the terrors of his mind from consuming him. "The images, they always haunt me."

Dhar's eyes were concerned. "It is not that simple…"

On impulse Terr extended his hand, palm up. Dhar looked down in surprise at the proffered hand and slowly brought up his own. When they touched, Terr longed to feel the connection he knew must be there, but there was nothing. He let his arm drop and turned to watch the calf suckle. He swallowed hard and blinked rapidly.

In the Shadow of Death

"Your touch. I thought—"

"My wounded brother, it takes more than just telling it," he heard Dhar say behind him. He turned and gave a wan smile.

"I knew it wouldn't be that easy. Well, I'll find out how easy it is soon enough."

Dhar glanced at the pack. "You are riding tonight?"

Terr chuckled. "Sidhara said it was time." The nervousness clear in his voice.

"Do not dwell on your fears, my brother, for they are of your own making."

"It's the uncertainty…"

"I know. When you return, I shall be here for you."

* * *

It was cold and the air crisp, washed by clean desert winds. Terr's breath a white fog. He cast a furtive glance at the silent form of his master. Beneath a purple sky of an awakening dawn the jagged buttresses of the escarpment waited for him in silence. Overhead the twin moons made the lesser stars flee. The constellations stared down at the desert with brittle indifference.

The oark mounts grunted, tossed their heads and chomped at the bits. Pressure on their flanks reassured them and they padded along quietly. After six days of travel, everyone was weary. They were strange days, new and yet familiar. Terr knew he lived through something Dharaklin had already experienced, and the memory of it terrified and excited him. He hadn't talked to Sidhara about those memories, but he suspected that somehow the old Wanderer knew. His master did not help during the scorching days and the frigid nights, waiting for Terr to guide them both through the desert, setting camp and finding grass for the oark. It had been another test, and the fact they arrived safely showed he passed.

There was a stillness like a waiting. Only the hissing of sand beneath the oark's footfalls broke the silence. When the dark cliffs grew before them, the sand gave way to smooth slabs of rock and patches of pea-gravel.

Terr's lips were suddenly dry. He turned to look back at the dunes. They lay thick in shadow for the dawn was yet to break. After all the waiting and the teaching, he now found himself afraid, unable to take this final step.

In the village, before the mud huts of the Wanderers, watching the shifting dunes, it had all been so simple. From what he gathered, the teachings of the Discipline had no rules and made no demands. For a while, that had been enough, but the road he took, chosen for him more likely, had no turnings. Now that road ended before the cliffs of Athal Than. Ahead of him, he faced an unknown past and an uncertain future. Dharaklin's memories had deserted him. This, he realized, he needed to face alone.

To turn back time, he had to walk the canyons of Athal Than and bare his soul to whatever god would listen, so his master said. Failure meant death, or worse still, insanity even deeper than the one from which he was struggling to emerge—if the gods didn't obliterate him for his presumption.

A fleeting breeze tugged at his robes and the sands whispered to him. With a shake of his head, he clenched his teeth as the oark padded softly toward the black walls of the escarpment.

When they stopped, light bathed the tops of the cliffs and the sky turned pale amber. The stars died, leaving Aribus and Rima glowing yellow orbs. Terr and Sidhara dismounted, leaving the oark to nuzzle at the small shoots that clung to the rocky ground. The cliff tops suddenly turned golden and the shadows swept over them. Sidhara reached and touched Terr's shoulder.

"It is time," he said gravely and Terr began to tremble. "Do not fear, my son. My spirit shall be with you."

Terr turned to stare at the dark, forbidding folds of stone before him. The hidden crevices terrified him, as did his dark nightmares.

"I don't fear the questions, master, only the answers," he said at last and Sidhara nodded.

"Just so, but you have no choice. You have felt the call. Your memories and past cannot be denied."

"I know, master." He accepted that he had no choice. Ever since he woke in the village, all choices were denied him.

"I will wait for you here, my son. This is a thing you must seek for yourself, but my spirit shall not leave you. Remember, the gods do not seek to punish, and whatever fears you experience in there are only those that you take with you. Clear your mind and welcome the god's embrace and love."

That was easy for the old man to say, Terr reflected.

"I feel unworthy…"

Sidhara nodded. "That is the beginning of wisdom, my son."

The dread of the unknown held him rooted in place. For a time, he could not move. He could feel the cliffs calling him even now, pulling at him with irresistible force. It was almost a physical sensation. Now that he was here, it seemed the gods were in a hurry to claim him. One of the fissures lay deeper in shadow. For no better reason, he took his first tentative steps toward it, and hesitated before the darkness that was like a warning.

He stepped through.

His master's strength flowed through him and he was comforted.

The gorge narrow, winding, and gloomy, its sides polished by the ceaseless winds and driving sand. He could easily touch both walls with outstretched arms. Where the cliffs met the sky, amber light painted the dark browns and reds of the rocks. His footfalls muffled, the shadows parted to let him through.

The soft texture of the smooth walls reminded him of another place, but the memory refused to surface. He walked on, hollow footsteps sounded behind him. He stopped, but he couldn't hear anything. His imagination had betrayed him. The trail curved left and he walked deeper into the Keep of Death. The very rocks seemed to whisper to him and his skin prickled. He had an urge to run from this haunted place. Life back in the village wasn't really bad, even if he was insane. Did he want to know who he had been if it meant a real death?

The shadows crowded him. *It isn't real*, he kept telling himself. *Do not fear…do not fear…*

Suddenly, it seemed darker, colder. He felt someone behind him and slowly turned his head. There was no one there. *It isn't real*, he kept telling himself, but his inner terrors were ready to burst forth from his mind and consume him. 'Fear is only what you bring with you,' he recalled his master's words. He exhaled loudly, forcing his mind to clear, and started walking.

He didn't know where he walked or why. He only knew he must not stop. Not knowing, that is what scraped at his nerves. The shadows moved with him and he felt tangible power emanating from the smooth cliffs around him as *something* peered into him. He knew the face of real fear, then, for it was his. It wasn't the fear of imaginary terrors, but one of being judged for transgressions he didn't even remember committing.

His mouth went dry and his heart thudded in his chest. It was almost painful as a compulsion bade him stop. Is this where he would die? A numbing cold swept through him and he froze in place, unable to move. If gods really did exist in this enchanted domain, he was certain one of them looked at him now with detached scrutiny. A scrutiny that reached into his very core.

The cliffs around him faded and reality shifted, leaving him disembodied. Small blue lightnings flickered around him and crawled over his body. He did not feel their touch as he stood in a cocoon of light. He remembered Sidhara's words and struggled to compose himself. If the gods of this place wanted him, he would not resist. In a way, it would be a release and an end to his nightmares. Slowly, he spread his arms and waited for judgment.

Reality shifted and he saw a young man dressed in a strange, hauntingly familiar gray uniform slumped against a peelath trunk. Red cliffs towered over him. He felt the heat of the day and saw that the man's face was sunburned and cracked. Terr felt the man was close to death, but the Saffal had claimed him and would not let him go. Then the man looked up and Terr felt a shock of recognition. He was looking at himself.

Slowly, other memories came on fleeting gossamer wings.

A small, dirty face appeared among the shadows and he knew the boy. Alasi stood there in his rags, sullen and defiant. Then he smiled. Terr's heart stirred and he reached for the boy, but it was just a passing image. He saw the pursuing M-3s, the envoy and the mines of Anulus. Yet somehow, the memories seemed pale, insignificant and shallow—vain and without meaning that left his soul bare.

New images came and flashed before him: of his joys and sorrows, loves and hates. They swirled around him, through him, and swept him into oblivion. He watched it all, detached, stripped of emotion. Beyond the village of the Wanderers and the sands of the Saffal, his horizons expanded to encompass the stars of the Serrll, the Fleet and his crash. They were like scenes in a Wall, surreal and unreachable.

Why hadn't his master ever told him of those worlds? Why hadn't Dharaklin?

His yesterdays coursed through him in waves, sometimes painful and tearing, at other times pleasant and mild. He felt being turned inside out. Not all the memories were worthy.

It all came back.

How long was he lost in the village of the Wanderers? Certainly months. He would have to find out. The world he had known crowded him and he felt a tug of duty and responsibility. There came a twisting in his chest and he cried out in pain as reality shifted again.

In the mud hut, he saw Sidhara standing beside him. The

shadows lifted and there was a body lying on a mat of peelath leaves; sunburned, naked beneath a rough blanket of oark hair. Shock made him stop and stare. He was gazing down at his body, but that could not be impossible. In a kind of duality, he saw that the alien was not of the Saddish-aa.

Fear and terror lay in those eyes. The pale skin dry and cracked, drawn tight over a strong face. He was whimpering, shaking his head at the torment within him. He stepped to the mat and the woman moved aside. It was suddenly very quiet. Then he reached out and grasped the other's hand.

"Do not fear, my brother," he heard himself say and wished his strength to flow from his hand. "Rest, I am with you."

His grip was returned with surprising intensity. Then the alien's eyes began to change and expand. They were orange eyes with vertical red slits. Dharaklin…Nightwings, the shadow who walks at night—his brother. Terr felt himself falling into those eyes and everything exploded around him.

Eyes of fire peered into his soul and Terr saw the face of Death.

It all faded and there was a moment of utter stillness. He did not want, he did not need, he was nothing, a mote in an endless expanse of nothingness. After a time, he didn't know when, almost like a caress, a creeping warmth steeled through him and he felt comforted. There was a sense that he had accomplished something important. For a long time, he stood with his arms spread as he basked in the shadow of Death.

When he stirred, the sun was high in the sky, bathing the cliffs of the small clearing with harsh light. He looked down at his hands and marveled.

"I remember," he whispered in startled wonder. He lifted his arms wide and laughed. "I remember it all!"

Holding his arms high, he began to chant the ancient litany. The words from the *Saftara* came unbidden and he paid homage to the god of Death.

In the Shadow of Death

"I shall walk in the shadow of Death," he intoned the words and his voice grew deeper. "And it shall be with me all the days of my life."

A warm tingling slowly spread from his middle, consuming him, and his skin was on fire. It passes quickly and there is a presence around him, in him, and he felt detached as he grew. He looked down at himself, arms upraised, and heard the creature chant the litany that had invoked the god. He was Death, and everything that lives was his, and he breathed his essence into the one who called him and they were one.

"With shadow shall I smite my enemies, and with thunder shall I purge their land!" Small lightnings slithered and crackled between his arms. "And all who stand with me in the shadow of Death shall know my power, and be comforted. With shadow and thunder shall I walk their land!" he cried and clenched his fists.

Sheets of blue light danced around him and the power surged through him in rippling waves of prickly, painfully pleasant sensations. He squirmed with pleasure as Death embraced him, and he gave himself willingly. Around him, rolling thunder grumbled over the escarpment.

Lightning lanced at the cliffs, sending stone chips flying off the walls. Thunder shook the ground beneath his feet. He felt immortal and invincible. Nothing could stand in his way. It was a terrible, giddying power and he cried with joy at its release.

After a moment, he lowered his arms and basked in the quiet glow of being. Knowing again who he was, he pondered his new heritage. He had to relive the horrors of his mind to have his sanity restored, and he wasn't sure whether the journey had been worth the price. Hadn't Sidhara warned him? The gods, it appeared, were whimsical, and he received more than he bargained for—the power to walk in their shadow.

That would take some getting used to, he mused wryly, then laughed with the sheer pleasure of being whole again. Thunder echoed his laughter. The Saffal had fought hard to take him, but it seemed that he had outsmarted the desert. Then, sobered, he knelt on one knee and bowed low, muttering a silent thanks to the god who had touched him. Whatever waited for him tomorrow, he could face that future re-newed…with Death in his hands.

Transformed without understanding how, he took a turn-ing through a narrow canyon. The cliffs parted and the desert stretched into the distance before him. The brown hooded fig-ure of his master stood unmoving, contemplating the sands. The oark beside him picked at the thin brush that dotted the dunes.

When Terr walked up to him, Sidhara's eyes looked back approvingly and he nodded once.

"The gods have judged," he said gruffly. "That be enough."

Only then did Terr comprehend something of the power that lay in the old man's shadow, an aura of invisible light that manifested an unfathomable being. In his period of ignorance and madness, he hadn't known Sidhara for what he was, or he would never have dared approach him. Compared to his puny power to merely wield the destructive hand of Death, Sidhara could shape the destiny of worlds—or destroy them. Who or what was Sidhara, really?

Without realizing it, he covered his eyes, sank to his knees and lowered his head before the old Wanderer.

"Master, I crave your blessing and forgiveness for burden-ing you with my shadow."

Sidhara looked down at the alien before him and pondered. This was the first time in anyone's memory that the gods had touched an offworlder. He did not even know it was possible. Not for him to judge. Done, he was not displeased. He reached with his hand and touched Terr's head.

"Tah, it was the god's will, foolish creature. We could not turn away from your suffering."

"Master," Terr said rising, strong with the power in him. "Why didn't you tell me?"

In the Shadow of Death

"Twice more shall you walk within the shadow of Athal Than before you are complete," Sidhara said sternly.

"When will I know?" Terr was still coping with the realization of his release, and the old Wanderer who had taken him under his wing.

"You will know. The call will pull at you and its summons cannot be denied. Each time you answer the summons, you must come to me."

Sidhara did not call Terr 'foolish creature' again. That was something at least.

That evening, cloaked beneath the canopy of stars, they had a small fire going. It crackled and snapped and the shadows lay thick about them. Nearby the oark snorted and stomped. The spread of stars was their blanket and the black walls of Athal Than their protection. Shortly, they would begin their long track to the village.

"All who pass the first trial are in a manner reborn," Sidhara was saying, his voice rumbling, coming from somewhere far away, as though he was remembering something. "As you were reborn. Although for you, the trial was much more than simply an acceptance by a god. You may now bear a name befitting a Saddish-aa Wanderer. From now on, we shall call you Sankri, the strange one. For indeed the work of the gods is strange."

Terr felt the shock of it go through him. In Elexi mythology, Sankri was the god of death. Could Sidhara have known? It didn't seem possible, but after having survived his transformation, what *wasn't* possible? He knew the words of the *Saftara*, but even armed with the wealth of Dhar's memories, he knew so little of its practitioners.

After a time, Sidhara pointed at a group of stars low in the sky. "Behold, Amulran the Damned. He stands bent between heaven and earth, holding up the sky. Should he fall, chaos would engulf everything." Then he turned and showed Terr another pattern of stars. It didn't take too much imagination to

241

see a man holding an outstretched bow.

"The Stalker. He is locked in his moment of revenge, unable to loose the arrow of eternity. The gods touched them, hurling both into the sky to stare frozen at each other until the end of time."

"Why does he want to avenge himself on Amulran, master?"

"For betraying a friendship, my son."

"And the gods punished him for that?"

"Not punishment, but an exercise in restraint."

A hell of a way to teach someone restraint, Terr thought. His master stared at the flickering flames for a time.

"You may feel the Stalker has been dealt with harshly. But consider, my son. Had he loosed his arrow, Amulran the Damned might have been killed, and chaos would have swallowed everything. Frozen in time the Stalker may come to realize the consequence of carrying out his act of revenge and relent. Both will then be free.

"The gods refused to pass judgment on them, willing the Stalker to make the choice himself. And so, you too will face choices of moral judgment. You will be tempted to use the power within you to resolve a dilemma you may not clearly understand. Or the expediency of the moment will be too tempting, as is the desire to wield Death. For we are all imperfect and prefer to force action in order to change the conditions of the conflict. For you as for all of us, that choice will always be a dangerous one."

Terr was confused. From elation and renewed confidence, Sidhara reduced him to uncertainty and doubt. If this gift was so dangerous, why was he pushed into its acceptance? Only to regain his memory and past? He saw the possibilities of his power, but Sidhara went beyond its mere application and personal gratification. He sure could have used Death back on Elexi.

Sidhara's eyes touched him.

In the Shadow of Death

"You feel strong with the power now, invulnerable. Your imagination is full of its potential. Is that not so?" When Terr didn't say anything, Sidhara gave him a fond smile. "You are the first offworlder to have undergone the trial and survived. But enough said. It will come with the waiting. My son, I have not dwelled much on the underlying teachings of the Discipline. That was deliberate. Even though you had the words of the *Saftara* within you, your spirit was not free to comprehend them. Now, I can tell it, even as your brother's memories come to you fully. There is still a lot you must learn, but fundamentally, there is only one underlying lesson that encompasses everything, and you may have already realized what that is."

Terr thought of the Stalker and Amulran frozen in time, and about the gods who put them there. Sidhara didn't talk about justification or the reason behind their conflict. He didn't moralize or judge. There was only the consequence of their actions. Restraint by the gods? He thought he had it then.

"The Discipline is not a religion as you said, but a guideline for resolving moral and social conflict."

Sidhara nodded with satisfaction. "A penetrating piece of insight, but not quite right. The teachings are not for *resolving* conflict, but to give one the capacity and patience to live in harmony *with* it. For conflict is a pattern of all life that endlessly tests the spirit."

Terr grinned at its exquisite simplicity.

"I am pleased that you see the humor of it," Sidhara said dryly.

"Forgive me, master. I laughed at myself, at my ignorance. The use of any power implies responsibility, of course. But to use it effectively requires judgment and an understanding of all the related issues."

"Just so."

"But you're telling me that we cannot always know what the issues are, or judge the right or the wrong of it."

"Judgment requires a superior moral position, my son.

There is always a question of fitness. Before you are tempted to use your power, you must ask yourself whether you are fit to judge another's imperfections amidst the distractions of your wants and desires."

"So we do nothing?"

Sidhara didn't say anything and Terr realized that in their past the Wanderers too must have had instances of abuse. Moral restraint is learned, not given.

The old man stirred the embers of the fire. "In the waiting, most things resolve themselves. Sometimes we are forced to act because the situation has become intolerable. Beware of Death, for it is the ultimate judge. Unleashed, it cannot be recalled, but I did not mean to frighten you, Sankri, my son from the stars. You have gained a measure of insight into yourself, and that is always good. I can tell you this. When tempted, refrain. Let the power feed your spirit rather than the storms of your wrath."

They sat there, listening to the night. After a time, Terr looked at his master, having to ask the one question he was avoiding.

"What now?"

Sidhara did not pretend not to understand. "You have returned to reality and the past is open to you again. Your future is now for you to make."

"I don't want to leave," Terr said in anguish.

"I know that, my son," the old man said heavily. "But there is one more trial you must face before then. You must face your nightmare. You must face Katai Than."

Chapter Ten

The morning broke mild and refreshing.

With the sun hardly above the horizon, the sky already full of commuters and freight shuttles. Celean Park still in shadow, and light mist hugged the ground. It would be a few hours yet before the sun broke through the ring of towers of the various administration buildings.

In the comparative luxury of the executive cable-tube, Enllss watched the city fall away beneath him. An external image painted in real-time inside the tube. Some preferred undersea vistas or the deeps of space. He could not be bothered.

He'd been angry all night and his jaw ached from having it clenched. The alternative was to mouth frustrated obscenities.

The cable-tube doors flashed amber and the outside scene faded into a neutral interior decor of soft pastels. Still scowling, he strode toward his offices, daring anyone to say something. Sensing his mood the early few of his day shift staff avoided his eye.

His personal aide was there waiting for him. An Assembly rep in her first term, competent and learned quickly, he took her with him when appointed commissioner. She put up with his quirky moods for the last two years, something of a milestone. The last one hung around for six months and was now a backbencher in the Assembly, recovering from the experience—or was it trauma? He almost smiled then.

His staff had a pool going on how much longer this one was likely to last. The bet was another eight months. If she managed to stick with him for three years, she would be promoted to more responsible duties.

He planted himself before her and pointed a long finger at

her face.

"I want Sill here, now! If that son of a bitch is out of Captal, then he's out of a job!" He stomped into his office. The translucent doors barely got out of his way.

She raised a slim eyebrow and reached for the comms pad. The boss in one of his testy moods again.

"Send tea!" Enllss bellowed. The doors clicked shut behind him.

The discrete ceiling panels of his office brightened to brilliant blue, offsetting the orange glow of the walls. Tempted to shut off the window screen, he decided to leave it transparent. Mist shrouded some of the towers as it lifted from below.

He paced. The rage and frustration of the previous evening came boiling back. Finally, he stopped pacing.

"Comsec," he growled and looked at the Wall.

The Wall faded into full holographic mode. He scanned down the list of secure messages left for him overnight by members of the Executive Council and other commissioners. The items were for his eyes only, and of such importance that even his closest personal staff were forbidden access. Nevertheless, the facility had become cluttered again with personal trivia and nonsense.

Only one message interested him and the cause of his irritation.

"Show item four, Diplomatic Branch preliminary. Summary only," he commanded.

The words hung there, cold and indifferent. His lips curled in anger. He set slow scroll and scanned through the summary. It was all there, and Sill could not or would not see it. The fool had his nose so far up Anall-Marr's ass, his eyes were full of crap. Terr had seen it months ago. What was more, he'd had enough sense to put it into that emergency beacon burst to Rayon.

Where are you now, my boy?

He paced the length of the office.

A panel opened in the side of his desk and a tray of herbal tea rose from the cavity. He stopped, breathed in the fresh aroma, and poured himself a cup. Holding it between his hands, he sniffed at the tendrils of rising steam and took a sip, savoring the delicate taste. Maybe a fraction too hot, but otherwise excellent. It stilled the emotions churning within him.

The comms alert beeped. He reached across the desk and touched a pad.

"What is it?"

"Diplomatic Branch Director Sill-Anais is here, sir."

He broke contact and frowned as the translucent doors slid away. Sill walked in, smiled cheerfully and nodded. Enllss sat down his cup with a loud click and pointed at the Wall.

"What the blazes kind of report is that, by damn?" His eyes flashed at his director, his rage restored.

Sill glanced at the text and raised an eyebrow. "What's the matter? I left out a period? Ach!"

"You left out a blasted sight more than that, you old fart. I've been racking my brains trying to tie Kapel and her brood with the Karkans. The best thing you managed to come up with is to suggest that she's aiming to nominate as Prefect when Anall-Marr gets his selection as Primate. Utter drivel! Have you forgotten she once campaigned for the General Assembly? Tell me, Sill. When in the whole Deklan history has the Ecumenical Synod permitted a prefecture to fall into outside hands? Tell me that?"

Sill was a bit taken aback by his friend's outburst.

"Well, no such case—"

"Then what kind of worm crap are you shoveling here?" Enllss demanded and pounded the desk. "Your agents told you what I want to know and you refuse to see it. Right there! Last paragraph. Read it!" he snarled and pointed at the Wall.

Miffed, some of Sill's good humor evaporated. "What's all this about—"

"Just read the blasted thing!"

By all accounts, Rayon's mission was an outstanding success and Sill felt justifiably pleased with himself. Even now, Anall-Marr was putting in advisors to monitor changes in Kapel's administration. On the official level at least, the question of slavery had been successfully resolved. His agents had done a great job and he couldn't understand why Enllss was so pissed off.

He scanned down the paragraph and began to read.

"A possible scenario to interpret Kapel Pen's policy of passive resistance and subversive media campaigns against Deklan rule, coupled with the unprecedented integration of Kunoid Minerals' operations into the administrative structure of the Four Suns, it is suggested that Kapel—"

Enllss waved him to silence. "Enough! Ignoring the long-winded verbal diarrhea, the bottom line is that she's planning to cede the Four Suns to the Karkan Federation!" Enllss grated and shook his head in disgust. "Why can't your people write plain reports, huh? This drivel is almost as bad as the garbage I get from my staff," he muttered petulantly.

Sill was in shock. Cede the Four Suns? He picked a form-chair and sat down, more than a little disturbed.

"It hides their own ignorance," he suggested absently. "But look here, Enllss. I cannot believe you're serious. Ach! I can't."

Enllss glared at him. "I can see that, by damn. You've lost your objectivity, you senile old fool. Why do you think the Karkans poured megaserrlls into Anulus when they could have used those resources to open up one of their own worlds? And don't tell me they don't have any. Not as rich perhaps, but they've got them. Kunoid is a con job, I tell you. We've been pounding our brains worrying about market monopolies while all this time the Karkans were planning to steal the lot. The whole system! Other border systems could follow the Four Suns; beads on a cut string. It would be a strategic disaster."

Sill wrung his hands in agitation. "Enllss, listen to me. Kapel Pen may bear little love for the Deklan Republic, but that's a far cry from ceding the system. Ach! And for what?"

"Power, that's what!" Enllss snarled and prodded Sill on the chest. "She may have been thwarted once, but the gal has vision and ambition, and she's smart. I wonder what the Servatory Party offered her to come across. Directorship of a Branch? Maybe even a commissioner's post. They would deliver, too."

Sill looked outraged. "From controller to commissioner?"

"You kidding? For the riches of Anulus and the resulting political fallout at stealing the Four Suns? I would make her an Executive Director!" Enllss looked tired as he slumped into his formchair.

Sill shook his head. "I'm still not prepared to believe it. If it's true, it could ruin Anall-Marr."

"It might not be such a bad thing," Enllss said harshly. "I think Deklan would be better served without him."

"Ach! You're a cold-hearted bastard, Enllss."

"That's right. I don't give a crud about Deklan or the bleeding billions on Elexi. I cannot afford to and neither can you."

"Rayon's mission?"

"He's done his job. Your people have done theirs."

"We do nothing, then, and let her do it?"

"Not my department, Sill. Admin Affairs can do the sweeping up. In case it slipped your mind, the Bureau of Cultural Affairs is Serrll's intelligence arm. While I run it, its objective is to maintain stability between the Revisionist and the Servatory blocks. First and foremost!"

"What about the Four Suns?"

"What about it?"

"Ach! The secession!"

"There is nothing we *can* do about it. Strictly speaking, it's a matter for the Ecumenical Synod. Your government will have to come to terms with losing one of its systems. Tactically, a shift of one system to the Karkans won't mean a thing. Strategically, though, it will be a phenomenal propaganda coup. It wouldn't do the Revisionist cause much good either," he conceded.

"Ach! I don't believe you're serious, Enllss. You're going to allow the Karkans to walk off with one of the most critical assets we have without lifting a hand. It will set the Deklan's economy back by decades."

"Take it easy, Sill. You knew what your government planned when they allowed Kunoid Minerals to develop Anulus. Didn't you?"

Sill shifted in his seat. "I had an idea—"

"I'll bet you did." Enllss smiled with satisfaction, his eyes hard. "You knew the Synod was going to use Anulus to pressure the Paravan Trading—"

"As a representative of the Deklan Republic—"

"Oh, cut the crap already. We all do what we have to. Legally, Deklan is in a knot. All Kapel needs to do is announce her decision and hold a referendum. If the general plebiscite supports her, the Karkan Federation owns the Four Suns. Under the Articles of Association, your revered Synod cannot do a thing about it, unless you kill the bitch. Not that I give a crud." Enllss picked up his cup and took a long swallow. "Not bad. Want some?"

Sill waved him away.

"You should try it, calm you down."

"Enllss…"

"Okay." Enllss put down his cup. "What do you think the Karkans will do with Anulus once they gain control? It could make life uncomfortable for some of our industries."

"To use your own words, Enllss, I don't give a crud about the Paravan Trading Association or the Sofam Confederacy either. And I don't like your glib talk of killing. We're beyond that. The question is; how do we stop Kapel Pen?"

"Not we. You!"

"Ach! If she's allowed to go through with this, it will damage the whole Revisionist coalition, and our careers."

"Not as much as it will damage Deklan," Enllss said easily. "But you're right. Neither one of us wants that to happen, do we. As for our careers, inform your government, Sill, I'll give them one day, twenty-two hours, to figure out their own deal with Kapel. Afterward, if you still haven't got it worked out, I, and by that, I mean the Sofam Confederacy, will go public."

"Why, you dirty—"

"Unless…" Enllss raised a finger.

Sill glared. "Unless what?"

"We reach an understanding…right now."

"The Sofam worlds have always been a godless and sinful people," Sill hissed. "We were right not to trust your kind."

Enllss laughed and pointed at the door panels. "If you don't want to deal with us, Illeran and his Servatory Party thugs are in the next building."

"Hypocritical asshole. Ach! You know I won't do that, but I cannot commit the Synod to anything."

"Your problem. This is the deal. For an equal Anulus concession with Kunoid, I'll tell you how to stop Kapel from ceding the Four Suns."

"Without compromising Anall-Marr?"

"Without compromising Anall-Marr."

"I don't need to make any deals with you or Sofam," Sill said evenly. "Once Anall-Marr becomes aware of Kapel's treachery, he'll have her—"

"Have her where?" Enllss demanded coldly. "What's he going to do? Come marching in with a squad of priesthood guards and demand her resignation? All she needs to do is file a formal referendum motion with the Bureau of Administrative Affairs and he can fulminate all he wants. What of your other border systems? They're only waiting for an excuse like this to become openly hostile. You forget my friend, Anall-Marr has his hands full trying to become Primate. He cannot afford any unpleasantness. Not now. If he doesn't handle this just right, he can forget all about being Primate, and Deklan could lose more than the Four Suns."

"You evil, scheming—"

"Twenty-two hours," Enllss said flatly.

Sill gazed at his old adversary with grudging admiration. He knew Enllss would rather deal with Deklan than allow the whole stinking mess to boil over. Only the Karkans would benefit from a brawl within the Revisionist coalition. He had no idea what Enllss planned, but he had learned long ago not to underestimate his friend's abilities. Still, one day didn't seem at all long enough to sort out a mess of this complexity. Then again, Kapel could announce her secession at any time.

"The Synod may not listen to me," he temporized and Enllss shrugged.

"Their choice."

"As you always intended," Sill said bitterly. "Very well. I will take the necessary steps. Rayon must be told."

Enllss shook his head emphatically. "No! In time, but not now. There is too much risk of a leak and I don't want Kapel making any preemptive moves before your Synod is ready to act."

"From the messages Rayon has been sending me, I wouldn't be surprised if he hasn't figured it out already."

"Then tell him to keep his mouth shut!"

Sill didn't look very happy. "There is one more thing, Enllss, that must be said. I didn't expect this kind of treatment from you. I thought we were friends."

Enllss nodded, his mouth a hard line. "Yeah, but neither of us is permitted to forget his loyalties."

"Ach! A dirty business."

"No, only dirty players."

Sill looked tired, old and disappointed. "Perhaps you're right. Sofam has nothing but derision for the way of the Path. Ach! That may have given you a more objective perspective of us. I wouldn't know. What I do know is that you're prepared to sacrifice everything we've had between us for a moment of personal satisfaction and a desire to see Deklan humbled—"

"As you sought to humble Sofam," Enllss said.

Sill averted his eyes and his shoulders sagged. "Perhaps."

Enllss felt an urge to reach out to his friend, to tell him…what? That he was sorry? His pang of conscience was momentary. He remembered that Sill was a master manipulator. They both had a job to do. Sill was mistaken if he thought that friendship would prevent either of them from doing what they thought was necessary in the interest of their faction.

Dirty players? The lowest.

"Have you discussed your plan with Illeran?" Sill ventured.

Enllss shook his head. "My boss has a lot on his mind these days. There is no need to add to his worries…unless Deklan rejects my deal."

Sill sighed and nodded. "They called off the search for your nephew," he said after a while.

"Yeah, I know. Anabb told me last night."

"They found his survival blister, or what's left of it, in the middle of some desert. It appears that his containment cell failed. It's a pile of slag now. He must have survived his crash, for they found tracks leading into the desert."

"Then he could still be alive?" Enllss demanded and Sill winced.

"Doubtful. Ach! Face it, my friend. It's a four-day walk to the nearest Wanderer village. The survival pack didn't hold enough water to last a day in those temperatures, let alone four."

"Were any of the villages contacted?"

"Anar'on refused permission for overflights over the deep desert. We carried out several stand-off orbital scans, but they came back negative."

"Well, maybe one day, he'll just walk out," Enllss said with a dull ache of loss. "What about the M-3 commanders?"

"Ach! They drew a reprimand and were sent to the bottom

of the promotion list. That's an effective showstopper as far as their careers are concerned. The COMDEKOPS investigation could not prove criminal intent. The only thing they've got them on is not following standard procedure."

"I don't want them at the bottom of the promotion list, Sill. I want them on Cantor, counting rocks for the next two hundred years!"

* * *

"Sankri! Sankri!"

The cry went up from the boys as they ran to meet the two weary travelers. The men hung back and nodded to themselves, grinning approvingly. The sharp heat of the afternoon was beginning to fade and the long shadows were welcome.

Terr and Sidhara slowly led their drained oark mounts toward the village. The boys clustered around them, chattering excitedly. There was undisguised joy and pride in their faces. The more adventurous jostled to touch them both, while the timid were content to simply be close. *How did they know*, Terr wondered. He turned to Sidhara, but the old man betrayed nothing.

Their unpretentious pleasure had moved him more than he cared to admit. He smiled reluctantly, then laughed with them and returned their touch. They accepted him completely, alien and all, and wanted nothing in return. He felt a sense of belonging that disturbed and comforted. He realized it could also be an emotional trap.

In the square, surrounded by tall peelath, the villagers waited to greet them. They were all there, the women, the men and the Rahtir. The unpaired maidens looked fondly at Terr and the youths smiled indulgently. The elders maintained their solemn dignity as was fitting and only nodded sagely.

Terr stopped his oark and handed the reins to one of the boys, who immediately lifted them high in triumph. The gesture provoked good-natured jeering from the others. The saddle creaked as he dismounted. He rubbed his butt to some general laughter around him. Even a few of the Rahtir cracked a brief grin. The journey had been long and he was justifiably weary. There was no shame attached to that.

Everyone suddenly raised their arms and cried, "Sankri!" A tingle ran down Terr's spine and his hair stood on end. He was unaccustomed to such attention and he felt self-conscious. He remembered how it had been before, but he was someone different now. He wasn't even the person who had crashed. The realization was sobering as he pondered what the god of Death had wrought.

There came an abrupt hush among the villagers and they fell back, forming an opening. A tall figure strode toward him and stopped. Thin as a weed, wearing a surtaf with a yellow hood, his eyes were alive and smiling and Terr knew him. In the days of their journey back from Athal Than, he often wondered about the inevitable meeting with his alien brother. That they would meet, he had no doubt. Now that Dhar stood before him, he wasn't prepared.

The shock of seeing the tall alien standing there was like seeing his alter ego. He had never been close to another person, always feeling himself complete, confident and in total control. Now, Dhar's most intimate memories and experiences were intertwined with his own. His feelings toward this alien who so unselfishly risked his sanity to save him were a turmoil of gratitude, uncertainty and a measure of timidity and fear. He may walk in the shadow of Death, but Dhar was its very embodiment. He wondered what Dhar thought of him.

Dhar covered his eyes for a moment and bowed before Sidhara, then turned to Terr. His face an unreadable mask. Slowly, he extended his left hand, palm raised.

"My brother Sankri. I soar with joy to see you again, and whole," he said heavily and Terr reached up with his hand. Their palms touched.

"Nightwings," Terr whispered, and in Dhar's eyes, he found compassion and love and the bond that was between them would be unto death. He need not have worried. "Our shadows have crossed and we're one."

The villagers roared their approval, then drifted away, leaving the two of them to their thoughts. Sidhara smiled indulgently, patted Terr's arm and shuffled away. Terr stared after the retreating figure, then looked at his new brother.

"Dharaklin," he said, savoring the rolling thunder of the name. "My brother of the night. Fitting."

"In your days as well, I hope. You need looking after. Wandering alone in the Saffal..." Dhar hissed and shook his head. "Even for us, it just isn't done."

They both had a chuckle, suddenly comfortable in each other's presence. In a flash, Terr realized they may be different physically, but they were closer than any blood brothers could be. He felt a real rush of warmth and affection for this giant man. Then he sobered, compelled to ask something.

"How did they know my name?"

"Let us walk, my brother," Dhar said, instantly serious, refusing to explain.

Terr weary from his trek in the desert, as Dhar must know, but he would not have asked if it hadn't been important.

They walked in silence toward the rocky flats that sprawled behind the village, for the moment, content in each other's presence. Terr could not keep his eyes off Dhar, drinking him in, trying to understand why he had done what he did.

The small gorge opened before them, already filled with dark afternoon shadows. Tall peelath covered the steep slopes. Tarad grass crowded around their trunks. Dhar made his way down the worn path with easy grace. Evidently, Terr was not the only one who made use of the gorge. When Dhar stood at the bottom, he looked around briefly and breathed deeply of the scented air and leaned negligently against a peelath trunk.

Terr picked a convenient boulder and parked himself on it.

In the Shadow of Death

He looked around with new eyes at the familiar rocky outcrops, the stands of peelath, and shook his head.

"I must have spent days here, staring at nothing. Now, it's only a blurred memory of someone I never really knew. A shadow of someone else."

"How do you…feel, Sankri?" Dhar asked diffidently. Terr tilted his head and chuckled.

"How do I feel? I feel transformed. I have my past again and more than I bargained for besides. I feel…alive! But there is a qualitative difference from what I was before. It's the duality I find disturbing. And I don't mean only your memories. I…"

"I know," Dhar said softly. "It was the same with me, the feeling of being reborn as someone else. The same, yet different. Do not force it, my brother. It will come with the growing, and though it will take time, the force of my memories will fade. Then again, perhaps not. No Saddish-aa has ever joined with an alien before."

"I didn't mean that. To wield such power!" Terr clenched his fists. "I can feel it in me even now, coiled, ready to unleash Death at my bidding. It rages inside me. To stretch out my arm—"

"That is not the way of the Discipline," Dhar admonished sternly and Terr nodded.

"That's why I fear what I have been given. I'll tell you something, Nightwings, my brother." Terr looked at Dhar, savoring the name, and smiled. "I like how that sounds."

"I like hearing it."

Terr's smile faded and his face clouded. "Before, my days were filled with madness and my nights with terror, but for a while there, I was almost happy. There was only the village and the world of the Saffal. No one wanted anything from me and I didn't want for anything. I had a kind of peace," he said and hung his head.

"And a kind of death as well," Dhar said firmly. "But you

left out the pain, my brother, and the nightmares. I saw."

"If that was death, it wasn't so bad after all." Terr scooped a handful of sand and watched it trickle between his fingers. "Now, I must face a new life, I guess, or remake an old one. Your arrival here is timely." He cocked an inquiring eyebrow and Dhar grinned.

"Officially, I am on extended compassionate leave. A family matter, you might say," Dhar said dryly and Terr laughed.

"How long has it been?" he ventured.

"Since your crash? Two months."

"A lifetime."

Dhar stood up, suddenly grave and hesitant. "Sankri, I am gladdened that you are whole again. I have watched your torment and felt your pain and I was powerless to help you. Difficult as this is for me, these words must be said. When I first saw you, delirious and lost, I could not bear to leave you thus. Some may consider my actions noble, but I know now that I have forced myself on you without your consent, exposing you to a terrible risk. Sidhara warned me, but I wouldn't listen. Call it pride or arrogance. Both were equally wrong. Because of me, you are now torn between two destinies, struggling to come to terms with a culture not your own, facing an uncertain future. My memories are in you, but they are not your own. You will forever be part of the Saddish-aa, but you also stand apart from us. It is one thing to grow up with the teachings of the Discipline and another to have it thrust upon you, as I did. If I can atone for my actions, remember this. Through all your turmoil to come, for there will be turmoil, and if you allow me, I shall always be with you, my brother."

The breeze stirred the grass around them. Terr felt the impact of Dhar's words and the hair on the back of his neck bristled. It was all there just as Dhar told it, and the words could have been his.

"You must live with the burden of my memories as well," Terr said softly. "Not always honorable."

In the Shadow of Death

"You haven't led a sinful life, Sankri," Dhar said in a rumbling whisper. "I cannot deny you the gift the gods saw fit to bestow upon you. Tah, it is destiny. In your old life the Wanderers were nothing to you, primitive desert nomads, a curiosity. I know how it is and you should not feel shame. All of us are products of our environment. Your background is proud and you walk in the shadow of a powerful and sophisticated family. You achieved much in the Fleet and done with honor. I shall understand should you choose to turn away from us...and me."

Terr felt the pain and the effort this display of emotion must have cost Dhar. The Saddish-aa were a proud people who didn't reveal their emotions easily. The desert made them hard so that they could survive. Beneath that protective scab, it also hid a complex and sensitive people. He understood that all too well now. Admitting to his needs did not come easily either.

How *did* he feel about this alien who had risked his life and sanity for a stranger, no matter what the motive? Gratitude? Yes, and love. Yet he also feared commitment. He needed time for his emotions to settle. As for Dhar's uncertainties, he didn't even hesitate. He stood up and took the one step that separated them. Heart pounding, he reached across the space between them and touched Dhar's chest with the palm of his hand.

"Nightwings, alien we may be, but I am humbled and proud to stand in your shadow, and proud to call you a brother. I was dead and you gave me life. We're one, always. Knowing me, could you ever doubt?"

"A memory is not the person," Dhar said softly.

They stood like that for a time before Dhar brought his hand to Terr's chest.

"All is well, my brother," he said simply and Terr felt the heat of his hand.

"As our master is often want to quote, the gods have judged," Terr said gruffly. "It be enough." Emotions raged within him and he looked away. He perched himself on a boulder and hugged his knees. "I'll just have to come to terms with it. Besides, I never had a brother and I'm kind of curious to see how I'll feel. Tell me. What's been going on while I was busy dying?"

Dhar's mouth twitched. "You stirred up quite a storm. As far as the Fleet is concerned, you really are presumed dead."

"Don't everybody grieve all at once."

"You cannot really blame them, Sankri. The Old Man—"

"Old Man?"

"Anabb," Dhar said and Terr grinned. "He's got an M-6 prowling the Four Suns. Last time I heard, he had it parked over Elexi. The Bureau of Administrative Affairs has extended the Envoy's tenure to oversee the changes being implemented in Kapel Pen's administration."

Terr looked incredulous. He couldn't believe that Rayon hadn't acted.

"You mean, she's still in charge?"

"She is the Controller, if that's what you mean."

"But that's incredible." He realized that Dhar didn't know, or hadn't been able to piece it together from the knowledge he gained when they merged. Apparently, shared memories did not instantly translate into automatic understanding. It was an interesting observation. "I think she plans to cede the Four Suns to the Karkans. I also think she wanted me dead because of that knowledge."

Dhar's only reaction was to raise an eyebrow. "An interesting theory, my brother."

"I could be wrong."

"And given your memories, I should have seen it."

"So, the memories don't immediately integrate into a coherent whole," Terr mused. "Fascinating."

"Something for the Rahtir to contemplate, my brother. Anall-Marr has his people all over her administration. If you are right, Sankri, he has not gotten wind of her plans or he would have moved against her."

"He may not be able to. A scandal right now wouldn't do his campaign much good. It could also mean that Rayon hasn't been able to figure it out either."

"Or the Bureau of Cultural Affairs is holding him back," Dhar said quietly.

Terr nodded. "It would make sense that my uncle is cooking something. All the more reason for me to return."

"Sankri, you must have considered this, but when you resurface, whoever tried to get rid of you before could try again. Given what's at stake…"

Terr was thinking along those same lines. He may have enjoyed a blissful period of anonymity, but that didn't mean events around him had necessarily stopped. Even after all this time, the envoy may still find his suspicions relevant, if the beacon's burst was recovered. Terr could not afford to assume anything. Better to raise the alarm than assume that everyone else was on the ball.

"Nothing I can do about that until they show their hand. What of you? You're on Talon, right?" he said, the memory surfacing. Rit! This duality, it was going to take some time getting used to.

"I am sweating out a tour as one of the base commander's administrative assistants," Dhar said evenly and winced.

"Tough."

"Your sympathy is appreciated, but it could have been worse. It's only for a year and then I will rate Third Scout senior grade. It was either Talon or two years in Sargon in an M-4," Dhar said grinning. "Your career seems to have taken somewhat of a turn as well."

"Not for the better if I'm considered dead," Terr said darkly and Dhar laughed.

"And now?"

"I know, I know. I found something here that has been missing in my life, Nightwings. I found fulfillment, a purpose and an acceptance. There is still so much that I need to learn of the Discipline. I don't want to go back."

"My brother." Dhar's eyes were full of understanding. "You cannot escape your destiny. You will always be one of us. This land is now yours, as are its people, but your heart soars between the stars and you would not be content with the simple life here. It may keep you for a while and you may even be happy. But at night, with your eyes lost in the blaze of The Arch, you would feel its pull. I know, for I feel it also."

"Yeah," Terr said wearily.

* * *

In the west the sky was still washed deep red. Overhead, Aribus appeared as a golden crescent. Torches blazed among the peelath. The men were tending a large fire, joking and laughing. Poultry and other meats crackled on the barbecue. Delicious smells of cooking drifted in the warm evening air.

Drums were beating to the soft strands of the leetas. The girls danced around the fire with abandon. Clapping their hands the youths urged them on. The fermented peelath berry juice flowed freely amid loud talk and jesting. For this was a special occasion.

Sitting among them, Terr tapped his foot in time with the music. The melodies tugged at his heartstrings. There was a density and texture to the lives of these people that transcended the hardship of the land. They have found contentment, he decided. They were fortunate, but they lived under such a terrible shadow. Or was it so terrible? Looking at them, they carried their burden lightly. However, that acceptance had come after lifetimes of living in the shadow of Death. Would *he* be able to accept his burden just as easily? He pushed the thought aside and shared in their simple pleasure, his tomorrows and yesterdays forgotten.

A hush fell over the crowd when the Rahtir emerged out

of the communal hut. The men gathered before the fire and squatted on the mats of woven peelath leaves. The women sat opposite them, leaving a wide path between them. The Rahtir, wearing plain or purple hoods, made their way along the path. They sat at the head of the two columns. Sidhara took his place of honor at the head of the group.

He gazed at the assemblage with regal dignity. "Let it begin."

A young maid emerged from the women's communal hut. She was dressed in a pale gray robe that reached her knees. Her orange hair fell down her back in a swaying tumble. Dried desert flowers adorned her head. In one hand, she held a brown cape with a yellow hood. In the other, she held a ring of yellow flowers. With quiet dignity, she walked to where Terr and Dhar were sitting. Out of darkness, drums began their slow beat.

The beat quickened until it reached a crescendo as the girl reached Terr. They took him through it, but he still felt nervous. He looked into the serene composure of her face and the fire of her eyes. She leaned forward and placed the ring of flowers on his head. He stood up. Together they walked toward the Rahtir. The drums began their slow beat again.

Sidhara was standing, watching them approach. When Terr stopped before him the crowd waited for the drum roll to fade. Sidhara seemed cloaked in power. Terr fancied he could see its glow about the old Wanderer.

"The gods have judged another among us fit to stand in their shadow." Sidhara's heavy voice carried the power of the gods. A low rumble of thunder rolled among the dunes. "He was not of the Saddish-aa, yet his blood has now mingled with ours. Is there anyone here who refuses him?" He glared at the assemblage, almost daring dissent. Only the crackle of the fire disturbed the expectant hush. "Just so. In recognition of his trial, he may bear a name and stand tall with the rest of us, as a Wanderer."

"Sankri!…Sankri!" the shout rose and Terr felt goose-bumps all over.

Towering over him, Sidhara unclipped Terr's old cape and allowed it to fall. Saying nothing, he reached out and the maiden placed a new cape across his arms. He clipped the cape with its yellow hood on Terr's shoulders and the drums began to beat again. Terr felt a stirring deep within him and Death settled over him. Sidhara felt it, nodded and stepped back.

The drums were suddenly silent.

Terr found himself looking at two realities. One was an alien, staring at a people who took him for one of their own. The other was an overwhelming power gazing down at the crowd with detached benevolence. The images blurred and merged while terrible forces burned through his body.

The girl looked at him, hung her head, and sank down on one knee. "I ask for your blessing, Sankri," she husked.

He leveled his hands, shocked to see them glowing. Bright blue sparks crackled and danced between his fingers. To touch her meant death—if he willed it. A lapse of concentration or an instant of carelessness and she would die. She must have known, as all of them must have known. Still, she waited for his touch.

His hand brushed her hair. The sparks washed over her and spilled across her shoulders. A murmuring of surprise came from those around him, but he did not hear it. Power surged through him and it would not be denied. He had an urge to lift his arms and laugh. He shrugged back the impulse and the desert rolled with thunder.

He pulled back his hands and the girl stood up, the fires falling away from her.

"Tabe," she said and her eyes glowed with wonder and contentment.

Then they were around him, shouting his name as they touched him. With a cry, he raised his arms. Blue fires played between them and the lightning went forth. There was a clap of thunder and he leaned back and laughed.

Sidhara stared thoughtfully at his alien protégé and wondered what he had unleashed. The image of Sankri, suspended in night with two stars at his feet, flared bright in his mind. The future yet to be written, and Sarumajan, the destroyer of worlds, need not walk the land.

* * *

The morning sky had a dull haze and fine sand filled the air. The wind whistled among the peelath, hot and urgent. The oark stomped restlessly in the corrals and men hurried to secure extra lashings around the fences. Children drove alarmed poultry into the coops, causing panic among the squawking birds.

Terr drew back the peelath mat from the door and squinted against the stinging sand. Dhar stood beside him dressed in the working grays of a Third Scout. Dhar took one look at the coppery sky and shook his head.

"Marrakan," he growled, sword of the wind, they called it.

It was one of those late fall storms that swept across the Saffal with undisguised fury. It lifted a wall of sand that marched inexorably across the desert. The storm lasted for days of howling wind and driving sand, or disappeared in only hours. For anyone caught in its path it meant death.

"My brother," Dhar said, looking uncomfortable. "Storm or not, I am compelled to return to Kanarath. You are under no obligation to come with me."

"No, I will come," Terr said heavily. "I must finish it."

Terr found it hard to say goodbye. He had grown to love this land and its strange people. They were now part of him and he part of them, but he needed to find out where he fitted in the life of his yesterdays.

He had nothing to pack, and Dhar, he would learn, was always ready. Sidhara waited for them beside the combie, hands crossed before his chest. A brown hood covered his head, his cape fluttering stiff behind him.

"My two sons of the stars," he rumbled. "Do not forget the roots of your fathers and follow the teachings of the Discipline."

Power radiated from him in waves. Now that Terr could feel it, he couldn't understand why Sidhara had deigned to look at him in his days of madness.

"Master," he said brokenly. "I must go, even though it pains me."

"Just so," Sidhara said and nodded. "But our shadows will merge again, my strange son, and you are still to walk to Katai Than."

Terr knelt before him and bowed until his head touched Sidhara's sandals. The old man placed his hand on Terr's head and he felt the Wanderer's strength.

"Tabe," Terr murmured and stood up.

The villagers began to gather around them. Even though parted, they would be in his thoughts. The bubble opened with a hiss and the combie shifted beneath them as he and Dhar clambered in. The power plant spooled up to a soft whine. Terr lifted his hand as the bubble closed.

He whispered a farewell.

Through the pickup mike, he heard the chant of their names. Dhar didn't linger. With barely a tremble the combie lifted. In seconds they were deep in the storm's haze. The village but a smear in the sand that left Terr dejected and excited all at once. Just like that, he became cut off from something he had come to cherish. Looking down, he realized how keenly he felt its loss.

They broke through the cloud of dust into brilliant sunshine. The bubble polarized immediately. Dhar pointed with his hand and Terr stared in awe.

The wall of sand must have been over two talans high as it reared above the Katai Than escarpment. It looked solid, a brown wave rolling inexorably over the desert. Small lightnings played in its depths.

"Marrakan?"

"A big one," Dhar confirmed, his voice filled with concern. "Without a met scan there is no telling how long it will last."

"Can we outrun it?"

"Easily. Inside the front the winds are fierce, but the front generally moves fairly slowly. Generally."

Terr looked at him. "I would hate to be the poor bastard caught in its path. How long to Kanarath?"

"Just over eight hours. We'll be there by mid-afternoon."

Terr worked that one over. A combie can push up to three hundred and eighty talans per hour. After eight hours…

"That's over three thousand talans!"

"About right," Dhar agreed.

"And nothing between us but desert? That's a whole lot of loneliness."

"A few villages here and there. Not a good place to crash."

"I found *that* out!"

"I just remembered," Dhar said with a nasty grin. "I will have to call you 'sir' when we get back."

"Only fitting for a swabbie Third Scout," Terr said with a straight face. Dhar punched him on the shoulder—hard.

Massaging the tender spot, Terr watched the desert move below them. The sand broken by ridges of red stone, scattered scrub and stretches of tarad grass. An occasional clump of peelath that flashed by provided a splash of darker green. The desolation of the landscape was striking and he marveled how he could be so drawn to such a hell, but that desolation also held a strange and compelling beauty that had filled some deep need in his soul.

Only the whisper of the power plant broke the comfortable silence. He relaxed and enjoyed the company of his newfound brother, not worrying about what waited for him tomorrow. The two of them fitted in a way that transcended culture and custom. An understandable gulf of accomplishment lay between them that only time would bridge, but he trusted Dhar completely. A glow new to him and he savored its sensation.

When the proximity alert gave a soft beep, they exchanged glances.

"You expecting company?" Dhar asked and Terr shook his head.

"Not that I know of. You?"

"Same here. More likely your friends than mine," Dhar suggested.

"Came to finish the job you think?" Terr ventured. "But how would they know where I was, and in this combie?"

Dhar gave him a tight smile and Terr answered his own question. Someone had to be watching from space. His M-3 pals had probably sowed S/14 sensor pods into low orbit and kept an eye on him. As to why they haven't struck before, it was likely that they were as wary of the Wanderers as he had been.

Dhar tapped the small nav display plate and sighed in exasperation. "This thing cannot tell me anything. Could be a local freighter off course, or perhaps not. They're coming in for a pass."

Terr turned his head as a dark shape flashed past. It certainly wasn't a military job.

"I thought I saw Palean markings. Could be a raider."

"Raiding us?" Dhar chuckled without humor.

Terr kept his eyes on the approaching ship. "Watch his shields! They'll pulse before—"

When the raider fired, he tensed, but Dhar had already sent the combie into a barrel loop. The yellow beam came close enough to make their hair stand on end from the near-field effect. Small sparks danced on the console.

"That was a burst from a Koyami military projector!" Terr shouted in outrage. He wanted to take the controls, but Dhar was already doing the only thing possible. It was hard to simply sit there unable to do anything.

In the Shadow of Death

Dhar sent the combie plummeting toward the desert. The flat oval shape above them stood on its edge and plunged after them. Even a near miss would finish the combie. Apart from the single environmental nav shield, they were defenseless. Terr felt cold anger well up and watched as the ship maneuvered overhead.

The combie rolled and slued as another beam brushed past. The desert came up fast and he braced himself for impact. Despite the restraining field, he grunted when the combie groaned into a sudden hover. It rocked in the raider's wake when the black shape overshot them, almost scraping the desert.

"They mustn't disable the combie!" he hissed urgently. If they crashed, he had a hunch that neither of them would be surviving it.

"I know," Dhar muttered, wrestling with the controls. "Hold on. I'm landing behind those rocks."

"He'll simply climb and pick us off!"

"We cannot fight them here!"

"Fight them with what?" Terr demanded ironically.

The combie came down beside a small ridge of jagged rock. The bubble was still opening when the raider lifted above the ridge. A lance of yellow death seared the air above their heads. Dhar jumped out and turned toward the black shape as it glided toward them.

He raised his arms and Terr heard the words. He knew what was happening. He hurriedly climbed out and shouted, but Dhar was already touched by Death and blue sparks crackled between his fingers.

A roll of thunder shook the ground. Dhar leveled his arms at the ship and lightning stabbed at the hovering shape. Its nav shield flared yellow-white as a bolt of yellow light pierced the hull, shooting out through the other side. Massive backsurges crackled against the hull where the bolt had struck.

They both dived for the sand as the ship shuddered, pierced like an insect, rolled on its side and plowed into the ground. The explosion lifted them, then slammed them down hard. Terr looked up and spat sand as he rubbed his ringing ears. Rock and metal debris rained around them and the sound of the explosion boomed across the desert. When silence returned, he stood up. The raider had disintegrated completely and the landscape was strewn with blackened wreckage.

This was the first time he had seen the hand of Death used in anger. He looked at Dhar and felt the power about him. When his brother turned, the red slits of his eyes were bright, burning with fire. The fires faded slowly and Dhar stared at the column of black smoke coiling above the wreckage.

He picked himself up, brushed off the sand and looked tragically at Terr.

"I should not have done that," he whispered brokenly.

"If you hadn't, we would now be a smoking heap, not them," Terr said softly. "I ought to have thought of it myself."

"This was the first—"

"Look, Nightwings. I wouldn't waste my sympathy on them. I'm glad you acted when you did."

The smoke thinned, curling in small fingers above glowing pieces of metal. He took a last glance at the smoking ruins and climbed into the combie.

"Come on. We better get out of here."

As he waited, Dhar glanced down at his hands—the hands of Death.

* * *

Hugging a meandering coastline the topaz sea followed a dark line to the horizon. Kanarath rose out of the surrounding profusion of green. Where the belt of vegetation ended, the desert waited to reclaim the land. Long rectangular patterns of green and olive hugged the shore.

For the first time on this world, above the sea, Terr saw clouds.

In the Shadow of Death

Dhar hadn't said much since their encounter with the raider and Terr left him to his thoughts. Then again, he also had things on his mind. In a gentle turn the combie headed for the towers of the Center.

Beyond the farms, out in the desert deeps, the gray expense of the inter-star terminus shimmered and swam in the heat. A few liners lay tied to the landing rings of the civilian terminal. A solitary M-4 sat parked near a maintenance building in an otherwise empty field.

The place was not exactly a tourist trap.

By outworld standards, Kanarath wasn't even a city. Nonetheless, at almost one million inhabitants, Anar'on's administrative center, and capital of the Kaleen group, Kanarath was a sprawl. The fabled hanging gardens were ribbons hung between buildings. Communals, combies, and cargo haulers crowded the sky.

The combie banked and headed for one of the white towers clustered in the city's center. Two sled-pads stood parked on a landing ramp that protruded from the side of the building. The combie settled with a sigh. A wave of heat rolled in when the bubble opened. Sitting in the cool comfort, Terr had forgotten the heat.

An MP, clad in crisp working grays, phase rifle at his side, stood to when Dhar climbed out. No respect for rank, Terr mused when the MP scowled at him.

"Ah, this is a military establishment, sir," the MP said, his eyes measuring Terr's surtaf with distaste. "Off limits to civilians."

"It's a disguise," Terr told him and winked.

The MP's eyes flickered at Dhar. "I'll have to ask both of you to validate your IDs, sir."

Dhar waved him inside. The surtaf swirling about his legs, Terr grinned despite himself. The booth little more than a simple panel of controls and a display plate. Dhar pressed his palm against the plate and stepped back to let the MP check the readout.

"All clear, sir," he rasped reluctantly.

When Terr pressed his palm against the plate, it flashed yellow. The MP looked at him suspiciously.

"It says here that you're dead…sir," he protested.

"Doesn't seem likely," Terr said. "Besides, it's something I would know, don't you think?"

"Well, you check out—"

"Right," Terr said and headed for the cable-tube.

The MP still gaped at them when the door clicked shut.

"I wonder how he's going to explain me away," Terr mused. "Not being dead will mess up accounting something bad."

"The error can always be corrected, you know," Dhar said dryly. Terr glanced at him and frowned.

"To think my brother said that."

"Level please," a soft contralto voice inquired. It sent pleasant images through his mind. Dhar merely chuckled.

"Admin," he said with a smile. "You have a low mind, Sankri."

"It has been a while, you know."

The MP downstairs must have talked, for another muscular individual waited for them when the tube opened, the corridor carpeted powder blue. Dark red walls glowed from indirect lighting. Terr nodded in appreciation. It looked like the high and the mighty lived well out here.

The MP stopped before a paneled door at the end of the corridor and stood at parade rest. After a time the door slid away. A young Palean first scout gave the two of them a close look.

"Second Scout Terrllss-rr?" he asked. Terr nodded. "Prima Scout Se Iklin will see you directly." He bobbed his head in a characteristic gesture, his bulging eyes barely moving. "If you'll follow me."

He probably meant it as a request, but it came out as a clear command. Obviously, some suspicion still lingered regarding Terr's identity.

Soft-grained yellow peelath doors hissed open, revealing the gloomy interior of a large office. The two corner walls took up ceiling-high tinted window panels. The Wall on their right cycled through scenes of hissing surf. Terr heard the boom of muted breakers. A low desk stood before a wide window screen. City buildings towered in the background.

"Come in, gentlemen," a deep sonorous voice came out of the gloom and Terr turned toward the sound.

Se Iklin looked old even by Palean standards. Probably pushing one hundred and twenty and close to mandatory retirement. Terr figured Anar'on was likely to be the man's last appointment. His mottled skin shone with a sweaty sheen. He may have been old, but his large black eyes were alive with interest.

The prima scout walked deliberately to a small flower tray parked on a wall shelf. Judging by the way the Palean hovered near the tray, it looked like Se Iklin's idea of excitement was to fondle his prized konica bulbs; three of them, each with a purple-blue cup flower. That explained the gloom of the office. Konica bulbs were native to Palean rain forests, Terr knew, and didn't do well in the glare of the sun.

As Se Iklin moved toward the desk, his long thin hands twining, the ceiling brightened. It left a strip of gloom above the wall shelves where the konica stood. He turned to the first scout and gave a small nod. The young Palean threw Terr a searching look and withdrew.

"Please make yourselves comfortable," Se Iklin offered and waved at the formchairs.

Terr sank down with a grunt into one of the seats positioned before the desk. Se Iklin looked with amusement at Terr's Wanderer robes.

"So you're the young scamp who has caused all that trouble in the Four Suns," he observed, hands working. He glanced at

Dhar and inclined his head at Terr. "And how did you happen to come across him, ah, Third Scout Dharaklin, isn't it?"

"The people of my village found him in the desert, sir," Dhar said gravely. "I happened to be on leave when they brought him in."

"And you did not see fit to report his presence?" Se Iklin asked in mild surprise. "As a Fleet officer, your duty—"

"As a Saddish-aa Wanderer, sir, I had no choice."

Se Iklin gave Dhar a probing stare. "No matter. We can leave that one for the debrief. Your arrival here is fortuitous. I received a report of a projector discharge in the southern Saffal. A military projector. The Anar'on administration is understandably curious and has asked me to investigate. SC&C places a freighter and a combie in the area."

"We were attacked by what appeared to be a raider bearing Palean markings, sir," Terr said evenly.

"Indeed? And you managed to evade?"

"Well, not quite," Terr said and Se Iklin chuckled.

"I have more than a passing familiarity with the Wanderer Discipline, Second Scout, and of its practitioners."

"You'll find the log of our engagement in the combie, sir. Right now, I would appreciate it if I could get in touch with Prima Scout Anabb Karr."

Se Iklin's face betrayed the questions he wanted to ask. "I dare say. Very well, then. Since you insist." He issued crisp commands and the Wall cleared. He must have used a private code for Anabb himself came into view.

Anabb took one look at Terr and his eyebrows creased in a frown.

"You're supposed to be dead," he said sternly.

"I assure you, sir, the rumors are exaggerated," Terr snapped, somewhat peeved at this cool reception.

"Some people will wish you were," Anabb added dryly. He turned to the Palean and cleared his throat. "Iklin, can you give me a few minutes with this wayward officer?"

In the Shadow of Death

Under strict protocol, as the highest-ranking Fleet officer in the Kaleen group, Se Iklin was entitled to hear whatever Anabb had to say. He also appreciated that some things were better left alone.

"Undercover skullduggery. Bah!" He snorted and stood up. "I'll want to talk to you about this later, friend Anabb."

"You don't want to be mixed up in this," Anabb growled.

Terr and Dhar pried themselves up and stood to. The old Palean gave them a nod and walked out. When the door clicked shut, Terr turned to the Wall.

"Sir, may I present Third Scout Dharaklin. He saved my life."

"I know of him. Part of Talon base commander's staff." His eyes rested briefly on Dhar before they returned to Terr. "A Wanderer surtaf, isn't it?"

"Well, sir, my uniform took the blister crash kind of hard and wasn't quite up to it."

"Hah! It would have been better had you brought back the M-1."

Terr didn't say anything. The old fossil more worried about a piece of hardware than a life. The ungrateful...

"You're different somehow. A quality..."

"It's the desert, sir. Toughens the character."

"I dare say. And you wear a yellow hood. I thought only initiates of the Discipline were permitted to wear a colored hood."

"That's right, sir."

"Mmm. I'm sure there is more to your story, but I haven't the time to go into it now. I want you on Talon for a full debriefing. An M-3 will pick you up—both of you. I'll arrange it with Prima Scout Se Iklin."

"Sir, about my mission—"

"Is finished as far as you're concerned, Second Scout."

"A few loose ends to tie up, sir. Personal things."

Anabb pointed a stubby finger at Terr and glared. "If you

275

have any plans regarding the M-3s that attacked you—"

"It's not that, sir," Terr said hastily. "Although the thought had crossed my mind."

"We'll talk about it when you get here."

"Sir, I must tell you that we were attacked by what looked like a raider on our way to Kanarath," Terr said and left Anabb to think it through.

"I will take appropriate measures to see to it that you get here alive," Anabb grunted, his eyes appraising the boy. "For a milk run, you made quite a mess while on Elexi. They're still picking up the pieces."

"Just distracting Kapel's intelligence machinery, sir. As per orders," Terr added with a straight face.

"Thunderation! I can see you have not lost your sense of humor."

"Talking of M-3s, sir. About my ship—"

"Your exec has it." Anabb raised his hand when Terr was about to protest. "Don't worry. I'll have him recalled and you'll get back *Ramora*, but you'll lose your executive officer. He deserves a command after surviving your encounter with Maintenance. An M-2, I think it is."

"As long as it's not *my* ship. I'll need another exec, then."

"Making demands already?"

"And I have him right here," Terr said and felt Dhar stiffen.

This was a delicate moment and he wasn't sure of his ground. Having someone else's memories was one thing. Judging actual reactions was something else, but he could not tolerate the thought of losing Dhar now.

Anabb looked stern. "Still a Third Scout. Hardly enough seniority or experience—"

"I want Dharaklin, sir," Terr said and Anabb frowned.

"Report to me when you get to Talon. And son, I'm glad to see you safe," he said gruffly and the Wall faded.

"Well…" Terr stared at the Wall.

"He must like you, my brother," Dhar said. "I would not have dared talk to him like that."

"After what I've been through, what can he do to me? But Nightwings, you heard what I said. My old exec has finally wrangled a command and I really need a replacement. I would be honored if you would consider it."

Dhar looked wistful. "An M-3 is a fine ship, Sankri, and a heavy responsibility. My heart soars to hear your words, but Prima Scout Anabb is right. I am not qualified, even though it would get me off Talon."

Terr looked at him steadily. "You're wrong, my brother. You *are* qualified."

Dhar stood there puzzled, then his eyes widened. "Your memories, yes. But I cannot rely on them as a substitute for experience. I could let you down at a critical moment, endangering not only the ship, but everyone in it. And the memories may fade over time."

"You don't know that," Terr persisted. "Look. You'll pick up experience and I'll help you. Anabb will not refuse me and it will mean an immediate promotion for you to full Third Scout."

"If he agrees—"

"He'll agree," Terr said with wicked relish.

Chapter Eleven

Like some ancient lord watching over his manor, Enllss stood before the window screen and stared at the city spread before him. A hint of dawn crept into the sky. Below, the city sprawl lay in a blaze of light. Serving the needs of the Serrll, Captal never slept. The nameless faces of the bureaucrats may change between night and day, but the wheels of government moved ponderously on.

Holding a cup of herbal tea, he sniffed appreciatively at its aroma.

For him this moment was especially sweet. In one stroke, he had managed to neutralize the potentially devastating political damage the Four Suns secession could have caused to the stability of the Revisionist coalition. At the same time, he had broken the Servatory Party's threat of economic reprisals over their planned control of Anulus.

Discussing it with Illeran, the Karkan made a few pithy comments and approved his actions. Although Illeran was the senior Karkan representative in the Assembly and one of the most powerful figures in the Servatory Party, he was also an Executive Director for the Bureau of Cultural Affairs. As such, his responsibility transcended any inter-party rivalry.

Enllss enjoyed working with his boss.

Admittedly, the victory yet to be consummated, he was too shrewd a tactician to rely on its certainty. He had seen too many well-laid plans founder through premature disclosure. In this case, he felt justifiably optimistic. His sources on Deklan confirmed the confusion in the Ecumenical Synod generated by his proposal. The twenty-two hours were up and he expected Sill momentarily, a figurative begging bowl in hand. Early and a cruel way to start the day, but the moment was indeed sweet.

He admitted that politically it was the best solution. Having one or the other of the two power blocks controlling Anulus would always be a prospect fraught with temptation for economic blackmail. Properly controlled, enough raw material existed for all. Perhaps Sill was right. Sofam had been squeezing Karkan's access to strategic metals a bit tight. He reminded himself that someone should talk to the Paravan Trading Association about that. Those guys were getting too heavy for his liking. There were limits, by damn!

No, it was a triple victory. With Terr safe, a load greater than he'd been willing to admit, lifted off his shoulders. Was he becoming paternal in his old age? Without children of his own, the boy had become a son he never had, and he was fond of the young scamp. Terr had a promising career and should go far unless he got shot for insubordination first, he mused wryly.

From what Anabb told him, Terr had been changed by the experience. He did not doubt it, and an initiate of the Discipline? Well, time enough to find out all the details when next they saw each other. He knew Terr was going home to Kaplan for leave, and he had arranged a stopover for him in Captal. He looked forward to seeing the boy.

The comms alert beeped, catching him wearing a satisfied smile.

"What is it?"

"Diplomatic Branch Director Sill-Anais to see you, sir," his aide announced.

The whole office knew that something big was brewing. Wild speculations were circulating around the departments of his Bureau.

"Hah! Show him in, will you?" He took a sip of tea as the doors slid away. He placed his cup down with a loud click.

"Sill, you old sand slug!" he boomed at the figure and pointed at a couch. "Make yourself comfortable. Care for some tea?" he gushed, grinning hugely. He could afford to be mag-nanimous in victory.

Sill's tall wiry frame looked bent and his shoulders drooped visibly. His eyes had dark bags under them and his long hair had lost some of its gloss. Clearly, he'd had a long day and an even longer night.

"Enllss," he piped, bobbed his head and sagged gratefully into the couch. "I'll have some of that sewage water you so loosely call tea," he said, his long face now even longer.

"Some way to treat my hospitality," Enllss said with mock severity.

He noted the crumpled clothes and the lines of fatigue and felt a twinge of regret. Whatever had transpired during the last twenty-two hours had obviously left Sill very unhappy. No one liked to back down. Blinded by their prejudice, Enllss had known the Deklans were unlikely to find a solution of their own. Forced to accept a proposal without any details, and from Sofam. It must have been particularly galling to acknowledge defeat. That's how the game was played and his twinge of sym-pathy only a momentary one.

He drew another cup and focused on the issues at stake. In Captal, friendships were a bonus. An exception, not the rule, and for a good reason. Where the fate of worlds hung in the balance, personal involvement left one vulnerable and subject to emotional blackmail. Many an Assembly rep had resigned, shattered by the impersonal thrust of political maneuvering, not least by his own party.

Tough that Sill was involved in this one, but Enllss could not afford to worry about that. Deklan had miscalculated, sim-ple as that. They were fortunate the price exacted had not been higher.

Sill nodded and accepted the steaming cup. Enllss picked a formchair and sat down. Sill took his time sipping the tea.

"My government concedes to your proposal," Sill said with obvious bitterness after taking a cautious sip. He placed the cup on the small table between them and looked pointedly at Enllss. "As you knew we would."

"As I knew you would," Enllss agreed evenly. "You couldn't risk Kapel Pen announcing the secession while you maneuvered for position."

Sill ran a hand through his hair. "I must also convey to you the Synod's disappointment at this treatment by a coalition ally."

"I bet. Bleeding dry tears while you held Anulus and Kunoid Minerals over our heads," Enllss said with plenty of bite. Sill had the grace to look away.

"What are the details?" Sill demanded.

Enllss leaned back and relaxed. "The Deklan Republic cannot afford to lose Anulus, and the Revisionist coalition doesn't want to lose the Four Suns. Anall-Marr is boxed into a corner and he knows it." He paused and took a sip of tea. "I think it's time he reappraised the situation and went back to first principles," he said over the rim of his cup.

"What do you mean?"

"Let's look at the situation on Elexi. You have a matriarchy in a loose coalition of factions controlled by various members of the Pen Family line, right?"

"Ach! I know that. What's your point?"

"So testy." Enllss shook a finger at him.

"Get on with it, damn you," Sill said irritably and Enllss chuckled. Swearing by a priest of the Path? It must have been a very heavy night.

"You'll like this. Kapel has stayed in power because she has managed to satisfy the needs of her Family. Or at least managed to prevent any of the other factions from ganging up on her. Coalitions are inherently unstable. Members constantly jockey for ascendancy. Judging from our recent—"

"Ach! You don't need to rub it in," Sill growled and Enllss laughed, enjoying himself.

"Just kidding, but the situation with Kapel is essentially the same. What you need to do is tip the balance of power in favor of one of the factions hostile to Kapel."

"How? The Ecumenical Synod does not interfere directly in the administration of its systems."

"I don't believe that any more than you do."

Sill glared, but held himself in check. "Okay, but we have no influence with any member of the Pen brood. Besides, those bitches are not exactly gushing with adoration for Deklan or the Path. Ach!"

"Then change their mind. Offer them a prize they cannot refuse."

"Such as?"

"Get Anall-Marr to nominate Kapel's sister Talia Pen as his successor. Talia is ambitious and could be receptive to such a suggestion."

"Ach! You're crazy! The Synod would rather lose the Four Suns than see its power eroded. No, contaminated! Who brought them the enlightenment of the Path? We lifted them out of darkness—"

"Sill! You don't have any choice. Now listen to me and stop fulminating. Why does Kapel Pen want to cede the Four Suns? Does she think the Karkans will treat her people any better? Of course not. They offered her a prize she couldn't refuse. Same thing here. Talia Pen doesn't give a crud about the Karkans or the Deklans, for that matter. Can you imagine her pride and boost to her ego? For the first time in history, a non-Deklan will ascend to a Prefecture. She's not going to mind the enhanced status of the Four Suns among the other border systems either."

"This could ruin Anall-Marr," Sill pointed out miserably. "You said that you wouldn't compromise him."

"This won't compromise him."

Sill didn't hear him. "It will set back the progressive movement throughout the whole Republic for decades."

"Worm crap! Now listen to me. Properly marketed, this

move will be seen as a fundamental shift in the Synod's policy toward the border systems. It will signal a new era of cooperation, away from the intransigent views of traditional hard-liners in the Synod and the Ecumenical Order. Far from selling out, Anall-Marr will be held up as a visionary who is willing to take that first step toward greater maturity and understanding between all Deklan systems. After all, doesn't the Path itself dictate such a course?" Enllss pointed out mildly.

Sill shook his head in admiration. "Ach! You know us so well, but it isn't that simple, my friend. Changing the course of tradition will encounter a lot of opposition. Even from Anall's own supporters."

"It's either that or Anall-Marr's career will be ruined when Kapel Pen announces her secession," Enllss said bluntly. "And what of the other border systems not rich in mineral wealth chafing under your merciful rule? They bear no love for the Deklan Republic and would gladly follow Kapel's lead. You could lose more than the Four Suns if you don't handle this right. We all could. A split within the Republic can only weaken us and benefit the Servatory Party."

"Perdition to the whole Pen line. Ach!" Sill hissed and stood up. He paced, hands twining in agitation. Then he whirled and pointed an accusing finger at Enllss. "Even if we do what you suggest, it will leave a power vacuum on Elexi. Short of killing her, Kapel is quite capable of mounting an insurrection."

"Then you see to it that she doesn't. Get Talia to appoint her sister Relina in Kapel's place. Admin Affairs won't stand in Relina's way should she choose to resign her General Assembly seat; owing to pressing domestic circumstances," Enllss added dryly.

"And her replacement?" Sill demanded and Enllss shrugged.

"Tamara Lin would make a good choice. It would satisfy

her ambition and remove a probing thorn from the Elexi administration. I'm not so naive to believe that a change of administration will relieve the general suffering of Elexi's population. But who knows? With Talia as Prefect and under greater general scrutiny from everybody, she'll have to polish up her act. The position carries with it *some* responsibility, as she will find."

Sill studied his friend and nodded with grudging respect.

"I was wrong, Enllss. Ach! You *do* look beyond Sofam's immediate interests."

"None of us have much choice in this."

"I don't know," Sill mused and pulled at his chin. "It could just work. Thankfully, I don't have to make the decision. I wish I had never heard of the Four Suns."

"I am sure that others will share your sentiment," Enllss agreed equitably.

* * *

For what seemed like another lifetime the only sky Terr knew had been amber. He still found it strange to look upon the blue-green of Elexi.

On the darkened deck, he sat back in the command couch. Even the whisper of status reports seemed muted and far away. Navigation bubble transparent, Elexi showed as a sliver of light when the ship came over the terminator. Even now there was something unreal about his past. It seemed elusive and dreamlike. He had a flash of panic when he imagined waking in the desert—insane. A cold chill swept over him and he shifted uncomfortably.

At least Anabb had not begrudged him the use of another M-1, but he looked stern when he said that he would be less than amused if Terr lost this one as well. No sense of humor, that was his trouble, Terr decided. The ship pitched and slid into the atmosphere.

In the Shadow of Death

SC&C brought him down beside the envoy's M-4. He knew an M-6 normally stood picket off-planet while the excitement died down. To see it sitting on the far side of the field still came as a shock. It towered over everything: ugly, silent, and menacing. Its inverted triangle emblems looked subdued, adding to the utilitarian image of the warship. Somewhere in his past, he longed to command one like it. Now, its deadly purpose only repelled him.

He walked down the landing ramp and wrinkled his nose in distaste. A pall of brown smog hung over the city. It was cool despite a clear sky until he remembered that by Elexi standards this must be a hot day. He pulled the zip-jacket tight around him and shivered. He would take the heat of the Saffal any day.

A combie bearing official triangle markings sped toward him from the terminus building. He looked around trying to figure out the subtle difference he knew was there, but could not see. Then it dawned on him. There weren't any flags. The terminus building lay bare. Even the flagpoles were gone. He hoped that Rayon had managed to change more than merely getting rid of some flags.

The combie slowed to a stop and the bubble retracted. The driver stepped out quickly, opened the back door and stood stiffly beside it. Terr watched with amusement as a Deklan in civilian garb lifted his long legs and stepped out. The Deklan glanced at the M-1 before his searching empty eyes came to rest on Terr, then gave a stiff smile.

"Second Scout Terrllss-rr? Please allow me to introduce myself," he said, using his best diplomatic polish. "I am Rayon's special executive assistant. The Envoy wishes me to express his liveliest pleasure at your safe return and is looking forward to meeting you."

"Well, I guess I can spare him a few minutes," Terr said. The Deklan stiffened, then relaxed, giving a polite chuckle.

"Ach! A man with a sense of humor, I see. If you will, please." He extended his hand at the combie.

The driver hurried to open the door. Terr climbed in and sank comfortably into the upholstery. The material squeaked and groaned as the Deklan slid in opposite him. The bubble closed over them and the combie rose quickly.

They exchanged inane pleasantries on the way to the Center. Terr declined the offer of a drink and there were a few seconds of silence while the Deklan indulged. Terr didn't mind. They were never going to be pals anyway. Two MPs stood to when the combie came down on the main landing ramp of the Center's executive tower. The driver opened the door and waited for them to file out. Terr barely hesitated, wondering if one of them would turn out to be a plant and finish what started above Anar'on.

"This way," the executive assistant said after straightening his smile.

The cable-tube took them directly to the envoy's offices. When the door opened, Rayon stood before the window, staring at the city below. He turned and smiled warmly.

"Terr! I am so very pleased to see you again. Pleased," he said in his clipped voice.

"Thank you, sir."

"If you will." Rayon extended his hand at the formchairs. He glanced at the Deklan and nodded. "I'll call you later."

The Deklan stiffened and shot Terr a poisonous look. "If you don't mind, sir—" he started, but his words died when Rayon frowned. The poor man flushed, mumbled something and stomped out.

"Ignore him. I do," Rayon said comfortably as he seated himself behind the desk. "He is one of Anall-Marr's creatures sent here to monitor the changes. Competent and means well, but resents my authority. It's natural enough, but he is foolish to show it. Foolish. Tell me of yourself. You are well?"

"Well enough, sir. Prima Scout Anabb Karr allowed me to come here before I take some leave while my ship is being recalled. I need to tie up a few loose ends."

"I dare say." Rayon looked at Terr with amused appraisal. "I'm told you walked in wearing the robes of a Wanderer."

"It seemed the appropriate thing to do at the time," Terr said with a faint smile.

"Quite. These last two months, you actually lived with the Wanderers?"

"Yes, sir."

"Two months. Well, I'm sure it must have been a fascinating experience. Fascinating. You'll have to tell it to me sometime. Have to." Rayon nodded, then grinned. "Things have changed around here, as you were no doubt told."

"So I've heard."

"The local media is full of your return. Some of the commentary is really quite fantastic. The *Morning Tribune* channel has been making all sorts of allegations about Kapel Pen and the Karkans. Quite fantastic. Quite."

Terr wasn't fooled by the sparkle in Rayon's eyes. "You know of Kapel's plans then, of course?" he asked and Rayon nodded.

"Enllss outlined the whole sordid scheme to me while you were still on Talon. I admit to some personal pique at being left in the dark until recently, but I appreciated its need. Appreciated. That didn't mean I liked it, although I had a good inkling of the whole thing already. And you, my young friend, played no small part in sabotaging Kapel's grand scheme. No small part. Well done, my boy."

"Then you received my beacon's message?"

"Bah! I passed it directly to Sill-Anais and his analysts, and I received the abridged version. They caved in when I started making a nuisance of myself. A nuisance. Without the corroborating evidence in your message, I doubt whether Enllss would have been convinced to act. Doubt."

Terr sat back in the formchair and shook his head. "I still find the whole thing incredible. It was a bold and imaginative plan nonetheless."

"And Kapel almost brought it off. Almost. Tell me. How did you happen to piece it all together?"

Terr smiled ruefully. "To be honest, sir, I didn't. Not quite. I only outlined one possible scenario." He sat up, suddenly concerned. "Tamara Lin, is she all right?"

"Why, yes. There was a bungled attempt on her life while we were on Anulus. She demanded an audience with me a few days later, claiming Kapel planned to cede the Four Suns to the Karkan Federation. As you can imagine at the time, I found her story less than credible. Less."

"Well, sir, she provided me with all the clues I needed. I received a comms signal from her while in orbit over Anulus. I never got to read it as the M-3s jumped me, but I had plenty of time to pick at it while on my way to Anar'on. I couldn't understand why those M-3s were after me. I always figured it was because of my survey scans. I thought Kapel Pen may have been afraid I would pick up a new mine site or something—"

"You did."

"—but that didn't make sense. A mine would have been an embarrassment, but not a reason to kill me. I figured it had to be something personal. However cryptic, the contents of Tamara's message confirmed it. I now believe the attack was ordered to prevent me from getting that message, sir. Or if I did get it, to see to it I never got around to telling anyone about it. Namely you," Terr said and shrugged. "I guess eliminating Tamara was the next logical step. In itself, her message didn't amount to much, but they didn't know that and couldn't risk me talking."

"By they, you mean Kapel Pen?"

"It all pointed to her."

"Well, your reasoning was consistent if nothing else. Consistent."

"What of Kapel Pen, sir?"

"She has not announced a referendum, if that is what you mean. Hasn't."

"I would have thought—"

"Family politics, my boy. The executive palace is buzzing with rumors of a power spill. As yet there has been no word from our illustrious Controller. No word. She has withdrawn into a shell ever since the news broke of your return." Rayon paused and smiled. "Talia Pen will be leading a delegation to see Kapel later today."

"The Proctor of Raman?"

"None other. You will be representing me, and indirectly, the General Assembly."

"Me?"

Rayon laughed at Terr's bewildered expression. "I'll fill you in later. I suppose you're also anxious to know what happened to your late slave. Anxious."

"Alasi! Yes!"

"He and his family are back on their farm and fully compensated. Fully," Rayon said with satisfaction and tapped his fingers against the desk. "As were all the other illegal prisoners. At least that part went well. You cannot see it now, but for a while there, every available ship here was used to repatriate families off Anulus. Every ship. It threw the mining operation into chaos, but Kapel was uncharacteristically cooperative. In the light of what we know now, she obviously wanted to divert attention from her, ah, other activities.

"Soon afterward, Relina Pen was recalled from Captal and Kapel carpeted her for that complaint to the Bureau of Administrative Affairs. Carpeted. My sources tell me that Relina's been spending a lot of time with Talia lately."

"A Family plot, then?"

Rayon's smile was sardonic. "More like poetic justice, I should imagine."

Terr didn't know what to say. "What about you, sir? When are you getting back to Captal?"

"Shouldn't be long now, I expect. Shouldn't. Some details still need to be sorted out in Kapel's bureaucracy. Between

Anall-Marr and the Admin Affairs people, they seem to have the matter well in hand. Well in hand. When I return to Captal, I will have the satisfaction of seeing slavery abolished here. Abolished. Despite the primary agenda for my visit here."

"Do you really think it will die out? Once the excitement fades, things will return to their old ways."

"Cynical, aren't you? But you're right, of course. At least there won't be blatant violation of citizens' rights. It will be a brave administration to allow things to slide again. Brave. Between us, Terr, I'll be glad to sink back into the anonymity of Captal bureaucracy. Glad," Rayon said and Terr smiled.

"Somehow, I don't see that happening, sir."

"You think so? Well, we shall see. And you? Back to your M-3?"

"I don't mind it at all. This has been a most unusual assignment, and I've had enough excitement to last me quite a while," Terr said dryly and Rayon laughed.

* * *

Kapel reached across her desk and tapped the inlaid console pad. Two of the window panels slid away and a refreshing breeze stirred the drapes. She sat back into the formchair and relaxed. Gazing fondly at the city, she took a deep breath and exhaled with satisfaction.

She had never liked the sterile sameness of air-conditioning, preferring her air raw. Sometimes it *was* pretty raw. Fluky winds would occasionally bring with them the unrefined smells of industry. To her, rather than being an embarrassment, it was a smell of power. Power she had carved for herself and her Family out of the rock of Anulus. Today the air crisp and clean. Invigorating was the word she looked for.

She could afford to relax now. The pressure was off and it felt grand. She raised her hands above her head and laughed. And Anall-Marr thought he had her beaten. After years of scheming and bullying the reluctant Family factions, she was ready to burn the ground from under his feet. She hoped the fire would catch on in other border systems. There wasn't much chance of that, though. She knew the Ecumenical Synod, once stung, would make it difficult for anyone else to follow in her footsteps. That didn't matter. The political damage would have already been done.

In a few minutes more than one ambition would be realized; hers as a General Assembly commissioner, and Talia's as controller of Elexi. Even as a little girl, Kapel remembered that Talia was always the troublesome one. As the second oldest, she resented Kapel's privileges and Family patronage. Naturally ambitious—it ran in the family—Talia had never been content taking Kapel's leavings. Now, she could have it all to herself. Kapel was prepared to be generous in victory. Even to Relina, her wayward Assembly rep. Being the youngest of the three, Relina found it tough going taking her share. Thinking back, Kapel and Talia had played some cruel pranks on their youngest sister.

Only the strong survived in the Pen line.

When the comms alert beeped, she stood and tapped the console pad. "Yes, Garner?"

"They're here, Dama," he said woodenly, but worry creased his face. Kapel didn't seem to notice.

"Well, don't just stand there, silly man. Show them in." She cast a last glance around the room.

Everything was set and the long conference table in the far side of the office properly lighted. All the chairs were in place. Although this meeting was a formality, she was always careful to observe the proper forms when dealing with the Family. It didn't cost much and made the proceedings all the more pleasant. It had taken her two frustrating months to finally get the Family behind her. Later today, she would make the announcement, savoring the image of consternation on Anall-Marr's face.

Garner opened the big floor-to-ceiling door and stepped aside. Kapel smiled coolly at Talia, then frowned when Relina and Tamara walked in. She felt a flutter of premonition when she saw the Scout officer Terrllss-rr.

"What is this, Talia?" she demanded imperiously. "What are they doing here?"

Talia smiled demurely, acknowledging Kapel with a nod.

"My dear sister," she said sweetly. "Let's not spoil this with pouting."

Kapel shot Garner a glance and he fled, but not before casting a glare of hatred at Terr.

"I suppose there is an explanation for this?" Kapel tried hard to conceal the disquiet in her voice. Where Family maneuverings were concerned, anything unusual was a cause for apprehension.

"Of course." Talia extended her hand at the conference table. "But let's get comfortable first. I so hate talking business while standing."

The silence palpably frosty as they arranged themselves. The shifting of formchairs and the squirming of upholstery broke the tension. Kapel took her position at the head of the table and folded her hands over the polished top. Somewhere, things had gone wrong—badly, she realized, looking at the tableau before her.

"What's going on, Talia? Why him?" she snapped, not at all comfortable.

Terr studied Kapel, recognizing the personality instantly. Power, authority, unshakable confidence and an iron will. It was all there. Anabb could have been sitting in her place.

"As a representative of the General Assembly's Envoy, I'm here to observe the proceedings," he said, surprising himself at how unemotional and detached he sounded.

Kapel examined Terr as though he was one of her rock specimens. Finally, she gave a small nod.

"I see. And where are the others, Talia?"

In the Shadow of Death

Talia watched the interplay between the two with amusement. "That's just it," she said easily. "There are no others. You see, darling, there has been a change of plans."

"Change? What change?" Kapel's heart pounded. They betrayed her; she knew it! After participating in more than one such session, she could read the signs. "And what is *she* doing here?" she demanded with a glare at Tamara.

"She is Family," Talia said simply, fully in control. "And this is a Family matter."

"She's no Family."

"It's only a marriage accident that put you where you're now, dear cousin," Tamara said primly, her eyes flashing fire.

"You bitch! They should have drowned you at birth."

"Quiet, both of you!" Talia snapped and shot each of them a hard look. "Kapel, let's not make this any more difficult than it has to be. The senior Family has decided it wouldn't be in our best interest to cede the Four Suns to the Karkan Federation."

"I knew it, you sold out!" Kapel squealed in rage and jumped to her feet. "You sold out to that Deklan pervert, neh? A religious hypocrite, him and his Path. Bah!" She flashed at them and ground her teeth in disgust.

"I haven't sold out anyone," Talia said coldly. "And do sit down. You were the one planning to sell us all for personal gain, my dear. You abused your power as Controller, allowing the population to be exploited far beyond what I would call normal prudence."

"This sudden concern for the suffering millions is really touching," Kapel said with a sneer. "I expected better from you, Talia. From all of you. What brought on this belated feeling of righteousness and breast-beating?"

"Some harsh realities, I'm afraid. I'm not defending my complicity in this—"

"I am relieved to hear *that*!"

Talia brushed the sleeve of her jacket. "As I was saying. We all must share some of the blame, neh? What you were doing brought the Bureau of Administrative Affairs—"

"They only wanted to find out about our plans for the secession," Kapel said and raised a finger. "Do you really think that Enllss or Captal give a sniff about our populace?"

"Perhaps not, but deporting innocent families to Anulus to satisfy Kunoid's labor demands was ill-conceived. Granted, you may not have been aware of the duplicity of some of our officials—"

"Officials under *your* control."

"As I said, I am also culpable, but you condoned it nevertheless. We all did, even though some of those officials suddenly found themselves heading for Anulus. I'm afraid the gesture came too late, darling. But, enough of this, neh? I am here to inform you that you have lost the confidence of the senior Family and the position of Controller of Elexi and Prime Director of the Four Suns has been declared vacant."

"You can't do that!" Kapel spluttered, her heart sinking with the dread of certainty. Talia looked serene, her eyes devoid of any pity.

"I've just done it," she said with ringing finality.

"A vote of no confidence requires a closed ballot of all the senior Family—in my presence. I only see three of you here," Kapel said, trying to salvage something out of this mess. Time, she needed time to reorganize and take action. A few arrests…

"I have their ballots, duly registered," Talia said and pointed at the Wall.

Kapel looked at the stony faces around her and laughed. "You always wanted my job, Talia. Didn't you? Well, it's not going to be that easy, dear sister. I'll fight you all the way on this. I will fight all of you."

"I don't want your job," Talia remarked and glanced at Relina. Kapel frowned, then laughed outright.

"Her? She hasn't the will. Besides, this must be ratified by the Prefect, neh?"

"Oh, it already has been," Talia said and smiled secretively.

"What do you get out of it, if it isn't my job," Kapel demanded.

"Anall-Marr's job," Talia said sweetly and Kapel's mouth sagged in astonishment.

"Prefect? I don't believe you. What if he loses his election as Primate? You won't last a day."

"He won't. In any case, to contest the election, he was obliged to resign his position as Prefect and I accepted the nomination—effective immediately."

"You mean the Ecumenical Synod has already ratified this?" Kapel whispered in shock and Talia nodded. She sat up straighter and her eyes bored directly into Kapel.

"As Prefect of this sector, I am formally endorsing the decision of the senior Pen Family relieving you of the office of Controller, in case you harbored any thoughts about contesting the Family's decision. Second Scout Terrllss-rr, as the General Assembly's representative, you will duly note that the forms have been observed."

The words echoed around the table with a finality that left Kapel shattered. Shaken, she began to realize the enormity of behind the scenes deal-making that had gone into this. Everything she had worked toward for years had come crashing around her feet. She had nothing, she realized. Nothing. She looked at Terr's impassive face, then at Talia, and blinked back the sting in her eyes.

"You sold me out to the priests," she whispered, choking back emotions threatening to overwhelm her.

"You sold yourself," Talia said, regretting what had to be done. "Whether you believe me or not, dear sister, this move will strengthen the Republic by healing a long standing rift between the core and border systems. It represents a major shift in Synod policy and I'll take every advantage of that. Whether the shift was imposed by Captal or not, I don't know, and frankly, I don't care. It will give the Four Suns a powerful voice on Deklan. It will be a voice for all the border systems."

"And I won't be a part of it," Kapel gushed.

"No, you won't," Talia said bleakly. "As commissioner, you would have achieved greatness, but it would have been yours alone."

"I would have been a voice in Captal for everyone to hear," Kapel said with a spark of defiance. "A voice in the *real* center of power."

"Your voice, yes. But not the voice of the Four Suns, or that of the border systems. It would have been a Karkan voice."

Kapel turned to Tamara and forced a smile. "And you, my dear cousin? What is *your* payoff?"

"I am replacing Relina in the General Assembly."

Kapel said nothing and nodded. Then she stood, placed her hands on the table, and looked at each of them with utter scorn.

"Damn you! Damn you all!"

Epilogue

Low in the east a band of dark clouds hugged the horizon. Along the river, stands of tall mud gums basked in the afternoon sun. Branches swayed and creaked in the breeze. Dark brown and oily the river ran swollen between low banks. Tall grass leaned far over with the gusts. Bush clicks chirped among the jeer brush.

The western sky clear, the suns hidden among the branches of the gums. The combie settled and the grass gave way beneath it. The valley lay open before Terr, following an ancient river basin until it lost itself among low hills.

Gray smoke streamed from a small cottage below. The skeleton of a double-story extension stood surrounded by piles of building materials. A new barn adjoined the corral. Dry hay stood stacked high against its side.

Two small girls were prodding four reluctant animals toward the corral. Poultry fluttered around their feet. The girls paid them no attention. Out in the field a tractor left freshly turned soil behind it, the man driving it barely visible in the transparent cabin bubble.

There was something idyllic about the rustic simplicity of that scene and Terr felt its pull. After what felt like a lifetime with the Wanderers, he could appreciate the link between the soul and the land, and saw it now with different eyes. Still, he could not forget the sweat of the brow or the unremitting labor such a life demanded. Maybe if things were different...

With a surge of power the combie lifted and angled down into the valley. He swooped over the yard and banked for a landing. The girls looked up with open mouths, then ran shouting into the cottage. Alasi stepped out on the porch, holding back his sisters with an outstretched arm. One of them clung to his hand. His long hair washed and tied into a neat tail. He wore an old coverall, torn at te knees. Terr smiled. When the bubble opened, Alasi's expression of stern suspicion melted into a wide grin of delight.

"Terr!" he yelled and ran toward the combie.

He pranced while Terr climbed out. Then Alasi was on him and they embraced, laughing. After what Alasi went through, Terr glad to see the boy able to laugh again. He pulled back and clasped the boy's shoulders.

"It's good to see you again, you little scamp."

"I don't believe it's you," Alasi gushed. "Everyone said you died. Only Tominoy never gave up hope…Maw! Come see who's here!" he bellowed at the open doorway. "Let's go in, neh?" He tugged at Terr's hand. "I want to show you off."

"Wait." Terr leaned into the combie and placed the system on lock. Alasi prodded one of his sisters on her shoulder.

"Run, get Paw." The girl stood there and started at Terr with big yellow eyes. "Git," Alasi said kindly, but the tractor was already gliding toward them.

"He's comin' anyway," she said gleefully, stuck out her tongue and ran inside.

Alasi's mother stood framed in the doorway, wiping her hands on an apron. Her eyes swept over Terr and she smiled. The years were light on her shoulders and the agony and terror that was there before now gone. She had filled out and her cheeks glowed with health.

"Dama," Terr said and bowed.

"My young master." She nodded, then turned to Alasi and scowled. "Well, you ruffian? You going let him stand there or what?"

"But, Maw!" Alasi protested and rolled his eyes.

Terr grinned and followed him inside.

Cooking smells pervaded the interior. Steam rose from pots on a wood-burning stove. Soot smudged the wall above the stove. Rough clay tiles covered the warm floor. A small bench partitioned the kitchen from the common living area. Pots and other utensils hung suspended from hooks set in the low ceiling. Beside a large window stood a wide wooden table. A vase of dried flowers sat on the embroidered tablecloth.

The girls hovered around their mother.

"Please, sit," she said and hurried to the stove and did things with the pots.

"I'm not interrupting, I hope?" Terr said, unsure of custom.

"You is always welcome here, my young master." Alasi's mother flashed him a warm smile.

Terr pulled back a carved wooden chair and sat down. Alasi sat beside him, not taking his eyes off him. The girls peered at him from behind the bench partition.

Outside, he could hear the spooling whine of machinery. Heavy footsteps preceded Alasi's father. Terr stood up and nodded.

"Master Terr," the man said gruffly as he patted dust off his shirt.

"I am glad to see you settled back on your farm, Tal," Terr said.

Alasi's mother turned from the stove and snorted. "Hah! After what they've done to us? If it hadn't been for the publicity and the Envoy, we never would've gotten anything."

"It's over now, Maw," Alasi's father said kindly. "Let it be, neh?"

"Heavens above! It won't be over until that Pen bitch is run out of Raman."

"She's gone," Terr said.

"Gone?" She stared at him. "You mean she's out? Praise the—"

"When did this happen?" Alasi's father asked and pulled out a chair.

"Earlier this afternoon. It was a Family spill."

"Well, don't expect me to shed no tears," Alasi's mother muttered.

"So long as they leaves us alone," Alasi's father said. "But what of yourself, Tal—"

"Please, just Terr."

The man nodded and his mouth twitched. "I heard that you crashed on the Wanderer world."

"Hey!" Alasi's eyes lit up. "They say that the god of death rules their lives, neh?"

"Hush, boy. Don't interrupt," his father admonished.

Terr smiled. "If it hadn't been for the Wanderers, I *would* have died. Everything they say about them is true and more. For indeed in their hand lies the shadow of Death." Alasi gaped, his eyes round with wonder. Terr frowned at him. "Didn't Tominoy tell you?"

"Nah. He never said. Bet he has the power, neh?"

The image of the old Wanderer came to Terr. Tominoy's inner calm and commanding presence had impressed him from the first, reminding him so much of his master.

"I wouldn't be at all surprised." He turned to Alasi's father and inclined his head. "I see an extension."

The man shrugged. "Be up before winter. Can't say it won't be welcome."

"Welcome! Listen to him," Alasi's mother chided. "The least they could—"

"Someone's coming!" One of the girls ran to the door. She skidded to a stop and her small hand flew to her mouth. She shrank back from the doorway. "Daddy! Daddy! They're here again," she cried and ran to her father. She clung to his leg and sobbed. He glanced at Terr and placed his daughter on his knee.

"There, pet. Who's here?"

Alasi's mother dropped the ladle, wiped her hands against her apron, and hurried to the door. When she looked at them, her eyes held the horror of slavery.

"Please don't let them take us again, Daddy." The little girl searched his face. He wiped her cheeks and jerked his head at Alasi.

Alasi padded to the door. "There's an M-1 coming down in the yard, Paw," he said darkly.

Terr stood beside him to see the sleek ship settle. The landing ramp lowered and two priesthood guards brandishing rifles, ran out. They scanned the area and took station on either side of the ramp.

Garner walked down and looked around the yard. He saw the combie and gave a tight smile.

"It's him," Alasi's mother hissed. "He was there at the Field when they brought us back from Anulus."

"What's he want here?" Alasi demanded and Terr shook his head.

"I don't know," he said, trying to hide his concern. "Whatever happens, stay behind me."

"They won't take us again," Alasi's mother said with grim determination and Terr smiled at her.

"They won't. I promise you."

He walked out and Garner looked at him with interest. "Your Excellency," Terr said and bowed formally.

Flanked by the guards, Garner walked closer.

"So, Second Scout Terrllss-rr. We finally meet under more informal circumstances. I must say, you're not at all what I expected. Rather young to have caused so much trouble, neh?"

"Tal Garner," Alasi's mother said from the porch. "This is my land and you're not welcome here."

Terr took in the two guards. They stood at rest, but ready. Professionals, he decided. One of them caught his eye hoping he would do something. The guard had a white scar from temple to mouth. It didn't do anything for his looks.

Terr knew then that he would have to kill him.

Garner sneered and shook his head. "After all I did for your miserable family? That's all the gratitude I get?"

"What've we to be grateful for, neh? After being oppressed,

sold into slavery and tortured? No amount of compensation can wipe that out."

"Perhaps not, but Dama Kapel has paid dearly for that."

"So I heard. And I cannot say I'm sorry," Alasi's mother said with relish.

Garner laughed. "You have spirit. I like that. You'll need it where you're going."

"Tal Garner," Terr said. "If you're contemplating something against this family—"

"I'm not contemplating anything. I'm here to do it. You're no longer the Envoy's aide, Tal Terr. That uniform will not protect them, or you."

"You risk much for a hollow gesture."

"Not really. I should have eliminated you earlier. Instead, the guards bungled my warning, but there won't be any bungling now. I shall see to it personally."

"You mean to exile me to Anulus?"

"I mean to avenge myself on you. I want you to face the same kind of humiliation I watched Kapel Pen suffer. You played a prominent part in overthrowing one of the greatest leaders the Four Suns ever had. Destroying you may wipe away some of that shame."

Garner's eyes were bright, already seeing him in the mines. How could Terr reason with someone like that?

"Garner, listen to me. She did it to herself."

"Guards, take them away!"

Scar-face raised his rifle and the girls broke into sobs. Terr turned to see terror on Alasi's face.

Rit!

He didn't want to go through the whole crap again.

"Garner. Take me, but leave these people alone."

He could see that Garner was almost tempted. Then he shook his head.

"No, it's better this way." He jerked his hand at the guard.

Scar-face smiled with anticipation. Terr stood there, torn

with indecision. He could swat them like insects, but he wasn't ready. The image of his master eluded him just when he needed to know what to do.

"If he resists, burn him where he stands," Garner ordered.

So be it.

Unbidden, Death stirred and came to rest on Terr's shoulders. The power coursed through him and he felt invincible before these puny forms. His hand twitched and a rumble of thunder rolled over the hills. He had an urge to raise his arms and let loose the lightnings.

Forgive me, my master.

"Don't provoke me, little man," Terr said in a voice that came from Death itself.

Garner gaped and his eyes opened wide. "A Discipline adept," he whispered and whirled at the guards. "Kill him!"

Scar-face frowned, not sure what was going on. The rifle twitched in his hands.

"Don't even think about it," Terr said and the guard's face twisted into a sneer.

What happened next seemed to take forever. Scar-face raised his weapon and Terr reached for him. A bolt of light touched Scar-face and he screamed and his body jerked like on strings. There was a peal of thunder and the ground shook. Scar-face dropped his rifle and crumpled. His chest was a charred, stinking hole. A wisp of smoke rose from the burnt uniform where he lay.

Terr turned his eyes to the other guard. The goon opened his nerveless fingers and the rifle fell with a clatter as he shrank back in terror. Terr raised his hands then. Blue lightnings crackled between them and he laughed. Thunder echoed his laughter.

Garner trembled in shock. Terr lowered his hands and bared his teeth.

"Go mortal, before I forget myself. If you harm this family, I will find you. Anulus will be pleasant to what I'll do to you."

Garner fell back and seemed to shrink into himself. He

turned abruptly and stumbled back toward the M-1. The guard gave Terr a fearful glance, then crept uneasily toward the charred body. With some groaning, he got it on his shoulder and staggered toward the ship. The nav shield came on and the M-1 rose.

It disappeared quickly beyond the valley.

Tempted to throw a bolt after it, Terr clenched his fists and shrugged. Thunder grumbled. The hand of Death lifted and he felt the emptiness of its passing. He stood there, marveling at what he had done and how it felt to be a god. It was a heady feeling. He turned.

Alasi stared at him, trembling. His parents held each other's hands, their faces pale. The girls gaped, eyes round with awe.

"They won't be back," Terr said gently.

Alasi knelt and bowed to the ground. "Sankri." He stretched his hands before him and began to chant a litany.

Terr felt the hair on the back of his neck rise. He walked to Alasi, lifted him up and looked into his eyes.

"Stop this! It's still me."

"No!"

Terr shook him. "It was the only way the Wanderers were able to save me after my crash."

Alasi took time to digest that. "You mean, you're like Tominoy, neh? You're not a god?"

Terr nodded and ruffled his hair. "No, I'm not a god."

Alasi's mother stood beside them. "Our master has saved us yet again," she said breathlessly, her smile uncertain.

Terr slapped Alasi on the back. "Let's go inside. I have a lot to tell you."

About the author

Stefan Vučak has written twenty-one novels, which include eight SF books in the Shadow Gods Saga. His *Cry of Eagles* won the coveted Readers' Favorite silver medal award, and his *All the Evils* was the prestigious Eric Hoffer contest finalist and Readers' Favorite silver medal winner. *Strike for Honor* won the gold medal.

Stefan leveraged a successful career in the Information Technology industry, which took him to the Middle East working on cellphone systems. Writing has been a road of discovery, helping him broaden his horizons. He also spends time as an editor and book reviewer. Stefan lives in Melbourne, Australia.

To learn more about Stefan Vučak, visit his:
Website: www.stefanvucak.com
Facebook: www.facebook.com/StefanVucakAuthor
Twitter: @stefanvucak

More Books by Stefan Vučak

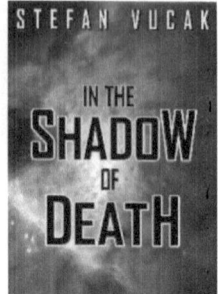

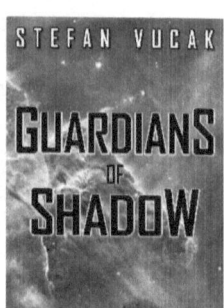